Riding the Tiger

Milena Banks

iUniverse, Inc.
Bloomington

Riding The Tiger

iUniverse books may be ordered through booksellers or by contacting:
iUniverse
1663 Liberty Drive
Bloomington, IN 47403
www.iuniverse.com
1-800-Authors (1-800-288-4677)

Cover painting by author

ISBN: 978-1-4759-5637-5 (sc)
ISBN: 978-1-4759-5638-2 (hc)
ISBN: 978-1-4759-5639-9 (e)

Library of Congress Control Number: 2012919316

Printed in the United States of America

iUniverse rev. date: 12/3/2012

For Erik and his infinite patience

HUNTERS FOR GOLD OR pursuers of fame, they all had gone out on that stream, bearing the sword, and often the torch, messengers of the might within the land, bearers of a spark from the sacred fire. What greatness had not floated on the ebb of that river into the mystery of an unknown earth! The dreams of men, the seed of commonwealths, the germs of empires.

Joseph Conrad, Heart of Darkness

Contents

Prologue

Hong Kong *1997*

How I came to know these people begins with my name.

The nuns christened me Jardine after the intersection where they found me, Wo after the cross street. You see, Mum was carrying only me when she died—no papers, no ID. In death, she carried off my identity, leaving me to strangers, so that my entire connection to the past has been this intersection—two roads and a crack in the pavement. It's a busy spot, a constant colored blur of trucks, taxis, and overloaded bicycles, all stopping, speeding, parting, in frantic yet hypnotic rhythm. I watch them glide by like the passage of time, yet somewhere in this continuous flicker of bodies, motion, and lights, time stopped for my Mum in the form of a bus.

To be exact, she was run over by a double-decker passenger bus just here, on the corner of Yee Wo Street and Jardine's Bazaar, in 1970. When she was struck dead, she threw all her luck with mine. I was dropped as a baby, but I was fortunate, they say. I was caught in a basket of long beans on its way to market, so now, twenty-five years later, instead of lying six feet under over in St. Michael's cemetery with Mum, I'm wondering how luck and green beans brought me here. But I'm beginning to understand. Time has stopped again with a lurch.

His name is Algernon Worthing and he says he knows me. I went to his flat today with a strawberry cake, thinking I had a gig, and turned on the boom box blasting Little Richard's "Tutti Frutti." I was about to burst into his flat dancing when a horrified elderly gweilo emerged. "You are Mr. Worthing, aren't you?" I shouted over the music. "I got your phone message right, didn't I?" I was already cringing inside with the suspicion I'd confused party orders.

The old Englishman was speaking to me but I couldn't hear. He stepped out into the bright lit hall only to be even more dumbstruck by my banana yellow sequined outfit with its plunge neckline, Madonna bra, high-cut thighs, and bobbling cherries sewn head to toe. I switched off the music and put down the cake box.

"Hmmmm. Indeed," he said, a bit shattered by the noise but studying me intently.

I caught a glimpse of my anxious face in the hall mirror. No one who knew the flat-chested schoolgirl in combat boots and tartan mini would recognize this vavoom vixen. But the Carmen Miranda banana headdress paired with red lipstick and false eyelashes, normally a rather saucy and dashing combination, appeared ridiculous in this light. Yes, even being disguised as a self-confident stripper made no difference; I was still me, a Chinese Jane Doe, 5'7", slim, oval face, amber eyes, and a few freckles hidden under makeup. I felt crushed and lost.

The old man leaned back, and taking his glasses off, polished them on a handkerchief. Turning to an old amah behind him he said, "Get us some tea, will you, Auntie?" But "Auntie" stood there glaring and barring the entrance.

I didn't wait to hear her snotty assessment. Exasperated, I yanked off my banana turban and pulled on my raincoat, shedding plastic cherries that bounced and clicked all around us. I was so upset I thought I would cry. Worse still, set free, my long black hair fell to my shoulders, porcupined with embarrassing hairpins. Suddenly, I felt a calming hand on my shoulder that stopped me from leaving. It was the old man.

"Actually," he said, as he stooped over and began picking up cherries, "actually, I did call you, young lady. I know you." Seeing the cake box, he asked, "What kind of cake is that?"

I started to say, "Strawb—," when I was rudely interrupted.

"Hai-yah!" The old amah's cry was telling. She just knew no decent Chinese girl would ever take up a profession like mine and was mortified that he was complicit in my being there.

"I thought this was a *birthday*," I said defensively, speaking to him but looking at her. "My roommate and I have this business, Banana Rama, you see? I just *dance*, that's all. Fully *clothed*, of course." I looked back at him. "Did you say you *knew* me?"

"Come in. Take the cake, Auntie, and make some tea."

Auntie snatched the cake box, peeling herself away, but her ears were turned back like satellite dishes.

"I see you have an American accent," he said.

I followed him into a thickly carpeted room cluttered with antiques. "The nuns at the orphanage taught me English, and then," I said squeezing in past a Ming chair, "I was sent to an international school courtesy of an unknown bene–."

"Have a seat," he cut in and took up a cigar from a humidor, pinching off the end.

The noise of the teakettle came whistling from the kitchen and she was back, sliced cake and all, her pointy eyes sticking into me like thumbtacks. The old man waved her off, but with a hovering smile; he enjoyed her angry chicken attitude. "I was born during the final years of the Empress Dowager, 1903," he said, lighting the cigar. "Imagine that, the whole of China about to fall, and Hong Kong filled with masses of peasants." He stared at me across the room, all debonair like Cary Grant, with strong pleasing features. He wore a silk smoking jacket over a crisp shirt, pin stripe slacks, all finished off with an elegant bowtie and impeccably cut gray hair. "Do you know your history, young girl?" he demanded like a headmaster, his face suddenly stern. But the sparkle in his blue eyes made my heart beat faster and his rich musical voice tickled the tummy like deep ringing chakra bowls. "No? Well, when Ci-Xi died, the peasants believed the Manchus had lost the Mandate of Heaven. God's permission to rule.

The Manchus began chopping heads across the border to keep their dynasty in power. A God-awful mess, I'd say." He abruptly stopped and appraised me through his glasses. "So you're a performer. Well, that makes sense."

"It does?" I was starting to sweat in my raincoat, and picked at my cake slice, trying to look nonchalant. I knew he was an old China hand and wondered what moldy prejudices he might retain from the glory days of Empire. I certainly didn't like an English guy telling me *my* history. He was flipping noisily through the *South China Morning Post* while I swallowed some fluffy pink frosting. Just a few more months and the British would be handing Hong Kong over to Communist China. They'd won it through an unfair treaty during the Opium Wars; too bad for them. 1997 was going to be a bad year for the Crown. I felt like poking my tongue out at him, but then he startled me, suddenly slapping down the newspaper.

"The woman," he said, folding over the paper, and pointing to the *obituary* page, "the woman who has kept you from knowing who you are, has recently died." Auntie turned in gaping disbelief to look at me and then at the paper.

I wondered why was *she* was so shocked. I glanced at the small print. *Violet Summerhays Morgan.* "But, but *I* don't know her. Is she my benefactor, er-tress?"

He frowned, "A benefactor would be a person motivated by goodwill, I should hope." He stared at me. "You're young and this is hard to explain but, a person who suffers terribly might call upon the devil to take away their pain. Anyway, there was a heinous crime committed years ago and—" Clearing his throat, he broke off. "Look, I've been authorized to speak to you as there's no one left alive who can be hurt by what I have to say."

Hurt? I sank back deep into that chair, my energy spinning off like water down a drain. *This felt wrong—it was supposed to have been a gig—that's all.*

"I knew your grandmother," he said, eyes narrowed and voice pained, like a doctor about to give a shot with a very big needle.

I stifled a groan. It was as if all the dusty furniture around me and this living antiquity itself were reaching out from the grave to connect to me like hungry ghosts and bad luck. I wanted to bolt out into the sunshine on Hollywood Road and never come back. But I couldn't run off; at some point, a Jane Doe has to know.

"We met at a very auspicious moment some fifty years ago. You see, there were a lot of us riding the tiger when it got hungry … Anyhow, you've come in time. I'm nearly dead myself." Just then Mr. Worthing went into a coughing fit, and in the midst of it he tried to speak, "You," he said, his hand vaguely flapping about in the air, "are that tiger's child."

"But what do you mean?" I cried, dismayed as he turned blue in another fit of coughing. *How could this gweilo know anything?* I jumped up. "Do you know who I am? Do you know my people? But, I'm Chinese!"

The amah hurried over with a glass of water, and I understood our meeting was over. Oddly enough, she now seemed well disposed toward me and pushed something into my hand when he wasn't looking. "Mieng tien lai. You come back tomolo," she whispered tapping the piece of paper in my hand. Then, looking me in the eyes, she added, "That woman she die, but story not stay bury! Hab honey in mouth, but dagger in heart!"

Suddenly I was outside, standing in the noontime traffic like the whole encounter had never occurred—but I could still smell the cigar smoke and see his warm smile. *Dagger in the heart?* I looked down at the paper in my hand, blinking in the light. It was an old, creased wedding photo of an elegant gweilo bride, flapping doves, and a startled-looking groom. I looked closer at the bride's hard, colorless eyes. They stared boldy back at me. I felt mesmerized; she was terrifyingly beautiful. As my finger traced the cracks in the surface, I looked at a dark blotch on the paper and scraped it. Brown dust crumbled under my nail. I tasted it. Could it be—*blood?* I flipped it over. It was a postcard. On the back penned in strong elegant script was the date, *1 November 1937,* and beneath that, *Violet Summerhays, Hong Kong socialite, married today.* As the taste of iron spread through my mouth, I knew my life was about to change. And I knew in my heart, that if I was to move forward, I had to know the past, however terrible it might be.

Book One

1926-1937

Sea Voyage

1

Peninsula & Oriental Steamship *July 1926*

THERE WAS A LOT of blood in the water when he was pulled on deck just off the Malaya coast, a few hours out of Jahor. He'd nearly been eviscerated, but Jack couldn't remember much after being heaved out of the sea like a tuna, sailing half drowned over deck.

He revived consciousness a week later in a fever and found himself in Hong Kong with an old English nurse peeling off his bandages, asking how it was possible he did not remember meeting *the* Mr. Summerhays. "He's a taipan, you know." She pushed up her glasses. "His account of your heroism is printed right here in the *South China Morning Post.* Says, 'Destiny has seen fit to save the lad for something better …' Better than dying, I should say. You're lucky you're alive. And Summerhays says he'll do you a good turn. Now, that's as good as gold."

There was little Jack knew about destiny or taipans, but lying on the hospital bed with nothing but time on his hands, the strange, fateful event on the Celebes Sea slowly began to come back to him. His ship had set sail from Port Said the week before, but Jack had been sick below deck until that evening, when he'd come up for fresh air. Everything around him was so new, so strange—the wet touch of tropical heat, the sharp smell of human sweat commingling with onions and curry frying below deck, and the people of all races and colors speaking at once. Jack turned and stared westward toward home, his throat tight with grief. At the horizon the hazy sun was sinking lower and lower, flaming as it touched the rim, then it dipped out of sight. Kentucky was a world away, as good as lost to him; he'd spent all he had to get this far. On deck, lamps were lit, one by one, and the moon came out with the stars. The excited gabble of passengers waiting for dinner distracted him and he eavesdropped. Listening to their polyglot of gibberish, however, made him realize how little he actually knew about the world, its languages and its people. Even the clipped speech of the English confounded him.

Dismayed with his own lack of sophistication and learning, he leaned over the side, watching the water rushing far below and wished his mother could have been there—this had been *her* dream. Jack had spent six months doing two shifts at the mine to earn the money needed for her medical treatment, but a month ago when he'd returned home with an envelope bulging with cash, he'd found her—eyes and mouth wide open, arm dangling off the side of the bed. She had removed the silver tiger charm she'd worn all her life and it sat in her palm, winking in the lamplight. It had been her most precious possession, brought back from French Indochina by her father, a sea captain. She had always wanted Jack to have it, to pass on. He took it from her dead fingers, weighing it in his hand—*cold*. He looked at the stack of money he'd saved in vain for her and didn't know what to do.

A priest from the mining company was sent over after the funeral. "Son, don't take it so hard. In time you'll find it's not death that's a bitter struggle, it's life."

Jack wondered about that as he sat in the dark kitchen, the oil lamp wick burned up, the old clock ticking. Mother had filled his head with so many seafaring tales that as a little boy he'd shout, "I'll never work in the mine! Never! I'm going to sea like Granpapa!" She would caution, afraid of what she'd stirred in him, "Jack, we're tied to the mine by the fire in our bellies." But he dreamed her dreams, seeing the beautiful exotic faces Grandfather had described, and the open skies above sails filled with wind—all as he worked hundreds of feet down a coal chute in perpetual blackness. There and then, he decided mining was not a daily struggle he wanted a part of anymore, and without a word to anyone, he picked up and left Kentucky—for her sake as well as his own.

Thousands of miles away in the growing darkness over the Celebes Sea, Jack didn't notice the real-life skirmish beginning farther down deck from him where two Chinamen were struggling silently. Mesmerized instead by the translucent water, he watched as it streamed away full of stars and in its depths saw his mother's eyes. When the two bodies separated with a sudden flash of steel and a quiver, he didn't hear the groan, or see the body fall overboard, but a terrible scream raised the hair on his neck, and he stood back, startled.

A Chinese girl was rushing about on deck, pleading, but the passengers kept back, almost frightened by her desperation. "Save life! Save life!" Running along the rail her warm hand found Jack's, and his heart stopped.

"*Please*, Tuan!"

His eyes, which had been searching for a place to bury himself in the sea, had found hers instead—slanted and dark above flower petal lips.

Shouting for the nearest crew member, Jack rushed a coxswain: "Stop the ship, there's a man overboard!" Pointing over the side, Jack didn't notice the strange air on deck, how he, the bewitching girl, and the crewman were standing between the white passengers on one side, and the Chinese on the other.

The crewman, enjoying the situation, stood arms akimbo, not moving. Looking over Jack's threadbare clothes with an oily grin, he guffawed, "A man? You mean a bloomin' coolie! 'Is own bhoys threw 'im ov'r for bad debts at Fan Tan. I don't see thim 'elping 'im." It was true, Jack now noticed, that neither the Chinese who stood laughing nervously at the rail nor the white Christians who wrung their hands did anything to save the man. "If 'twere a white man," he was saying to Jack, "we'd 'ave shtopped. But costs money to shtop 'n' 'tis no use av shtoppin' whin t' bloomin' divils can be bought for a fiver in Malaya. 'Oo's to rhisk losin' thir hand fohr shark grub?" The man pointed at the girl. "All fohr a poxy yellow thart?"

All Jack could think of was the body drifting farther and farther into open sea and the pretty woman on deck. His clothes came off easily, and he could feel the tropical wind on his hot skin like a breeze from another world. He didn't hear the shocked gasp of the passengers behind him. Instead, he leaped up onto the railing barefoot and, recalling his dives into the rain-filled quarries as a child, judged the huge drop to the sea below. "Stop, you there!" came the startled cry from a boatswain who rushed forward to grab Jack's leg, but he was a moment too late. Jack was flying straight down in a swan dive and, for the first time since his mother's illness, he felt a tremendous surge of peace in his body, lifting his soul as he remembered his failed promise to her—*I will save your life.*

Then he hit water. It was as hard as a rock face and shocked the air out of his lungs in a blast. Gasping, choking he saw the ship sweep past silently, and suddenly he was alone in open sea.

He called and called for the man, but the blowing spray filled his lungs as he tried to see over the waves. Powerful, cold, and black, the sea drained his strength until he finally stopped fighting it. Then it buoyed him up, salty, indifferent, rolling him down long glassy sheets of moonlit waves. Whitecaps foamed above, and he was sent reeling down deeper and deeper troughs. When the moon emerged from cloud cover he spotted the face, flotsam gray. Jack called, waved, then began to swim toward him. The heaving troughs at first brought them closer together, when suddenly the coolie was lifted up up, up, as Jack dropped. And then the wave crested. Simultaneously they both began to fall, down, down, down—the man at his tail, faster and faster, until they were tumbling over one another in a tunnel of water.

The moment it passed Jack made an attempt to rise and suck some air into his lungs, but the man was clawing up Jack's body like a ladder out of hell, pushing Jack under as if he could climb up and step out of the sea. Underwater the silence was startling, and then came churning confusion; a knee banged into his head, a foot cracked him in the ear. Jack pulled the man down and rose up himself, breaking the surface, gasping, but found himself once again shoved down into the eye-burning roil, his lungs bursting for air. Suffocating, the pain in his chest growing, he discovered he was not ready to die, and on his way up he clubbed the man, knocking him unconscious.

He was an excellent swimmer and did the sidestroke, pulling the body along by the chin so that the unconscious man could still breathe. In time his arms grew numb and heavy, his legs ached. The man was bleeding, but Jack made his promise over and over—*I must save his life.* Every now and then he was reassured by the sight of the ship, far off like a low, bright star and growing in size. But as time crept by he became faint, losing his sense of direction, and the sky, speckled with stars, appeared above and below—the color of the universe, deep blue and fathomless, spinning as he swam. And then blackness …

The next time he opened his eyes he found himself blinking up at two silhouettes in a brightly lit room. One was leaning over him. "Look at those stitches. A shark or the coolie's knife—who's to know? But it's as ugly a stitching job I've laid my eyes upon. Imagine—jumping overboard for a coolie."

"Ay," the other said, musing. "But he's got bollocks and not a thought for himself. I need someone like that."

"Well then. Let's hope he pulls through."

"Young man," the voice said loudly. "Can you hear me? Oh, never mind. I'm going to hire this lad. Give him my address when he comes to."

"Yes, Mr. Summerhays. I most certainly will."

Auspicious Beginnings

2

St. John's Cathedral, Hong Kong *November 1, 1937*

Jack Morgan stood partway up Victoria Peak at the fork in Battery Path, already late for his wedding. Ten long years had passed since his leap into the Celebes Sea. In that time he had turned Mr. Summerhays's firm around, and risen to second in command at China Coast Navigation; today he was to marry the man's only daughter. Jack squinted, and eyed the deep-water strait far below filled with seafaring junks and cargo ships. The blue swath of water cut Hong Kong Island off from China and the rest of the world, and from his past, too. Jack looked to the right. Only fifty feet away, the doors to St. John's Cathedral yawned wide open—a hundred guests and his bride waited inside. Jack looked back across the sparkling strait. Less than a thousand miles directly north into China, the Japanese Imperial army was hunkered down in trenches, bleeding, stinking, training—also waiting. Disparate peoples and cultures, yet aligned with his life they were a bullet and a gun. If he could have seen—could have made the connection and looked down that barrel at the life he'd been pushed into choosing he might have shot himself then and there. But there are slower ways to die.

Up above, the clock tower began chiming out the hour. He was now a half hour late, but still, he didn't move. He couldn't. Under his formal jacket, in his shirt pocket, now damp with sweat, there was a telegram and it felt like a cold palm pressed to his chest, chilling him even on this hot day. He couldn't disprove its contents, he didn't dare. But he told himself, *To run from blackmail and lies is impossible.* Even so, his instinct urged, *Leave Hong Kong.* Instead, he stood still, fingers tapping the hip flask in his pocket. *If I leave,* he reasoned, *I will lose everything I've worked for ...* He didn't, however, consider what he'd lose by staying.

Good-looking and still in his thirties, Jack had every reason to think the future was in his lap. He was an important man in the colony. Tipping back his head he emptied the silver flask of its burning contents with a silent toast to his future and his luck—whereupon he choked, and then coughing with dismay, turned the bottle upside down. He watched the last shining drop soak into the dry ground. *All gone.* The past was all gone too, this was true, for no one from his family was alive to see him marry, or witness his heretofore-amazing success. *Poor Mother*, he thought, she'd have marveled at the elegance and finery of this wedding—not to mention the guest list. Surely mother would have loved old Percy, his generous father-in-law and chairman; he could not be so sure about his intended.

By formal standards Violet Summerhays was a striking girl, who also knew when to speak and when to hold her tongue. She kept herself busy with a full social schedule attending dances and parties, and hacks at the Fan Ling Hunt. As far as club gossip went, however, she was thoroughly disliked by her friends, who, when pressed, declared she went beyond the pale. Some even said she paid her way through life. As for luck and the business of marriage, unknown to Jack, these too had been contrived by the wallet. Violet had secretly consulted native wisdom for an auspicious wedding date and had hired a geomancer to review his charts for the year of the ox. Violet had also pressed her father into her service—"Make him marry me, Papa." Percy could not have been more willing and saw to it that his right-hand man accepted the proposal. So when the Heaven and Earth chi aligned, and the contour of time was decreed positive, November 1, 1937, was selected. On this day, with the geomancer's blessing, she was to marry this most eligible bachelor to the great envy of many Hong Kong society girls. True, they said it was ambition on both sides, but no one ever said, *Serves him right,* for Jack Morgan was well-liked and still possessed that earnest glow of youth that made so many people smile in those early days when they looked at him. His bride, however, preening in St. John's vestibule, was champing at the bit, the taste of victory in her mouth. She could hardly know that Jack would be her final prize, and that fate, like bamboo, though it parts for the wind, would no longer part for her. Had she been told, she would have laughed. Everything had always gone her way. Nor was she troubled that he was late; she threw a satisfied glance at the large cage of doves, cooing and flapping, knowing that in a short time they would be released and she would walk out into the sunshine with the biggest catch in Hong Kong on her arm.

Outside across the road, just a stone's throw from the vestibule, Jack held the empty flask in his hand, transfixed by the silver reflection of the wild bamboo grove at his back and the long green stems that moved across the surface of the curved flask like beckoning fingers. Abruptly, a hand on his shoulder startled him out of his stupor. It was his best man.

"So Jack," Algernon sneered, a note of warning in his voice. "I see you're relying on liquor to get the job done. Never have before."

Jack pulled his shoulder free, stumbling, and then crossed the road into the sheltered forecourt of the cathedral. Empty as a cage, its hot silence enclosed him in a small airless pocket of beauty—stone arches, bricked walks, shrubs shaped like clouds. Moving closer toward the church, he passed through moving shadows and spots of sunlight, not knowing if it were the trees that were swaying or if it was him.

Algernon followed just behind. "I say! You really going to *stagger* through it like *this?*"

Feigning deafness, Jack gazed at the foliage high above. Shifting and illusive as a whiff of jasmine, there was dazed poetry to drunkenness, a transient sense of well-being. Even the stench of sewage was barely noticeable. Nearby a coolie snored gently, and some pretty amahs added to the charm as they sat by a stone nullah sharing a meal of rice and fried fish. But as he stepped into the sunlight the chopsticks and the black eyes halted—and followed the shaft of light to this white man who seemed marked out for something special. He sensed their interest, and his deep-set eyes locked onto their curious gaze.

The girls blushed. Jack made a comic formal bow and they broke into giggles, hiding their faces. It was only when his eyes turned back to the beautifully printed sign, "Summerhays-Morgan wedding," that he paused, and a tiny jolt, a premonition, penetrated the haze. His captive eyes went down to the next line: *China Coast Navigation, Hong Kong.* Below that, the prestigious crest of the company seal granted authorization.

"You wanchee ride?" A voice called out as if from a dream. It was a coolie, harnessed in the shafts of a rickshaw, standing over by the French Mission building. Gesturing in the direction of town, he was holding up three fingers.

"A cheap price for freedom," Algy said, his voice kinder now. "Please think about it, Jack. You've got two legs, a brain, and you work hard. There's a future for you anywhere you go."

Poised at the outermost edge of the church, Jack thought of the immense self-sacrifice it had taken to rebuild Percy's firm single-handedly. It was now regarded as a top company up and down the entire South China Coast, and old Summerhays was the first to sing his praise. But some months ago, Percy, drunk and unable to look Jack in the eye, proposed a deal. "Jack," he'd said shamefacedly, "I gave you a chance when no one would. Violet wants to marry you. I can't accept no for an answer."

Suddenly he felt himself being pulled away from the doors.

"Wake up, for God's sake," Algy whispered in a low, desperate voice. "Don't do it. She's hard as nails. Even Percy's jumping hoops!"

Jack jerked his arm away. He didn't like being pushed and pulled; it was one reason he'd held out so long against the marriage. And now this insinuation that Violet, his younger by some ten-odd years, could possibly be choreographer of his future was beyond belief. He pulled on the white gloves Violet had asked him to wear and moved again to the center of the open doors. It was then a face popped out of the church, spotted him, and immediately ducked back in. He heard the sound of a hundred guests turning in their seats to look, felt their eyes on him, then stepped onto the red carpet. Immediately the organ struck its chord, smashing the silence like a tray of dishes hitting the ground.

After that, all he felt was his pounding heart and the slow pace of his legs. The blur of faces and feathered hats turned to follow him as he passed, but it was like a fever-induced dream and the smells of dripping candle wax, perspiration, mothballs, and heavy perfumes brought wave after wave of nausea over him. Oddly enough, he did not stagger, but in his whisky-soaked mind the image of the empty, waiting rickshaw suddenly appeared before him. Rather than turn and run, he almost laughed, for his common sense had long since drowned in a fluid bubbling extinction at the bottom of his glass. And yet here, here in the church above the roar of the organ, now of all times, the strange woman's face suddenly became real, calling him, calling from that one sanguinary place in his heart which still remembered. He turned, mystified. *Even over the organ, he could hear her distant voice.* His eyes raked the crowd. They'd spent three days together in China, six months ago—three days he'd tried hard to forget. Dismayed, he looked back ahead of him and walked to the end of the carpet. They hadn't even kissed, and yet—*And yet.*

It was too late to do anything but stand at the altar. The best man at his side seemed to vacillate between tense hysteria and doomed silence. A murmur swept over the crowd, and they both turned to see the bride. Her father and a queue of maids, step by step, led her in toward the pulpit, a veiled pupa in white. The hair on his neck rose. For the life of him, he couldn't see or remember her face—he felt embalmed, unable to wake. Oh sure, he'd gone to parties with her, danced two summers of balls, his name filling most of the blanks on her dance card at Percy's insistence, and he'd dined with her and her father up at Peak House. All that evaporated. As she joined him at the altar, he looked sidelong at this veiled figure with whom he was to spend the rest of his life, and realized she was a stranger.

"Will you take this woman … sickness … health …" Jack's responses were short drowning gulps. He stared at the veil that drifted eerily with her breathy responses. When the voice paused to ask if there was anyone present who objected to the union, Jack didn't hear, but when it said, "I pronounce you man and wife," like a gunshot his mind flew back to the moment six months ago in Shanghai, when the city was falling to the Japanese—yes again, he could hear the bombs, see the buildings crumbling, and superimposed over the flames, over this bridal veil, he saw the face that had secretly burned into his heart and dreams, the face that matched the inner voice. *Ana.*

The veil came up on Violet Summerhays's triumphant face, the wrong face, and realization caused a spasm in his chest. Jack quickly suppressed this disturbing self-knowledge to the farthest reaches of his thoughts, and leaned forward to kiss his new wife. But at the very moment when his lips pressed hers, and their eyes met, the shock was like that of a door slamming, and Jack knew with dead certainty that he had made a terrible mistake. He let out a small, futile gasp—*Too late, too late.* The seed of destruction was already planted deep in his heart.

Out on the church threshold, Jack thrust his hand into his pocket. He'd always kept the tiger there. And all these years he'd planned to give this link from his past to his future wife. But the pocket was empty. He'd given it to Ana on a whim, taking a chance on love. He stared at his empty palm. A sudden roar of wings startled him and, as he looked up, he felt the hot flash of a camera.

Violet grabbed his arm. "Carry on, Jack, it's all over now," she laughed through her teeth, and led him into to the boisterous crowd pelting them with rice.

"God save the King!" a voice cried out. Two parallel lines of uniformed men raised their swords in salute and Jack and Violet ducked, passing under and into their new life. "God save the King," the guests echoed back as the flock of doves whirred higher and higher up over the Crown Colony, disappearing into the blue of the sky. It was a perfect day for a wedding, and none of the guests congratulating the couple could have believed that in four short years the Japanese flag would be flying over Hong Kong and that many of those lining up for the group photos would be in internment camps, dying. But that day did come.

China *1 November 1937*

IT HAD BEEN AN auspicious day for departure. November 1 was Tai-an, O-bachan, his grandmother, had pointed out. Good day for weddings, departures, coming back alive. Yoshi Sakura closed his eyes trying to forget he was so far from home. He'd never killed—didn't know the feel of an animal's blood on his hands, much less that of a human. The train swerved.

Yoshi opened his eyes. He could see nothing through the slats but the endless sky over China. He sighed. The sound of the train was finally lulling him to sleep. It had been the longest day in his life, though actually he didn't know how much time had passed since he'd left Tokyo—only that he hadn't slept. He did know that all the train cars were loaded to burst with the fifth and sixth companies of the third battalion of the sixth regiment. Infantry—378 fresh soldiers heading to central China. Back at Tokyo headquarters a new marker pin was stuck in a map, marking their progress in this war of great casualties. Yet it was an exhilarating war, he could sense it in the air. "Remember, what you lack in experience and hardware you'll compensate with your sense of duty and Yamato spirit!" This had been the urgent send-off in Tokyo. "With spirit alone we can win!" He'd believed them, he didn't want to be a slacker.

"I'm going to the front lines." It was with these words that he'd announced his good-byes to all the people in his village: schoolteachers, neighbors, and the girl he secretly desired. "We will honor you!" they all repeated, excited and proud as they signed his flag. He didn't

even know what he expected to find in central China, but when his younger sister had asked, "O-nichan, what will you do there?" he'd answered her boldly, "We'll march," for he'd had much training in the past weeks marching. He'd been issued a rifle too. "We'll shoot at the enemy," he added. "And where will you sleep, elder brother?" "Ah, barracks, I suppose." Yoshi had no clue, not even now, one week and thousands of miles from little Yumiko's awed gaze. He asked himself, *At which city will we disembark? Where are they taking us?* But he didn't dare ask his fellow soldiers, fearing even innocent questions might be looked upon as dissent. So Yoshi squared his face, trying to appear as stern as when he scolded Yumiko, and silently repeated what he knew. *I am a soldier of the Imperial Army. Yes, I would be proud to die for my Emperor.* But it wasn't exactly true.

Last year his asthmatic uncle had rated Class C and had been posted to Hong Kong! Imagine that—women, sake, food! Healthy as a horse, Yoshi had been rated Class A, and was assigned to the infantry. All he could do was bow with humble thanks to the town official who handed over the notice, and accept his congratulations. "Please don't worry," the man had said that sunny day at the front door of the family minka as he'd handed Yoshi a folded red-disk flag, "for if you fall in action we will enshrine you in Yasukuni." *If I should fall?* He had watched as the flag was tied to a weeping cherry tree beside his house and thought of Uncle dancing to jazz records whenever he was drunk. *He'd gotten off scot-free.* But it was shameful to complain, it was un-Japanese. *It was never done.* And so it was the front lines for Yoshi.

Now far away on the train, and hungry, he reached into his pack feeling around for stray crumbs of O-sembei. *None left.* It was then his fingers touched the soft folded flag inked full of signatures and encouraging words. *"Gambatte! Endure for our sake!"* the villagers had written. Next to it he felt the final photograph taken last week. Mother, father, the family stiffly lined up in front of their thatch-roof minka, and he in his new uniform standing a little to the side, already apart.

Unable to work the fields, O-bachan was eighty-seven and unlikely to see him again. She alone had traveled all the way from

Kamakura to Tokyo Station to say good-bye to Yoshi. His smooth brow dimpled slightly as he thought of her so far away now. He and his fellow soldiers had taken a train to Yokohama from there, then a ship, then a ferry at the embarkation office. Finally, here he was in an open slat train car somewhere in China. He leaned on his rifle, fingering his bayonet. *If I die so far from home, how will my spirit find its way back to Yasukuni?* His Commander had cut off all such thoughts in training. *Fight to the end!* he'd screamed over and over. They would step, and thrust, step and thrust, and plunge the sharp dagger into a dummy made of straw lying on the ground. *What is the spirit of the bayonet?* Commander would roar and they would answer, *To Kill, To Kill.* And they moved as a group, possessed with spirit in a mechanical dance full of kill.

"You are ready," training Commander reminded as he saw them off. "Fight to the end!" he bellowed as the train departed Tokyo Station. Yoshi could also see O-bachan's bent form waving a handkerchief at the edge of the platform. He knew what she was saying. "Remember the tiger, Yoshi-chan. Even wounded, the tiger returns alive." All Yoshi could think of was Uncle going to Hong Kong and living it up in jazz clubs. *I'll get there myself,* he thought, *by hook or by crook and I'll never have blood on my hands.*

Foreign Devils

3

Three months before the wedding …
Peak House, Hong Kong *7 August 1937*

The previous night had been chilly, and at dawn an opalescent haze had gathered on the opposing shore, sparkling in the sunlight over Kowloon. High up here on Victoria Peak's dark northern slope however, the same haze had a cold, smoking opacity. Coiling and uncoiling with damp stealth, it was as if it had a conscience, as if it were somehow waiting, judging but patient, Oriental in nature. When the sun finally did clear the high ridge above, stabs of light penetrated the gloom below, and brilliant jewel tones flashed—cerulean butterflies, potted orange trees, emerald green tennis lawns … Between snatches of mist, coolies too could be spotted on the jungle path, bent double under bamboo poles as they hauled up provisions for the English who resided at these elevations. When the first strong gust of wind blew, Peak House, too, finally emerged from its shroud, terraced, with white pillars and arches, a magnificent example of British colonial taste. And there, drifting down its walkway in a cream satin dressing gown was the mistress of the house, her red hair and jewelry catching the light as she waved and cooed in her plummy voice. "Jaa—aaaaack. Oh Jaaaack!"

The two men on the driveway glanced back uphill at Violet, half smiled, then looked past her toward the house where there had been a sudden bark. It had come from the kitchen, as a small terrier darted out followed by Cook Boy Number One. Jack's face broke into a grin as the dog tore straight down the hill.

"Agh! Ling-Ling, you old bitch!" Percy said with great affection, leaning over to pick up the leaping terrier who simply adored the old man.

Violet cringed. "It's a filthy beast. Put it down!" She rushed forward and her abalone fan came down hard on the dog's nose. But the terrier was quick; snatching the fan away, it shook it like a rat, tearing the silk concertina, so when Jack finally was able to hand it back it was wet and shredded. Wide-eyed, Cook Boy scooped up his dog and hurried off toward the house.

Percy looked at Jack, "You see? Women are like that, always jealous!" They laughed heartily as Violet opened her fan in dismay.

Jack got into the car and the white-gloved chauffeur closed the door behind him. The old man stooped to look in. "Why not put this trip off? We'll know by September if there's war."

"Percy, you can get in, or you can get out, but you can't do both."

"It's not worth it," the old man frowned. "You might not get out alive this time." When his future son-in-law didn't answer, he shook his head. "You'll learn one day—there are forces beyond your control."

Violet snapped her fan against the car. "You going alone?" She was watching Jack closely.

His brows furrowed a second, then he said, "No. Algernon's meeting me at the ship. There's a bit of accounting on this trip. Why?"

Violet shrugged, looking away, restraining herself from rolling her eyes while her father scribbled down an address for Jack. "Call my banker in case there's trouble," he said, concerned.

She stood a few feet apart, observing how their mutual affection and private jokes excluded her from their world. *Jack could do no wrong in Father's eyes.* She frowned, twisting her engagement ring, a cushion-cut Golconda diamond. The jeweler said there was nothing bigger than this in Hong Kong, but she'd been expecting far more from Jack. He hadn't even noticed her new gown was transparent. She pulled it tight around her, suddenly cold.

"See you," he said with a blasé wink as the car pulled away down the steep driveway and out the tall iron gates.

Jack was a man who had been hard to catch—still wasn't caught—and had raised the red flag in her mind by putting off the wedding several times already. Violet stood, arms crossed, wondering if Jack had a lover in Shanghai. "Father, I don't appreciate the comments you make in front of him. Me, jealous, like the dog?" She kicked at a pebble with the toe of her French silk pump.

"I meant nothing by it," he said turning back toward the house, his face flushed from blood vessels in his red cheeks that looked like maps of rivers with all their tributaries.

"Off the cuff, is it?" she snapped her fan. "Well, these comments have a way of insinuating themselves."

"Violet Summerhays," he scolded sharply, his blue eyes flashing under craggy white eyebrows. "Sarcasm is *not* attractive in a young lady. Besides, Jack's risking his very hide with this trip." Seeing the dog nudge its way out of the kitchen door, Percy encouraged it again.

Violet felt all her wrath and frustration focus on the small bobbing point that came running back to Father, who took it in his arms, speaking to it in coddling tones, letting it lick his face. The terrier wriggled with joy, its brown eyes alive and its pink tongue panting. But when the dog's eyes turned to look at her, tongue lolling, teeth smiling, Violet felt as if it were taunting, for in a way, she understood; her heart, clenched and shrunken like a fist in rigor mortis, would never open up, never love—*didn't dare love*—and it was as if that dog were flaunting this secret knowledge of her. By God, she'd have liked to have taken up her fist and hammered that dog to death with it. Instead she pulled a tight smile, holding in her disappointment at being so misunderstood, and entered the house. Pausing at the hall mirror she straightened her bob. She had very large blue eyes, high cheeks and thin lips she always painted red. Even her friends misjudged her, and out of envy called her Ice Queen behind her back. Violet may have had everything, but what they didn't know was that she was hungry for more. For what, she didn't exactly know, but it was eating her alive.

Five days later ...
Cathay Hotel, Shanghai *12 August 1937*

ALGERNON RAISED THE BLACKOUT curtain as he poured a drink. He could hear gunfire and explosions pulsing at the outer edges of the city like the true heartbeat of China, troubled and erratic, growing louder by the hour. Just north of Shanghai at Woosung Port, on the Yangtze River, he'd heard the wireless announce that Chinese peasants were falling to the Japanese troops in their steady victory march south. Here, in Shanghai proper, the mandatory blackout had yet to take effect, but all the clanging and hawking noises that symbolized healthy fortune and the getting of money had stopped dead.

Any fool could see that Shanghai was about to hurtle into its future and instead of getting out of the way, Algernon Worthing, China Coast Navigation's junior accountant, could only stand in his bathrobe in the Cathay Hotel and stare at his useless ticket. At dawn that morning the Blue Funnel Line had pulled away from shore, leaving him and Jack Morgan in Shanghai. They'd come all the way to China for the sole purpose of meeting a client who hadn't had the decency to show up. Jack had been in a lather over it and as a result had gone and foolishly extended their stay in search of another client.

"Well, bugger him!" Algy flicked his ticket onto the red Chinese lacquer table. Staring at it, he was struck by the sharp contrast of the small white paper surrounded by the immense redness. Far from England, far from the rest of the world, he too was swallowed up by China. Algy tipped back his shot glass, then gazed out over Shanghai as the lights came on, reassuring himself that he was safe in the confines of the luxurious Cathay Hotel. But as he looked toward the blackened rubble of the decimated Chinese part of town, Nantao, an awful sense of doom came over him. *He'd been attacked yesterday; what might happen tomorrow?* The Communists and the Kwomintang in China were engaged in a bloody civil war and the Japanese were only using this to their advantage to divide and conquer. They were secretly said to be assisting the Kwomintang Nationalists under Chiang Kai-shek. But how was it that Chiang didn't see—once he defeated the Communists, he would be next?

Algy heaved a sigh as he dropped the curtain. *Certainly a raise was no good if he were dead!* He sniffed and took up a handkerchief moistened in eau de cologne and dabbed at his temples. Back at the home office, Percival Summerhays was "setting an example" by forcing all his employees to pay up liquor debts around town by Monday next week. Because of Jack's delay Algy would now *miss* this deadline and face disgrace back in Hong Kong—*perhaps even blacklisting.* Feeling nauseous, he stretched out on the hotel bed closing his eyes. After a few moments however, his eyes popped open; there was a cracking noise. He sat up. *Gunfire?* Silence. After a minute he lay back down. *If only I hadn't gone to market yesterday. How gruesome.* Algy took a thermometer from the bedside table and slid it under his tongue. *I could have gotten typhus, even died in the melee! And would Jack have cared? Not a whit!*

It had happened in the morning, just after he'd finished up some business. He'd paused at the black market and purchased a lucky rabbit's foot, then, just as he was inspecting cut-priced American cigarettes, an armed Japanese guard troop marched by, parting the local Chinese horde with an air of disdain. Algy barely had time to duck as a rotten cabbage flew over him and thunked a guard in the head. Before he knew what was happening, a mass of natives surged every which way—rifle butts cracked down on heads, people groaned, screamed. Algy lurched backward, lost his topee, and fell into a massive tray of eels; the whole thing gonged as it hit the pavement spilling eels everywhere. There he was, struggling in a bloody, writhing mess of snakes when suddenly he'd become aware he couldn't move; an individual with an eye like an egg over easy was pinning him down and breathing hard in his face. Algy tried to pull away as the mouth opened and gasped its warm, vaporous threat: "*Foreign devil, get out!*"

Back at the hotel, visions of the rotted mouth, the eels, and the tumult haunted him all night until finally this morning he'd mentioned the incident at breakfast. But Jack would have none of it. "I say, that would put the wind up anybody. Mind your step, Algy." This was maddening. Algernon had again attempted to point out that politically things were deteriorating quickly and that he also needed to get back to pay his liquor bill when Jack had cut him off. "So that's what this is about. You little rotter! We're here on business! I'm not interested in the Communists, the Kwomintang, or the Japanese. And you dashing about Hong Kong, drinking up and then not paying for months on end, is positively the limit! You'll give me a fucking stroke if you keep this up. I'm not leaving, come hell or high water! And neither are you!"

Algy removed the thermometer, squinted. *No fever—yet.* He pulled up the blackout curtain. Well, the weather report was correct. *Typhoon approaching.* That must be the high water. And hell? Well he had a good view of it from the window. Hundreds of junks, sampans, and other spindly insect-like craft were slowly covering the entire Wangpoo River like a black stain, all presumably seeking refuge in the shadow of the gargantuan warships. He couldn't tell if it was the war or the storm they were escaping, but an hour ago he'd noticed the refugees had started pouring in by land. The International Settlement was closed off by barbed wired—completely separate from the rest of China, its civil war and starvation; but now they'd broken through. Taking his tea at four o'clock in the lobby he'd looked out onto Nanking Road. *He'd never seen anything like it.* An endless crush of people flowed past the hotel swinging heavy bundles on bamboo poles, staggering under the weight of household goods, umbrellas, and babies; they'd come to the heart of the Settlement for protection. All it would take now was one incident and the war would be upon them; for all he knew he could be facing Japanese bayonets in his pajamas tonight. Algy quickly drew down the blackout curtain. Until now the International Settlement had been a safe entrepôt for business and provided a cushy lifestyle for the expats from mainly France, Britain, Holland, and the US. But for how much longer? The Japs were late to the game and now wanted the whole show for themselves.

It was half past ten. Algy was supposed to be getting dressed after his bath, and in an hour's time be on his way with his boss to an evening of smutty establishments, lugubrious thrills, and illegal transactions. Jack had dug up a fresh client this afternoon, Lucky Chan, some opium dealer, and was charged up about the prospects of a deal. Algy looked at the white suit which lay on the bed, as if waiting for him to decide. *In a pig's eye I'll go,* he thought. *To the Jade Gate Club? With a notorious opium dealer in the dead of night? Hah! Not my idea of a rattling good time.* Again he heard the distant crack of gunfire and a low grumbling. Algy snatched his cigarettes and dropped back on the bed, lit up, and stared at the ceiling. *Am I the only sane person here?* It seemed that way, for all over town foreign residents of Shanghai, at home in their villas, were settling down for a pleasant weekend. He'd heard their plans earlier at tiffin. He'd been invited to croquet and charades and turned them down, stupefied. "But the International Settlement is safe, young man." That was their mantra, and their case in point was that in '32 the Japs had taken over the Settlement with a few deaths and bombings—then realizing they'd lost face internationally, they backed down. This was the worst case and it had proven insignificant—or so Jack said. But what did he know? He was Percy's lapdog, living for the old man's approval, worshiping him. Algy slammed down his lighter. *What an ass! I'm a fool to depend upon him.*

He got up and paced the area around the bed following the pattern in the carpet, then practiced the mambo for a few steps, when the hair on his neck stood up. Turning his head from door to window he held his breath, listening. Noises came from the hotel's rooftop tea garden, the ting of porcelain teacups, the quiet laughter, and the calls for the Chinese boy serving drinks and appetizers. *There!*

He heard it again. In a second he was at his window peering out onto the rooftop of the building across the street. Three barefoot Chinese were running stealthily in the twilight, hunched over, carrying guns. Quickly they passed out of his sight. Even though he was in his bathrobe, Algy wasted no time donning carpet slippers and running from his room, down the hall to the elevators where he could get a better view. Throwing open the window, he peered across the threshold, and then leaned out even further to see. The window jamb was pushing hard against his stomach but in that position he could observe a sniper lying flat out on a ledge, motioning downward. Algy, holding onto the voluminous pongee silk curtain and putting his leg out the window, straddled the sill, and tipped out as far as he could without falling.

Far below, a uniformed patrol of about a dozen Japanese soldiers was marching in one body, a caterpillar creeping to an uncertain fate. Algy thought of shouting or throwing his slipper down to warn them, but in his agitation to hold his robe together he felt the sill slip from his hand. Losing balance, he cried out, gripping the curtain on his way out and over. There was a loud rip.

It was the foot inside that saved him. It bumped up against a table leg and he stopped, frozen—hanging in space, robe whipping upside down—and a cold breeze fanning his naked nether region. In a panic he worked his foot down, hooking it on the table leg, and slowly brought his body back upright. The Chinamen on the roof opposite were laughing while one of them raised a revolver at him. Algy dove back inside, landing on his ass in front of the elevator doors with his heart in his throat, face flushed, waiting frozen—expecting gunshots. None came, but the elevator bell tinged. An elderly lady stepped out and then looked straight down where his robe had fallen away. She choked out a throaty scream and ran off down the hall. Algy gasped, and leaped up, pulling his robe about him, then hid, quaking behind the torn curtains until the elevator doors closed and the hall went silent. He must have flushed three shades of Communist, but eventually curiosity got the better of him. He peered out the window again—tentatively, keeping well within the frame.

In the stillness he heard a rifle sliding along the cornice and his gaze moved over the rooftop. Instantly his eyes were on it as it pointed downward. Algy peered over to see the trajectory and nearly swooned. Far below, a guard in black Japanese uniform marched out of the hotel onto the street, striding diagonally across the road through crowds of pedestrians and hawkers.

The shot was not distinctive at all, a low pop. The laughter in the hotel tea garden continued, even the people nearest moved without stopping. Algy watched as the guard crumpled, and suddenly was lying flat on the street like an x. There was a shout and screams as people spewed away from the black spot, and in seconds the street was empty. Algy hung in the frame, frozen, and then slowly looked over to the sniper thirty feet away. Their eyes met. Sudden noise came from the street and they both looked down. The guard troop was returning at a clip with guns raised, and as they scanned upward they began shooting at random. Windows cracked in the building opposite, and glass rained down onto the street.

Racing back to his room Algy made a dash for the telephone. "Concierge!" he said after breathlessly waiting for the connection. "Yes. Boy, this is of utmost confidentiality, do you understand?"

He could hear the concierge grinning in that deprecating manner of the seasoned hotelier, "Yes, Mass-itah Worthing. Of course."

"I *need* to know which *ship* is departing *this evening* for *Hong Kong*," he said slowly enunciating. "I want—to book—a *single—passage*." This was not the usual concierge who spoke impeccable English.

The boy cut him off with more cheerful effrontery, "No can do. Ship go Hong Kong side now. Everbody leave. Mei you. Ticket all gone."

"How so?"

"Some white man aflaid of Japanese mosquito," he said, bursting into peals of laughter.

"Listen," Algy said, "You get me a berth on any ship. I want to leave now. Savvy?"

"You wait. I maybe find."

"Where is the concierge?"

"Him sickum. No ploblem."

Algy rang off disconcerted. If only he could sneak down and look up the schedules himself, but Jack would be heading down to the lobby any minute. He raised the edge of the blackout curtain and peered out. Here and there, artillery fire flashed, momentarily outlining the seven Japanese warships, guns like quills on their backs, and not one embassy or foreign bank was out of their range. The Yangtze, thick with mud, glimmered under the darkening sky, while in the east it was black as spilled oil. The American warship, *U.S.S. President*, was nowhere to be seen. Algy checked his watch and looked at the silent telephone, then, chucking his robe, began to dress, hands fumbling with his shirt buttons. In exasperation, he opened his valise and took out a vial, carefully adding several drops of laudanum into his gin and bitters. Tipping back his head, he was gulping it down when there was a sudden pounding at the door. He choked, spluttering, and dabbed himself with his handkerchief, feeling gin up his nose. "W-who-?"

"It's Jack, for God's sake! Open the door."

Algy unbolted the lock, and peered round, sniffling.

"Aren't you dressed yet?" He glared at Algy's shirttails, bare legs and carpet slippers. "Our new client will be here in less than an hour!"

"I'm not feeling well," Algy said pinching his nose as the liquor stung his sinuses.

"Yes, you've been sick all week. What's the disease today, dysentery? Typhoid? Never mind. Security told me a man exposed himself to a lady on this floor. I suppose it wasn't you," Jack snickered, looking him over. "Anyhow, I'll be down in the lobby in twenty minutes. Get dressed, and here," he said pushing an envelope through. "I've checked your paperwork and want you to go over these tonight with Chan. A lot hinges on this, so do your damnedest. And be on time. Eleven sharp!"

She'd told security already? Algy shut the door, cursing under his breath and throwing the envelope onto the bed. *What if the old bat identified him? No—impossible. It hadn't been his face she'd been looking at.* He began to pour another drink when the telephone shrilled.

"Yes. Yes. This is Mr. Worthing," he answered quailing, with a glance at the door while pulling on his slacks with his free hand. "What? Oh! A steamer for Macao?" He couldn't believe his luck. "How do I get there? A rickshaw on Poo Tung side to the wharf? There? Why, I'll be murdered! No, no—it's all right! I'll take it!"

Algy put down the receiver and in a burst of energy began tucking in his shirttails. Across the river at that very moment a Portuguese steamer was loading on coal and would set sail in an hour's time. In the distance, a single-engine plane roared, louder and louder, and passed just over the building rattling all the glass. Algy cursed, losing a button off the snowy white trousers. *Oh dash it!* In a wild sprint about the room he skimmed his things from every surface, threw them into the suitcase, tied on his favorite checked cravat for luck, and lit a fresh ciggie. He was pulling on his tan shoes when the floor trembled with impact … *God, they're in Woosung already.* He was about to pop out the door when he remembered the papers that he'd spent hours writing up for tonight's client. He almost put them into his briefcase, then paused, taking a puff. *He's going to fire me anyhow,* he muttered then raised the curtain, and unlatched the window. A strong wind was blowing when Algy tore open the envelope and, before he could reconsider, Jack's papers ripped away instantly, fluttering out into the dark night like lost doves. "Oh bollocks!" he grimaced.

Peak House, Hong Kong *12 August 1937*

In the morning a note delivered by hand was waiting at breakfast for her; a letter from a friend's mother. Violet opened it without interest, then gasped.

"Are you all right, dear?" Percy tipped down his newspaper and stared over his spectacles.

Violet folded the note carefully.

He put down the paper slightly. "Well?"

"Pippa's just eloped!"

"Is that all? Well, bally good for her." He raised the paper up again.

Violet stared, furious. "Father, I was supposed to be married before Pippa, but here I am, still engaged a year later!" Her head throbbed as she wondered what to do. She hadn't slept in days and now felt faint. The doctor had prescribed pills for her nerves.

"No one's keeping score," he said from behind the paper. "And I'm tired of that topic, my dear."

"But I'm the last of my friends to marry. It's humiliating."

"Friends?" He stood up, removing his napkin. "You mean *rivals*. You only keep each other close so no one steals a march; that's not friendship."

"I don't care. I want a firm date."

"Later, my dear. I'm off to the office just now."

Violet threw down her own napkin and went to the library, closing all the shutters. "*Pippa eloped. A love match,*" she read in the dark—then crumpled the note … *Love?* Pippa had flirted shamelessly with Jack and Peebles all summer! Her eyes glazed. And now she married—*who—some nobody!* Pulled him out of a hat, no doubt. Violet took out her pills, but then was so tired she just lay down on the sofa. It must have been the tried-and-true manner, she mused—*Pippa* was *certainly pregnant.* She reached under the sofa mattress and removed the broken section of elegant glass walking stick she'd hidden there. It sparkled in the darkness as she ran her fingers over it. *My little trophy*, she thought with a sneer. Violet stroked it for a while, then closed her eyes and drifted in and out of sleep. Suddenly she jerked. Sitting up in a daze she heard Father's Studebaker and her pills fell onto the floor. *Was he coming or going?* Disoriented, she quickly combed her fingers through her hair, hid the cane segment in her sweater sleeve, then went out through the long hall, passing under Father's magnificent white tiger trophy with bared fangs. Unlike the city below, Peak House was perpetually dark and cool with its wide uncluttered spaces, ebony-stained teak floors, and high ceilings; Violet pushed open the verandah doors not knowing if it would be day or night. *Day* … A distant panorama of the harbor sprang into view beyond the trees.

Father was just sitting down at the verandah table. "What have you been doing all morning?" he asked over his shoulder, reaching for a cucumber sandwich from the heap on the silver tray.

She joined him on the shaded terrace while far below Hong Kong caught the afternoon sun, its rank odors and squalid dwellings concentrated into a single swath of clean-burning silver. "*What have I been doing?* I've been thinking how *Pippa* will soon be buying a house, starting a life while *I*—" Percy held up a finger silencing her and turned to look at the cooks stumbling about in long white aprons and wide black trousers, playing at croquet on the lawn for his amusement.

"Harder! Harder," he bellowed. The cook's apprentice looked toward the old man for direction with an exaggerated expression of doubt etched on his face, raising the mallet like a question mark. "Yes!" Percy shouted from the terrace. "That's it, now swing!" The ball chucked off sideways.

Her jaws clenched as she observed his sickly features. Father had been ill for ten years after his heart attack and she was forced to languish alongside him, wings clipped, caged, grasping at things through the bars—diamonds, rare butterflies, men like Jack—whatever she could reach from Father's house or tempt to his doors. *It wasn't fair.* Worse still, if Father remarried or died, she'd lose everything—unless, that is, she married his right-hand man. Only then could she be sure to secure the house, the firm, *and* the fortune—and Jack was that man. Unfortunately, he was turning out to be rather pigheaded, and she wasn't exactly sure what *he* was playing for.

"So," Percy turned at last to her, his wicker chair straining. "Don't you have enough here? Parties, servants, clothes—he'll keep his word. Why this monomania?" He frowned, then clapped at the cooks for attention. "Boy! Boy! Keep your eye on the ball! Then, SWING!"

"And what if he has a woman in Shanghai, Father? Then what?"

A moment later there was a hearty clunk, and the ball flew over the grass, ricocheted off a tree, and then shot down the steep drive with both servants in hot pursuit. Percy guffawed, "That's my boy! They'll have to sprint all the way to Wan-Chai to fetch that one!"

"Father! I need you to talk to me! But instead you arrange this spectacle of playing at golf with croquet mallets?"

He tapped his knee, signaling for the terrier to jump up, then paused, rubbing his sternum as if it pained him. "You're seventeen, Violet. You've time. Remember doctor's orders; Avoid excitement—and this monomania over infidelity. It's poison for your nerves!"

"Nothing's wrong with *my* nerves. And he *has* had countless lovers."

"By golly, he needn't go all the way to Shanghai for a lover!" he said getting up. "Foolish girl. China is about to fall and everyone wants a bigger share of the pie. He's representing my interests—and *yours!* Take up a hobby like other women."

Violet turned away to look over the railing, trying to quell the emotion that as a child would send her into fits of coughing. Pippa would have children before she and Jack ever stepped inside St. John's Chapel—*if he ever did. For what if Jack backed out again?*

"What is it, my dear?" Percy asked, coming to stand by her, his voice gentle and pitying, his hands reaching to her fists, undoing them finger by finger as he had when she'd been a child. "You know this match suits me like no other. He's a wonderful lad. But remember, men are simple brutes when it comes down to impulses. Like a bullock, he'll need time to settle into collar or he'll be that much harder to hold when married. Otherwise, what'll keep him here in Peak House?"

"A lock and key!" she said, thinking of Father's dalliances.

"Love and trust, my dear. And this needs time."

"Time? Father, you spend it at work with him!"

"Because I'm grooming him to take over. When I die I want to know the firm will continue and you'll be taken care of. In my judgment it's nigh overdue I sign control over to Jack's discretion. He puts all he's got into this job. I admire that and I *will* reward him."

Violet felt her face grow hot. It was the last straw. After Mother died, Father had courted a common shop girl, and then carried on for years with a *Chinese* woman. If it hadn't been for her own clever interference he might have even married one of them. Now it seemed that Jack would be edging in on her control, taking over the firm—and perhaps not even marrying her in the end. "What about me? Don't I have a say in anything?"

"Listen, my child, I've been too easy on you these years since Mother died and—"

"Mother?" she cried out, wretched. "I may have been born from a cabbage leaf for all you care for her memory! If you raised me wrong, then it was *your* fault. I refuse to be brushed aside by you men, your 'big jobs' and responsibilities." She cast her eyes about in desperation thinking she should just do like Pippa and get her man. Violet set her jaw. "You know, neither Jack nor you will set a firm date—it's all just high-jinx and drinks with you both!" Her insides trembled with agitation as she spoke, but she couldn't stop herself and the little voice that warned that she and Jack had never slept together … *that she was still a virgin* … that little voice—*just died.* "I'll tell you something," she said, flushed with rage. "I was going to spare you, but why? Legitimate or not, you can be expecting an *heir* to Peak House. Now. I believe we will get a date! Am I wrong?" It was an amazing feeling.

Percy's face reddened as he stared at her in disbelief. "Young lady, don't you ever, ever joke like that again!"

"Hardly a joke," she said watching father go white with shock. "I'm pregnant." Violet stood up and turned her back to him, dismissing the cooks who were returning, and felt a tingling flush, a thrill of power over the old man—*the first time.* In a light careless voice she said over her shoulder, "It happened recently, only six weeks ago." She was not entirely able to turn and lie to his face, for she was afraid she might laugh. *Was this madness?* She didn't know, or care, and trembled at the edge of hysteria. *At least someone will take me seriously now.*

Father was stammering.

"Too late for sermons," she said closing her eyes, holding up her palm. Her head was still throbbing.

The old man was addled and pulled at his collar, his face as pale and transparent as paper, revealing purple veins in his temples. "Jack didn't say a thing to me."

"Ah-hah! So now you see he's not your estimable Jack! Well?"

"Good God, you'll marry straightaway. You must." He was shaking his head, and then he reached for her arm, breathing heavily. "Gracious!" he muttered aloud, "What will people say?"

"They'll say terrible, terrible things. Shall I dispatch a telegram to Shanghai? I'll tell him you know *everything* and that you *demand* a date be set."

"By Jove, don't be so punitive. What's done is done. You can send that devil my congratulations. After all, I *am eager* to see him permanently settled here at Peak House." Then wandering ahead of her into the house he muttered, "And me—to be a grandfather—"

"And what about the fact that I am now a shamed woman?" But Percy hadn't heard. "Well, then," she announced, "I'll write him to *return* from Shanghai *immediately*."

"Let him do his job, dear. Let him stay as planned. I'm going to have a rest and a drink in my library, in peace, thank you."

"But father! I need to have a *say* in the business too."

"You?" He laughed. "Go. Send him a letter with my warmest congratulations. We need this all to work smoothly. There's not to be a breath of this around town." Then he firmly closed the door.

Congratulations? *Unlikely!* In her room, Violet wrote the note several times over, unsure how to word it. She hadn't even thought it out. *Pregnant?* Jack would have apoplexy. The thought made her laugh. She slid out the cane—her one proof of his infidelity, and spun it around. The question was—*would he contest her pregnancy?* To be sure, he'd want to know whose child it was. But would he have the temerity to face Percy and say—*I can't be the father; your daughter's a lying slut?* Violet lowered the pen to paper, laughing, gasping, writing out the telegram. As she signed her name she was a little horrified, rolling the swirling glass along her table top. It was as if she were driving, careening round the sharp curve at Magazine Gap Road with hands covering her eyes, tires squealing.

Auntie Rose entered the room and Violet jumped when the servant spoke, as she hid the glass segment.

"What for writum? I herim you talkee foolo ting!"

Rose's eyes were suspicious. But Violet imagined she wouldn't know what the glass segment was even if she had spotted it. "Why do you say that?" Violet said covering the paper. "Why do you listen to things not intended for your ears!" Most servants spoke pidgin, a bastardization of English, for the Chinese prejudice against the foreign devils prevented them from condescending to learn an inferior language. Violet found it all amusing; she herself could speak Cantonese like a street urchin.

"Hah!" the amah blurted. "What for you maritman, you no likum tru?"

Violet felt herself redden. "Take this to Number Two Boy. Make him go to telegraph office, chop-chop. Whom I marry is none of your business." It amazed her how Rose understood her proper English perfectly, and Violet suspected her sweet amah was a rebel at heart—breaking the back of every English word on her tongue on purpose and with distinct pleasure.

Rose snatched the paper. "When you lik-lik gir' you telle, 'Auntie Rose, same likum mamma,' now you talkee Auntie bad. Nogut Chinee coolie. Same likum dok. Troimweium." She headed out of the room, but added over her shoulder, "One day you needum dok."

"Throw *you* away?" Violet leaned back in the chair. "I'd sooner throw Poppa over! He makes me so cross. And—I don't need a dog, thank you. I'm marrying one who can't seem to keep his trousers on. Now *hurry!* I'm sick of his business in Shanghai. This note will *make* him return." As soon as Rose left the room she took out the piece of cane, spinning it between her fingers, watching it sparkle.

Kita Kamakura, Kanagawa Japan *12 August, 1937*

CALL IT A VISION or a visitation, but weeks before he got it, Yoshi had known his red call-up notice was on its way. He had gone to sleep by the kitchen one night with an eye on the brazier, tasked with keeping it lit until dawn. It had been hot out, and he left the shoji screen open to cool the room until he could drift off. But at midnight he jerked awake, touching his forehead. *Something wet had touched him.* He looked up at the ceiling; it was dry. He peered into the thick darkness. *Could someone be in the room?* He couldn't see anything but he could hear the wind over the rice paddy like steam hissing endlessly from a kettle. He could also smell cold incense ashes from the family shrine blowing through the house. *I could have been dreaming.* He rose and added three coals to the brazier then lay down with a heavy sigh. Sometime later he rolled over onto his side, and opened his eyes, chilled again. Even his breath frosted. He listened carefully. The room was pitch-dark, the coals an orange dot in the blackness. He thought he'd heard someone sloshing out in the flooded rice paddy. *But that was ridiculous.* He listened harder, but only heard his rapid heartbeat. Yoshi's gaze drifted over to the window. *No moon tonight.* Out of the corner of his eye, however, he sensed a movement and turning his head towards the open shoji screen, he saw it. *Blacker than the night, a dense shadow was moving out of the darkness at him!* Yoshi closed his eyes tight. *Tap, tap, tap.* He could hear water hitting the tatami floor. He opened his eyes. To his horror a ghastly woman with sooty eye sockets was looking into his face! Her long black hair hung down like seaweed and her decayed kimono stank of rot. Yoshi attempted to scream, but couldn't. Staring at her gaping mouth he was shocked, for all her teeth were blacked out. *Was she speaking? She had no tongue!*

"Yoshi—Yoshi chan …" She was talking to him without moving her lips—and oh! The terrible blackness of that mouth! He could hear a coy, sharp voice asking, "What side does the foreign devil mount his horse? You will find out soon and in a foreign land …

And there you will dirty your hands with human blood!" Incredibly, he heard these words in his head, though they did not come from his own mind. "You will die an old man, but you will never return!" Her fist suddenly appeared near his face and from it burst out a big red centipede which fell to his chest.

Yoshi screamed and jumped up, brushing himself off in terror.

Everyone in the house awoke. After they calmed him down and gave him cool barley tea to drink, he told them, "My call-up notice will be coming, Father. I am going to war."

"Why do you say that, Yoshi?" they all asked, concerned.

"I saw a centipede."

"In your dream?" his father asked.

Yoshi stared at a trail of water across the floor, numb with fear. He couldn't answer.

"But that is a good omen! It's victory in war! Victory, my son! Why don't you speak?"

Fire over Chapei

4

Cathay Hotel, Shanghai *12 August 1937*

JACK MORGAN NEVER HAD trouble with women. He had pleasing, masculine features, deep set blue eyes, a broad mouth and a square jaw, but how he hated that scar. Three stories up from Algy's room, Jack stepped out of a claw-foot tub, and reaching for a towel, caught his full naked reflection in the mirror. More than an inch wide, it ran from his hip, jagging up across his chest all the way to his ear. Over the years, many a woman's lips had traced it downward over his sternum and belly to his satisfaction. But Jack considered the scar a guilty reminder; he'd gotten his big break that day but the Chinaman, who'd gone overboard, had died. Nonetheless, Summerhays had hired him and had opened all the doors for him out of the kindness of his heart. Jack thought of the deal with Chan he'd set up for that night. *If he failed, Percy would be ruined.*

Jack removed the pistol he'd hidden under a clean stack of towels and loaded it, knowing he couldn't play by Percy's rules tonight, or ever. If he had, China Coast Navigation would have gone broke years ago. It was amazing to him that Percy hadn't guessed, and yet the old man was content to sing Jack's praises all over town and had ostensibly handed over the reins to the firm. However uneasily, Jack viewed his trust as complicit approval, for Percy never asked how he'd done it. Percy only stepped back and watched the money flow into his coffers. At least it made the old man happy, but with the depression becoming global, it was getting harder and harder to keep succeeding and Jack found he was forced to take greater and greater risks keeping Percy in the red. But making Percy proud of him had become Jack's raison d'etre; having lost his father at an early age, the old man's kindness overwhelmed him with gratitude.

He picked up his pad of paper and checked the numbers. His current order: three American ships, only slightly used, from a firm no bigger than Percy's—going out of business. Price: $140,000. Jack had bought them on credit alone. His eyes moved across the page. His problem was a caboose, originally custom-made for a European Royal. Jack had picked it up at auction in Austria for a Chinese warlord; it had been a sure sale and he'd shipped it out knowing it would pay for the deposit on the ships. *It had been returned. Client dead—hijacked in a skirmish.* The meeting and the sale were the entire reason he'd come all this way under threat of looming war. Jack crossed out the dead warlord's name and wrote in *Lucky Chan*—then threw down the pad, hoping luck and Algy's paperwork would suffice; it was a perilous situation to be in. He looked at his watch. He was expecting a call from an informant doing a background check on Chan.

As Jack pulled on his shirt and tie, he thought of the cursed train car. It came replete with mahogany walls, red mohair seats, oil paintings, gold fixtures, and heavily armored sides—the latter an especially important attribute in China. Besides warlords, few citizens had enough disposable cash to buy it outright so Jack had paid a finder's fee to a local Frenchman, Edouard, to procure this last minute connection to Lucky Chan. He hoped the man had deep pockets because if Chan didn't buy the caboose, Percy would get the calls for the cash next week; Jack's name in the colonies would be ruined and Percy's firm would be put into liquidation. But Jack liked a challenge. After getting up every morning for years and going down those mine shafts, not knowing if he'd ever return, he'd found there was little he feared.

The telephone shrilled. It was the informant from Nantao with important news. Lucky Chan ran a sing-song club in the French Concession, but he had regular business at the Chung Wai Bank headquarters, a front for the infamous Shanghai mobster and arms dealer "Big Ear Tu"; Shanghai's "*other*" mayor. Tu's "bank" was funded entirely by opium and it was said he was financing the rise of Chiang Kai-shek's Kwomintang with his ready cash and "influence." A sing-song club with prostitutes was small potatoes, the informant said. It had to be a front. With a contact like Tu, Lucky Chan was certainly involved in running smuggled goods and opium all over China. Jack rang off pleased, for this was just the sort of wealthy client he needed. Tucking his handgun into his jacket, he rushed out the door nearly colliding with a butler poised to knock.

"*Dien pao!*" Proffering a tiny silver tray the man repeated, "Telegram!"

Jack instantly feared that Percy had become ill, and as he rushed down the hall, tore open the envelope, heart pounding. Entering the elevator he removed the paper, but nothing could have prepared him for the shock: *I AM PREGNANT. RETURN AT ONCE. FATHER KNOWS.* He broke into a cold sweat and tucked the telegram in his breast pocket just as the attendant announced, "Ground Floor!" The boy pulled back the gleaming brass gate, gesturing with a gloved hand into the lobby.

A Chinese stood blocking Jack's way out.

"Mr. Morgan?" Dressed in a black Mandarin robe and cap, he bowed in greeting.

Flushed, Jack bowed back slightly, stepped off the elevator, and tucked the telegram deeper into his pocket. "How did you guess?"

Chan smiled. He did not look at all like a raunchy club owner. He had vivacious, intelligent eyes, wore glasses, and had a schoolboy smile, at once humble and supercilious. "Mr. Manet here described you to me," Chan said looking at Edouard. "What did you say?"

Manet, Jack's French contact with the heavy accent, came up and they all shook hands. "I said, 'A han'some American football player wis za brhoken noz.'"

They all laughed. "I'm grateful you had the time to meet with me on short notice," Jack said, still reeling from the telegram. "I feel this could be a very fortuitous occasion for both of us."

Chan nodded obliquely. "Yes, possibly. But perhaps you know that too much luck may also be suspect." He tapped his cigarette holder against a potted palm. "A trap, you understand?" Edouard had told Jack that Chan had excellent English, having attended a Baptist missionary school as a child, but it did not explain this complex man before him.

"Ah well, at times the Chinese can be too superstitious for us westerners. You must find us rather simple." Jack grinned and lit his cigar, playing for time. "I always kowtow to good luck myself… But I *am* sorry my employee has delayed us," he said, looking around for Algy. Chan had arrived early, making it appear as if Jack had been late. He cringed. The night was starting out awkwardly already.

"Have you heard of the tale of the citrus fruits gourd?" Chan asked. "No? I will tell you. This citrus gourd was delivered to a famous temple during a very long and difficult fast." He adjusted his long cigarette holder, smiled, then continued, "This gourd was rumored to come from the abbot of another temple, a gift, very lucky, no? But the hungry monks noticed it moved. Suspicious, the head priest cut it in two. And what did he find, but a *poisonous* snake inside, its head cut right off by the very knife itself!"

Jack nervously touched the pocket with the telegram, feeling himself turning crimson just thinking of it. He took a deep breath. He needed his wits about him, for Chan was setting up a cultural minefield. "That's insightful," he said and winked. "But I prefer the old Chinese ballad of Li Chi, the little girl who slays a dragon." Here Jack switched to Chinese and said, "Looking upon the skulls of its long dead victims, she exclaims to them, 'for your timidity you were devoured!'" Chan laughed, but Jack could see the cold glint in his eyes as Chan assessed him, and he knew it was going to be a hard sell. He couldn't imagine the evening starting off any worse.

Yet Chan was it; he was unlikely to turn up a better client with so little time remaining.

Cathay Hotel *8 August 1937*

A SUDDEN, LIGHT TAPPING on his door startled him. *It couldn't be Jack again, could it? Surely not.* Algy straightened his suit, and then opened the door. "Ah, the bellboy! Come in. Come in." He snapped his suitcase shut then, glancing in the mirror, smoothed his eyebrow. There was bound to be a party on the steamship tonight; no, things couldn't be better.

He gave the boy an extra coin, which brought a beam of joy to the lad's face; then together they slipped quietly down the hall, the boy pushing the luggage cart. On their way, Algy pinched a pink rose from the arrangement on the landing and deftly tucked it in his lapel. He wanted to look festive on the steamer, and noting the boy headed to the rear elevator, was pleased that he had understood they were to escape unseen. The rear lift, "*For Asians Only*," opened and they stepped in. As it glided down, Algy felt giddy. *If only Jack knew! Why, he'd have his head. And too bad Jack didn't know, for he was sick of never being taken seriously. Yes, for once in his life, he was taking a stance.* Algy adjusted his cravat in the elevator mirror just as the bell announced the ground floor. *Now, to avoid Jack on the way out …* Excitement fluttered in his stomach at the pull of the suspension cords on the lift. It seemed to swing there for a moment in space.

"Hai-yah!" The boy tapped importantly on the button to hurry the doors.

Algy smiled at him, nodding. Now they would disappear out the rear exit and—the doors opened on the ground floor. "Hurry, chop-chop!" Algy encouraged the bellboy pointing to the service entrance but the boy suddenly veered at a clip toward the main entrance where the rickshaws waited!

"Wait!" he whispered hoarsely after the boy. "*No. NO! NO! We mustn't go that way. Stop!*" Algy felt faint. The bellboy was already past the lobby and almost through the front door when he stopped to turn and look for Algy.

"Mass-itah," he said, beckoning, coming back through the lobby where Jack and his client were certainly seated and waiting. He could even discern the scent of Jack's "superlative" evening cigar. Obviously, the concierge had neglected to inform the bellboy of the confidential and sensitive nature of his departure. *Bloody hell! They had used the rear lift! Couldn't he put two and two together?* He motioned for the boy to come back—yet the boy stood resolutely pointing outside. Algy pursued as far as the potted palms without coming into view of the lobby and, holding out another coin, attempted to lure him from behind the plant. At that moment, however, the front doors opened and in strode Jack.

"It seems there are no cars for the evening," he announced, waving a cigar. His voice carried, and he appeared confident and amused. As a group of men joined him by the doors Jack must have sensed something and turned.

"Ah, Algy! It's about time. But—but why are you standing behind that *palm*?"

In stunned fright, Algy was still holding the coin up in the air.

The group of men all turned, craning to see through the plant. Coming to his senses, Algy chucked the coin, and stepped out from behind the vegetation, aware that he was grinning ridiculously. "Ah, I just dropped something, there, actually." The sound of the rolling coin resounded on the marble floor and made a loud ping as it hit a wall. Algy surreptitiously tried to push his small wicker suitcase behind him.

"What the—? Never mind." Jack's baffled disgust vanished as he recuperated his authoritarian demeanor. "We didn't see you come out of the elevator here. Come meet everyone. We're taking rickshaws tonight."

He shook hands reluctantly with Frank Minton, Lucky Chan, and Edouard Manet. He also proffered his hand toward another Chinese but the man only glared. Algy flushed, "Ah—Chan's *bodyguard*. Sorry!" He laughed nervously. This sort of crowd was nowhere on Percival Summerhays's regular client list. "Isn't there a painter, Manet?" he said trying to lighten things up.

Edouard scoffed, "I am an artist of sorts, vouldn't you say, Frahnk?" The men laughed and Algy felt himself go crimson. The man was a thorough rogue; his ridiculous alias and expensive clothing did nothing to hide the fact from Algy. *How was it that Jack didn't notice—or didn't he care?*

As the group moved out to the street the boy followed at their heels with the heap of luggage. Panicking, Algy motioned to him to go away, but the boy was excited by the tip he'd gotten upstairs and was eager to show his gratitude publicly. "Mass-itah," he said loudly, "Mass-itah Werzing!"

Algy pretended not to hear, though the boy tugged at his jacket. He tried to shake him loose and muttered through clenched teeth, "Go away!" The boy looked utterly perplexed and Algy gave him a discreet kick, which only increased the boy's amazement.

Jack, too, had a puzzled look and said, "What the devil's going on? Algy, this your luggage?" He was pointing to the suitcases and the boy.

It was Algernon's chance to come clean and tell him he was leaving on a steamer, but with the entire group of men staring, he crumpled. "Ah, *no*. The urchin's mistaken." And then, "Go away, boy," he rebuked, his voice cracking.

Luckily, there was an abrupt commotion which deflected attention from him. When the coolies squatting under their rickshaws realized the prospect of money was at hand they leaped up and fought over the clients. Seizing the moment, Algy hurried past the bewildered bellboy, the struggling coolies, and claimed the first rickshaw. At this, the coolies stopped quarreling and, when the others in the party followed suit, Lucky Chan's bodyguard shouted out directions. It was the end of his predicament, at least one of them.

Moments later they were streaming through the night behind barefoot rickshaw boys, who were breathing heavily with their loads. A last stolen glimpse toward the hotel doors had revealed the lone bellboy standing at the curb with the heap of abandoned luggage. Algy reasoned he must double back as soon as possible but he was feeling a bit woozy from the laudanum and couldn't remember any landmarks ... Left and right dark cavernous buildings whisked by, horrible odors, crumpled forms. Algy covered his nose with his perfumed handkerchief and focused his eyes above the shoulders of the man pulling him so that he didn't have to consider whether the claims of famine and cannibalism were true.

After some time the rickshaws slowed and came to a halt under a blue lantern on Bubbling Well Road. Stepping over litter they stood under a discreet sign, *Jade Gate;* Chan's bodyguard tapped and an eyeball appeared in the slot, looking them over. Immediately the door unbolted and a lavender-turbaned Sikh in immaculate white emerged and bowed, while a piano sprinkling out a light jazzy tune invited them inside. Like their hotel, it was another world—glamorous, richly decorated, shocking against the poverty outside.

Algy looked around and took in the scent of gardenias, liquor, and cigarette smoke. The group assumed a place at the bar under a limping ceiling fan, but it wouldn't have occurred to them to loosen their collars, even in such an establishment, for Shanghai was a formal town, even in summer when it was renowned as one of the three furnaces of China. A mural of the Alps decorated the walls all round and the muted lighting produced a most soothing effect. Here and there lovely young things in high-necked silk cheongsams with buttock-high slits were dispersed among the crowd. Bee-sting red lips, moon-white faces, and not a day over fifteen, they graced the room like an arrangement of white flowers nestled in darkness—shining, unblemished, except for the blight at the heart, for the ravages of civil war could be seen in their eyes. Algy smoothed his eyebrow nervously. At least he had a ticket out tonight, but these young girls would expire here in service of these *customers.* Jack, standing beside Algy, already had two on his arms.

"Ah yes," Algy said, unable to restrain himself, thinking about the raise in pay he'd been denied. He noted Jack's lecherous grin. "A veritable cornucopia of pleasure, this place. But what would it take, Jack? One well-placed bomb and out goes the power, out go the ceiling fans, away with the liquor!" He took the olive from his drink and popped it into his mouth. "Ah, yes! Away with the native servants! And we would have one dirty mass of foreigners, quaking, stinking, begging for home."

Jack slapped him on the back. "Gentlemen—you must forgive him. Algernon here, my *killjoy*, has been yearning for the comforts of Hong Kong all week. And," Jack said, eyeing him, "it appears he has been drinking! *Alone*." This last word was delivered with a poignant glare. "Let's tip back a few ourselves, gentlemen."

"Ah, the comforts of Hong Kong," Lucky Chan said pushing on his gold wire spectacles, interpreting the comment to be a slight on Shanghai. "But we have *everything* here that one can imagine, and more! Do we not? Shanghai is the cosmopolitan heart of Asia." And, as if Chan thought Algy was going to slip away, he took a pincer hold of his shoulder.

"I'm speaking of safety, gentlemen, safety," Algy muttered, trying to shrink into himself discreetly—but Chan wasn't letting go. *This was no time to be involved in a lengthy discussion of China. His steamer was certainly boarding passengers by now. Just under an hour!* He thought of the docks where he was headed and shivered. He didn't stand a chance unarmed. At the bar, a clock gonged the hour. He looked at his boss. *There was always Jack's revolver ...*

"He fears za myopic Jap-anese," exclaimed Edouard, laughing at Algy and slapping him hard on the back. "But you know, zey cannot see to drop ze bomb. Zey miss constant-lee!"

"We depend upon it!" Frank Minton said, raising his glass and eyeing the two girls hanging onto Jack. "How is it they cling to you? Are you covered in honey?"

As Jack's smug face tipped down to the girl in pink who whispered in his ear, Algy muttered, "It's the money they smell." He cast a glance toward a slight bulge on Jack's chest—*Was that the gun hidden there?* It would be tricky getting it off him.

"Ah! I have a wet ear now," Jack said, amused. The other girl reciprocated with little kisses on his face. "Take one off my hands, Algy, will you?"

"And—is it not true, Frank?" continued Edouard, "Ze rhail-road 'as not taken a direct hit in maaanths!"

"Another," Algy said ordering a fresh drink. At that moment the lights dimmed and the bar mirror and glasses rattled. People looked up and when the lights came back up everyone laughed. Behind him the door opened and he turned to look, catching a glimpse of the street. He must leave that very instant.

"Where'd you find this blighter?" Frank said to Jack. "You should 'ave left 'im in the 'ome office."

"You're absolutely right," Jack said giving Algy a nasty look, and then in a forcefully cheery voice he said, "You hear what she asked me, Algy? The little vixen speaks American!" As Jack pushed the girl over to Algy, saying, "Tell him what you said to me," Algy was quick to note the slight bulge of the weapon.

The girl in the lime cheongsam pouted, "I say you wanchee play-play yes? Fuckee-no." Then she burst into peals of laughter.

"Det is exactly what *he* needs," Edouard sneered. They were all staring at Algy. "Poor lad's sick wis' worry." They laughed heartily.

Algy tried to extract himself from the taxi-dancer and felt himself tottering. He didn't need to act tipsy at all; the laudanum was doing it all for him. When he reached for the fresh glass he had no trouble spilling it all over Jack. "Oh, so sorry!" Algy cried out. Jack turned beet red but didn't say a word as he removed the wet jacket and Algy, ever so helpful, hung it over a chair for him. Abruptly, a spotlight came on at the piano, distracting the group. A trickle of applause began as a dark-haired woman made her way through the tables, and Algy neatly fished out the pistol.

"Why do you fear the Japanese so?" The voice was in his ear. Algy nearly dropped the gun as he hid it at his side. *It was Chan.* "Yes, you Mr. Worthing. Why do you lose face in front of your superior? Have you no pride?" Chan's eyes went down to Algy's hand and he seemed to give the slightest smile.

"Er, *no pride*?" Algy looked Chan in the eyes. Small and narrow but very dark; in them Algy saw the Japs goose-stepping into China, making Asia their own, *just like a newsreel.* "Oh, *Pride!* I capisce. One of the seven sins!"

"You are an imbecile!" Chan spluttered.

"That may be. But I do recognize when I'm at sixes and sevens." He pulled out his matchbox, pointing to the text. "My hotel. How do you pronounce this? I wouldn't trouble you, but I fear the rickshaw boy can't read Chinese either!"

Chan spat on the floor and headed off to the others who were facing the stage, putting a hand onto Jack's arm to guide him. "I especially want you to meet our new singer, Jack. She comes to us via Austria. A *white* woman. So beautiful, see?" Chan's high-pitched voice was at once ingratiating and condescending. "Ah, but no touching," he broke off in gleeful laughter.

Algy couldn't help thinking a web was being woven around them, and Jack, whom he had always esteemed as a man of the world, and rather attractive, now appeared quite ingenuous in Chan's grasp. Leaving his boss to his own ruin, Algy gained the front entrance, Jack's gun in his pocket.

Out on the street he stood under the blue lantern, now extinguished, surprised it had been so easy. The mandatory blackout was in effect, and the street was silent and eerie, almost abandoned, but there was a pervasive sharp hot stench of charring wood he hadn't noticed earlier. In the distance he could hear a squadron of planes buzzing, maneuvering under cover of the night sky. Like a cluster of crucifixes they approached, no ensign visible. He waited looking up for them and suddenly they passed overhead shaking his very lungs. *Bollocks!* Algy made a beeline toward the rickshaws at the end of the street.

"Boy! You there!" Algy cried out halfway to the corner. No one looked. The coolies were the same miserable wiry lot as anywhere, naked sunken chests, bare feet, and khaki drill shorts. They were arguing among themselves and Algernon, taking out his matchbox, pointed to the name, *Cathay Hotel*. "Take me here," he demanded. He expected a battle over who was to take him. "To the Bund," he repeated. The air was thick and he choked, "Cathay Hotel. Savvy?"

Not only was there no response, they completely *ignored* him. "For goodness sake," Algy said with great annoyance, and turned to look where they were pointing. He almost fell back in shock. *The entire North West quadrant of the sky glowed red.* "Here, here!" he said. "Take me to my hotel, *Ca—thay—ho—tel!*"

One of the coolies looked at the matchbox and simply took it and withdrew into the group discussion which was getting louder and louder by the moment.

"You, boy. Return that at once!" Algy's voice was not heard above the din which in typical Chinese fashion was arresting, yet at this instant, it was so agitated that even people in the filthy black tenements above began sticking their heads out the windows. He tried to interest the coolies in money but all at once they dispersed, leaving him alone in a foreboding street without his hotel address.

Algy raced back to the safety of the bar, only to find Jack dead center of the group discussing a Borneo hunt in a loud hearty voice. Algy could have shouted *FIRE*, but they wouldn't have given a fig. The problem was, he really *needed* Jack to find his way back to the hotel—but Shanghai could be falling for all Jack would care. He had business on the brain, and God help the bastard who got in his way.

"You know, Frhank," Edouard was saying, "You've nevah bean to Borneo and you couldn't mek a deal to sev your vorseless life, ah? ah? I em right! So! Fermez la bouche, ijiot! Or you'll be in prison wis' your friend."

Frank Minton stood up, kicking his chair back, "Why don't you bloomin' sod off?" His chair tottered, then fell to the floor with a clatter, and even Jack stopped the Borneo story as Frank stormed off.

Chan jutted his chin impatiently toward his departing employee, 'You see, Frank is not so steady up here." He tapped his temple with a fingernail. "Last year he killed a man for pushing him in the street. I had no end of trouble with the police."

Edouard slapped his drink down, "'E's bloody estyupeeed! Dan'gher'us too! I don't know why you keep Frhank on et all. Even sa British Navy didn't keep 'im. And that gun wis za 'air trigger! Why do you let 'im carry it?"

Jack puffed his cigar, "Sometimes—you need a fool and a fall guy all in one."

They all looked at Algy, then laughed.

Chan's eyes glittered, "You, Jack, you could have been Chinese!"

Algy felt himself going crimson and it was all he could do not to scream. He'd missed his damned ship, his luggage was on the curb, and here was Jack thinking the sun shone out his ass. Algy frowned. *Jack needed a lesson in humility, a real kick in the pants.* Taking a step away from the group, he followed Frank out of the main room down the dim lit hall tapping the gun in his pocket.

He could hear Jack call after him, "Oh Algy, where's the paperwork? *Algy?*"

Algy laughed, stalking off. *I'll turn his damned deal upside down. I'll do it if it kills me.*

ANA

5

Bubbling Well Rd., Shanghai *12 August 1937*

JACK HELD BACK HIS temper and, craning his neck, looked over the banister where Algy had just disappeared. *Had that fool even brought the file?* The last thing he needed was another distraction, and for the first time on this trip he was starting to feel a slight sense of panic.

"Ah, I see you are admiring these," Chan said resting his hand on the sparkling curve of the banister. "But it's not so special; *cheap*," he said.

"Eh?" Jack cast an eye over the fine crafted metalwork. "Bronze d'or, isn't it?"

"You've a good eye. But they arrived from Paris damaged. Very inferior." Chan announced happily tapping the golden railing.

"Is that a fact? Well, our company has very ordinary stairs," Jack countered, continuing the humility game according to Chinese protocol, but knowing it could go against him. However, before Chan could declare, *If your company is so poor, then I shouldn't do business with you*—there was a shout and a thud on the dance floor. Couples surged away from something in the darkness, and they discovered Pablo, the bar manager, on the floor warding off blows from a man in a tux. Upon hearing Chan cry out, "Mischa, stop!" the man suddenly stood and bolted. Jack spun about in pursuit, collaring him—when a sudden collision stopped him in his tracks, and he let go. Breathlessness gave way to the sensation of large yielding breasts crushed up against him. The delicious feeling lit up his primordial mind. Dusky perfume, dark glossy hair. A mermaid of a woman, in a skin-tight sequined gown with a heart shaped face, looked up at him with the big green eyes of a sea goddess. He felt a shock to his very core, but Chan interrupted. *I wish I could come back for this one,* Jack thought, reluctantly releasing her to the darkness.

A moment later he and Chan were walking back to the bar talking, but the impact remained on his body for some time. He forcefully reminded himself of the three ships crossing the Pacific—ships he'd been so excited about. At that very moment they were heading for CCN's dock like messengers of doom because this deal with Chan was going nowhere. "You know, Chan," Jack said, making another try without being too direct, "we have a lot in common."

"Is that so?"

"Yes, you see I was educated in the West, and 'colonized,' so to speak, by my British sahibs in Hong Kong, and I learned Chinese as my second language. A hodge-podge of multiculturalism for an ordinary American, wouldn't you say?"

Chan laughed, suspicion in his black eyes.

Jack re-lit his cigar, thinking how the Chinese had traded masters: Out with the English and in with the Japanese, who were taking over large tracts of the Chinese coast all the way up to the Russian port city of Vladivostok—terrorizing all shipping therein, and confiscating it for their own war efforts. Chan knew it too; they were determined to break the back of Chinese unification. "I know some entrepreneurial Chinese," Jack said, looking Chan over carefully and thinking of the opium the man was dealing, "They're desperate for small craft that can be easily hidden, that can ply shallow waters and land goods up muddy rivers where Japs can't patrol. But I say, why not go by rail instead? Open up *all* of

China, not just the coast! Imagine the potential," he said. "I've got an armored luxury train car that I plan to show Chiang Kai-shek."

Chan's eyes sparkled over his drink, perhaps considering the bait.

Jack took a puff of his cigar, rolling the smoke in his mouth, waiting. He knew his own energy, size, and Western bravado had impressed Chan, but he also knew the Oriental mind. Trained in patience and fatalism from birth, they understood the insignificance of humans in the Cosmos; the Chinese did not deceive themselves as white men did. As much as Chan might admire Jack, he sensed his Western arrogance must have irritated the Chinaman. It lay between them, a stumbling block, and Jack wondered if Chan could be lured into crossing it. As for himself, as a westerner, all this was tiresome. He saw everything in black and white and drew a direct path between himself and any goal—no face saving or wagon circling involved. Jack wanted to sweeten the deal by adding a crane to the armored caboose to facilitate moving opium stock with ease, but if he did, it would only acknowledge that he knew the man's *real and illicit* business. *Patience* ... He clenched his jaws, and ordered another drink.

At that moment a page boy came up out of nowhere and whispered something to Chan.

"Ah!" the man sighed, "It appears that the son of an old friend has returned to my opium establishment upstairs against express orders of his father. I must send him away without having him lose face. May I leave you in the capable hands of Edouard?"

Jack was unable to disguise his dismay. Emptying his drink as Chan departed, he turned, looking for the brunette. He'd not forgotten her. She was there, behind the bar, tears and sequins flickering as she wept silently. But she must have sensed him even from across the room for she suddenly looked up and into his eyes, startled. They held each other's gaze, yet the moment he stood to make his way to her, the spell broke; she looked away with a deliberate frown.

Jack was neither a blackguard nor a cad, but the fact that she'd rebuffed him made him act against his better judgment. "Edouard, can you excuse me for a minute while Chan's gone?"

"Ah, someone 'as caught your attention?" Edouard gave a devious smile toward the girl. "Of course!" he shrugged expressively. "But don't forget, mon ami? Ze man, he chases za voman until she *captures* 'im." He broke into laughter as Jack walked off.

Bubbling Well Road *12 August 1937*

ALL ANA HAD WANTED was a chance at a decent life, yet it would be that much harder now. Chan paid her less to sing than he charged her for room and board, and her brother Mischa, upon thrashing Pablo, had gotten himself fired and had ditched her with an enormous opium tab. As it stood, her situation was now hopeless; as of tonight, Chan owned her. She wasn't even allowed to leave the club unescorted. Mischa's drug habit had ruined them both and now her biggest fear, becoming a prostitute, was closer than ever. Ana crept to the back of the bar, waiting for her next set to begin, trying to stop her tears and think of a way out, but even her legs were trembling.

The man in white was persistent and irritating, and when he came across the room to stand beside her, Ana had the intention of sending him away. Magnetic, impossible, inappropriate, he stared at her from deep-set eyes, inches away. This was exactly *not* her type. She knew the men in these places, their intoxication, their wild spending in the face of China's tragedy; they were revolting. After being a refugee in Shanghai and Berlin, she imagined she no longer needed men, certainly not a stranger. But, in the end, it was the seduction of sympathy.

"Well? Am I so objectionable?" he asked in a smooth, confident voice. "It may surprise you, most women find me charming."

Ana took out a cigarette and laughed at his audacity. He said nothing, but tilted his head toward the dance floor, and she found this confidence annoying. "Haven't you been told that true beauty needs a flaw," she asked sharply. "Something besides that little break in your nose."

"I have a handicap, but I suppose cruelty is yours," he said, his hand squeezing hers very hard as he led her between other gliding couples.

"Ah, you *are* the beast I imagined," she quietly laughed, then hooked her hands up over his neck. "So then," she whispered, "handsome stranger, what is your handicap?" She expected a lie, some lude confession. *And so what?* She felt his lips on her ear, a kiss? No, it was a whisper. Breathy chills coiled through her body.

"Trouble?" She echoed, leaning back to look in his eyes, and removed a hand from his shoulder. "You kill a man? No? Well, then I wouldn't worry. Everyone's in trouble in Shanghai. *You're* not *special.*"

"Thank you. You're too kind." He grabbed her hand so she couldn't leave.

Looking into his eyes, his intensity excited her. "Release my hand," she purred with disdain, but he brought it to his lips. Somehow, it pleased her to toy with him.

"So, who was that troubled soul who punched out the manager?" His voice was soft. "Anyone special?"

"Jealous already?" she asked with contempt, brushing her finger slowly across his lip.

"Maybe," he said against her fingertip.

"My brother, the main piano player here," she sighed taking her hand away. "But let's not talk about it."

"Fine. Then tell me, you're a woman of the world. Could you marry someone you didn't love?"

She raised her eyebrows. "I'd wait until after the first drink to propose to me. You could use that afterward as your excuse for being ridiculously romantic."

He had the slightest smile in the corner of his mouth, "I'll have you know, no one's called me that before."

"No? A pity. It's rather an endearing trait." They made a few turns about the dance floor.

"Well, have it your way," he said. "But tell me; I'm sure you've had good offers." The last comment stung and she tried to get away from him. "I'm not finished," he said in her ear.

Ana felt her despair returning. "You're an odd one, for Shanghai," she remarked bitterly. "A bit of an orangutan."

He looked down at her, "Better that than a mercenary, no?"

"I'm still working here, aren't I? That's proof enough I wouldn't marry for money," she answered, dancing slowly now, gazing at people who entered and left the club of their own free will. They didn't even know what freedom they had. She hadn't had to sell herself yet, but she'd seen starving women on the street in winter raise up their skirts as men went by, and then go with them into an alley to do it just to be able to buy a scrap of bread. Her fear returned at the thought, her heart pounding. Mischa hadn't cared about anything but opium, but she'd had him at least. Now alone, she felt herself slipping downward another rung. The street was not far off.

"I'm sorry. I didn't mean to upset you. Don't stop dancing."

Ana sighed, submitting to his pressure, and they glided along for some time until then he murmured. "You smell so good."

"Chanel No. 5, comes in a bottle," she said, then looked up at him. "Tell me. Why this talk of marriage and money?" She felt she was going to cry.

"I was told that's all there is," he said looking directly into her eyes.

Her heart fluttered at his look. "I hope not." They did a few turns about the floor when she spotted the man Chan had tailing her so she couldn't escape. He was eyeing her suspiciously. Ana turned back to her partner, feeling their time together was limited and suddenly afraid for it to end. "This is really about you, isn't it? You must know, you're not the first to sell yourself." His gaze moved away and she knew she'd hit a nerve.

"What's your name?" he asked gruffly and they introduced themselves. "Well, Ana," he said, "I'm no different from any of these foreign devils running away from something, hoping to strike it rich here at the ends of the earth. Even you, I believe."

She laughed. “The end of the earth it is. And when you return home all wealthy, life at home will somehow be shiny and new. All this will be forgotten!” She said it gaily, but this capitalist had become all too human, his bravado not different from her own. They remained silent after that, moving across the dance floor among the other couples, between pillars, tall leafy palms, in the intimate darkness of the room. The song ended but Ana found herself resting comfortably in his arms; he didn’t seem to want to part either.

“I confess, I’m feeling a little reckless,” he said holding her.

“Oh?”

He looked into her eyes, his own, warm, searching hers. “I ought to be going … My business deal is going pear shaped.”

“That’s not good.”

He was gazing at her lips. “No.”

Ana turned her face, resting her cheek against his chest so he couldn’t kiss her. She’d already imagined those lips parting hers, and hers opening to his. Everything she’d kept tight and closed up inside seemed to blossom under his touch, even her fear transformed into butterflies—and she lingered in the safety of his embrace, her rapid beating heart keeping pace with his. Still, Ana tried to haul herself back into reality. *This man will walk out that door at the end of the night and I will remain a prisoner at the Jade Gate.* Tears stung her eyes and she turned her face away.

There was a sudden, hard tap on her shoulder a few minutes later. “Ana, Pablo says you are to sing along with Cedric for tonight.” The bartender’s eyes darted from her to the stranger with curiosity. He pointed to the man in the spotlight playing the opening notes of the latest hit and Ana turned to look.

When the bartender left, Jack kept her behind. “Meet me afterward,” he said, hands hot on her bare shoulders. “Ana? Will you?”

From the corner of her eye she saw the bodyguard in the shadows, watching.

Bubbling Well Road *12 August 1937*

FRANK WAS STANDING AT the urinal when Algy entered the lavatory, veered to the sink, and turned on the squeaky tap, letting the brown water run clear. Touching his temples with his scented handkerchief, Algy smiled in the mirror. "Damn hot weather, isn't it?"

Frank's upper lip curled with disgust. "That your 'stink-water' I smell?"

Algy frowned, "My handkerchief? It's *cologne*," he protested. The man was certainly touchy.

Buttoning his trousers, Frank sniffed, "What do you want, you bleedin' fop?"

"I—I want nothing from you, my man," he said, stepping back toward the window. The view gave onto a vile alley below and he noted the perilous drop. Hearing Frank leaving, he added, "But you might want something from me. Edouard's scalp perhaps?"

Frank flushed red. He had small unpredictable blue eyes that cast about in a rapid manner, but now, sharp with anger, they were like tracer bullets coming round the door. He stepped back in, letting the door drop shut behind him.

"He's double-crossed you, hasn't he?" Algy said, feeling sly.

"Has he! He beat me out of a morphine deal, then called the customs agent on my lad. Milt's in a Chinese gulag now." As he spoke his voice trembled with growing rage, "I gonna fuckin' rip 'is 'ead off and stuff it up 'is arse, that's wot."

"Indeed." Algy lit a cigarette, fingers trembling with nervous excitement. "I—I *see* the reason for the animosity. But why'd he set up this lousy deal?"

"Don't you know? CCN's reputation's impeccable. Harbor police aren't likely to check cargo with your company flag flyin'."

"So that's it." Algy tapped his ash off in the sink and noticed outside the window, the sky was flashing wildly. He took a few quick puffs and stared at Frank. *What would set him off?*

"I thought you were the bleedin' accountant. Don't you know anything?"

"I just find it amusing," he said. "Listen, Frank. You do realize this deal will fall in on itself, don't you? I mean, Chan wants passage for cargo—and Jack thinks he's selling you a train car. *Complete mismatch!*"

"What's that to me?" he snorted. "The frog put this one together for Chan. It's 'is problem."

"But it's your chance to turn the tables!"

"Wot 'r' you sayin' exactly?" he asked, suspicious.

"Ah! But I want a deal first," Algy said. "You see, I need you to get Chan to throw *Jack* and myself out of the Jade Gate, capisce? Blow the deal, for my own reasons. I have to get back to Hong Kong right away."

"What for? What do you 'ave on the Frog?" His eyes narrowed suddenly. "Don't you fuck with me," he said jabbing Algy in the chest.

"Oh, but I *have something*. Morgan doesn't even *own* a single ship and he's got three being delivered that he hasn't paid for!" Well, it was *partly* true, yet Frank still hadn't lost it. "Don't you see? Chan will have a zero in his books after *this* deal evaporates. And the frog's on the take as well! I *know* Jack and Edouard have cooked this all up."

"Right-o, but none o' this'll get Milt out of jail, will it now?"

"No," he said, dismayed. "Nothing will help Milt, I'm afraid. But, you see, Frank," he said smoothing his eyebrow quickly, deciding to take a different tack. "Edouard's gone and exposed Chan's heroin and morphine operation to Jack."

"So?" The word hung in the air between them.

"So?" Algy shifted his weight. "So, Jack could cause a lot of trouble for Chan's reputation. Um. Think of his honor. Yes. And, and you might be caught up in an investigation too. A stint in the slammer with Milt, perhaps?" Watching Frank's face, he saw he'd hit the bull's-eye. "Ah-hah! See? Now let's you and I hatch a—"

Frank stared, then in a sudden rush, threw open the door and stalked back toward the bar in a fury.

"Frank!" Algy ran after him, catching up. "Stop! I spoke in confidence! As a fellow Englishman!"

Frank paused and jerking Algy aside with a hiss, stuck a pistol in his ribs. "You'll keep your mouth shut if you know wot's good for you." They returned to the bar together, Frank keeping himself between Algy and the others. Algy thought he was going to throw up from sheer nerves.

"Everyone knows za piano player's prhobleme," Edouard gestured broadly. "De *opium*!" Algy tried to catch Jack's eye in the bar mirror in attempt to warn him Frank was armed.

"Siddown," Frank said, boxing Algy in between himself, the bar and a pillar.

"As Conrad says—ah? Sa very death of our young men!" Edouard snorted. "And za young ledee. Such a good singah, but the Chinese sink large breasts are vulgar," he said laughing, patting Jack on the back. "What a shame, anh? Sey bind sem, you know?" he said with a gesture across the chest. "But Chan says she's our investment for foreign clients." A moment later, Jack got up and excused himself. Algy tried to flag him in vain but found he was being pinched so painfully below the table he winced aloud.

"Where's Chan?" Frank asked the bartender after Jack had gone. The man pointed upstairs. "Typical!" Frank spat, then abruptly jabbed a finger into Edouard's shoulder. "Don't think I didn't hear you, either. Investment? I *found* the broad—or are you just going to pretend you don't hear me! My Milt's in that Chinese gulag, you sack of shit! Been there a month! You owe me!"

Edouard shrugged at the bartender, "Do you hear a mosquito in here somewhere?"

"Mosquito?" Frank's breath reeked like petrol. "I'll blow the stuffing out of your ears. Just you wait. Oy! Bartender. Another shot."

Algy grimaced, "I don't think that's smart," he said. Both men were already filled to the gills, eyes glazed.

An elegant hand with long nails suddenly came down between Frank and Edouard. "We Chinese are the only ones with restraint,"

Chan said tapping his jade ring on the bar top. "Watch your temper, Frank. I told you before."

"Temper?" the cockney sniggered, "You'll feel *your* temper when I tell you wot I know," he said jerking his thumb at Algy. "I found this 'owling blunder 'as a secret that'll interest you. Especially the frog."

"Him?" Chan frowned at Algernon over his shoulder. "What could *he* say?"

"Wait till Morgan returns," Frank scoffed.

Algy felt sick. Seeing Jack now would be utter humiliation or else he'd be shot out back.

"There's a school of chaps whose closest men are fools," Chan sighed inspecting his ring. "Though it has its purpose, I suppose."

"Oooooo-lalalalala!" Edouard said gesturing to the far side of the dance floor. "Our Jacques seems to have a keen interest in our singer."

Chan tapped his cigarette holder on the ashtray. "I wonder how long her cash will hold out now."

Edouard laughed uproariously. "Eh, quoi? Salop!" Chan and he exchanged amused glances.

"That's ungentlemanly!" Algy protested, hoping to turn Frank's attention to Edouard.

"My little friend," Chan coughed elegantly. "Russians are a dime a dozen in Shanghai. Their clocks stopped in 1917."

"No papers, only grand stories," Edouard added, smiling into his drink, swaying slightly.

"Don't you pay her enough? Frank says she works for *you*."

"I'm fed up with this!" Frank slammed down his empty glass, removing the gun from Algy's ribs at last. "E's over there dancin' with that coaster and we're 'ere like a lot of fools waitin' for some deal Edouard promised. So, what are we waitin' for anyhow, Edouard?" He sat poised at the edge of the stool, like a taut spring, eyes red, a foot on the ground, ready.

"Mon ami! I see no need to explain to *you*. You are fortunate det you are even here zis evening. Is that not so, Chan?"

Chan's eyes sparkled with keen attention as he appeared to gauge Frank's mood and gestured to the bartender to stop refilling his drinks.

"A coaster?" Algy asked.

"You've got them in Hong Kong too—these beguiling white women, drifting up and down the China coast, leaving a trail of victims in their wakes."

"That's you," Frank hit Edouard on the back. "Living on wits alone!"

Edouard leaped up ready to fight.

"Enough!" Chan burst out, bringing his lit cigarette a hair's breadth from Frank's face, quashing his attempt to stand to the challenge. Raising a finger in warning, he then reproved, "We're all gentlemen here, are we not?" His gaze went down to Frank's lap. "I told you not to bring that in here."

Frank flinched away from the burning ember. "But Chan, Edouard's tricked you. Ask 'im wot 'e told me!" He jerked his thumb at Algy with one hand, while he slid his revolver out of view, his eyes darting left and right away from the cigarette tip.

"Look at 'eem!" Edouard's elegant face contorted with indignation and he jabbed the air with his finger like a pistol. "I can't imagine what zis animal is talking about—and ze accountant? It's a joke, a foolish one! Get Jacques over here. We vill soon see 'ou dis cock-nee is calling a liar! Be-cause—"

"Cockney? I'll give you cockney!" Frank said, eyes narrowed. "My lad's in jail!" he said grinding his teeth. The sound put Algy on edge.

"My lad, my lad!'" he mocked, flapping his hands about. "Your Milt deserves all 'e gets! Why should I care about zet cretin? Pah! You Jaques Tars are all za same," he gestured, then losing his balance, knocked his glass to the floor along with his barstool.

Startled by the crash, Chan turned away from Frank for a split second.

It was all Frank needed.

Algernon had the sense to step back as Frank leaped up with his gun and squeezed the trigger. The rest seemed to happen in slow motion. Edouard's lovely white suit spurted red, his eyes widened in disbelief. Falling back against the wall, he sank down, hand raised, as if trying to get in the last word. But it was unlikely. Red faced and shaking with rage, Frank emptied his gun into the body.

The Lavatory Window

6

Bubbling Well Road *12 August 1937*

THERE WAS A MOMENT of silence in the bar, then pandemonium—everyone was up and running for the doors. Only Frank stood still, gun in hand, watching Edouard gasp. Jack found himself grabbed by the arm, and the next moment dragged into the men's lavatory with Algy locking the door and pushing up a window, ordering him to follow. There was screaming all around. Jack was thunderstruck. "What the devil have you done?"

He got no response from Algy, who began to shimmy out the window frame. Jack grabbed hold of his collar and attempted to heave him back into the lavatory and nearly succeeded, but there was a loud rip, then a yelp, and he was gone. Jack stared at the gaping window, then leaned out only to see Algy in the alley below. He was about to slam it shut when Algy waved up at him.

"They'll get you as well. Hurry!"

Jack turned away disgusted. He could hear a growing commotion outside the door, someone pounded, then it was Chan, calling him and laughing. "Mr. Morgan? Are you hiding in there? The attendant here says two foreign devils will take his cumshaw."

Someone pounded again and an insolent voice broke in, "I'd'a never suspected you was yellow, Jack old boy."

Jack marched over in a huff, reaching for the latch, but caught himself—and just to be sure, braced his foot against the wood. It was a good thing, too. The moment they heard the latch go, there was a huge push and Jack found himself sliding backward on the tiles. It took a monumental effort on his part to shove the door back those few inches and, as he came closer and closer to the door jamb, a pair of hands pushed in to get a better hold. Jack took a deep breath and slammed it shut, bolting it. There were loud cries of pain on the other side, followed by curses. They didn't want explanations—Jack heard the unmistakable click of a gun. He quickly felt for his own, only to find it missing. This left him no choice.

He squeezed out the window and dropped to the ground outside just as gunshots splintered the door inside. Heading toward the junction with the road he caught up with Algy and pulled him back. "Not that way!" Algy turned to gape, confused, and Jack punched him squarely in the jaw. "That's for my deal. Now, come back," he said. "Your way's the front of the bar." He turned a blind eye to his reeling companion and vaulted over a wall, but hearing Algy crying out for him to wait, Jack stopped. Algy's hand was clutching the top of the decaying mortar. "Heave ho, for God's sake," Jack urged. "They're behind us!"

The sound of running feet confirmed this and put new life into Algy, who suddenly appeared on the top of the wall.

"Down there," came Frank's voice in the distance.

Algy dropped down beside Jack and they were off, stumbling through a courtyard filled with shrubs and dwarfed trees. They crashed through fragrant jasmine, ran along a flagstone path, and stumbled into a carp pond. The men were clambering over the wall behind them and the thud of bodies dropping to the ground announced their arrival. Immediately there was the sound of gunshots emptying wildly into shrubbery. Dogs everywhere awoke, barking.

Jack and Algy approached a rock garden and ran up an ornamental stone bridge that led them a good two meters straight up. From there they leaped onto a tiled roof and, scaling it, dropped into another stinking alley. Algy was breathing hard, but their white suits marked them out and there was no question of stopping and hiding. Sunrise too had begun to light up the horizon like a crack under a door—but for the moment the alleys and courtyards remained in darkness. The two men ran at a good pace, stumbling through heaps of garbage, scaling crumbling walls, and ducking through more gardens and private entrances; they would have been rid of the their pursuers far sooner had they not tripped over a sleeping guard who got up banging a gong shouting, *"Stop! Stop thief!"*

It wasn't until they slid down a tiled roof and dropped into an especially quiet enclosure that they finally caught their breath. All around, shrubbery shifted like crouching figures in the strong breeze and paper lanterns drifted eerily, candles blown out. Pestered by mosquitoes and gnats, they hid in the shadows and listened. The delicate tinkle of a wind chime came on the jasmine-scented air, punctuated only by the *glock-glock* of bamboo knocking on stone and water. Looking up, Jack distinguished the writing on a lantern then stepped out to the middle of the garden. "*This is that Japanese inn across the road*," he whispered. "*We've made a bloody circle!*" He sniffed at the air. "Say, what's that burning?"

"Chapei, I imagine," Algy said dusting off and pointing northwest. "Not that you'd care."

Jack noticed their white suits glowed orange in reflected light and looked back quizzically over the rooftops and trees. The entire sky glowed ominous red in the north, buildings standing out like black cutouts. It left no doubt that much bigger things were in motion. "You knew all along?"

Algy came forward, lips pursed bitterly, adjusting his boutonniere, "Well, why do you think I wanted to get you to leave that dump? But, no! You wouldn't listen until there were bullets at your heels. Why I ..."

Jack gave him a warning look, then turned, making his way down a mossy bank toward a stone basin overflowing with water. Taking up the bamboo drinking cup, Jack splashed water over his face, realizing for the first time in years he didn't know what to do. *Saturday morning and he still had no deal.* Percy's firm was teetering on ruin.

"Well Jack, what next?" A stronger wind drifted across the garden and the sudden clash of a wind chime seemed ominous. "Aren't you talking to me?" Algernon sniped, rubbing his jaw.

"I'm doing all I can to not pummel you."

"I didn't *do* anything," Algy whined.

Jack bit his lip, then exploded, "I leave you for an hour with that idiot, Frank, and before I know it, there's been a shooting, someone in our party is—I presume—*dead,* and you're pulling me out a lavatory window! Try to get an understanding of that! I've a bloody caboose rotting in a godown on Pootung wharf and you tell me you did nothing? What the hell happened back there?"

"I know things look black indeed, but there was a misunderstanding of sorts." Algy grimaced. "Frank's rivalry with Edouard …"

"What's that to do with *me*?"

"Ah? Right." Algy wiped his brow. "Let's try to find a steamer to Hong Kong instead. You can sell the train car later." The wind chime crashed as if struck by a stick and bushes whistled in the growing wind. "Looks like the typhoon's arrived."

"Sell it *LATER*? You're a goddamned accountant! Don't think for me! I've a bid out on *three* ships in *Percy's* name—something he has no knowledge of! And the train car was to give me the *deposit* when they arrive next week. Our firm may be ruined because of your blunder. In fact, I'll have your severance check cut Monday. You're a fucking liability I don't need."

"Wait up!" Algernon was following him, "Jack! You can't leave me here."

"Oh no? I'm meeting someone back at our hotel. You're free to do as you like."

Algy stopped him. "Not that woman?"

"I gave her my room key."

"*Are you mad*? But that's the first place they'll look for us!"

"And pray tell me why?" He jerked Algy's hand off his sleeve. "What have *I* done?"

The wind blew in a heavy scent of brackish water and smoke, drizzling them with rain drops. Jack slapped at another mosquito then looked up. *It was no insect.* There was a sudden louder buzzing. He ran out onto the middle of the lawn and stood out in the open when the entire northern sky lit up in a violent burst of light. There was another loud series of crashes. The Japanese had started shelling again. Jack took off across the lawn, passing under wildly shifting pines, and headed out over a low bamboo gate. However, before Algy could follow, Jack was already returning in a sprint, "Get back," he said fiercely, pushing past him.

Confused, Algy caught up on the terrace just as Jack slid open the paper and wood shoji, and both of them ducked into the ryokan, an old-style Japanese establishment. Gesturing from the safety of the interior for him to look, he let Algy peer out between the doors just as steel-helmeted Japanese marines with machine guns rushed past the gate. They could hear hundreds of boots stomping past. Jack slid the door shut. "Satisfied?"

"I suppose we're stuck here for the night," Algy said, uncertain.

In the room behind them, an all-night party was winding down and they walked past three girls in kimonos dancing in slow motion to the sound of a shamisen. Japanese businessmen, in advanced stages of inebriation, lay scattered here and there on the tatami mats, snoring, knees bent upward at the ceiling. A lovely geisha in a floral yukata came up to them and led the way to the front desk. "Dis way, gent'ermen," she chirped, giggling shyly behind her hand.

Minutes later they were sprawled out in their room and lying on their futons in the darkness. On the paper shoji, shadows of branches danced against an orange glow of sky.

"What are we going to do?" Algy asked sitting up on his futon. "There's a deck of cards here."

Jack rolled over, pulling a pillow over his head. "Fuck off, Algy."

Tiger Moth

7

Bubbling Well Road *12 August 1937*

In just minutes her life was about to change and a man would die. And yet clients at the cocktail tables were foot-tapping to a snappy opening, the horn section was playing call and response, the drums were backing them up, and the clarinet was squealing away with delight. Ana had no idea she was coming to a fork in the road as she came around the piano, hands on hips, blowing kisses to admirers in the audience who cheered. Picking up her cue from Cedric, she snapped open her fan, slinking past men at the tables, singing the lines to "Goody Goody" with the spotlight following. Now and then she cracked her fan at a patron who grinned, eyes going to her cleavage or hopelessly to his date. "So you gave her your heart too?" she sang, then added, "Just as I gave mine to you, and you broke it in little pieces—now how do you do?" Clutching at an older man's tie, she stared him down to the great thrill of the audience, then released him with mock disgust—only to find Jack had returned and her heart soared. He was standing in her path, leaning against a column. The audience laughed when she poked him in the chest with her gloved finger, but hooted when Jack held on. By the time Cedric and his swing band took over with the refrain, Ana found Jack had surreptitiously passed a tiny leather case to her.

Joining Cedric on the piano bench for the next number she finally allowed her eyes to look down. *A key. Cathay Hotel 1401.* She looked back up at the notes, not wanting to believe what she had seen: *One dance with him and that's it … He thinks I'm a whore.*

Cedric turned the page with a sidelong glance; she'd missed her cue. With the spotlight on her, she had to sing on, unable to fling the key at him, but his certainty that she'd take his offer made her eyes blur over the notes. Worse still, his offer was not repugnant to her, and she felt a chilling fear as she watched Jack disappear into the crowd. The last singer had hanged herself when Ana had started this job—Chan had demoted her to a prostitute. Ana looked out over the crowd, then spotted the back staircase. At the end of every night, just as the sun was rising, she would mount the filthy worn stairs exhausted, with eyes burning from cigarette smoke. Up past the liquor-soaked ground floor bar, past the first-story opium den, and then past the second floor rooms where the prostitutes lived and worked, she would climb her way up to the attic apartment where she lived with the young Chinese girl, Ming-po. *Now it is just me and Ming-po.* Ana bowed as the song ended, blinking back tears. The spotlight was so bright and she turned away for a moment, gathering her strength.

Chan's ancient father hadn't seen seventy in decades, and each night Ana had to sing him to sleep. This task itself wouldn't have been so bad, tired as she was, but the old man had recently gone into a decline, and Chan, as eldest son, wanted to do all in his power to keep him alive. At the suggestion of a herbalist, Lucky Chan had procured a wet nurse, Ming-po, as a source of nutritious breast milk for old Chan. Horrified, Ana would pick up the missionary songbook the man had sung from in his distant youth and flip to a page. No matter how intently her eyes followed the lines in the book, or how loudly she sang, she could still hear that awful sound. *The sound was driving her mad.*

Ming-po had had a child recently, but the baby was nowhere to be seen. Dead, most likely, or sold, Ana suspected. Still, Ming-po did her job with a haunting stoicism and her young round breasts did seem to revive the old man, for the sudden glint in his eyes as he considered the round flesh was remarkable. His sloppy lips smacked and choked on the white stream as he nursed, and his sunken black eyes would watch Ana as she sang, watch her with that toothless gobbling, and it seemed to draw the life out of Ana too. Ming-po sighed at times, and said cryptically in Chinese as she pointed to her blue veins, *Bad luck is my sister, same blood.* Ming-po was lying back into the arms of her fate, like a child to its mother, and every day she got thinner, her eyes duller. She did not even talk of escape, even when Ana urged her to consider leaving.

Each time Ana put money away towards the same end, she was thinking of that sound and Ming-po's face, and each time she saw Ming-po she had thought—*At least I have my brother to console me; I can keep my dignity.* Yet he'd spent her savings, and now he'd left. Applause drew her back into the present, and she smiled dully.

Her eyes scanned the crowd, and she watched the main door opening and closing as patrons left. *If I could just stand up and walk out . . .* But everywhere Ana went, one of Chan's bodyguards was her shadow. "Shanghai is a dangerous place, my dear," Chan always said. "Man-kwok, my guard, is keeping an eye on my collateral. You won't get away." Indeed, he was always within reach, as now, sitting in the first row. Even Mischa wouldn't escape China. Chan's men would surely track him down for his debts and kill him. Ana's hand went unconsciously to her earring. These matched diamonds and the gold bracelet she'd hidden upstairs were all the security she had left. No good buying a ticket out of China; she had no papers—but there were other towns, other jobs.

Ana turned the page for Cedric, and in the second it took for her to look back up, something had happened. An explosion. Screams. Customers began leaping to their feet, chairs went flying. More bangs—*gunshots.* Ana stood dumbstruck, observing the bedlam from the stage as if in a dream, until she looked at the seat below her. *Man-kwok was gone.*

Unlike the others who were seeking cover or heading out the exit, Ana turned and ran up the back stairs. Up three flights of dingy stone steps, past the prostitutes' quarters, the opium den, and Chan's counting room, she climbed to her chamber under the low slanting roof. Her carpetbag was under the bed and she jerked it out, throwing her dresses and shoes inside. "Ming-po!" she called, thinking the two of them could run away together. Ana could still hear shouts from downstairs as she got on her knees and lifted the bamboo bed. Feeling inside the hollow leg she searched for the little leather folder. Nothing. *The bracelet was gone.*

Standing up she looked all around the room and saw the suede wrap she'd kept the bracelet in, on the floor. *Empty.* She dropped her carpet bag in despair. *I can't leave without money … Yet Mischa did this to me?* Downstairs the noise was subsiding and she thought of the street whores. Ana went to the roof window and pushed it open feeling tears running down her face. The thick, humid air of the coming typhoon struck her like a wet pall and looking up she suddenly noticed the sky was on fire. *What did it matter? Now I'm here for good,* she thought. *Perhaps Ming-po had gotten away.*

From downstairs a voice cried out, "He's dead!"

In the next room, old Chan was calling her name and calling Ming-po. *It was strange.* Ana went in to check on old Chan, who was bald and toothless and very thin. He lay in the dark cave-like space of the heavily carved wooden canopy bed and his eyes met hers, hollow like the bottom of a well. *One more day,* his eyes seemed to plead. In pity she went to him to pull the tangled sheets from his body, but when she came close he clutched at her with a wild frenzy. Fighting him off, she had only a moment to notice the white glow of the face behind the old man. Lying still, eyes rolled up dead, was little Ming-po. Ana wrenched herself away, falling to the floor, almost taking him with her. As she lay there panting, old Chan's supine form balanced on the edge of the bed, and the whole image was framed by the open window behind his bony silhouette—a red sky with black trees like an omen from the next world.

She thought it was a black bird, but above the trees there was a sudden roar, deafening, and a dark plane descended from the sky. Ana got up, running to the window as it approached, certain it would land on the club. It didn't, nor did it drop a bomb, but whizzed over so low it shook the air, its landing gear visible—and then it vanished below tree level. Before she could give it more thought, a volley of gunshots came from below. Leaning out the window Ana was in time to see Chan and his men disappearing down a back alley. Watching Chan leave she thought of the tip jar downstairs. It would be stealing, but it would be enough to get her out of Shanghai, away from Man-kwok, the Jade Gate, and her growing debt to Chan.

Chan's driver was in the basement staff kitchen, hunched over a bowl of soup, when she came bursting in through the door carrying her carpet bag, her purse heavy with coins. Three servants were squatting snapping string beans into a huge pile on the floor and they froze, gaping open-mouthed at her and her sequined gown, unaccustomed to seeing the "talent" in the kitchen.

"Wong," she barked in her most authoritative voice, "You're to drive me to meet Chan." The entire kitchen staff turned to stare at him.

He got up confused, deliberating between his half-eaten soup and the white woman, suspicion, hunger, and inertia working his face.

Ana hurried him, "Now! Chop-chop!" Her request was unusual, but he'd driven her twice before, and she only hoped the element of surprise would work.

"Ta shr zher," he said looking confused, or perhaps thinking aloud.

"No, he's *not here*, Ta shr zai *Cathay Hotel!*" Ana turned her back and marched out of the kitchen, her shoes clicking as she flung her wrap over her shoulder.

The staff laughed uproariously at Wong's confusion, saying, "He doesn't want to miss the fried bread!"

In the garage Ana took out several silver coins and handed them to Wong. His narrow eyes grew wide as she explained they were going to look for her brother. "Take me to every opium den in the area. We must find Mischa." He didn't argue; he needed money like everyone in Shanghai and opened the passenger door.

As they drove off she looked at her reflection in the rain-streaked automobile window, and saw the earrings Grandma had worn to her wedding some fifty years before. She removed them and placed them in a little red pouch for safety. She would pawn them with Vassily, who was a constant fixture at the Cathay Hotel where Jack was staying. And she would return the key. On a small piece of paper she wrote, *Getting married? Goody-goody for you*, and tucked it into the key case, then looked up as Wong pulled up at a club Mischa frequented. She went in, hopeful, but he wasn't there.

Wong stopped outside of every opium joint they knew about and waited while Ana went in and asked for her brother. Over the next hours they slowly began to run out of places and began hitting the lower-class joints, which frightened her. Wong took over the search but without luck. Finally by Soochow Creek he slowed, pointing out the window as sounds of fighting came through the fog. Japanese machine guns were rat-tat-tatting in response to lone snipers. After that she lost all track of time and some hours later opened her eyes; Wong had apparently pulled over to sleep as well, and it was now past noon, Saturday. He awoke to her prodding, and sleepily told her he had to return before Chan fired him. Ana nodded, then asked him to go to the Cathay Hotel first and to then drop her at the train station. Wong relented and turned the car back toward the Bund.

They passed a crowd on the way to the Cathay—an air show appeared to be in progress. Turning the corner Wong pulled up under the familiar iron and glass awning and Ana told him to wait while she stepped out onto Nanking Road. It was full of shoppers, carousing sailors, elegant tai-tais, beggars, and globetrotters. Several of the Chinese fighters buzzed overhead doing loops. She ran through the traffic into the hotel, handing over Jack's key at the desk, then rushed through the vast lobby of gilded glass, clutching her purse, carpet bag, and the tiny red silk pouch with her earrings. Tiffin was beginning, and she could smell the food and wine. Waiters in crisp black and white uniforms whisked by with menus, and some carried food-laden silver trays. She glanced around the lobby at elegant people who came and went of their own free will. She and her fellow White Russians were stateless prisoners in China—unable to leave or enter any country without papers. Her heart ached with fear and envy as she hurried away, and pushing open the Lalique door to the Horse and Hounds Bar, she looked for Vassily, the pawnbroker. She spotted him as usual, holding court at the bar.

"Heard the weather report. Looks like we'll just miss most of the typhoon," Vasilly said, making room for her, with an admiring look at her décolleté. "My dear, remind me to introduce you to Sassoon, who ought to be getting tired of shiksas by now. You know what he says, 'There is only one race greater than the Jews and that's the Derby.'"

Ana smiled, wondering how many shots he'd had. "Yes, you've said that before," she added drily as his hand slid over her posterior, but she didn't move it away for fear he'd give her a bad price on her earrings. "What is going on outside?" she asked.

He shrugged. "The Chinese are upping the ante. Last week they killed a Japanese lieutenant and his driver. Now, who knows what monkey business the fools are up to. Teasing the battleship, the *Idzumo*, I'd say, until it starts shooting its antiaircraft guns at them."

Ana took out her diamond earrings and passed them to him. She couldn't bring herself to speak.

Vassily looked up at her, with an odd expression. "You know, my dear, I just saw your brother. Lent him some money on the bracelet you sent over earlier—and now I see you! But, it's a bad time for loans my dear. I suggest you keep these. A woman always wants a sparkle by her eyes."

"My bracelet? Mischa?" Ana flushed, looking down. All the faces at the bar were turned to her.

"Gentlemen," he said to his companions, "I must introduce you to my beautiful and talented—"

Vassily never finished that sentence. At that moment the loud roar of planes was heard overhead and before the startled patrons could grasp what was happening the entire building shook to its very foundation. Plaster fell from the ceilings, glass broke, chandeliers swayed madly, and a deafening crash sent people scattering, falling, screaming. Three explosions rocked the hotel from the top. Ana was thrown to the floor.

She opened her eyes seconds later only to see the entire place covered in a thick coat of plaster and debris. Vassily was before her, lying on the marble floor, a glass shard in his head; others stood dazed or unconscious. People began screaming, shouting for loved ones, crying. Standing up, ears ringing, Ana limped toward the door, her feet sliding on the floor and plaster. She had to get out. She had to find Wong … but nothing could have prepared her for the carnage outside.

In front of the hotel, fires were burning. Debris littered the street, and the place where she'd left Wong was marked only by his burning car. *The dark form of a man was at the wheel, crumpled over—outlined in orange flames.* Ana fell backward in terror. Above, glass windows were bursting, and black empty sockets gaped with shooting tongues of fire. Visions of Russia so long ago came back to her. She watched in shock, hypnotized; Shanghai too, this most formidable city, was going to fall.

Nanking Road *13 August 1937*

THE WALK TOWARD THE Bund and the Cathay was not long, but it was arduous as thousands of people swarmed the streets in human rivers of misery. All were escaping the typhoon, escaping China, going to the foreign settlement as if it were another country. To struggle through them was to know firsthand what it was to be a living thing in the soup of life, smelling sweat, camphor in clothing, cooking oil, illness, and fear. Bodies—slippery in the drizzle, warm, clammy, grabbing, pushing, bracing, falling. Several times Algy was wrenched away from Jack's side but always managed to keep him in view. As they came closer to the heart of the International Settlement the masses gradually dispersed into doorways and alleys. Nearly back at their hotel, Jack and Algy were startled to hear the reverberations of airplanes buzzing high, then low. They paused in the spattering of rain, looking at each other mystified—then decided to go to the Bund for a view of the sky. A block farther, they came out into the open by the Whangpoo River and stood on a grassy bank, shielding their eyes from the glare. Chinese bombers from the Lungwha airfield were performing stunts below heavy cloud cover.

"I can't imagine the logic of doing this with the edge of the typhoon battering them," Jack said.

"A frightful risk. I think there are four of them," Algy said counting them out as they flew into sight from the southeast. "No, two more."

"Well, there won't be if they get any closer to the *Idzumo*." The Japanese battleship was moored north of them toward Soochow Creek, about six blocks up from where they stood; their hotel was at the midpoint. They could see the battleship's hull bristling with guns while thousands of people lined the shore watching. Rooftops and observation decks were also crowded with spectators pointing up at the planes. "I'm going to go see our concierge; maybe I have a lead from another client waiting for me," Jack said. Up above, the planes flew low, closer and closer to the warship with every pass, and in perfect formation.

"But Jack," Algy cried out following him. "What about Chan? Don't you think that …" Algy was not able to finish the question. As the planes swooped down again in a show of bravado, the *Idzumo* began to fire shell after shell. Explosions popped in the sky around the planes, puffs of smoke following their path as they banked upward; and suddenly to the amazement of the crowd, there was a loud whine, then another, and another. The planes had released a hail of bombs! The crowd could see them falling from high up. Some spectators stood in disbelief, while others threw themselves down on the grass, covering their heads. The first bombs exploded in the Whangpoo sending huge columns of water more than two hundred yards up into the sky, soaking people on rooftops. Jack and Algy raised their heads, unable to look away while the last two bombs began to tip and drop rapidly. They ducked and two earthquakes struck one after another, shaking the ground in a crash of cement and glass, leaving their ears ringing. Getting up, Jack cried out pointing to the rising columns of smoke as thousands of people screamed, running en masse, inland, away from the Whangpoo and the *Idzumo.* People pushed past them, dropping possessions, littering the road behind them, trampling children, carts, anything to get away. Jack pushed his way back through them heading to their hotel, which appeared to be on fire. Algy followed in confusion and when they both turned left from the Bund onto Nanking Road they stopped dead still.

What lay before them was carnage. The pride of Shanghai, lined with European buildings and shops, was deserted but for the dead. Glass fell down onto the street like the sound of crystal rain. Then antiaircraft guns began firing again from the river, deafening them. Jack sprinted into their hotel, but Algy stood still, looking on in shock.

He saw all sorts of mangled metal tangled in downed tram-wires; vehicles were overturned and ablaze; charring remains of human bodies were scattered higgledy-piggledy. Directly opposite the hotel, blown into the road, was a crater three feet deep, a man's shoe balanced on the edge. The few cars not burning were freckled with shrapnel, tenanted by corpses. Flattened rickshaws, hawker carts, apples, a tram car—everything was blood spattered. Algy didn't know where to look or run but he heard more planes in the sky buzzing louder. He thought to go find Jack but at the hotel entrance where the Lalique doors had once gleamed there was a gaping hole. People were emerging, covered in plaster and looking as if they'd been dipped in flour; as they stepped out onto the street they stood dumbfounded by the burning car. Jack suddenly appeared among them, with Chan's sing-song girl dazed and clinging to his arm. Then the air raid sirens began their deafening wail. Algy waved to Jack, who hurried over.

"Where are we going?" Algy hollered. The girl was looking back at the burning car.

Jack pointed down the road, steering the girl away from the chaos and dead bodies. When the infernal siren cut out at last, Jack took Algernon aside: "We're in a bit of a fix." They both looked at her.

Her eyes went wide and she grabbed Jack by the forearm. "Don't, don't leave me here!"

"But Ana," he put an arm around her shoulders, "Algernon and I have to make it all the way to the airport. I'm not sure it's a risk you want to take—"

"No. I won't stay," she cut in, green eyes flashing, voice thick with emotion; then she suddenly broke into shuddering tears. Even Algy was taken by her beauty.

Jack held her and she wept against his chest. "Don't cry," he whispered looking confused; then he leaned down and kissed the top of her head.

Algy raised his eyebrows, then cleared his throat. "Ah-hum. Without a vehicle, I don't see how we're getting to the airport, much less out of here alive." A sudden loud series of reports like thunder ricocheted off the buildings and they all stepped into a doorway.

"The airport's north of town," Ana said between thunderous crashes, still tearful, but peering out at the sky. "It's no good. All of Chapei is on fire … But I did see an airplane land back on Thibet Road. I was at Chan's when it came down."

Jack looked surprised. "*Thibet Road*?" He had a hand resting comfortably at her waist. "But that's the racecourse!" A look of cunning came over him. "Wait in here," he said abruptly, then dashed out across the road into the rain and wind.

Algy sneered. "He is a veritable ass. And you needn't bank on anything he might say. He's just fired me, and that's the second time in one year, mind you." He was about to add another unflattering remark when they heard a loud metal scraping. To their amazement Jack drove up in a partly crushed vehicle dragging a mangled bumper behind it.

Their drive across town was perilous with blockades and detours, and it was already late in the afternoon by the time they pushed through the abandoned entry gates at the racecourse.

"Wait! There it is! Back there," Ana pointed over the guardrail where a plane teetered in the wind, apparently abandoned. "Looks like it might flip over!"

Jack backed up the twenty feet, and pointing to a gate that read, Ewo Stables, commanded, "Algy, get out and open it."

"But—you're not—going to—?"

"Do it, damnit!"

Algy climbed out into the driving rain and unhooked the gate, then hopped back in as Jack hit the accelerator. They tore across the green, skidding through rain-bogged turf, and barreled full speed toward the plane. Algy suddenly saw a white man leap out and come running toward them, waving his arms frantically. Jack hydroplaned to a swerving stop in time, but before anything could be said, they distinctly heard an airplane rumbling in closer and closer overhead. Jack cut the motor just as the noise swooped in low and the sound of guns came blasting from behind. Then a monstrous shadow passed over and it was gone.

"Hurry, get out! Get away from the car!" the man shouted in an American accent, pointing to the sky, "It might be back!"

They all scrambled onto the field watching the plane disappear over the flat rooftops. However, it did not return. They looked around them—the turf was shot full of holes.

"What was that for?" Jack asked.

The man shrugged. "Potshots for now."

"Didn't hit the plane, though," Jack observed. There were more shots in the distance and they all turned to look toward the Bund where the *Idzumo* was still firing away. "Look," Jack said, pointing toward a plane in the distance that was trying to outrun Japanese artillery fire.

They all gasped as it tore ahead of exploding smoke puffs. *It was headed straight their way.* It came closer and closer at full speed, too low over the tops of buildings, and then suddenly banked. Two bombs dropped as it lifted up ahead of the artillery, but the group on the racecourse had no time to run. The ground shook, once, twice, in rapid succession as the bombs struck a block away on Thibet Road leaving their ears buzzing.

Jack stepped forward, his voice terse, "I don't know how long your plane's going to stay where she is. Come on, I'll help you stake her down against the wind."

The pilot had a southern twang as he spoke, "Don't have any rope. My 'assistant' in Hanoi offloaded it by accident. Don't matter anyhow. They've spotted me now."

"Ah, a fellow Southerner! How do you do?" Jack said, holding out his hand, suddenly his charming self again. Algy rolled his eyes as he introduced himself, "Jack Morgan—Kentucky, via Hong Kong."

"Sam Johnson, out of Alabama, USA. And I'm not doing well," he said shaking hands reluctantly. "I've got cargo for Chunking but I'm out of fuel and I can't see how you could help. That plane could be back any minute for us."

"Your plane's going to flip over before then," Algy said gloomily looking at the wind lifting at the wings.

Jack glared at him, and then turning to the pilot spoke in a low voice so Algy couldn't hear. Leaning closer Algy thought he heard him murmur, "I'll have the rest for you in Hong Kong. What do you say?"

Algy looked over at the plane, the *Alabama Girl,* which had a voluptuous gal barely contained in a bathing costume painted on the side. *Looks like poor old Percy just bought himself a plane as well as a caboose!* His gaze wandered over toward Ana and Jack. They were looking into each other's eyes, and Jack had her hand in his, holding it to his chest. *Could Jack seriously be taking this femme fatale back to Hong Kong?* Algy stared, dumfounded, thinking of Violet. "You're barking mad, old chap," he muttered, "barking mad."

Macao

8

Shanghai Racecourse *13 August 1937*

"We'll be heading into the wind," the pilot drawled a half hour later glancing back at her and Algy in the fuselage as he secured the door. "Due east, over battleships. Gotta be quick about it, too, before the typhoon pulls a fast one. Let's hope there's no break in the cloud cover. This is one time we don't want moonlight," he said, returning to the cockpit where Jack was seated.

Ana gave a quavering smile at Algy. "Imagine buying a plane outright! Amazing, isn't it?" He seemed cross to her, angry she was coming along. *It was as if he were jealous.* "I've never flown before," she added with a smile.

He shrugged. "The real trick will be seeing how Jack explains this escapade." He lit a cigarette, then shrugged again. "Not that I'll care when our remains are scattered from here to Timbuktu."

"But Jack said this plane was safe and highly maneuverable," Ana said.

"I wouldn't get my hopes up if I were you," Algy sniffed bitterly, glancing over his shoulder at her. "He'll say anything, my dear, to appear interesting but he's a crashing bore and a cad. You'll see. He thrives on female attention."

Ana studied him a moment. He was nervously stroking a rabbit's foot. "I gather you rather like him." When Algy flushed at the insinuation she knew she'd hit a nerve.

He looked away testily. "You can put him out of *your* sights. He's to be married soon. It's all been arranged."

"Yes, he's told me," she said quietly. *Soooo, we both have a crush,* she thought. Glancing up towards Jack in the cockpit who was sitting with the pilot at the controls, and her gaze lingered on his broad shoulders. He truly was an enigma, smooth and cavalier one moment, and the next rolling up his sleeves and siphoning benzene out of their automobile tank for the airplane; even the pilot was in his pocket. At that moment Jack suddenly looked back at her and winked. Ana couldn't help feeling a flash of excitement.

The engine noise was increasing, and when the brakes let go the aircraft suddenly buzzed forward. She looked out the window. They were passing all the cargo they had off-loaded for seating room and when the tires began sliding and bumping through the mud and potholes she felt them pick up speed, the pitch of the motor rising in intensity. Soon it was a deafening roar and the entire plane was vibrating; outside trees and buildings were speeding past. *How was all this metal to become airborne?* Several sudden thumps knocked the airplane body, boxes fell, then Ana abruptly felt her stomach drop and sway with an abrupt swerve and lift. She hardly dared look. They were off the ground—and it was exactly how she'd felt in his arms. She glanced up at the back of his head, dismayed. *I'm not in love,* but felt her face flush at the thought of him.

Higher and higher they flew, rising over rooftops, over Chan's, over stately European-style buildings, over the snaking Woosung River that gleamed black so far below—Shanghai and all her troubles—*gone*, just like that. The airplane tipped, bringing a final dark vista of the city to the porthole. In Chapei, the fire was still burning like a red wound in the heart, and Ana touched the cold glass. She hadn't thought China would have let go so easily. The plane dipped as the motor stuttered and she gasped. This modern age terrified and fascinated her, like Jack. And *people, flying like thoughts—it was amazing and unnatural.* After some time, as she sat in the dark, clutching her seat, the plane settled into an even roar and Ana felt the cold coming on, inching through the metal, into her bones; aided by the noise, she began numbing toward sleep. Some time later and frightfully cold, she was startled awake. Jack was pulling a coat over her shoulders—*his*, and still warm from his body. She felt the warmth in her own body responding to him, to his presence.

"We're going down in Hankow," he shouted, and indeed, the plane was losing elevation in the dark. Algy had gone to the cockpit and now Jack sat down beside her, demonstrating how to brace. There were few lights below, almost nothing to see by, but the landing wasn't rough, and before she knew it the door had been flung open and cool night air was coming in. *All the way down she'd been holding his hand.*

"Algy said we were very lucky," she said retracting her hand to her side self-consciously, "you know, that the airplane could run on Red Star auto fuel!"

"You have quite the grip," Jack said staring into her eyes and Ana looked down quickly. She did not want to be tricked into feeling happy and then have her hopes dashed yet again. The pilot and Algy had already hopped out onto the airfield when Jack said, "Well?" Taking her by the arm, he indicated the exit and she allowed him to help her down. What if it was true, that he *was* a cad, and that it was *him* marrying for money and not the woman? *Oh, I'm so stupid!* Unable to hide her bitterness, Ana said hotly, "Algy claims you buy anyone and everything, whether for sale or not."

He tilted his head, smiling boyishly. "Oh, not everything. Some things are free of charge."

She had no rejoinder, but to her surprise he began to laugh and then went off to see the pilot. Caught in the undertow of her sorrows, she was captivated by a man who created his own destiny, limited only by what he could imagine.

He returned after a few minutes. "Ana, Sam's off to arrange for someone to store this extra cargo, but we also need more fuel.

Shouldn't be too long. You coming?" His gaze went down from her eyes to her sequined décolleté. "Algy's going to pick up some vodka at a Russian bar."

Ana declined and turned away to walk along the perimeter of the landing strip, looking into the darkness of the surrounding fields. Once away from him she found her fears returning, and looking up at the night sky felt very small. Here she was, somewhere in China surrounded by death and war, with no friends, and she hadn't even said good-bye to the few Russians she still knew in Shanghai. *I will have to start a whole new life again, alone. I will be on the street, somewhere, tomorrow.* It was a sobering thought.

When she returned she found Jack unloading boxes with his sleeves rolled up, breathing heavily, heaving crates onto the grass.

"I thought you were going with them," she accused.

"I couldn't leave you here alone," he said. "Besides, I knew you were particularly interested in speaking to me."

"You assume a lot," she said quietly.

"Oh, Ana. You just desperately want to know what makes me tick."

"I've far greater concerns," she said annoyed, then her voice broke. "But, I *am* grateful that you helped me leave Shanghai—*really I am.*"

"No need of that," he said holding out his arm. "Why not come for a walk? What? Don't you trust me?"

"You're the one who gave me your room key."

"Ah! So I did. Well now, I give you my word of honor; I won't succumb to your charms again, and that silly German accent. *Dahlink?* Come on." He pointed out the moon and taking her arm in his, led her into the wide open field. Breezes moved through the long grass, flowing in waves. He squeezed her hand in his and a hush of peace washed over her. Ana saw him shake his head.

"What is it?"

"Ana. I've already succumbed, but—" He gave her a cryptic look, taking out a scrap of paper. "But, 'goody goody'?" he asked holding up her note.

She laughed and removed a cigarette from her clutch.

"Why'd you write this?" he asked.

"Because you assume too much about me."

He took her cigarette and lit it. "The first time I saw you," he said puffing, then handing it back, "you reminded me of someone."

Ana took it between her lips, watching him closely as she drew in the hot smoke. "Oh?" She didn't like reminding him of another woman, yet her own quick jealousy startled her.

"A girl who worked in a hat shop back in Hong Kong," he said, gesturing to a wide stone seat by a stream and they sat down together.

"I gather she's not the woman you are marrying?"

"What? No," he said. "It's just that the girl died so strangely." He looked up, troubled. "Last year she was crushed by the Peak Tram. Fell off the empty platform, just like that. She was crippled in one leg but she always carried a cane. Anyway, I've gone over it so many times. She knew her foot wasn't right so why walk near the edge? The cane she always carried was never found …"

"Indicating someone else was there and removed it?"

"Precisely."

"But Jack, you walk near the edge—am I wrong?"

"I do." He looked at her. "How about you?"

"I don't like uncertainty."

He raised her hand to his mouth. "Adventure?" he asked, his lips brushing her skin.

"No adventure." She peeled her hand away, afraid she would cry.

"Not even with me?"

"You, my dear sir, are a one-man-beehive of adventure and contradiction."

Jack threw his head back and laughed and Ana found herself smiling, then laughing with him. He turned unexpectedly, "Then I take that as a *yes*."

"You do?" She didn't like being propositioned—didn't like finding herself sliding toward him mentally and emotionally as if the stone seat they sat on was tipped toward him.

"I like a challenge," he said, eyes soft and dark. He took her hand in his and kissed it gently.

"Well then, I hope your new *wife* will comply with your expectations."

He looked surprised. "You *are* cruel."

"Am I?" She attempted to pull her hand back. "You've said that twice now."

"Ah well, so I have." They were silent for some time watching the moonlight, silver on dipping blades of grass, and listening to the quiet trickle of water over stone. "I think I'm going to make a very big mistake," he finally said.

She got up feeling confused, but his palm slid around her waist, stopping her from leaving.

"A mistake? How so?" He drew her to him gently and held her until she relaxed. She didn't know how long they stood like that, or if she was even breathing, but the feeling was like no other. For the first time in her life her nervous thoughts felt stilled. An amazing sense of peace filled her. For the first time ever, Ana felt safe.

"A mistake," he repeated, whispering it.

Headlamps were bobbing in the distance, approaching. "Algy's back," she said quietly.

"Ana, don't deny it you felt it the moment we ran into each other." His thumbs were pressing into her upper arms as he tried to force her to look into his eyes.

Blinking back a few hot tears, she was thankful for the darkness. "Your life's arranged." She removed his hand from her body, then headed slowly back toward the plane and climbed inside just as the truck came to a stop, shutting down its engine. *Was this how he pressured all the girls as Algy had implied? Did he expect a quick fling at the back of the plane?* He didn't follow her in, and Ana sat inside alone, staring at the floor, her tears falling freely, tapping on the floor. *He's called me a mistake.*

From outside she heard his voice. "Sam, you can see my banker at Jardine's, he'll settle the balance. I'll call him as soon as we land in Hong Kong."

The two men chatted in a jocular way, then climbed up into the cockpit. When he didn't come to see her she found a tarp on the floor and stretched out, having had no sleep for two nights. She wanted to wait to see if he came back to her, but slowly she gave in to a deep, exhausted sleep.

When she opened her eyes again, a hot breeze was blowing over her. Sitting up, she looked at her watch. *Hours had passed!* The door of the plane was open, and straightening her hair, she stood up and put her head out. *It was not Hankow.* Jack, Algy, and the pilot were outside the craft standing in the blazing sunlight talking to a uniformed official. Ana bit her lip—*she had no papers. Could they send her back?* She ducked back inside until she heard the army jeep drive off, then emerged cautiously. *The sunlight was dazzling.* Behind the men there was a long strip of twinkling blue water and on the opposite shore a broad mountain that towered over tiny ships below. *Hong Kong!*

Jack turned, and seeing her, began striding back toward the plane. He had a sparkle in his eye and a playful twist to his lips. "Sleep well?" He reached up to her.

Ana decided to say nothing about passports and reached out, taking his hand. He gave a mischievous little pull and she landed in his arms. Jack's eyes were like the water behind him, dancing blue, and her heart caught in her throat as she looked up at him.

"I have to see you again," he whispered, eyes warm, searching hers, then added, "I had a devil of a time seeing you sleeping by yourself, you know. I wanted to wake you and—"

"Please, put me down. Please," she interrupted, holding back tears. "What about my—my papers?"

"All taken care of."

"Just like that? But—"

"Stick with me," he said swinging her down, then taking out his wallet. "You'll need …"

"I—I'd like to change my dress," she said turning to the steps, feeling her face burning with shame at the suggestion of money.

"Wait," he restrained her, grabbing her hand on the railing. "Ana, I'm sorry. I'm in business to think quickly. He fished in his pocket with his free hand and pressed something into her palm. "I was going to give it to you on the plane last night. I thought we'd have time to talk."

She looked down at a sparkling miniature tiger.

"He's my lucky charm. Keep him safe for me, will you? This way I know you'll see me again. *Promise?*" He squeezed her hand tightly and when she nodded, his eyes flashed in quiet triumph. Her heart skipped a beat as he leaned in for a kiss. Just as his breath was upon her lips, a horn beeped. They looked up, startled, as an open flatbed lorry appeared speeding towards them across the tarmac followed by a car. The truck was piled with people holding "welcome back" banners and kept honking. Jack pressed a finger against her lips. "Wait for me here, darling," he whispered. "I'll be back."

Minutes later, in a fresh day dress, Ana lowered herself from the aircraft and was just about to approach the small, well-dressed group when she spotted Jack at the center of the hubbub. He was smiling broadly, one hand patting an old man on the back, and attached to his other was a tall, willowy girl in an excessively broad sun hat. She wore a scanty blouse with a white, crepe de chine skirt slit like a pair of trousers and a jeweled bracelet that sparkled as she laughed.

"Soooo," a voice carried in the breeze, "When are you two getting married, Jack old boy?"

Ana quickly turned away and hearing a motor start up, noticed Sam getting into an automobile. She waved, and grabbing her carpet bag, choked out, "Heading into town?"

"Kowloon side. But aren't you with him?"

Ana got into the car. "I don't even know him. Hurry, let's go."

Kai Tak Airfield, Kowloon *14 August 1937*

"Don't I get a kiss?" Violet pouted as they drove off the runway.

Percy already had his head in the newspaper and Jack was craning to see out the back, looking for Ana. Reluctantly, he turned around, his mouth tightened for the kiss; he was thinking of her provocative telegram. "I suppose congratulations are in order," he murmured low, so the old man wouldn't hear.

Violet shrugged. "The servants have prepared champagne tiffin for you and the whole gang," she said coolly. When he looked back at her, mystified, she raised an eyebrow, daring him to challenge her, here in front of her father. It was a side of her he'd never seen.

The auto made the sharp turn up Garden Road while the old man, oblivious to the undertones, noisily folded his newspaper. "By the by, Jack. I saw old Murphy while you were away. His son Stewart is going to build that shipyard over here on Hong Kong side."

"But what's wrong with the one on Cheng Chow Island?" Jack asked.

"Cheng Chow? That dirty fishing village?"

"But Percy," Jack said, "*those* villagers *are* the shipbuilders."

"Stew says he lives like a savage among them in a grass hut."

"But it'll cost him twice as much to make ends meet on Hong Kong Island." He froze, then eyed Percy with a sinking feeling. "You don't mean to tell me you loaned money to him?"

"Egad my boy! You're making profits hand over fist! Why not spread the wealth around? I owe him some money for gaming losses as it is."

Jack sat back in the seat and stared ahead thinking of the unsold caboose in Shanghai.

"Oh, Jaaaack. Always poo-pooing any expenditures. I've ordered the cook to make Yorkshire pudding for this evening and we've sent a boy to get some American steak for you at Wiseman's. Caviar, too. That should cheer you!"

Out the window, Central District with its banks and office buildings was getting smaller and smaller as the car turned up the steep incline of Old Peak Road. *His career in Asia would be over very soon.*

Percival tapped his daughter's hand. "There are other things in the world besides puddings and caviar, isn't that so, Jack?"

"Of course. Sorry," he said. "Things were pretty awful in Shanghai." He licked his lip nervously looking outside, "You don't mind if I make a few calls when we get up to the house?"

"Not at all," Percy said. Tapping Violet on the knee he added, "My little Poppet, look at today's *South China Morning Post.*" He passed her the paper. "Two hundred homeless people were killed just at the intersection of Thibet and Edward VII. Says the shelter was a charnel-house of flesh. Isn't that by the racecourse, Jack?"

Jack pictured the bodies at Nanking Road, scattered like chopped pork, and then the oncoming plane … And Ana, her catlike eyes and lovely lips. "Sorry? Oh, the racecourse. Yes."

Violet shrugged, fanning herself with the paper. "That's China for you. Yet another flap. But do tell, who was that woman on the plane?"

Jack looked into Violet's dramatic fleur de tête eyes, hard, without an ounce of tenderness. He'd once thought her ravishing.

"Yesss, *Ja—aaack,"* she purred through her teeth. "The *tart* in the *sequined ball gown*. I could see her two hundred yards away!"

"Her?" His heart skipped a beat. "She came over with the pilot."

"Very soon, my Pussums," her father wisely interrupted, changing the subject. "I'll hand over the reins so Jack can manage the firm at his discretion. I've chosen well for you, my dear." Jack noticed how the old man's hands shook.

"You know," Jack said. "There are still deals in Shanghai that could make you very, very wealthy,"

"I can't imagine what other business you're thinking of that Father doesn't already entertain," Violet spat. "And Shanghai's *rotten* to the core! You needn't go there for clients."

The car took another sharp bend and came into sunshine again, with a grand view of the China coast and Kowloon side's mountain range of nine green "dragon" humps. "Have you been taking your daily walks, old boy?" Jack asked, placing his hand over Percy's cold fingers. Percy was positively blue. It didn't help that Violet purposely left the Tantalus on the sideboard after Jack had particularly told her not to; Percy smelled of liquor, and it wasn't even noon.

He waved Jack off, "I'm fine—fine, and I won't be taking exercise. You're in cahoots with my doctor, I see. But, I want to tell you something," the old man said, clearing his throat. "My daughter has convinced me I should make her your assistant."

Jack glanced at Violet. "That's highly irregular."

"It's what I've been doing for years—helping Father and—"

"Jack," Percival cut her off. "You know your Hanoi rice deal alone brought in a clean $100,000 Mex. It's been sitting in my account and now that you'll marry soon," he coughed with a knowing wink, "you'll have that money to invest *together*."

"But, how's that possible?" he asked, uncomfortable with this first reference to the telegram. "We specifically decided you'd pay old debts off with the cash."

"Well, my solicitor had it in escrow, and frankly, it *was* about the time of my attack in February. I guess it slipped my mind."

Jack squinted. *February—it was February two years back!* "Percy, I believe we need to pay off those debts first."

"No so fast." He took out a cigar, offered one to Jack, then leaned back in the car seat. "A Dutch acquaintance is selling out of the rubber business. Albert Chiswick brought it to our notice."

Jack looked at him, incredulous. "And?"

"Well, when I buy his two thousand hectares our property will extend from one side of the peninsula all the way to the Indian ocean!" Percival put his hand into his jacket and fished out an envelope. "You sail to Java tomorrow. On the *Blue Funnel*. You're to buy the entire estate and see that it's put under new management. What do you think?"

Jack fumbled for his lighter, thinking it imperative he spend all day tomorrow around town begging people that were in China Coast Navigation's debt to pay up—yet here was Percy ready to invest in rubber! And all the while 150,000 Mex had been sitting idle! "Well, you've certainly surprised me," was all he said.

"Yes, I'm having the money prepared as we speak. It's in bar silver and gold and will be delivered to the steamer in an ordinary trunk at sailing. I've notified Albert, and since it's his idea—he's to accompany you."

"Percival, surely you know the Germans created synthetic rubber four years ago. It's only a matter of time when full scale produc—"

"No!" Percival cut him off. "This is my chance to have my name on all that land! Fathom that! His bank denied him the loan! The place can be had on the cheap! On the cheap!"

"Yes," Violet spoke up, "we'd be landholders and when things pick up we could build a tennis club for the planters. It ought to be rather amusing, I should think."

Jack thought quietly for a moment. "Percy," he said. "This won't be a pleasant affair. Buying the plantation out from under him like that? Think of the consequences. You were in his shoes only ten years ago."

"It's an opportunity I can't let go," the old man snapped.

Jack took a deep breath. "But surely you know there are suicides in the paper every day—planters are desperate. These people are burning down their own godowns for insurance money! There's been a global *depression* in *rubber*. It might not turn a profit again in years."

"We're making money, aren't we? How bad can it be?"

"But that planter will be *ruined* with no hope of recovering his debts. If he's an acquaintance, why not back his loan instead and take a cut of his future profits? That way he's happy and you're happy, and our money can be better allocated elsewhere—rice, for example. We can get immediate profits on rice. With the war and all we'll get double returns and no bad karma."

"Young man! I know a thing or two about business. I *want* that land!"

"To what end?"

"Damnit!"

"Jaaaaack." Violet cooed. "Ursula Van de Meres just bought a large tract—says she owns two *kampongs*. That's the native word for village. She says they treat her like *royalty*!"

"Imagine that," Jack cut in quietly. "Then you shall have it, I suppose."

"Yes, I knew you'd see it that way. And you know, Ursula tells me all the native children run up to the automobile as she throws sweets to them. They're infamously dirty, but I don't think she can catch anything from them that way."

"Catch anything?" Percy asked, confused.

"Well then, it's settled." Jack concluded, "As for the paperwork, the clerk I took to Shanghai will suit me fine."

"Worthing? That sententious lout? Albert won't like it," but then Percy sighed and said, "Right, my boy. As you wish. When you return we'll make plans for a big wedding, ah, Violet? What do you say?"

"I've never seen you men argue before," Violet observed, strangely pleased.

Percy winked slyly at Jack then looked at his daughter. "You'll soon be walking down the aisle at St. John's, my girl. Jack and I'll drink to that in my library."

"Indeed," Jack said, trying to smile but furious that Percy had been deceived by her, too. He glanced at her belly. Flat. *Who was her secret lover? Obviously someone she didn't want to marry. How pregnant was she?*

"Everyone marries at St. John's but I want it in *Macao*—at that *lovely* hotel! And the ceremony on the steps of St. Paul's!"

Percival spluttered, "St. Paul's is a ruin! And the heat! By Jove, consider my health! It has to be here at St. John's."

As they drove, Violet planned aloud, while Jack took out an envelope and scribbled a quick note to Algy. *Be on time. Blue Funnel Line. 7:00 ship to Java. Tomorrow. You have your position back with a rise in pay.* He signed it with a flourish and handed it to the driver to be delivered right away.

"Oh, Jack?" She slyly looked his way, pinning up the brim. "You haven't said a word about my new hat. I've had a dickens of a time finding a new haberdasher after that French girl killed herself."

He stared at her, incredulous, then smiled. "My dear, none can compete with your taste and breeding."

"You're amusing. At least I didn't wear *sequins* in broad daylight."

"No, you would never stoop so low," he said bitterly. He couldn't help thinking—*But you did. And low enough to send me that telegram.* She must have read his thoughts for she shrugged her shoulder and looked out the window just as Peak House came into view.

Up at the house, Jack helped Violet out of the car, taking her thin-gloved hand while the driver helped Percival. He was still pondering the old man's vanity—even cruelty. *Percy had no need for rubber, only a penny farthing signboard with his name on it! A sign he'd never even see!* But that subject was now closed, and Percy headed straight for his drink in the library. Violet however, paused in the hall at a cloying bouquet of lilies. Snapping off a bloom, she waited for him to pass her, her Burmese ruby earrings glowing like two red eyes as her lips cracked into hint of a smile. "Stanley Beach," she whispered, then slapped the flower into his hand, her eyes bright and accusing. "The night you passed out. Or *can't* you *remember*?"

Chilled by her audacity, Jack turned away into the library and closed the door, dropping her lily into a wastebasket. *Could she really think he'd not remember having sex?* "Percy," he said, "I need to make an urgent call, I'll be right back." In the hall he picked up the receiver and, checking that Violet was out of earshot, dialed Kai Tak. Some minutes later he returned to the library. It seemed impossible, but no one at the flight office had seen where Ana had gone. *Had he misread her?* He remembered those hours with her and it seemed like another life already—yet his short experience with the sing-song girl had cast Violet in an entirely new light. Svelte and very pale, she was waiting in library with her father, sipping a martini; and seeing Jack, she looked pointedly down into the rubbish bin at her lily. "You upset about something, Jacky dear?"

Jordan Path, Kowloon — *14 August 1937*

THE RICKSHAW BOY DEPOSITED Algy by the Kowloon Cricket Club where China Coast Navigation housed its lower-order clerks at nominal charge. He scrambled over a pile of stinking cabbage and refuse, making his way down the road around stalls of black century eggs, feather dusters, and frogs, wondering how soon he must move out. He wasn't officially *fired*—not yet. He nodded to the watchman who was squatting at the entrance to his building, eating rice. Normally polite, the man had an inexplicable grin on his face that set Algy wondering as he headed up the unlit stairs.

It wasn't until he'd almost made it to the top floor flat that he realized something was amiss and stepped back with a shrinking sensation. *Had vagrants been sleeping here?* There was no bad odor, but when he set his foot on the next step it was uneven and *soft*. "Foul!" he cried, and hurried back down quickly—then looked about him. *Rags—heaps of them!* In his flight, one had rucked itself about his leg and he kicked wildly about, thinking only of cholera and typhoid. "Allen, Fred! What's going on here?" he shouted up to his flat-mates. He heard sudden laughter coming from upstairs and a door opened on the third floor, the light slanting down on him. More laughter.

"Another hazing is it?" Algy swore and saw that the rags were clothes. And they were his own. They were scattered all up the steps and as he rounded the next landing shouting, a pair of shorts landed on his head. Algy looked up and saw a fat outline in his doorway. Albert Chiswick, the senior accountant! He tore the shorts off his face, *So that was it—all because I went to Shanghai and not him.* "Well, I just quit," Algy shouted up at them. "Your lousy firm will go under, just wait and see." They fairly shouted with laughter while Algy nearly cried with vexation.

It wasn't an hour later that he moved into the Young Men's Christian Association on the bottom of Nathan Road and headed to his bank. Unfortunately, when he handed over his passbook, the teller at the Hong Kong and Shanghai Bank pushed out a chit totaling his bills from bars around town. "I've been notified not to pay out your remaining balance until you've settled your accounts, Mr. Worthing."

Algernon was dumbstruck. "I say, you can't do that!"

"Recall Sir, Mr. Summerhays has frozen all employee assets until *these* are paid off." The clerk held up a voluminous pile of notes signed by Algy and showed him a long list of other names from the company roster, all blacklisted.

Algernon pulled at his collar, tried to speak, then, shutting his mouth, returned to the street. *Just as he'd warned Jack!* Standing in the merciless heat of Salisbury Road he was fit to be tied.

Tsim Sha Tsui Pier, Kowloon *14 August 1937*

ABOVE, THE TRAIN STATION clock tower gonged four times. All around the people were coming and going. Ana took a seat on a bench near some food carts where the scent of anise, cumin, and hot chicken broth wafted deliciously. She put her hand into her pocket and took out the silver charm, curious.

It was a beautiful tiger, with snarling teeth, ruby eyes, covered in paste diamonds. Meticulously done for a trinket, the stripes were inset smoky stones and his smooth belly was polished silver. *It was engraved.* She looked close, then quickly thrust it into her pocket, and standing up began to walk quickly toward the waterfront. *It was from Cartier and it was no trinket.* A hundred yards toward the water she became aware something was touching her—street children badgering for coins. She was tired, and their tugging here and there like so many flies disconcerted her. "Please!" she shouted, closing her eyes against the light. Things were starting to spin. A shadow passed over her and a dapper gentleman in white sent the children scurrying with a few flicks of his swagger stick. Ana forced her eyes to focus.

"Are you all right, Miss?" His eyes twinkled as he looked at her.

"Yes, thank you. Thank you so much," she said breathlessly and the man abruptly turned away joining a pretty girl with a parasol. Ana pulled out her silk purse, and counted her coins again. *Not even enough for a room.* She looked up and down the esplanade. Perhaps an idea would come to her after she had eaten.

At the noodle cart, Ana pointed to what she wanted, paid, and sat down at the table, her carpet bag at her feet, her purse in her lap. The whole coast blurred before her eyes. Just below her on the praya the children were chucking stones over the water. But one of them kept looking back at her and caught her eye. Ana clutched her purse in her lap, then leaned against the small table, startled when the steaming bowl was plunked down in front of her. Pale dimpled wontons floated like junks in a clear broth flecked with sesame oil and scallions. Ana's hands trembled as she removed her own chopsticks from her bag and felt the hot vapor on her face. The whole scene filled with colors and light appeared to move in a slow wave, and before she knew what had happened, she had fallen.

The sound of voices came to her from a distance, "Move away children, give air. Are you all right?" a kind voice asked, as if from a tunnel, and she heard the laughter of the children nearby. Ana sat forward for a moment and the blood rushed back to her head. A kindly old Chinese man helped her to her seat, scolding gently. "Be careful! Much heat in sun for white lady." He ambled off and Ana hadn't had the time to even thank him. Her soup was where she'd left it, her carpet bag at her feet. Taking her chopsticks up she began to eat and it was not until she'd finished her meal and prepared to put her chopsticks away that she noticed that the children on the praya were gone, and the coin purse that she had so assiduously guarded had vanished. Ana considered her empty lap. The children had an instinct for survival, she thought, *but it is obvious I have none.*

What to do—scream? There was no point. She got up and taking her carpet bag, walked along the pier toward a sign that read, Peninsula Hotel. There, she paused looking at a fleet of hunter-green Rolls Royces dropping off and picking up clients. Ana turned away and moved toward the next street and started to read signs again; *Nathan Road, Jordan Road.* After another twenty minutes her feet were beginning to ache and blister from the hot pavement and she put her carpet bag down. The red sign above her read, 'Nine Dragons, in gilt lettering. Ana pondered the wisdom of entering such a place unescorted, but since she had no one to soften the way, there was no choice.

A small woman came out of the door. "Missy, you come in, no?"

Ana smiled at the sing-song girl in the red silk dress with gold embroidering. "Are you a performer here? You have dancing?"

The girl nodded. "I dance for customah. We berry pop'lar club. Numbah one, Kowloon side! Name good luck, Nine Dragon, see?" She gestured up to the sign.

"I need a job."

The girl nodded and pushed Ana toward the stairs. Together they climbed up, the girl chatting all the way. It wasn't open for business yet but she directed Ana to the bar. "You wanchee drink? I get boss."

"Water, just water."

Ana leaned against the bar and sighed, unaware that she was being watched. To her right, at the dark end of the room, a fat man with a waxed mustache was smiling, and only when he stood up and approached her in squeaky shoes did she look.

"I'm Fausto," he said proffering his hand. "Manager of the famed Macao Golden Inn. I couldn't help but overhear that you are looking for a job."

"How do you do?" she said, as his lips touched her hand. He was golden himself in the reddish bar light, sweating nearly as much as the iced drink he held in his other hand. His eyes twinkled. "May I?" and he pulled up a bar stool. "I can see you're a lady of quality, perhaps down on your luck? Viennese, I think, from the accent."

"You know Vienna?"

"Ah, Wien, Prague. Paris. London—" He shrugged, grandly. "I had much business in Europe when I was younger, free to travel. But now, I'm married, five children. I'm responsible."

Ana leaned onto the counter with all her weight, in sheer relief. "I'm not as much a dancer, I sing. I've had training in the Viennese conservatory, but I do all the popular songs. They fare much better with these crowds, don't you think?"

"I see," he said, watching her astutely.

Afraid she'd put him off she added, "I've sung in Lucky Chan's Shanghai Club two years. They wouldn't have kept me so long if I hadn't done a good job."

"Ah, the Jade Gate!" he leered. "Those Chinese and their double entendres!" Throwing a quick glance over his shoulder at a doorway he lowered his voice, "You're overqualified for this place. And frankly, my dear, it's a bit dirty." He screwed his face in disgust and then cautiously asked, "Have you been to Macao? No! Ah well! Macao is much slower paced, less demanding, higher caliber. We do fewer sets, have more *cosmopolitan* crowds." He loosened his collar and took the opportunity to look about. "Aren't you here with anyone, no? Such a pretty girl, too. Ah, don't cry, *meine liebe fraulein*. Here, take this." He shook his handkerchief out and, putting his heavy arm around her shoulders, dried her tears.

When the boss came out saying, "That gweilo look for job here?" Fausto was waving him away, escorting Ana down the long stairs and into the coming darkness outside.

Kita Kamakura, Kanagawa Japan *14 August, 1937*

THE SHOP CLERK LEANED over a cedar tub, fishing out a fresh cut block of tofu. Pushing back her head scarf with the back of her hand, she laughed. "Hot, isn't it?" She had rosy cheeks, perfect skin and was always flushed from leaning over steaming vats. Carefully wrapping the tofu in brown paper she added, "Oh, did you hear? The Nakamura boy has just returned from China without his leg! Yes, crushed by a falling wall. And he, only a year older than you! How will he earn his rice?"

Yoshi did not know how to answer her and simply nodded, blinking back his shock. He folded the tofu into his indigo furoshiki cloth. They were all taught it was better to die for your country than be shamed and return alive. *Yet it could happen to me too.*

"Dozo! Here, try some okara," she said, offering up fresh soy pulp.

He didn't hear her but put his coin on the counter and distraught, hurried off, running down the narrow walled alley overhung with trees, his heart drumming in his ears. *Soon it will be my turn!* When he reached a tall wooden gate he stopped, breathless, and pushed the heavy door inwards. Stepping over the transom he entered a small forest of cedars on a hill; the garden of the Kyoka family. Once they had been Samurai, but now the master of the property was involved in politics in Tokyo. Yoshi earned extra income caring for the man's two horses.

Stepping over a spongy moss walkway, Yoshi passed the main residence and headed towards the bamboo grove where an old thatch building quartered the two black geldings. The other half of the building was a seldom-used dining hall with elegant painted screens and a wide sunken rectangular hole in the floor for grilling. Yoshi entered the barn and, setting down his furoshiki, went about his evening chores. It was dark and the pleasant nicker and chewing sounds of the horses calmed his nerves. He scratched them behind the ears and on their withers until at last his own panicked heart slowed. He carried in fresh water from the well, then climbed up to the loft. Once he had thrown down enough hay, he stretched out in the loft and closed his eyes. *The Nakamura boy, the village hero—ruined?* He sighed. Call-up notices seemed to always come at the middle of the month. *It was the fourteenth!* He shuddered. He did not want to go home. Sometime later he jerked awake to the smell of grilling fish and sake. He blinked. *How long have I been sleeping?* It was dark outside and he could hear voices coming from the room attached to the barn. Yoshi leaned closer to the wall knowing full well he was not supposed to be here so late.

"Kyoka," a low voice said. "You are too idealistic. How many have been assassinated because of your sort of thought? Look what happened—they killed Prime Minister Hamaguchi, and in '32, Inukai, and those bankers! Killed because of their ties to internationalism!"

"Takamatsu! Are you threatening me?" Kyoka erupted.

Terrified, Yoshi peered through a crack. His boss, Kyoka San, was hidden from view by a thick chain hanging from the ceiling which held an iron tea kettle over the heat. He could see three others seated around the central pit, where the coal glowed brightly. Smelt speared on long skewers, that were propped up in the sand, were slowly toasting above the fire. There was no woman there to serve them and this fact alarmed Yoshi; it had to be top secret. Worse still, the men addressing his honorable employer spoke to him as equals; his employer *had* no equals in Kamakura. These must be Tokyo officials! Yoshi wanted to run, but knew he mustn't move. *If they find me here they will kill me.*

"I'm not threatening you," the man said, pouring sake for the others. "But you know the people won't stand for this. How many are starving in the countryside, selling their *daughters* for *food!*"

"Enough!" Kyoka growled. "Things will turn around." He threw back his drink.

"No." Takamatsu went on quietly. "The foreigners are not buying our rice or our silk. What else have we to sell? Unemployment is rife! We need your support."

"But we lose face internationally with this kind of dual diplomacy." Kyoka said. "Japan fought for the English during the Great War against Germany, and alongside the Americans during the Boxer Rebellion. Now in one fell swoop, with our bold seizure of Manchuria, we have lost our good standing among developed countries."

"What do we concern ourselves with their opinion? The West wants to repartition the world to its own terms!" Takamatsu said, getting excited. "They have their colonies! We have a right to survive as well! Japan has *no* resources. We must protect what we have in Manchuria—especially with the Chinese going outside for help against our interests."

Kyoka looked around, studying the other faces. "We already have had insurrection after insurrection in our military. And in Tokyo last year, an attempted coup! Where is this leading, gentlemen?"

Takamatsu gestured to another man who had been silent. "Sato, from the Imperial Army, can tell you."

Sato nodded. "Russia is mounting its troops and defenses on the Siberian border of Manchuria to retake what we have rightly acquired. They are digging trenches, building airfields. They are mobilizing for war. Maybe not for today, but they will soon be at our throats."

"But we are China's liberators!" Kyoka said. "We must convince the Chinese we are trying to help them fight the Communists and the Russians."

"How? When they continually go to the West for help against Japan?"

Sato nodded, impatient now. "China is not even a legitimate country. There is no organization. What is to stop us from organizing China in our interests? You see already the West has caved in and conceded Manchuria. Not happily, but they have! They have no will to fight us. Now is our time to strike!"

Kyoka sighed. "All this, even when our Revered and Honorable Emperor is against you."

Takamatsu sat back a moment, then spoke low and steady, in a voice that frightened Yoshi. "The people have no more patience for international agreements. We have had nearly ten years of insurrections. Our country is fiercely divided and in ruins. Who cares what the Washington System proposed! If we deal directly with China those Westerners cannot cut us out of the riches still to be found in Manchuria. The Emperor must go along with this—the press is on *our* side."

"So!" Kyoka hissed. "Then you *are* going along with the military and its secret war against the Chinese! Why then bother with my view?"

"We are building a coalition. You would do well to join, Kyoka."

There was a moment of silence, then Sato spoke, his voice tight with indignation. "'If victorious, tighten your helmet chords.'"

Kyoka turned quickly to look at Sato who only stared back defiantly. "What are you *saying*, quoting Admiral Togo like this?" Kyoka demanded. No one answered, and Kyoka let out a long hiss, shaking his head in dismay, staring down at the fire.

"Prepare for total war," Takamatsu said. "A war like no other." The meaning of his words fell into the silence of the room like a rock.

After the men had left, Yoshi crept out of hiding, terrified, and returned home in darkness. He was right about one thing. Early the next morning the government official arrived on the doorstep with his red call-up notice. Yoshi thought of the red centipede, and mentally drew a line through his life up until that moment, voiding out the past. He was going to war, *total war. A war like no other.*

JAVA BOUND

9

Tsim Sha Tsui *14 August 1937*

IT WAS THE LAST call before the Kowloon departure and Ana stood near the gangway watching the sun descending over a string of islands to the west of Hong Kong. Fausto edged in between her and the gangway, chewing at his mustache. The ship's motors suddenly revved and the coolies below readied their mooring hooks. Observing Fausto's grimy Panama hat and five o'clock shadow unsettled her somehow, and she looked away toward the jetty where a small group of workers milled about fixing a smoking motor. A small creeping fear was niggling at her—telling her to run. As her eyes slid toward the Star Ferry that was boarding passengers for Hong Kong side, she saw Fausto's hand inching closer along the railing toward her own hand. A sharp whistle sounded and there was a clatter. The gangway hoisted up. *Too late.* Fausto gave a satisfied grunt, tapped her arm, and announced he was off to get a drink. Ana watched anxiously as fellow passengers filed below deck behind him, a drab and dejected lot carrying greasy paper sacks of food and makeshift luggage. An inexplicable feeling of dread settled over her as the steamer gathered momentum, pulling free from Kowloon under pink and purple skies. Sounds from shore disappeared in the growing wind and loud vibration of the engine.

Out on the choppy blue strait, seawater sprayed as the steamer slapped oncoming waves, engine churning. With her hair and dress whipping at her, Ana leaned onto the railing trying to watch as the sun vanished behind Victoria Peak. Below it, Hong Kong Island was already immersed in shadows, but hawks wheeling very high overhead were still touched with pink sunlight. As the steamer nosed closer, Ana spotted large isolated homes on the Peak, a few electric lights glowing against the darkness. She couldn't help but wonder if Jack were up there in one of those homes and in her mind his face appeared like a photograph, transparent over the water, his eyes watching. *Jack, Jack Morgan.* The sound of her voice disappeared over the water. After a time the strait and islands vanished into darkness and they were out on open sea. The wind roared like a furnace and Ana went inside to lie down on a bench, her heart heavy with regret. Hours later she jerked awake; the motors were reversing, there was a bump against the pier.

It was just before dawn when they disembarked at a shabby landing and Ana found herself walking up a steep hill with Fausto, away from town and the other passengers. Macao was still asleep and Fausto's close, labored breathing seemed unpleasantly intimate in the maze of unlit passages. Her sense of panic was rising as the sound of their solitary footsteps filled the narrow shadowy spaces between buildings. Outside a Portuguese-style stucco doorway he finally stopped, jangling a ring of keys. She waited. At last the grimy door swung open and Fausto led her down a long corridor to another heavy door. Inside, he lit a candle, illuminating the space; the floor was tiled, there was an iron bed and a small table with a basin of water and bar of soap. A picture of the Virgin Mary hung above the bed.

"Have a rest, and I'll be back."

Ana looked around noting there was no window in the room and was about to say something when he shut the door with a bang.

Victoria Harbor *15 August 1937*

ALL THE PASSENGERS HAD boarded and a church bell was ringing out the hour. In a last-minute rush to fill the remainder of the hold, coolies balancing enormous sacks of millet, cabbages, and boxes of government tea and opium overtook the praya and narrow gangway. Algy, who was already late, broke into a sweat as he pulled his luggage through this crush of workers, cursing Jack all the while.

"Ahoy there, ship's boy!" came the mocking voice from above.

Algy tipped back his solar topee and squinted. *It was Jack.* He said nothing and instead pushed onward, arriving topside after much effort. He found him sprawled on a deck chair, feet up, arms crossed behind his head, a cocktail on the table beside him. Algy dropped his things down with a deliberate thump, upsetting Jack's iced drink. "I'm here for one thing and that's an apology."

"So you say," Jack said righting the glass. "But you wouldn't be so snide if, say—you had a chance to move to Hong Kong side? Pay off your blasted liquor bills?"

"What do you mean, 'move to Hong Kong side'?"

"Well, I can't have my right-hand man slumming with company bachelors on Kowloon." The boatswain's whistle sounded and Jack gestured over the side. "Ah, take a look." Two coolies with a very heavy crate stamped with the CCN seal were moving up the gangway, holding up departure.

"What's that?"

"Let's head them off at my stateroom. We've got business to attend to."

As soon as the coolies had deposited the crate in the room and departed, Jack locked the door and rang for the steward. "Now Algy," he said relighting his cigar. "I've had a rough night of it myself, and we're both in a pinch." He poured out two shots of whisky then removed a portable typewriter from its case. "I'll not bring up Shanghai, the unsold caboose, and the folly of your conduct," he said, then took out a key and snapped open the lock on the crate. "You've your job back, a raise in pay. In turn, you'll do me a favor."

"A raise?" Algy peered into the crate, then gasped.

There was an abrupt knock on the door and Jack threw a rug over. It was only the steward. "Bring me an electric fan," he said, "and two more bottles, with ice." Algy was still dumbstruck and pointing at the gold when Jack pulled up another chair to the desk and took out a thick sheaf of papers from a leather valise. "I recommend you get comfortable because you're going to get old Percy out of an enormous financial calamity."

"Percy? Don't you mean *you*?" He narrowed his eyes. "What is it this time?"

"He means to buy a rubber plantation near Batavia."

Algy laughed, relieved. "Oh—right! Rubber's dead, you old sausage. Even I know that."

"Not Percy."

"You really mean this gold here is to buy a plantation?"

"Over my dead body."

"But dash it all! We're heading to Java!"

"Appearances, my boy."

"But what about the proof of sale documents—coolie papers? The gold?"

"We're loading it right back onto the next eastbound steamer and taking it directly to the bank. It'll secure the ships already purchased, and just in time I'll have you know. The sale document is where you come in."

Algy stared dismally at the papers and typewriter.

"Sit down and stop pulling on your collar. We've work to do."

"Ah well. Here we are—in the soup again."

"And one more thing, Algy. I want to find Ana. I'll need your help."

"Ana?" Algy just about laughed. "You sop. You've enough trouble as it is!"

Batavia, Indonesia *18 August 1937*

THE SUN WAS BLAZING when they docked in the Dutch Colony several days later and it was all Algy could do to keep his foul mood in check. Jack went off to hire an automobile while Algy smoked a cigarette and took a seat at the Alkmaar Café, ordering a thick Java coffee. He had a perfect view of the Amsterdam Arch at the center of town—it was as if the Arc de Triomphe had been set down in a poultry yard. An oxcart shambled through, then a donkey paused to defecate before walking on. Algy vigorously crushed his butt in the ashtray. He and Jack had already had several heated arguments over the course of their "accounting," and a thick silence now existed between them. As he drained a second cup, Jack finally drove up with a cheery beep and a cloud of dust. Algy turned crimson but got in, slamming the door so hard his teeth rattled. *If only I didn't need the money.*

Outside the capital the roads were terrible; potholes and erosion spoke of heavy rains and lack of funds. Jack drove recklessly, swerving past oxcarts, mangy dogs, and barefoot natives balancing baskets on their heads—stopping only once at a crossing as a train chuffed by slowly, carrying workers in and latex out. Algernon stared out his window as inner Java unrolled before him, reams of striped velvet kicked from a spool, endlessly undulating. Meticulous rows of rubber trees hypnotized with their regularity, while half-naked coolies in white loincloths moved silently among the trees. They stopped twice for directions outside rubber factories, open huts under corrugated tin roofs, honking. A white planter would come out of the darkness, dazed from damp smoky fires and carrying a whip, but visibly elated to see another of his kind. Most of them had apparently given up and gone home after the rubber collapse some years ago, for here and there they'd pass abandoned planters' bungalows, buildings on piles, collapsing roofs overgrown with creepers.

"Why feel sorry, Algy?" Jack asked, taking his eyes off the road to look at him. "Greed drove these people to tear up this land for their white gold. They made their fortune and now they've overplanted. No one to blame but themselves."

"Right! 'Forge this,' you say, 'sign there'!" He turned his head away, furious. He'd spent three nights compiling an extensive false ledger system by which funds gained from Jack's other affairs would be transferred to appear on the rubber ledgers as gains. He'd have to make regular deposits into the new plantation account as well. It wasn't a one-time lie; it was a network of lies, continual and ever growing.

"I didn't say it would be easy."

"No, it's bloody mad posting our *real* profits to the ledgers of a *dead* business which we don't even *own!*"

"Percy thinks there's a profit in it! That's all that matters!"

Jack had begun to enlighten him further, but Algy held up his palm. "I'll thank you to say no more." Jack deliberately hit a pothole and the scenery jumped, nearly bringing up Algy's two cups of coffee. For the rest of the ride, he clutched the dashboard and refused to look at Jack. This ridiculous job he was embroiled in included updating records and making reports on coolies—sick leave, deaths, new recruits. It was mind-boggling—he didn't know where to begin, nor did he even understand the rubber business. It was a total sham.

"Listen, Algy, you've got a hair up your ass about everything," Jack finally said with a warning look. "Try not to muck this up. We're almost there."

"Don't push your luck, taipan."

"Is that so? Kindly recall, Edouard's dead because of your meddling."

That put a damper on things and nothing more was said until Jack turned onto a gravel path lined with freshly whitewashed flower pots leading up to a tidy planter's house. Young Javanese children playing on the clipped lawn paused to stare as they drove up. Algy slunk down in the car seat wanting to die of shame. Up on the verandah there was the stirring of a newspaper and as they shut the car doors an old white man rose from a cane chair with a confused look.

Once they'd exchanged greetings and explained who they were, they were invited in with growing excitement and expectation, the planter asking if they wanted a tour. The man's native wife quickly poured out celebratory drinks and they all sat down at a modest table in the kitchen. However, before they drank to Percy's health and the sale of the land, Jack took a deep breath and began to unwind their lives with his explanation.

"But old Summerhays always coveted this land!" the planter exclaimed, incredulous. "Now he can have all of it!"

"But isn't this sale going to ruin you as it is?" Jack asked.

The man shrugged. "Probably. *Yes*."

Algy knew he would always remember this moment, the sound of the clock on the wall ticking, the man's hand as it clutched the bottle, and the look of the wife, slow and hateful as they drank her liquor and her happiness, these two well-dressed men from Hong Kong.

It was positively detestable. The relief Algy later felt as they scurried down the driveway was immeasurable. As soon as they hopped in the car and were headed back toward Batavia, he blurted out, "Don't you have an ounce of goddamned moral fiber?"

Jack gave a hard grin and after a moment said, "These trials bring out the best in us. You'll see, that planter will pull out of this somehow and be the better man for it. But I can't go around solving other people's problems. Look at those coolies, they'll die here and never see China again. Ask them, *who's been generous?* Not your planter. Look at this landscape—devastated by rubber. I'm indifferent to your romantic follies, Algy, because I've had to stand up for myself all my life." As they pulled up in front of their hotel, Jack paused, removing the key from the ignition. "Get washed up, and I'll meet you here in an hour. There's an earlier steamer coming through." He grinned with a particular sharp glint in his eye. "And by the way, remember that priest on the steamer I met on the way over?

"No. I was too busy forging documents."

"An amazing bit of luck. I received a tip for you on landing a cheap flat. It's attached to the Catholic mission. One of the elders died. It's close to the pubs, and you'll be able to afford it on your new pay."

Algy buttoned his lip. Now it seemed he had his job back because of a collapsing rubber plantation and, apparently, a new flat because a church elder had just died. He drew himself up, "Then I'd say the outlook seems rather black."

"Black indeed. But let me suggest you reserve a few negative adjectives for a truly grim occasion."

"Dashed sensible. Whose life do we ruin next?"

Jack threw him an irritated look but said no more. When they entered the lobby, however, he was quick to head for the concierge. "I want to place a trunk call."

"Who in blazes are you calling now?" Algy grimaced. "Violet?"

"Our solicitor. I'm making a loan,"

"You're broke, remember?" Algy shook his head and went to the bar to order a gin fizz.

Peak House *15 August 1937*

Had she really seen that cane? Rose headed down to the kitchen by way of the servant's staircase, perplexed, and a bit afraid. As Violet's keenest admirer, she had long passed off the girl's brazen antics as the ploys of an only child—until now. In a flash, the face of the French girl came to her—dead one year now. *Yet all children have a little evil in them,* Rose mused, reassuring herself. But Violet was a grown woman, and Rose had seen something very troubling three days ago when her mistress had been leaning over at her desk, writing that telegram to Master Jack. The object had caught the light, and Rose's suspicious mind. She'd seen it in the French girl's hand many a time ... *But why should Violet have a fragment of it?*

This morning, while Violet had rested in the library, Rose secretly hunted through all her clothes and shoes twice, turning everything over. *The thing must be hidden in plain view,* she thought descending the back stairs, frustrated. She pushed open the kitchen door, hearing laughter within. Hot in pursuit of a terrified chicken, "makee learn boy," the cook's apprentice, raced past Rose with a raised chopper. The staff was all in an uproar hopping out of his way, but merriment ceased the moment Violet herself appeared behind a cloud of billowing wok steam.

Old Wang, the chef's aged father, wiped the grin off his face and shuffled forth, head down, proffering the menu and stepping over the loose hen. Young Wang, his son, stood by blinking nervously while Violet studied the suggestions. It was an honor to be chef at Peak House, but it couldn't have been easy. Violet, an exacting employer, viewed her parties as a direct route to social eminence, and now she began arguing over the choice of sauces. Observing all the fuss, Rose had often wondered why the effort—*they were at the top already!* But a high-ranking Chinese in exile from Peking straightened out Rose's misconceptions. He had worked in the Forbidden City for the last Empress and had it on authority that the British in the Far East were bounders, middle class, and not what they made themselves out to be. This bit of information surprised Rose, but, being Chinese, she wasn't one to fault people for trying to rise above their station. *Yet how Violet tried*, she mused. *It was the source of all her troubles.*

If only Violet had settled for that rich boy, Peebles, who adored her. Life would have been easier for everyone. But several years ago Violet had decided to go for money as well as rank and had unwittingly begun a dangerous game in attempting to snatch Jack Morgan from the jaws of the competition. Her latest ploy, that telegram, had finally succeeded. *Pregnant!* Rose knew better, she did Violet's laundry. Rose shook her head in dismay. Violet's skill at manipulation, game-playing at its finest, had been perfected in her youth on her elderly widowed father. *Poor man.* Despite his attempts, Old Master had never remarried—proving the point; his daughter was well versed in the school of drama and dirty tricks.

Dirty tricks indeed. Rose felt her heart turn cold at the thought. Her mind flew back to that day one year ago when she'd discovered that the French girl, whom Violet suspected of sleeping with Jack, had died. It had been in all the Chinese papers, how she had fallen to her death under mysterious circumstances; her glass walking stick, always at her side, mysteriously absent at the scene of her death. Lacking suspects and evidence, the case was ruled a suicide, and closed.

Stink air, fill sky, she muttered under her breath. She glared at Violet across the kitchen thinking she deserved a good thrashing, but even that was too late and she wondered what would happen if anyone found out. But first she had to be sure. Yesterday she'd tried to empty all of Violet's handbags out but had again found nothing. The night before she'd gone systematically through all the desk drawers and bookshelves—*nothing*. Rose waited as Violet crossed out a vegetable dish on the menu, and as she leaned over, noticed how one kimono sleeve swung heavily across the table while the other fluttered lightly. Rose felt a tick of excitement in her heart. *She would check it later when Violet changed for dinner.*

"This b'long plopper," Violet announced in pidgin, looking at Young Wang. She tapped the menu. "My wanchee walkee-walkee fish, savvy?"

Tonight, like most nights, Percy was entertaining at Peak House, and there were always at least seven courses, starting with appetizers, moving on through the requisite soup, fish, and meat, finishing with sweet and savory items that went well with port. Rose always listened very carefully to the menu plans, for if there was any oversight she wanted cover for Old Wang, whom she secretly admired.

After further discussion, Violet handed back the menu and left the kitchen. That was when Rose stepped forward. "You makee squid!" she said. Old Wang argued back in Chinese that squid was not fish but Rose condescended to let him know it was favored by the honored guest that evening, a Frenchman, and departed, nose in the air.

Even though she had not been with the family the longest—Old Wang had been there even before the big plague of 1886 when Old Madam, Percival's mother, had died—Rose still held a special place at Peak House and the staff all deferred to her. She'd been purchased as a young mui-tsai, and had even been named after Percy's grandmother, Rose. She was proud of that, and thus kept her distance from the other staff, knowing her position was separate, higher.

Passing under the tiger head in the hall she scolded it as usual, *Bad joss!* To Chinese a white tiger boded ill, symbolizing war. *At least it explained all the arguments in Peak House.* Heading upstairs to help her mistress dress for the evening, Rose passed the hall mirror and paused to study her reflection. She had a high noble forehead, dainty butterfly lips, but still, she remembered how long ago the mui-tsai dealer in the busy Swatow market had hissed over her angled, knife-slit eyes. "Hard to sell! No good!" he'd said, pointing as she wailed. Number One wife had bargained hard right back, "Knife slit eyes, but tears still round!" She wanted a jade bracelet for the money she'd get by selling Rose and sold her the very same day Rose's mother, a low-ranking concubine, had died of fever. Hers was not an original story, nor special, but painfully, it was hers.

She leaned over the bouquet of tuberoses on the table, the thick perfume bringing back the past vividly, Young Madam's confinement, Violet's subsequent birth, and later Madam's death. Outside of the family, Rose had no life of her own. She'd raised Violet, taught her to speak Cantonese, was there for her first steps, attended her in all her needs, and prepared her for adulthood. Violet had recently entered society and Rose's job was nearly done, but she often longed for the early days when Violet had referred to her affectionately as Elder Sister, longing for closeness.

"Rose," she heard Violet calling from upstairs.

Rose smoothed her glossy black hair, adjusted her bun, then hurried up the servants' stairway. She looked forward to evenings after parties when Violet would sit before her dressing-room mirror. She would brush Violet's hair until it gleamed like polished rosewood and would murmur advice in Cantonese to her charge, and Violet would submit to this in a filial manner, half listening but answering in English and informing Rose of the latest club gossip. This was the only time Violet acknowledged that she knew the language, for she never let on in public when she abused the coolies and the staff in pidgin. *Rose forgave her.* In her heart she knew Cantonese was truly Violet's mother tongue, an intimate bond between them that Violet had learned not by rote, but with love's inflections in childhood. For Rose, Chinese and English were inside-outside languages, like slippers and shoes: slippers or Chinese for inside deeper feelings; shoes or English for outside, pukkah decorum. Hurrying down the hall to her mistress's bedroom, Rose picked up a hairpin from the floor and announced in Cantonese, "Young Wang's dinner looks good tonight! Mr. Morgan likes Chinese food, you know?" Stepping into the room she switched to English, her heart happy for a moment. "Mass-itah Jack say Wang bery, bery good. Good sign, ah? You' man eat happy, den he sindown home."

"Trust me, Old Wang is not part of the equation regarding Mr. Morgan," Violet snapped sarcastically, removing the red kimono and throwing it onto the bed. *Rose's eyes followed it carefully.* "And I told you; don't ever speak Chinese in the public rooms. Now, what am I to wear this evening?" She stood up in her gleaming silk camisole.

Rose hurried to show her the three evening gowns she had spent hours pressing and wondered angrily if Old Master had observed the changes in his child, like a hairline crack showing up to mar a perfect green jade. How she longed to have a talk with him about his daughter—*but this was unthinkable.* She eyed the kimono hem on the bed. One sleeve had flopped over lightly, the other hung heavy over the edge of the bed. *She must wait till Violet turned her back.*

"I don't want the pink one or blue. Rose, fetch the white. You never let me wear white, and it's so becoming. Birdy and Tuppy Westwood always wear white, and look so good," she cried fanning herself, irritated.

"Hai-yah!" she exclaimed, losing patience, realizing Violet was serious, but brought the gown out anyway, shaking her head. White was deathly, morbid. "They gweilo girl," she said, in English. "No savvy, i'-no-streit. Olsem you. An' you sendim tel'gram—i'no-streit! Makum trubul!"

"I'll thank you not to mention that again!" Violet slammed down her fan. "I don't want *him* taking charge of Peak House, or of me!" She got up and held the white gown before the full-length mirror. "For all I know he's got some woman up in Shanghai!"

Rose tried to keep her lip buttoned tight, but she'd taken out Violet's laundry that morning. "Hai-yah! My lukim-see *UNDERPANT!!!!"* she exploded. "Hab *BLUT!* You no catchee baby! What you say, ah?"

Violet laughed, "Sooooo, is *that* what this is all about! I saw you looking crossly at me in the kitchen."

"You makim lie! Bik ploblem. Olo Mass-itah soooo happy. Him tinkum you catchee baby. Mass-itah Jack—maybe he savvy you tellim lie!"

Violet sniffed, "You have no idea how to catch a man."

"I savvy," Rose muttered, switching to a Chinese proverb, "To cow play violin!"

Violet ignored the jibe and smoothed wrinkles in the fabric. "I'll wear the *blue* dress, but only because the white one would need an hour's pressing to be ready."

"One hour?" she cried. "All *day!*" She put the gowns away in the closet.

"You're lucky I don't fire you, the way you speak to me."

"Yeh, boss lady," she came out to glare at Violet. "Mass-itah Jack tinkum *him* boss, that *best* way!" She eyed Violet carefully, wondering what was going to happen to her if he found out. Her gaze moved to the dangling kimono sleeve.

Violet ripped out her hair ornament and tossed it onto the vanity. "For goodness sake, Rose, I'm Percival Summerhays's daughter! That company should be *mine*."

"Company? B'long father!" Rose said, carefully moving across the room and smoothing the bedspread by the kimono. She fluffed the pillows, then her hand moved down the bed, and over the red silk, folding it over casually. It was dense at the bottom. Her fingers slid across the silk, and slipped inside. Rose felt her heart stop and looked up at her charge in shock. Touching the smooth cold glass she wondered, *Could it be murder?* "You woman, tasol!" she said pointing at Violet with her free hand, while sliding the long segment behind her, keeping an eye on Violet, who was putting on makeup. *She would destroy this as soon as she got out of the room. "TRIPLE*

GODDESS, all you get!" Rose muttered, feigning anger, though her palms were damp with fear as she made her way toward the door.

"Triple goddess?" Violet looked up suddenly from her mirror. "A maiden, a mother, then, a hag? Is that *ALL* I can be? I'll *NOT* have it! That's your *Chinese* way, not mine!" She quickly jerked her head toward the kimono on the bed, then looked at Rose. "What's that hidden behind your back?" She leaped across the space in a flash and grabbed Rose by the arm, pulling it out of her fingers. "*This! This is mine!*" Violet snatched it away, the dizzyingly beautiful cane segment glittering in her long fingers, cherry red with a spiral of tiny silver rabbits.

"Bery bad joss," Rose whispered in awe.

"Don't be ridiculous," Violet said, setting it by her on the vanity. "He'll marry me yet. You'll see."

"See? See what!" Rose suddenly burst out in Chinese, "If Master Jack sees it he'll never marry you and you'll be a crone like me all your life!" She reached for the segment but Violet was quicker, and with a peal of laughter pulled it away, but as she did, it slipped and landed hard on the edge of the carpet, snapping in two. Violet gasped. Half lay intact, the rest was shattered on the marble floor.

Rose nodded, looking down. "You lucky. Only small hap left."

"You fool! This was evidence against him," she said taking up the remaining piece. "He must have had that *invalid* as a *lover!* Why else lavish this *gift*?"

"Gif'? He not marit den."

"He was courting *ME* at the time."

"Man catchee plenty woman. No can stop. But girl she die. Maybe you catchee rong, ah? Go prison?"

"Oh, really! For a lowly hat shop girl?" Violet switched to Cantonese, and spoke rapidly in a low rasping voice, while Rose crouched down, sweeping glass splinters into a heap and tuning her Mistress out. She finally stood up as Violet finished, saying, "Rose, it was *dark* at Barker Road. No one saw. So it's my prize, you see? He thinks *he* had his secret from me, but all this time *I have the very thing* he gave to her!" Rose stood quietly watching her as Violet turned it over in the lamp light.

Rose sighed. "I cookim joss stick, pray you no trabul."

"*What* did you say?" Violet's voice was teetering on outrage.

"I cookim joss for you. I wan-chyu hab happy, no sha chr, poison arrow from dewil-bilong-man-ee die."

"Poison arrows from ghosts? Rose, enough!" Violet said, dismissing her.

Rose pointed to the closet. "What for you keepum dead girl hats? Nogut!"

"Never mind, it's *my* collection."

Rose shuffled out of the room muttering angrily in Chinese, "Each situation, *more down!*" She heard a few dull thuds behind her and turned to see a perfume bottle bounce on the thick oriental carpet. Rose stooped to retrieve it. "Smellum water spensive!" she scolded. "Here, kostu maski forget," she said, removing a calling card from her pocket.

Violet scanned it. "Peebles? When did *he* stop by?"

"Morning. My talkee him, 'go way' like *Missie* say."

"Good!"

Rose sniffed the perfume bottle then placed it on the table. "Master Peebles got plenty something!"

"What about Jack?"

"Missie hab cold heart."

"You're as cold hearted as the next person."

"My—cold heart? Hah! Heart like tea pot, you pilim, cookim hand. Bery pain!"

"Look, Rose," Violet said putting up her hair, trying different decorative pins. "If I don't marry Jack, he'll run father's firm and marry some other club tart! Or go back to that bitch, Connie. And then I'd have to be congenial to her at evening parties, while she runs me and Peak House! Don't you see?" She pinned a long tortoise comb into her hair. "You don't have a head for business, you and your joss sticks and hokey temples! Peebles is my plaything, that's all."

"Peebles hab bik mansion Kowloon side," she said leaving the room. "*Bik muni, silly goose!* See? I *right.*" Nothing was thrown this time and Rose hurried down the back stairs to inspect the cook's labor before Violet had a chance to find fault, and pushed in the door to the kitchen.

"What this?" she asked in pidgin, playing the role of Madame, lifting the lids off steaming-pots and platters one by one. "*Hmmh!*" she said loudly over each one—shrimp spread appetizer, beef medallions, mutton curry, and then goose, "This one not 'nuf," she added disapprovingly. "Fat-kwai eatum plenty."

Old Wang replied in Chinese, "How gracious Heaven is to provide such a feast for man!"

Rose ignored him, feigning annoyance. Old Wang always pretended he was sophisticated because he came from Peking. *That was the northern Chinese for you.* But really, she was pleased, for she enjoyed his attentions and often spied on him when he quoted poetry to the caged birds on the terrace. Coming to the last platter Rose was taken aback. "Hai-yahhhh! What this?"

"This braise-fry walkee-walkee pish," Young Wang said sheepishly, reminding her it was the freshest fish at the market, just like Miss had asked, and he then added there had been no squid to be found.

Standing between the two cooks, Rose looked down closely at the dark jumble of little bodies. "This no pish!" she cried. They had deep fried a platter of scorpions.

"Blong pish!" Old Wang had the audacity to shout back vociferously, "Baby style lobstah! I makee bery good!!"

"Ah?" Intrigued she picked one up and bit it in two, chewing thoughtfully. Then looking at Old Wang she asked in Chinese, "So heaven make man for scorpion bite?"

The old man was flustered but his son was quick to answer her, mixing both languages. "Scorpion bite *man*—he die, but *woman* eat scorpion—*BERY GOOD*!"

The kitchen staff howled with laughter, but as Rose left the kitchen quietly she said, "You keep lik-lik lobstah, fat-kwai no savvy." As she shut the kitchen door behind her she shook her head, and wondered if Mr. Morgan understood just how fine a net *he'd* gotten himself into.

Macao *15 August 1937*

SHE'D BEEN A FOOL to think she'd end up with Jack. Ana pulled herself to the edge of the bed between the wall and the mattress, and lay there all night, stiff with revulsion. *This was what it was to lose everything.* She'd tried in vain to slip off of the bed, but the first jounce had caused Fausto's pig eyes to pop open. Nothing in them, but brutal rage and vulgar appetite. Waking him only brought repeated assault, and after he struck her with the back of his hand, heavy as a brick. Finished, he slept, trouble free.

Ana grew cold watching him, while inside rage and strength coiled tighter and tighter. She raised her cold hands to her eyes, cooling the hot bruise there. An image was coming to her, an image not of Fausto sleeping, but Fausto lying dead. Through her fingers, she could see the fat creases on his thick neck, glistening as he snored. Eyes wide, she began to move her hands in tandem like a somnambulist toward him and then suddenly she struck, and held with vivid force, digging with her fingers into that gasping, heaving neck, feeling tendons, feeling esophagus, feeling it swallow, gasp for air—*it was alive and she wanted it dead.* The body beneath her was struggling and suddenly, with a wild wrench, Ana was thrown clear, and her body hit something hard.

It could have been hours, or days, later. She didn't know. A tiny woman quick as a finch was seeing to the cut on her head. She seemed frightened too, for she didn't rest anywhere long. A few times Ana saw the door open and the wide shadow fell inward, but mostly the woman came with water, a bowl of rice with a small piece of fish. Ana tried to encourage her to say something, but she kept her gaze downward. One day Ana grabbed her arm as she was about to leave, begging in tearful Chinese where her clothes were. The woman had bound feet and easily lost balance and the rice bowl fell, shattering.

He must have been listening because instantly he burst in, knocking the woman aside and pushing Ana down by the throat.

"You're well enough to cause trouble," he leered over her. "Do it again, and you'll not wake in this world."

There were no clothes in the room, so she sat in the blanket and cried a little, but no tears came and she became silent. Time and the outside world were losing meaning. What she had, however, was the *hate*, and it coiled into something solid, undulating and alive, looking to strike.

Sometime later, the door rattled and he came in and threw down a dress. "Get up."

Ana felt tears of relief flooding her eyes. "Am I to leave?"

"Put it on." It was pretty mauve silk patterned with flying gold cranes. "You'll have a client this evening. I expect you to smile, and look as if you are enjoying it. If you disappoint me in any way, you will live a long crippled life."

The man was white, well-dressed, and smelled clean and fresh from the outside world. Her smile, as she stood awaiting his caress, must have quavered, but there was only candlelight, and he wasn't there to read faces or bruises. He did his thing, clung to her in his nakedness, grunting and crying out, then smiled guiltily, not showing his eyes, and left never thinking she was a slave.

As it had been at Chan's, her every move was monitored—so she decided to communicate with her body, to show she was a prisoner by giving love, and pleasure, selling her heart in the vain hope that they would awaken from the delight, and realize that this was another human before them. *But they didn't.* Instead, they enjoyed themselves, and as she performed exceedingly well, they passed the information on to Fausto. To her dismay, no one ever asked why she was there. Perhaps they assumed she was like a clerk at a bank, or a waitress at a bar—*as if it was where she belonged.* She thought about this long and hard and concluded that what spoils man most is having to comprehend his pleasure, rather than just pay for it. These men were here to buy oblivion, to clear their minds. As simple as that, and so different from what her expectation of sex had been. Two bodies struggling on a mattress together; *communion versus solitary oblivion.* The startling and tragic pairing of these wildly different aims in a single act opened her eyes. *And yet this was the foundation of life?*

Regardless of her disappointment, after some time her good performance granted her a little freedom. She knew from Shanghai that European women with voluptuous figures had an intrinsic value for European male customers who didn't share the Chinese taste for small breasts and boyish figures. Either way, soon she was bringing in repeat customers and bigger money for Fausto. After only a few days he moved her to an upstairs room in another building above his bar, where she could hear music through the floorboards, smell the acrid stench of opium, hear the sound of gaming, laughter, and voices of other women like her. It was Chan's all over again, but she was now one floor lower; *prostitute.*

Fausto began taking pains to dress her well. A wardrobe arrived, and she was moved into a room with a fresh coat of paint on the walls. Ana made a point of flirting with him, hiding her hate. One day two weeks after her debut she quietly suggested she could make far more money for him if he let her entertain the clients in the bar, or perhaps go to dinner. She said she could bring in an entirely different business, legitimate and high class.

It made him laugh. "Settling into your new employment, are you? But you can't run away, you know. I'll find you no matter where you go, and I'll bring you back."

"I am not talking of leaving you. I enjoy this work and if you let me I can work wonders for your profits. There's a future in this business."

"I'll let you keep your tips if you show me how I can charge more."

"I can do far better than that, Fausto. I can help you obtain European girls, and then your success here will be unlimited." He was astonished, and she left the conversation at that, allowing the idea to steep in him.

"European women," he said, enthralled.

Ana brushed his hair into place with a false tender smile and a cold sick heart. Desperate to escape, she imagined a long thread connecting her to Jack, wherever he was on the outside. She lived on the thin hope that if she just pulled on it in her mind, and if it didn't snap, she would be out of Macao and standing next to the man she loved.

White Wedding

10

China Coast Navigation & Co. *1 November 1937*

"THE RUBBER DEAL, A hoax?" Albert Chiswick trembled as he put down the telephone receiver. Beads of sweat broke out on his upper lip and forehead, and he sank down into his chair, forgetting to turn on the begrimed fan on his desk. This news was madness, but his friend in Java swore it was true. *Hadn't he seen Jack and Algernon board the ship to Java in September with his own eyes? He'd seen all the paperwork, the coolies, the rubber output. All those files! And today of all days the blackguard was to marry Percival's daughter.* Albert groaned. He'd been making inroads, gaining Percy's trust over the years in small increments, but in one fell swoop his life's work had been dashed.

He reached for the bottle of Martel's he kept in a locked drawer. This callow American had beaten him to the quick. *The girl, the house, the big promotion—GONE!* He got out a glass and filled it. *Yet could Morgan really be falsifying so many ledgers? Embezzling all that money with old Summerhays completely in the dark? There had to be records. He needed facts—facts.* From the outer office Albert could hear the excited laughter of employees leaving for the wedding at St. John's. *Why couldn't I have gotten this call a month ago? I could have DONE something about it—dug up evidence! Stopped the wedding!* The lift door rang, the Chinese operator called for remaining employees, someone shut the lights, then the metal gate slid shut and the heavy doors closed. *Everyone had gone to board the steamer to Macao.* He filled another shot, feeling sorry for himself. *I could've married her!* Tipping it back, he suddenly paused mid-gulp. *The executive file room—was it unguarded!?* He got up and peered down the hall.

Peak House *1 November 1937*

ON THE MORNING OF the wedding, things had started off badly. Ling Ling, Old Wang's terrier, had been found dead at dawn lying on the kitchen stoop, poisoned. Jack had sat with Old Wang for an hour, but the cook was inconsolable and cried like a baby. As preparations heated up and pandemonium ensued at Peak House, he grabbed his tuxedo and tennis racquet and headed into town. At last, in the silence of his office, he was able to take a deep breath and stood looking out his window. He had to grant it to her; Violet had contrived their marriage with the alacrity of a seasoned deal maker. He half swung his tennis racquet, then sighed. All of Kowloon stretched before him; sky, mountains, and harbor. Hundreds of junks, sampans, and ships nosed past one another on the strait. The sight had always excited him, but now it didn't seem to matter. At least he'd done one good deed—guaranteeing a loan for the rubber planter so he'd keep his land. Everything else in his life stretched out into a meaningless void. He couldn't forget Ana.

Jack put the racquet down and placed his hands on his desk, suddenly tired. He'd been unable to find her all these months. He'd even hired a detective who'd tracked Sam down in Hankow. Sam told him he'd left her at the clock tower in Kowloon that day, but there were no other leads; she'd simply vanished. The detective had concluded she had someone helping her, a lover perhaps, for a white woman couldn't disappear in Hong Kong. Jack sat down in his swivel chair and stared out across the water at the clock tower, dismayed. Now the theory seemed reasonable, but Ana had changed everything. Before, he hadn't been bothered by Violet, hadn't heard her endless conversations on the faults of friends, her criticisms of enviable successes, and her pleasures in their failures; somehow the veil had been pierced, and nothing seemed the same. The marriage, the job, even the view—Jack stood up and looked down five stories to the intersection of Pedder Street and Connaught Road where he'd stood penniless and broken ten years ago. It was a long drop. A sudden tapping at the door startled him and Jack turned around.

He was surprised to discover Violet's old beau confronting him with lackluster eyes. Hancock Peebles III was dressed for attendance at the wedding, but the details were wrong. "Peebles, you old dog. You look like you were dragged through a hedge!"

"Laugh if you want," Peebles whined, hair mussed, bow tie askew. "But I–I came here t–to tell you."

"What?" Jack said over his shoulder practicing a backhand stroke.

"Y–you can't marry her," Peebles gasped. "Th–there I s–said it."

Jack stared, feeling his eyes narrowing. *Sooooo—this* lout was the *father.* Jack poured him a drink. "Have a seat."

"No–no. I don't want anything. M–maybe a cigarette."

"Help yourself. You're looking pretty rummy."

"You're not surprised I'm here?" he said, taking one from the case.

"Nothing surprises me these days."

"Well. I–I just want you to know you can't marry her. I love her. She and I have been—"

"Been *what*?"

"N–no! It's not what you think," he said, wide-eyed. "Friends—*friends* for so long. Since we were that high," he said putting out a shaking palm. "Oh—it tries one's soul."

"What's this about?"

"Sh–she won't have me."

Jack sat down at his desk and sighed thickly. "You want my advice? Lay off the booze and find someone who respects you, loves you—then marry *her*."

"I'm done for," Peebles said.

"Someone else will turn up. Someone better."

"I spoke to Percy and he said it was up to Violet."

"He did, did he?" Jack laughed. "Well, take her, you can have her."

Peebles stood up, outraged, "H–how can you say that? V–violet is a w–wonderful woman, so lovely! Clever! She always tells me what to do. You d–don't appreciate her, you c–cad!"

"Listen, do you think Violet is looking *heavier* at all?"

"What?!"

"You didn't pay her an illicit visit, did you?"

Peebles gripped the desk with indignation, spluttering. "You d–don't deserve her!"

Jack pointed with the racquet, "The door's that-a-way. Don't mind if I don't show you out—and, if you change your mind, I have the ring." He turned his back to the drunk, but cringed when his office door slammed so hard his windows shook.

A minute later he heard it open, and he turned, half expecting Peebles.

"What the devil got into him?" Algy asked, kitted out in a tux with a carnation. "Jack, you're not drunk, are you?"

"Tolerably. Just don't slam any doors."

"Violet is arranging for the entire staff to attend the send-off on the praya. Everyone's talking about it." He pushed some papers across the desk.

Jack cut a tennis serve short. "What are they really saying? That I got this post by black favor?"

"What do you care? Here are the latest rubber files," he said.

Jack lit a cigar and took the papers Algy had deposited on his desk. "Ah. The coolie figures."

There was another knock and Albert Chiswick put his head in, wincing as he took in the executive view and the sumptuousness of the office. "Working to the last, are you? Thought you'd left, by now. Well, we're all rooting for you, old man!" he said waving his invitation. "I'll be missing the ceremony, alas—but I'll catch you at the party in Macao, taking a launch over this afternoon." Albert's beady eyes darted to the papers as Algy tucked them under the blotter.

"Sure, sure." Jack waved him out of the office, then when the door shut, quietly remarked, "Has he got his knickers in a twist! You see that look on his face? He actually thinks *he* could run the place!"

Algy looked at his watch. "Right-ho. We leaving yet? Because you're not even dressed."

"Know what I think?" Jack said, holding up a glass, eyeing the remains of his drink. "The world's full of lazy detractors who envy those who work hard for their rewards." He poured the last bit down his throat.

"Ah well, mediocrity *has* its perks. You should try it sometime."

"Well, it's got company, for certain. But, why the hell is Albert in today? Percy gave everyone the day off."

Algy sniffed, smoothing his eyebrow. "Albert has this job and his bottle—and if you persist, that's all you'll have too. Now Jack, you really need to get dressed," Algy said gesturing at the tuxedo hanging on the door. "You're to be married in exactly two hours."

It was a good hour later they tottered out, but at Jack's insistence they stopped at Gripps for a drink, and then at Café Wiseman's for another, until finally they were running up Ice House Street, twenty minutes late. "You're thoroughly drunk. Do you realize that? Any more and you'll be a complete disgrace."

"Just catching up with Peebles."

"Lovely. Now hurry."

Jack felt the ground sway. "I'm in no hurry," he snarled. "Violet's expecting."

"Yes, the whole congregation's expecting you."

"No. *A child*."

Algy grimaced. "Then you *must* go through with it."

Jack glared, "Damn her! It's not mine!"

Algy raised his brows. "Well, that puts the butter on the spinach." He pushed Jack along. "You drunken ass," he said under his breath. "You deserve one another."

Jack heard, only couldn't reply. He could scarcely breathe. The liquor had finally hit him and it was like a dream where he woke and couldn't scream and the pews opened up like a sea before him and all the heads turned his way. He thought he would vomit.

St. John's Cathedral *1 November 1937*

THE CHURCH INTERIOR WAS stifling and steamy, heavy with the cloying scent of gardenias, and the wall fans did little more than move the heat around. Algy looked about nervously. The pews were filled to capacity, had been for a while. Ladies wore hats, an aviary of pretty feathers; otherwise it could have been a funeral. The only thing on his mind was to rush through the ceremony before Jack fell over. He didn't give a hoot about matrimony himself, but for Jack to be literally standing on the threshold of married life and to suggest *that Violet was with child and that it wasn't his?*

He steeled himself, standing by Jack in the church, ready to catch him at any moment. Algy wanted to wash his hands of the whole affair and tell Jack to go boil his head. But as luck would have it, nothing untoward occurred. Rings were exchanged, there was a whirr of doves, a rain of rice, and Mr. and Mrs. Jack Morgan were finally married. *Thank you, dear Lord,* he said rolling his eyes skyward, disgusted.

The sun was hammering down on the festive party by the time the gaily decorated steamer pulled away from Hong Kong side. A Filipino orchestra was playing the old roast beef of England for the send-off and there was an opening dance, where Percy made a speech. Below deck Peebles spent the whole voyage vomiting in the men's room while Jack and Violet danced together topside, and it was lovely indeed to those who didn't know the details. Algy himself was thrilled when Macao came into view and was the first to disembark. Only later, up at the hotel, when he saw Jack over a tray of canapés he asked him, "You did put away the Java papers, didn't you? I left them under the blotter."

Jack was shaking hands with well-wishers, "Enjoy the festivities, my man. I've everything under control."

That was gratitude! Algy scoffed and as soon as the feast was over made his escape. The doorman at the Bella Vista was helpful, pointing down the road with a wink. "Best women in Macao! And opium served on silver trays!" Intrigued, Algy strolled along past romantic Portuguese mansions, smelling perfumed mimosa that spilled wild profusions of mini yellow pom-poms over ironwork fences.

The Golden Hind's arched yellow exterior was draped in bougainvillea, had a split tile roof, and gave the impression of an old grand manor. Inside, a mass of Europeans and nationals from every port crowded tables in the smoke-filled rotunda, and high up in the center, where a grand chandelier must have once hung, a pulley system hoisted a basket supplying the gaming floor with approvals on the way down, and cash and jewelry on their way up. Algy loitered about the tables until he noticed some of the wedding party.

"Worthing!" The company solicitor spotted him, and made his way over. "Sorry to bring up business but I didn't want to disturb Morgan at dinner. You see, I got an odd request out of Java today. Did he approve a loan for a rubber plantation?"

"Eh? A *LOAN?* Now, what's the sense of that, Duffy! We *bought* the rubber estate. You've seen the paperwork. Nix it. It's a mistake. Do it straight away."

"No worries, my lad," the solicitor tapped him on the shoulder. "It's easily repaired."

Algy nodded, shuddering as he thought of the rubber fiasco, and made a beeline toward the back stairs. On the second floor, mahjong games were in progress; on the third, an attractive young Chinese man showed him in. Opium beds lined all the walls, curtained off by gauzy drapes and heavy smoke. "I want to be near the exit," he said, recalling Mother's warnings about crowded places.

The warren of rooms stank of opium, and were lit by dim hurricane lamps. Here and there, punctuating the heavy darkness, he heard sighs of contentment. Algy followed to the back of the building, passing by a large open window and a door marked "exit" in Chinese. "This will do," he said, and lay down on the rattan bed, resting the back of his neck against a cooling porcelain pillow. He could hear the wind in the mimosa outside and the distant clatter from the tables below. In the dim light the man crouched beside him, working a black wad of opium with a utensil into a smooth ball. Algy found himself transfixed by the deft work of the man's hands and the deep yellow of the flame that softened the tarry opium. At last the pipe was handed to him, but not on a silver tray, he noted.

Algy settled into a comfortable position and just as he inhaled the first breath of the poison poppy, he was jolted upright by the powerful slam of a door. The shock to his nerves was enough that he dropped the pipe—which fell to the floor and snapped in two. *Bollocks.* He got up to summon the boy, but when he passed the window he heard two individuals in argument.

It was too discreet to have been a Chinese altercation, and this fine point interested him. He turned his head toward the patio below, hearing a gruff snarl. A woman's voice, barely audible said, "I don't think any harm would—" The sound cut off suddenly, and Algy leaned closer. There was a long pause and he heard the lap of the waves, the trees rustling, and night birds calling. Just as he turned to search for the boy there was a scuffle and a man's tight, angry voice rose in protestation, "Oh no, you don't!" Algy peered out into the darkness.

Directly below, between a rancid heap of refuse and a cobbled road, a lady in an evening gown and tall heels was attempting to pull away from a portly man, or perhaps lead him onto the street away from the club's rear entrance. Algy couldn't see much of the man as he was directly below, but he saw him jerk the woman toward him. "Where d'ya think you're going?"

They struggled off the stoop and onto the cobbles where the woman began to laugh—with a hysterical edge to it. "You're so strong. Do let go of my arm!" She whispered something, a flirtation, coercion perhaps, but there was a sudden wince of pain and she whispered, "Please, let's just take a little walk."

"I didn't pay for a walk!" he said pulling her by the hand, then by the waist, attempting to wrench her back into the door below. Seeing where this was leading the woman began struggling wildly, but he caught her dress and struck her hard.

"You there!" Algy leaned out all the way, "Stop that!"

The man looked up, and the woman broke his hold. Tottering backward, she fell onto the cobbles. The man cursed, and in a flash had her wrist in his grasp and was already half pulling, half dragging her back across the cobbles and up the steps. The strange thing was, she never screamed, but resisted with a passion that was startling. The man struck her face again. Alarmed, Algy stumbled about in the dark, feeling about for something to throw.

He found a heavy pail, and it wasn't until he'd hoisted it with great force that he realized it had a lid and that it was night soil, but too late—the whole ugly mass was already in motion when he called down, "You, Sir!" The man looked up—and the woman broke free again. The bucket, following the thick stream of excrement straight down, hit the man full in the face knocking him to the cobbles in a clatter. Algy gulped back a scream of hysterical laughter, then flew down the narrow back stairs. Throwing the door open he saw the man flailing about on slick cobbles like a shit-covered catfish, spluttering horrible oaths. It was worse when Algy pulled off the bucket and looked down at him. *GOOD GOD! It was Chiswick!*

Albert spit several times, then trying to stand, slipped again in the muck.

The woman standing in the shadows suddenly spoke. "Algy, but can that be you?"

"Ana?" Algy gasped. "My dear! We've been looking all over for you!"

Albert suddenly found his voice, *"FAUSTO! FAUSTO!!!"* The sound was more like a wretch with dry heaves. "Fausto, *HEEEELLLP!!!!"* This last cry he made ended in a squawk that seemed to open up his gullet—for he began vomiting prodigiously. Who could blame him, Algy grimaced, stepping away. The smell was awful, indeed—even from a distance, and surely he must have swallowed some.

Mortified, Algy grabbed Ana's arm, "Hurry!" They turned and headed down the hill and didn't stop running until they'd reached the end of the dock and were facing a full moon and the wide open South China Sea.

JARDINE

Hong Kong *1997*

It was Ching Ming today and first thing I headed for St. Michael's Cemetery to sweep mother's gravestone clean of leaves like a good Chinese daughter should. Listening to the sound of my broom rasping on stone, I could almost hear her whispering to me. She was probably angry I wasn't married by now or didn't have a professional situation like executive secretary, rubbing shoulders with bankers and barristers. *Luck begets luck*; I could imagine her scolding and looking me over disapprovingly. I was awfully slim, like a stick of gum people said. At least my hair was long and pretty. Still, I knew Mum wouldn't like how I dressed, pairing tartan mini-skirts *a la* Catholic schoolgirl with punk boots, but men liked it. Butchers and noodle makers would look up through their steamy shop windows at me and my long legs and I'd pretend not to notice. My friends were all girls from the orphanage. We had grown up together, each of us hoping one day someone would rescue us from the outside, but it never happened. We became young ladies and were released into the world, un-rescued. But all my life I kept the space in my heart open, watching from my table-for-one the noisy families at breakfast at big round tables, babies, aunties and grandparents passing dim sum around, laughing and arguing. Dim Sum meant touch of heart but nothing had touched mine.

I reached over and placed my offering for Mum by the stone urn, a perfect tangerine with a leaf still attached. Then I sat down to eat a lotus seed bun. I didn't want to tell her I had a gig tomorrow at a nightclub in Lan Kwai Fong, jumping out of a cake dressed as a cherub with wings and a lace corset. Instead, I tried to think back to the crash when she'd died—trying to inch my mind back as if it were a video, and I could rewind to a frame where I would suddenly discover her face. I couldn't. I had no memory of her, or her voice. Not knowing my lineage, not knowing if ancestral graves were well placed or tended, meant I couldn't appease their spirits with gifts each year. Because of this, I was told, no Chinese guy from a good family would ever marry *me*, a curse in this world and the next. Maybe it was true. How could I know?

Afterward, I headed over to Mr. Worthing's place, taking a double-decker bus through Central, full of hope that this old gweilo would at least point me to a line of graves and say, "Voilà! All these dead people, they're yours." I leaned against the window as we passed city hall. Chinese barristers happened to be posing for a group photograph on the steps. I craned my neck to look—they were all wearing powdered curly English wigs and pilgrim shoes. I guess I wasn't the only one with an identity problem. I shrugged and looked ahead for my stop. Mr. Worthing and I had arranged that I would come every afternoon when I wasn't baking a cake or sleeping late for a gig. Auntie Tam would serve tea and cakes and he would tell me things as we sat at his round rosewood and marble table, stories of his so-called glory days colonial life, rickshaws, servants and opium. I would frown or roll my eyes as I listened but—*but I kept coming back,* surprising myself; a friendship was developing.

Mr. Worthing lived with his housekeeper, Auntie Tam, the two of them knocking about in this dark flat with high ceilings above the racket on Hollywood Road, all the curtains shut. Every day I visited, he made me sit in a Ming chair with my back to a pair of double doors. Tall and matched like shut coffin lids, they gave me nightmares, and even now as I entered they distracted me and I looked toward them.

"How was the cemetery?" Mr. Worthing interrupted, and I turned around. Incense drifted lazily from a burner tickling my nose. The old man sat down across from me, toying with an origami crane, the air-conditioning unit humming on high.

"Hot," I said, sniffing and taking my usual chair.

He balanced the crane on his palm as if it were about to take off. Being so ancient, he seemed to me to be nearly on the *OTHER SIDE* and I wondered if he could see spirits yet. Like now. He was looking right *through* me—*past me. Was he looking at the doors?* "You know," I warned, "where you place these doors can't be random. Doorways are talismanic, a link between two worlds. Feng Shui?" This must have gone over his head. I looked at the incense. "You like sandalwood?"

He tilted his head slightly with a hint of a smile like I was daft. "It's Tam's."

"Oh." I sat there, uncomfortable. "Did you make that?" I asked politely.

His eyes slid over from me, to the crane. "A Japanese made it, 1941. Stanley Prison."

"Oh."

"You know, if I were younger, I'd have gone with you," he said.

"Where, the cemetery? Ching Ming Festival is not for … *foreigners*." I almost said gweilos. "Besides, you don't have family here."

He looked away, puffing on the cigar, a man of mystery.

Last night I dreamed of his doors again. In my dream they crept open slowly so I could see the bottom of a Chinese embroidered robe. My gaze moved across the silk to a pair of clasped hands—elegant hands, with long nails and jade rings. The hands moved, and I followed them higher, up across the yellow silk, and kingfisher blue flowers and vines, over the chest, high collar, but then, instead of a face, the fingers touched an empty oval space. I awoke, my pillow damp with tears. *I would never know my Mum.*

"You know, not everything is neatly buried, Jardine—labeled and tucked under stone. There's blood all over Hong Kong, and it's not all Chinese." He dropped the paper crane down in front of a framed picture; two men in white suits by a plane. One handsome, the other skinny. I looked at the two men, then at him. You can't smell a doubt or a lie, but something was between us—a question unfolding like the doors onto something dark. There was a reason he didn't just tell me who I was, what I wanted to know. It was all folded up tight, like that crane, like murder, death, or regret.

"Blood?" I asked warily, scared a horrid confession might be coming.

He pushed the picture away. "When we flew out of Shanghai that night," he said, "we hadn't imagined the siege would last, no one did. But Shanghai fell three months later in October, and a quarter of a million Chinese soldiers died fighting the Imperial army."

"Why didn't anyone help?" I asked as his cigar smoke dispersed in a blue haze sucking down the hall toward the doors.

"Well, the League of Nations debated about it. Of course they *did* nothing. There's no logic in appeasement, just cowardice." He looked irritated. "We humans have a lot of savage walking around in us. I learned this firsthand in China. War is just nations feasting, like people, but on a grand scale. Bigger mouths."

"But, what about *here*? People must have known what was going on across the border."

"You need to remember the English lived separate from the Chinese, physically and mentally—it began with the original cantonments. And later, our cultures remained mostly segregated by choice on both sides—Chinese with Chinese, foreigners with foreigners—that is, until the invasion and the slaughter began."

That word made me uncomfortable. "I can't imagine the Japanese running Hong Kong, but I remember the pictures at the end of the war, people at Stanley Prison standing behind barbed wire and looking skeletal."

"Jardine, we *invited* them in."

"I don't think so."

"But we did—call it ignorance, or neutrality, but after the carnage in Shanghai, there was a mere hand slap in the international newspapers for Tokyo. That was the green light for their agenda: Asia for Asians. It was the beginning of the end of white rule."

Well, not a bad idea, I thought, but said, "It was the end of *occupied* countries."

He smiled. "So, what's Tibet? A rounding error? Listen," he said putting down his cigar. "You do realize that the 'Great Game' is still being played, don't you? It's never stopped. Russia, Pakistan, Afghanistan, India? The old silk road and the struggle for control of the narcotics industry and oil. Those are the same old disputed stomping grounds from Kipling's days. Nothing's changed, only the stakes are higher because we've got atomic weapons and there's been a power shift East." He called out to the kitchen. "Tam, we need the pot freshened up."

"But, that's what the UN's for. To stop that," I said, hearing the slam of the kettle on the burner.

"You think so? I remember in the early thirties some American chap from the State Department would go to Geneva every year and force them to write up effective controls on Opium Suppression, and he'd even get all the countries to agree. When he'd leave, however, the "cooking of the books" would begin. The League of Nations Secretariat would sabotage everything, editing and weaseling out, word by word, any gains made. Narcotics are still king, and after all our efforts, bribery still thrives at the highest levels. The League of Nations was rotten then, like the UN is now."

Amah, who'd been listening while arranging an armload of yellow roses, added, "Drug everyplace. Wan Chai! Lan Kwai Fong District! Aiyaaah! You gweilo peopou bring drug, foreign wo'kah!" She glared at him then plunked the vase down in front of him when the kettle began whistling from the kitchen.

"Ah. Apparently it's *my* fault," he said quietly. He blew out a long smoke cloud with a distant look on his face. "In the '30s we'd say tracking down dope rings was like 'trying to catch a million fleas with teaspoons.' The League of Nations had made a world map shading it in two colors. The Victim Bloc, and the Opium Bloc.

China was the only country that was in both camps, a victim of its own product. Pushers *and* takers."

"How's that?"

"Drugs were one way the Japanese drove in a wedge. I think the Green Gang triad in Shanghai had a secret treaty, subjugating their own people through addiction for profit, siding with the enemy, mind you. You know, the Japs admire China, they copied everything here, but when I was in Stanley Prison the Japanese guards boasted, 'The Chinese have no loyalty to their own. How else can our small island nation win all of great China?'"

"So, you're on their side?"

"Absolutely not. But you forget, we're all human. We have weaknesses, but these run culturally, and clever outsiders can exploit them."

"But England paid its debts to China with opium too!"

"Unfair, yes, but not the only cause of China's fall. Remember, they were funding endless military campaigns while the West was undergoing the industrial revolution. China got left behind."

"Now the US is behind *China*. Everyone sees the tiger waking up."

He stared, amused. "You envisioning American coolies coming to build your railroads?"

"And why not?" I snapped. "We can buy up choice real estate, minerals, oil."

"You're welcome to the world, Jardine. It's China's oyster, this time."

"Then why so gloomy? Because the West loses?"

"It's a cycle, don't you see? In the '30s enormous political changes were happening on both sides of the world. 'Civilian' armies, Hitler's Youth, and Mao's Red Guard were squashing freedom of speech and dissent among their own people, clearing the ground for dictators. You see, Hitler's progressive belief was for science to manufacture all solutions for an ignorant public—it's appealing, yes, but dangerous. People are willing to give up freedom for trinketry—handbags, dope, electronics. You're the child of this progressive world, so you can't see it. But these wars are your parents, electronics and drugs are your bionic ears and eyes, but you still have a heart, I hope." He said this as studied me, then pulled out a thick yellow rose from the vase. I could smell its heady perfume. "On both sides of the globe, people sold out their neighbors for these ideals—and felt justified sending them to slaughter. It even happened here in China, as you know. They began with class warfare, demonizing the rich, the doctors, then the small businessman, and then finally teachers. They killed them all or sent them to prison camps—*Their own people* … Democracy is a rare bird."

"Yes," I said, looking down, and picked up the yellowed origami crane. It had strange block lettering on it. I set it down. "Did you leave before the invasion?"

"Leave? Things changed too quickly in the end—like a tsunami up close, you can't run, and when it's too far off, it seems silly." He sat back, impatient. "In Shanghai the night life continued, but all the money was being siphoned off to feed the Japanese war machine, and one by one, they cut off each coastal supply route that fed into China. Godowns on Hong Kong started filling up with food that the Japanese turned back until crates were simply dumped onto wharves. It all rotted waiting for transport inland while Chinese people starved to death by the thousands. Your generation all around the world is asleep, just a step away from darkness but you're too comfortable to notice, but most of history has been ruled by the iron hand."

I'd had about all I could take of this and looked to the kitchen as a radio came on. Auntie was doing dishes, and over the splash came the atonal wail of Chinese opera. I got the feeling that I was probably the only visitor that ever came here.

"She's a romantic old bat, isn't she?" he said. "Buys roses every week in Mon Kok and there's no modern canto-pop for her. It's strictly this stuff." There was a sudden clash of cymbals, then a metallic whining as a gong hammered spastically faster. "Turn that rubbish off!" The response from the kitchen was an angry increase in volume. He gave a hapless smile, raising his palms.

"Is that you?" I asked over the radio, pointing to a picture.

He pushed his glasses up squinting, then turned it over face down. Maybe he didn't like being reminded of how he used to look. Auntie turned off the radio and came out from the kitchen lighting a cigarette. "He got bad taste," she announced, satisfied she'd made her point. She had on a drab shapeless dress with a Harrods's apron over it. On her feet she wore sexy pink feathered mules.

"You listen to classical music?" I asked him.

"Jazz. Ana used to sing the one that's on the turntable."

I got up and opened the old Victrola reading the record label aloud, "These Foolish Things?" He nodded, so I turned the crank, setting the needle onto the spinning record.

Auntie grinned with the cigarette in the corner of her mouth and gestured to me to come over. Before I knew what happened we were slow dancing, me in my black combat boots and tartan mini, she in her pink mules. The lights in the room were dim and cigar smoke filled the air like in a Shanghai bar a long time ago. I closed my eyes pretending war planes were flying overhead, and as we drifted over Persian rugs I saw Ana, crooning her love song. When the music faded out, all that remained was the scratch-scratch of a needle going round a 78 rpm disk. It seemed to me that when you got old, the past became a vampire, sucking out all your energy as you did everything just to keep it alive. *Keeping it alive, that was him …*

"Ana had a sweet voice like that …"

I imagined Rita Hayworth in *Gilda* biting his neck.

"I fell in love when I heard her sing," he said distantly. "A lot of men did. Put the other one on, 'And the Angels Sing.' It was Ana's favorite."

Auntie Tam went back to her kitchen work and I slid the record out of its torn sleeve. I cranked the Victrola, and a woman's honeyed voice from the past came to life.

"We were all dancing to this in Hong Kong, but north of here every village was in smoking ruins. It was Chiang's scorched earth policy so as to leave nothing to eat for the enemy—but the poor Chinese peasants starved too." Mr. Worthing got up and went to a cabinet; he took out a silver flask and tipped some into his tea, turning off the record. He saw my eyes go round. "No worries; my warden turns a blind eye. She's not a bad gal after all. You know, she had a big-shot Chinese military boyfriend who told me she had quite a set of gams in '52. Did the mambo and the rhumba, really let her hair down, but don't tell her I said so."

I laughed and he smiled into his doctored tea. Just then the "warden" shuffled back in and put a copy of the *South China Morning Post* on the table. Mr. Worthing saw my eyes go to her sexy "gams" and the frou-frou pink mules. We both burst into laughter. Auntie, a respectable senior, gave a harrowing glance at our grinning faces, which we tried to hide by sipping more tea. But just try and sip, when your mouth keeps cracking into a smile. She glared at me first, saw the tea drool down my chin, then turned to point accusingly at him in an attempt to save face, "You bettah read papah. Property go down, old fool, lose money!" She stormed out, huffing, muttering in Cantonese.

We had a good laugh and when he caught his breath he said, "Dear old gal! Concerned about the stock market! Well, that's Hong Kong. You don't belong here otherwise."

"Was it always investments? I thought that things were more romantic back then."

He was still smiling, suddenly young. "It was always money, the romance of cash. When the Japs blockaded us, we said it like gamblers, 'Wait a season, and we'll be making money again.' My banker said to me recently, 'Wait till next quarter! See what happens with US interest rates.' See? Nothing's changed. This whole Sino-Asian conflict was only a 'manifestation of natives.' We wanted the return of our sovereign right of '*free*' trade." He cleared his throat sarcastically, "that is, trade under *Western specifications*? Either way, whatever side you're on, the problem comes back to complacency—an ignorant, malleable public. Beware of government." He pointed his cigar at me. "And never trust the son of man!"

Whatever. I shrugged. He was so naive. And conceited too. What did he expect, that I picket LEGCO in Statue Square then get hosed by water cannon? I sighed. "You really think educating people on history can make a difference? They would have to act on what they know."

"It's enough they know. It's the first step. For instance, I bet you don't know the Japanese built our current Government House here, or what the cenotaph is, or where the war memorial arches are on Garden Road. You know, one day they won't even take down the flag at sunset. Small details, but part of the growing fog. All sorts of people died fighting for Hong Kong, for what you have today. It's an amazing, special place."

"Then why hand us back to China? We might lose everything."

"How long can the West hold on out here? You've a legacy of a transparent, fair government. If you hold on to that, maybe Hong Kong can change China, instead of the other way around. It takes personal responsibility and keeping the government in line."

What a gweilo! Nobody in Hong Kong thought this pimple on the ass of China could change the beast. But I didn't argue. He was ninety-something and I still respect my elders.

He excused himself, getting up. *Too old to be my father, or my grandfather.* His cigar had given me a headache and I leaned back, thinking of all the years I'd stood in front of the mirror at the orphanage wondering who gave me up, who hadn't loved me enough, or who I looked like. Now I wondered why this crafty gweilo was interested in me of all people. *Could it be that he was just lonely?*

Before he was even out of earshot, Auntie came in and quick as a hawk spied the silver flask tucked in the armchair cushion. She scowled, then announced loudly, "He got cansah." She tapped her chest and I guessed it must be his lungs. "He no live long. No way!" She picked up the ash tray from the table wrinkling up her nose, waving a hand in front of her. "Fyew—fyew! Smell like fart! This kill him, one by one piece. He sit, smoke all day. When you here, he talk-talk-talk, no time smoke. You good person." She didn't smile as she said this, just slammed the flask down as if she'd had it. "Ask me?" she queried as if I'd asked. "I don' care." She shrugged and walked off, but a minute later came to offer a bean cake and tell me it was *he* who liked the yellow roses. "It remind him of her," she said knowingly.

Mr. Worthing was returning slowly over the creaking floor. "If you could cut him open," he muttered, then stopped. She had been watching him and I saw the worry pass over her face.

"Cut who?" I asked, startled, and he looked at me. Was he losing his mind? Or was it the cancer? A stroke?

"Ah! Again! He forget what he talk!" she accused as if delighted, then tapping the side of her head added, "Chee-sing gweilo! You got brain diso'-dah!"

He began coughing, turning bluish. I pretended it was normal, but mentally dialed the emergency room, ready to stand up, feeling a knot in my stomach. "Are you o—?"

Catching his breath, he barked, "Of course I'm all right!"

I recoiled as if I'd been slapped—my eyes filling with tears.

He ignored me, sat down and smugly re-lit his cigar, now perfectly composed, his lips making a perfect "o" around the Cuban. Being on the other end of his cigar was oddly intimidating. His gold cuff links winked in the light; his fingers were as thick as the cigar. And in that moment of the first audible kiss-puff of smoke, his blue eyes were perfectly round and open and seemed to suck in something from me too. Suddenly, I became aware of his stature, who he'd been and what power he'd wielded. I squirmed as his eyes crinkled slightly at the edges and a trace of a smile flashed; yes, he sucked in what he wanted, then turned away and let out the smoke and I *knew* right then he'd seen *THROUGH* me, *ALL* my little girl secrets, sins and wishes—*PICTURES* in his mind! I shivered, completely in his power and he knew that too. An amused smile tugged in the corner of his mouth as he began to speak. But now *I* could see something as well. In his vanity and power he had revealed himself. Yes. It all fit in. He was a completely different man from what I had imagined, a masterful person, a deal maker. *A liar! LIAR!*

He turned to face me, his eyes narrowed sharp and dark as if he'd sensed that I *knew.*

"Too dark!" Auntie came in suddenly and jerked aside the thick velvet drape, revealing a hazy twilight over Kowloon; the soothing smell of driving rain came through the tall casement window that was open a crack.

"Too damn early for typhoon season, only April," he said in a quiet voice. "Hate it. The air's a wet pillow, eating up all sound. People drink, make noise, work, but the silence is so deep you hear things you can't possibly know …" I heard the small desk clock ticking in the room. I thought of his cancer spreading like mold. And his furniture, all these things he couldn't take with him; the rugs, lamps, artifacts, memories, possessions—they were like wet clothes, smothering you when you're *drowning*, choking for air. Every item a sentimental attachment—a cement block tied to your ankles. And here he was, bailing out memories before he drowned. Then, I wondered, how could you hear things you couldn't possibly know? *Ridiculous.* What I did want was to be among the living, with loud music, spinning lights, blasting away all thoughts of death, old people and their ghosts. I began to stand up.

"Jardine?" He looked worried, yet chiding.

"What?"

"Won't you stay a bit longer?"

I hesitated, looking into his eyes. This stranger who bought my strawberry cake and a conversation was playing a complicated game. *Why? What did he have to lose?* I had butterflies in my stomach, I was unsure of him. *Why was Auntie Tam playing along? Maybe she wasn't trustworthy either.*

He opened a drawer and pulled out a picture frame, setting it on the table to face me. I didn't get a good look. Auntie hurried over and deftly turned the picture face down. As she moved away, I reached for the overturned photo. But Tam was quick and grabbed faster—and the frame propelled away from our fingertips, flying, bouncing off a Persian rug, then smashing loudly on the marble floor.

I heard a sudden, startled cry like that of a crow. *Was it the doors?*

As if in response, Auntie wagged her finger, full of some unexplained ferocity. "Bad things happen to China. No more tears. History, all gone." She took a few steps back, then disappeared down the hall behind me. *Could they be trying to trick me out of an inheritance?*

He put down his cigar, squinting, turning the tip slowly in the ash tray as if calculating something. "The house is burning, little Miss Wo. Will you wake up? Save your shoes and handbag? Or will you keep sleeping until everything is gone? The dragon takes all in its path … *Feng Shui*," he added with a sarcastic smile.

I was sick of his puzzles. "Why are you picking on me?" I choked out at last.

"Here's a clue." He tapped a book by Lao Tse on the table. "How do we kill the beast within without killing ourselves? What do you think?"

I froze, then before I knew it I'd stood up. "You're not Algernon Worthing, are you!" I was shaking.

"And you're no confluence of roads," he answered, unperturbed.

"But I'm an orphan! I've nothing, no family, no past! For God's sake, I'm named after a crossroad."

"Not crossroads, Jardine—but *William Jardine*. The man who tricked England into going to war against China. The man who helped take Hong Kong in that unequal treaty that still infuriates the Chinese—what was that, 1841? Anyway, I hope you appreciate the irony."

"You know what?" I cried out bitterly, "I don't give a damn if you're going to die! You're cruel!"

"Jardine Wo, you can't separate a fish from its bones, a rose from its bush, without both dying. You're leaving? Wait." He held up my purse, "Don't forget your—," he paused, squinting at the label, "your *Prada* handbag, Jardine. You'll want to save *this*."

I stared at him, then ran out, slamming the door behind me.

The air in the hall was like smog-scented fingers, cool on my face as I stumbled groggily down damp cement steps, my mind heavy with his dreams dragging me down. Unzipping, then digging in my handbag, I searched for my mini umbrella; instead, I pricked my finger on a yellow rose. I didn't understand why he'd put it in my bag, or how he'd done it. *No umbrella though* … Pushing the steamy glass door open, I stepped out of the AC into blinding sheets of hot rain. Rain was pouring off rooftops and cars, back-splashing with force. Instantly I was soaked. A river of tepid rainwater churned around my ankles, sweeping away papers, litter, broken umbrellas; everything let go. Rain slicked my hair into long wet noodles—my mini-skirt and tiny T-shirt stuck to me. All I heard was the rush of water. I sniffed the thick yellow rose and brushed the fragrant petal across my lips; veiny texture, luxurious lemon-apple scent. I squinted up at the sky, rain battering my hot eyes, clogging my lashes, blood dripping from my finger. I should have felt free and frivolous but instead I felt odd. Something had altered in me, as if someone had reached inside and twisted my heart; I was on the verge of crying.

Stepping out away from the building and onto the road, by chance I looked back at the building and froze. The glass door, steamed and rain streaked, had a dark shrunken head in it—*the ancient doorman.* Watchful with disapproval, he was staring at me. I nodded, a little scared, but there was no reaction on his face. *Why was he staring at me like that?* He had looked so incredibly sad—so sad that as I walked further and further down the hill my tears began to flow.

Book Two

1937-1938

The Naked Truth

11

Bela Vista, Macao *1 November 1937*

As dusk fell, bats funneled out over the orange tiled rooftops of the Portuguese enclave and Jack's horse-drawn carriage rattled up the cobblestone hill to the Bela Vista Hotel. The gold band had been on his finger barely a day, yet already they'd had their first quarrel and all because of a dress. When Jack had told her it would be best if they arrived first and greeted guests together at the banquet hall, Violet had raised her voice in a manner that shocked him. "I've a position to maintain. You're a man; you can't possibly understand." After a few angry words were exchanged, he glimpsed her silk negligée in the suitcase. "Very well, then," he'd muttered, for the promise of sex that evening tempered his response. So she remained shipboard, changing into a third gown with her dressers, and Jack had gone on without her.

As soon as his horse stopped, the white carriage was besieged by refugees outside the front doors of the hotel. The rich, hot scent of roasting meats and baked goods suffused the air, spilling out into the street where garlands of fresh gardenias and red paper lanterns drifted from the trees. It was like Lane Crawford's department store on the Queen's birthday. Jack hopped down among the crowd, embarrassed by the excess and poverty of spirit demanding such a display. He bristled with irritation, noting how the bedraggled onlookers were being beaten back from the entrance with swagger sticks, but before he could do anything, rickshaws with guests began arriving, adding to the melee.

Into this, the bride arrived with a clatter of hooves and the coachman's cry of "Whoa." The crush of spectators and the loud crack of the whip caused the horses to rear up under the black-limbed trees, and faces illuminated by the carriage lights appeared ghoulish, aristocrat and peasant alike. Wrapped in volumes of glaring white silk, Violet stepped out onto the carriage runner, her eyes thrilling with wild pleasure as she gauged her effect below. There was a terrified hush from Chinese onlookers, but somewhere a guest began to clap and this brought forth a smattering of polite applause. Violet kept bowing in delight until Jack swept her off her feet and carried her over the threshold where he set her down. He then ordered the concierge to make certain the crowd outside would be fed. It was not until hours later, after the eating, dancing, and rounds of champagne toasts that he was able to slip out of the main hall toward the back of the hotel and escape the charade, for that was what it was. He could only hope she would be lovely in bed. *At least she was experienced*, he thought, *and maybe it spoke for her passion, something he could understand.*

Leaning on the balustrade overlooking the bay, however, he noticed his hands were shaking. Heart pounding, he downed his drink as if it were a desperate cure, and then took a few deep breaths of the cloying gardenia-perfumed air. He didn't notice the waiter who removed his empty glass, nor the fat man in the shadows with blue slits for eyes.

Jack took out a cigar, remembering Ana and their dance at Chan's with a pang of regret and desire. Those eyes, quiet and fathomless, seemed to throw him a rope from their depths—uncoiling, falling straight into his heart. Jack looked around for his glass, and knew, if he stayed with Violet he'd never stop drinking. Not finding it, he leaned heavily on the balustrade wanting another shot but not wanting to go back inside for it.

"Pleasant thoughts?" a voice asked, startling him.

It was Chiswick sitting in a deck chair, watching him intently—hair wet, smelling of aftershave, and—could it be, *excrement?*

Jack grunted, "Enjoying yourself?"

"You know," Chiswick muttered, "every time I toasted to your future, and your happiness, a little thought kept coming to me." He raised an almost empty gin bottle, making a point in the air. "Not just that you stole my position, my seniority, my future in the firm . . ."

"You're drunk."

"Maybe, but I've a friend in Java at the planter's club. You know the place." He stood up wiping perspiration off his face. "Manfred Vogel. An insignificant little person in your world, but he saw you there. What I wonder is where all that bar silver and gold got to?" He then raised up his glass. "But damn you, I'll find it. *Chin chin.*"

Before Albert could say more, Jack had pinned him to the doorjamb by the neck. "See to it," Jack said glaring into the wriggling blue eyes, "that you wonder more about getting your own work done properly instead of blundering about stinking drunk. And you do stink." He shook Albert till the comb-marked hair jerked loose like noodles, and hair oil slithered onto his hand. He pushed Albert away, and headed to the ballroom, wiping his hands off on a napkin.

"Ah, Mr. Morgan," a company clerk said, "we were all wondering how a blackguard like you got such a lovely wife, weren't we, boys?" They all laughed, patting him on the back as Percy approached.

"Ah, look at me now," Percy said as Jack helped him into a chair. "In my youth you couldn't hold me down, but a man must have his vices, they're his only solace in the tropics."

"A bit unconventional as far as advice goes," Jack muttered, but Percy ignored him.

"You're the spitting image of myself at your age. Look at him, my men. I am so glad, so very glad, to have settled my daughter so well." He held up his drink, cloudy blue eyes shining with emotion.

"You're embarrassing me," Jack said.

"I'll not hear a word of it! You saved us from ruin, my lad."

As the other men moved away and the party wound down, Jack pulled up a seat. "You know I've wanted to talk to you about changes in strategy. We haven't discussed much and—"

"Just keep up the good work!" he said with a wheezing cough.

"Percy, why not reconsider and stay over tonight? It does no good to be overtired."

"No Sir, my responsibilities are finished! I'm heading back with the steamer. I've my own party tomorrow." He winked confidentially as the room emptied. "I'd rather die than miss it."

"You surprise me."

"I'll tell you something else," he said. "I've had a lady friend for some time now. I'd even bought her a ring. Yes! But Violet found it and insisted I withdraw my offer." He shrugged looking away.

Jack furrowed his brows. "So then," he hesitated, "is she—*Chinese?*"

Percy laughed out loud. "English, my lad. A seamstress! I'd have liked to make a decent woman of her."

"And why don't you?"

"Enough. It's too late for that. Let's have a final toast. I'm going to live, really live from now on." With that, the old man tipped the glass back.

"What are you saying, exactly?"

"Drink! It's good for you."

"It hasn't been good for you, Percy."

The old man looked at him with a steady eye, "Perhaps. But the older you get and the more you learn about the human animal—all that keeps a man from madness is drink or death." He winked. "A bit of wisdom for you, lad."

"I hope not."

"Injustice, corruption, ignorance … we're all flawed at the heart. Anyhow," Percy shrugged, "too often ideals outstrip abilities." He raised his glass, "That's why I say, best to look at life with blurred vision. Less troubling." Percy laughed and threw back his drink. "Now—you know my secret motto. Come, join me for another round and see if you can better me."

South China Sea *2 November 1937*

FAUSTO AND HIS MEN were busy with torches, combing the pier, but hidden on the deck of a junk, Algy and Ana slipped out of Macao right under their eyes.

"Come Monday, Albert will be waiting for me at the office!" Algy said with dread, keeping his head low but watching the searching lights bobbing along the waterfront. "I've had hazings before, but this time he's sure to drub me into a fine paste."

Ana laughed, wanting to say, *Albert Chiswick will never confront you about being in a house of prostitution*, but bit her tongue. After the lights of Macao safely vanished into the sea, they came out of hiding on deck to watch the stars together. Above them the patchwork sail, shaped like a dragon's wing suddenly stiffened in a growing wind. Ana felt the cool sea air sweep over her body, lifting her too, diluting her sorrows. The fisherman's young wife, with an infant strapped to her chest, brought out tea, and they all sat together cupping their hot mugs, rocking with the junk as it sailed over the South China Sea under a mist of stars. Free at last, Ana couldn't help but think of Jack, and if he'd waited. *But things were different now* ... The tiger charm was still pinned to her dress, as it had been every day since she'd seen him last, but now that she'd escaped, no man would accept what she'd become ... Ana lay down against a coil of rope and watched the stars, tears in her eyes.

Algy woke her as the warm yellow horizon gave way before them and Hong Kong Island rose up from a crouch to a sudden tall presence. Decked in lush green with a thick fringe of buildings around the base, it was magnificent. Ana gasped, looking up the steep slope of Victoria Peak, and Algy laughed happily at her surprise. Soon she could make out windows and signs and people, and the cheery hubbub on shore increased as they nosed in past hundreds of sampans, coming in to a final bump. "Pedder Street landing," he announced proudly. They stepped ashore among stacks of crates with the Queen's seal on them. *Hong Kong Government Opium*. She'd seen those before, at Chan's and Fausto's and even though she stood in the sun, a chill passed over her.

A rickshaw took them up Ice House Street, past the noodle shops and banks. Everything was moving and alive, a parade of life's boundless energy. "And, you must remember, dear," Algy said, interrupting her thoughts, "my flat is attached to the Catholic mission. The other tenants are all monks."

"Impossible!" Ana laughed. "An island founded on the drug trade, and holy men reside here?"

"Yes, I appreciate the contrast, but you can't show your face outside my door. I'll give you my hat and jacket, and when the coast is clear, you'll make a dash up the stairs. Otherwise, I'll be thrown out! Don't laugh. I'm very lucky, you see; only married men receive housing allowance. The bachelors all live in Kowloon. Look, take my jacket and topee, and when I signal, come running." A few minutes and several flights of stairs later, they threw themselves down breathlessly on Algy's sofa, weak with laughter and, finally, tears.

"I can't have you putting me up. Please," Ana protested, but Algy refused all further talk on the subject.

The next morning, before he awoke, Ana had crept out the back stairwell to a corner market and had come back with fresh papaya, mangos, some milk, eggs, and a beautiful bunch of white ginger blossoms. When Algy finally stirred on the sofa, she raised the blinds and opened the French doors. He sat up rubbing his palms together. "O-well, o-well, o-well! What have we here?"

Ana placed a hill of crepes rolled up with jam before him, and brought out a steaming-pot of Darjeeling.

"I could get used to this!"

His boyish happiness pleased her, the way he smoothed down his unruly hair, gave a wry grin, and eagerly took up his fork. But despite all the color and sunshine and her newfound friend, she couldn't dispel thoughts of Macao and her countless clients. The prostitutes would be waking up now and going down for a breakfast of congee and gossiping about their clients, some laughing, some tearful. And then Fausto …

When Algy finished his breakfast, Ana watched him fooling with his badminton racquet, tapping shuttlecocks into the waste bin, and she counted for him.

"I'm rather good, aren't I?" he said waggling his eyebrows. "The record's over a hundred at the club."

She nodded absently, fingering her tiger charm.

Bela Vista Hotel, Macao *2 November 1937*

VIOLET WAS STANDING IN the dark at the edge of the road, toying with her wedding band, realizing she could no longer put off losing her virginity. It was half three in the morning and rickshaws had just carried off the final lingering guests leaving the three of them. She watched as Jack gave Father a lift up to the horse carriage.

"He shouldn't be going. He isn't well," Jack muttered when the carriage started off with a jerk.

Father shouted back over his shoulder, "Off to celebrate bachelorhood! Jack, I leave you in charge!"

He was still waving as he disappeared behind a turn in the road, but Violet felt chilled. The matrimonial bed would be an arena and litmus determining the entire keel of married life—and for once she felt the situation beyond her control.

They both stood in the dark listening to the clip-clop on cobbles fade into the night. "Well, that's that," Jack sighed.

"Meaning?"

"Meaning we've an entire week to ourselves!" With that, he made a playful lunge, just missing her as a hotel clerk passed in the distance.

Violet stepped away, breathless. "Really, Jack. Not in front of the help." This reprimand seemed to work, but then she did have a lifetime of experience putting servants in their place. What it came down to though, was that she was afraid, and yes, *a little excited*—like before a Fan Ling Hunt on a strong, unfamiliar horse.

"I'm worried about Percy," he said once inside, fumbling for the keys to their suite.

"He's a tippler, for God's sake. Drinks himself unconscious. What do you expect?"

"He has trouble breathing, Violet."

"Well, who told him to eat all those puddings? Besides, he's not *your* father."

"Let's not argue." He opened the door and held his hand out to her.

She darted past him and Jack took up the cue, pinching her so that she squealed, until he grabbed her, pulling her onto the bed. The last move was too impromptu and Violet pulled away. "Don't be a beast!"

"You're always one for games, Violet."

"Games? I assure you, it's not a game. You disgust me with your brutality!"

"Disgust?" Jack stood over her, his face growing dark.

Violet shrugged with a coy smile but immediately his hands encircled her, moving down to her backside, pulling her toward him. "*No, no!*" she scolded in the voice reserved for cook boy, while her belly twitched. "Don't think you have rights!"

"Rights? I believe I'm not out of place."

"Place?" she asked, pushing his hand away. "I should wonder you know what that is."

"Are you yet again referring to the fact that I'm a 'hired hand' of your father's? When I met him, though, he did *still* pour his milk *before* his tea."

Violet felt herself flushing at this social gaffe. "I hardly think it proper form criticizing Father."

"No, maybe not, but—" He abruptly removed a folded piece of paper from his breast pocket. "There is this telegram. Proper form, is it?"

"How dare you!" Violet threw it to the floor, and rushed into the bath, locking the door and falling against it panting, but feeling a broad grin split her face. She whispered in Chinese, *Use egg hit stone.*

"You know, Violet," his voice came from behind the door, "Peebles came to see me today before the wedding."

She sat up. "Whatever for?"

"Maybe he's the one you want, seeing I disgust you."

She turned on the tap full, and water rushed into the tub drowning him out. The satin nightgown hanging on the door was a gift from Peebles last year in his vain hopes of getting somewhere with her. *No one had.* Rose had scared Violet with her talk of the man and woman thing. "Ebry mismis hab flowah. Can gib *one* time, tasol. Need be belly carefu'." But, Violet had countered, "Oh really! And what's this flower I can lose, but don't see?" No answer came or ever did, so that Violet clung to everything she had and peeled her eye out for things other girls had, that she could take for her own.

The floor creaked, and she heard him moving away. Violet jerked open the door. "So, you've really forgotten Stanley beach?"

He looked at her startled, confused.

"I see. Yet, you *still* married me—not knowing? But how sporting of you. Now you'll never know if it's yours, though, will you!" She watched the change come over his face, wanting to hurt him, yet she was equally afraid he'd see through it. She quickly added, "You may wait for me, if you like." Then, shutting the door, she felt a great surge of mastery over him. It reminded her how an older woman from the Fan Ling Hunt had recently advised her on Jack, saying, "Men are like horses. Keep that one on the snaffle, my dear, with a light and steady hand or else he *will* throw you over." Violet had colored, furious. "Not on your life, Bridget. I'll use a gag bit, thank you." *And it was working now, wasn't it. Why, he wasn't even arguing!*

Violet undid her dress letting it fall. She didn't feel too cavalier, however, and turned to listen but heard nothing beyond the door. Odd, patience was not what she'd expected from him. Violet opened the door to the terrace, and pulled on her robe. It was irritating how other women dispensed unsolicited advice on your horse and your man. *As if they could know!* Creeping along to the bedroom window she peered in, amused with her cunning.

For certain, she was shocked beyond her imaginings. Instead of having changed into his nightwear and turned out the lights to wait for her, Jack Morgan, managing director of Father's company, was sitting carefree and buck naked at the desk, writing what appeared to be a letter. Violet was utterly disgusted by his manly nakedness and the body hair completely exposed to the bright lamplight and chandeliers of the room! Not seeing her, he stood up in his nakedness, pen in hand, and paced the room, then sat down again leafing through a ledger. And that small shock of black hair, like a mustache! And that *THING* under it! There was something so savage—so hideous about it, as if he were a dog sitting in parody of man, holding a writing utensil! She hurried back into the bathroom and sat at the edge of the tub, staring into the foaming water trying to obliterate the image.

When Violet did finally emerge from the bath, she unbolted the door quietly, lowering her eyes, in case he was still indecent. She was surprised again, however, for all the lights in the room were out except for a lamp. He was not waiting, no, Jack was lying face down on the bed, covers askew, naked.

She hadn't seen a man this close and though she was curious, she was also terrified. He *smelled* like a man, emanated heat. It was not unpleasant, but overwhelming. She had to admit she quite *liked* the fact that he was her *own* man, claimable as such. She thought of parties they'd go to and how they'd be announced, *Mr. and Mrs. Jack Morgan*, and how everyone would turn to look, especially Connie, who'd failed to marry him. Lying there asleep, he seemed quite innocent. She unpinned her auburn hair which fell to her creamy white shoulders. Violet looked at her Golconda diamond in the dark. *How jealous they all were*—and this knowledge gave her a sense of ownership, a confidence to reach out toward his body …

One smooth stroke, though, and the back arched in response, and he rolled over, looking at her with those blue eyes. Suddenly, so suddenly, that thing also awoke too. "Jack," she began her little speech, moving back from him, feeling her breasts pressing against the tight lace. His eyes went down to them. "I–I want you to know that this is a marriage of equals, in every regard, business-wise, and in sexual congress as well."

"Equals in experience, you say?" His eyes had a strange light in them as he took in her face again, and then her transparent gown. He was staring at the outline of her nipples through the French silk. She tried not to notice his look, and tried also not to look down at It, but *It* seemed to have grown hideously in size.

"Really," she gulped down her shock, "first and foremost, Jack. This is a marriage of *convenience.* So—so you can *ignore* what Father says about *you* being in charge. In your interest I will forget about Peebles too," she added rather generously. *He was moving toward her.* "I—I will raise his child as *our own,*" she said haughtily, but inching away from him.

His hand grabbed hold of her arm, his voice thick. "How many lovers have you had, Violet?"

"I? Not so many as you, to be sure."

"Not so many, eh?"

"Well, you're not my *first,*" she laughed, giving a little sneer and touching her belly, "but you have your secrets, I have mine." Her supercilious reserve, however, had done nothing to put the chill on him, and nothing Rose had said about "pulim man" had prepared her for what occurred next.

She hardly knew how, but his hot nakedness was suddenly on top of her—he was pulling up her gown. Although her hands tried in vain to keep covered down below, and she cried for him to stop, his hands easily threw hers off. Prying her knees apart with one hand, he was feeling all up and inside with another. Violet felt disgraced, excited, exposed, and her heart fluttered with fear and desire—her private self completely open to him. Rising up suddenly, and poised between her open thighs, the rude-red thing was enormous now and pointing heavily toward her shame—and then as he moved in—*It* touched, burning hot.

"No!" she hissed pulling aside. It was so shameful, dirty, and from the sensation, she began to wonder if he was attempting to *put THAT in her too.* "No!" His hips moved, indifferent to her protestations, and the smooth head rubbing, pushed, shouldering its way inward—and just when she thought she could bear it, there was a searing shove. Violet let out an animal-like wail. Her hands clawed the sheets, and she found her insides assaulted. She lay, not breathing, feeling about to die. *If only she'd known ... if only she'd been warned ... for this was unreal.* He was pushing it in to her. *Pushing.*

The initial tearing sensation faded after a few minutes of pure agony, and looking away, she distanced her mind from what was happening by staring out the window at tree branches. Her attention was brought back some time later, however, by the sudden surprising discovery that It seemed to be moving into her more easily, and *inexplicably—It* had become *moist*, no—*wet*, and the pounding instead had become a silent rhythmic dance, penetrating deeper, smoother, swiveling, and that enormous snakelike thing sliding in and out, over and over, was slowly mesmerizing her with an amazing sensation. Violet turned to look at him in wonder, her own chest heaving as her stomach curled inside and she squirmed deliciously—then stopped in shock—realizing her own female part below, too, was participating in this transgression, holding to *It*, wanting *It* to stay, hypnotizing her brain into motionless acceptance—betraying her with Jack. *The shame of it!* His hips were moving faster now between her thighs and instinctively, and rather than try to keep him out, her hips now tipped for him to enter completely, and she held to the sides of the bed, gasping, thrilling as *his* smooth blunt instrument thrust so—*so* hard, her deep inner belly stretched with every reach, so painful and deep, tears came to her eyes. "More," she whimpered, finding her entire sense of self transported from her mind to this one spot he had known about all along, and perhaps had planned to possess from the moment he'd set eyes on her—undressing her, raising her skirt with his mind, planning her ruin as she innocently served him tea in Father's house.

Violet was startled when he abruptly paused, let out a racking groan like a strongman picking up heavy dumbbells, and stopped midair. She waited, noticing his face contorting, while she herself felt no ultimate satisfaction—and waited for him to resume—instead—he jerked *It* out. Violet gasped as if an arrow had been pulled from a wound. Staring at his retreating form, she watched as he disappeared into the connecting room, slamming the door against her new devastating knowledge.

Violet was furious. Furious, that her body wanted more from this man for whom she had absolutely no feelings. Worse still—she had spoken her desire for It aloud! *And yet—was this where life came from? Sanctified by God? Or the Devil?* She had no one to blame. Neither of them had done this for love—yet … It. *It* … It was the foundation of all relations. *And the florid red stain.* Violet gasped looking down. *Her disgrace. Her flower!* She immediately pulled away the sheet, taking it with her, so he wouldn't see and have the honor of knowing *he was her first* and *that she had lied.* Her insides burned as she walked, yet her inner belly still twitched, slippery and awakened to what he could do to her, and the space inside that now clamored to be filled by him. There was no doubt in her mind that Jack Morgan had done this many times before—it was a dance he knew well. No wonder Connie had eyes for him—Connie and other married women with whom he'd had his way. As she hurried across the room Violet began to feel a thickness oozing out of her. She looked down. *A strange white fluid.* Violet held back an anguished scream that arose in her throat—then choking on bitter tears, her disgust overwhelmed her—wrenched her very lungs. She ran to the bath, quietly locking the door and collapsed—and cried, and cried. *He'd gone to the bathroom inside of her—what else could it be?*

Toward dawn she realized, though—say what she would to insult him, the final insult was the power man had over woman, his knowing, and her own compliance in her defilement, this last thing was the crowning shame. With marriage, she had lifted a veil and witnessed the taboo of Life; a reptilian tango, vile and bloody, where everything decent fell away to reveal the glaring hypocrisy of civilized life. She looked in the mirror at the dark circles under her eyes. *Nothing would be the same after this*, she thought. *Nothing.* How different her experienced friends seemed to her now—*harlots, all.*

When Jack awoke the next afternoon, Violet was sitting across from him in a cinched navy dress, her hair pulled back tight. She had her sunglasses on under her broad hat, not wanting him to see her eyes. "I would like to leave Macao." As she spoke, she couldn't help but think of *It.* Where it had touched her, owned her, and that he had witnessed her naked desire for *It.* She hoped he did not confuse her lust, however, for a feeling for him—for she hated him now.

He stretched then said, "In a minute, dear," and pulling on a towel, sauntered over to the door, peering outside. "Boy," he said. Violet heard him asking about correspondence he'd sent out in the wee hours of the morning. It had been delivered, the boy assured him. Jack reappeared, "Violet, have you any small change?"

She fumed, handing over her purse, and he, perhaps not understanding her silence, doled out the change with great thanks.

"Now, what were you saying, dear?" he asked with boyish charm as he opened the paper. "Ah look. The Japanese are increasing war activity around Shanghai."

Violet felt incensed and cold hatred scintillated again in her veins. She stared at him. "I want to go home, today. *Now.*"

He smiled blandly, "As you wish."

It wasn't the response she'd expected, and she explained coldly, "Father is having a dance this evening. I want to surprise him."

Jack began packing immediately and even raced to make the boat. It only made Violet hang back with a growing sense of irritation. She had every mind to stop and return just to see the effect, unable to decide if he was deliberately stupid, or if this was *his* game rather than hers. She took off her gloves when they boarded, and went to her room. "I don't want to be disturbed," she said in the special tone she used on staff. But Jack listened. He didn't simper or hover, didn't try to win her attention, and unlike Peebles who clung to her every word, arguing with her, pleading—Jack agreed and did not knock on her door. It drove Violet wild. Not once did he even ask, "Was it something I said?" Violet found it hard to confine herself in that small stateroom, and even harder not to break things. Sexual congress, indeed, she thought ripping off her brooch and bracelets and staring into the vanity mirror. *This was something else entirely.*

Central China *3 November 1937*

So this was China, Yoshi thought. All around an unfamiliar landscape stretched in every direction—big, flat, unending fields. Japan, in contrast, had tiny quilts of green rice paddies, steep thatched cottages in cozy hollows, rolling hills covered with cedars. Here he didn't even know what crops he saw, what kinds of trees these were. The huts were squat and made of stone, not wood ... Yoshi stood swaying with the movement of the train car, listening to the clicking of the points, and let his thoughts drift back to his village. O-bachan had told him as he'd helped her out of the house on his last day, "Your mother will not tell you, but I'm old and unimportant. Forget Yasukuni Shrine, Yoshi. That is for the dead. There is no honor in death. Come home safe."

Yoshi thought of the famed Tokyo shrine Grandmother had referred to, the enormous arches that marked the end of a long journey. Some soldiers back in Tokyo had said, *If you fall, may we meet you in Yasukuni!* Emperor Hirohito himself, half-human, half-god, personally walked down that long path of somber trees each year to the special place marked with the Gold Chrysanthemum Seal. *Yasukuni.* The revered place for the honorable dead. The Emperor's visitation was the greatest honor bestowed on an ordinary human, and everyone in Japan knew this. *And she said forget Yasukuni*? Grandmother's words were treacherous. All over Japan soldiers were regaled with honorifics when they passed civilians in the streets. Everywhere people spoke of the new Japan, "Uniting the world from the Eight Directions." The soldiers said, *We'll bring great riches to Japan, we will overcome this depression and poverty once and for all! Think of those foreign devils taking what they please from China! What right do they have, the Americans, British, French and Dutch—helping themselves to Asia's treasures? What is to stop us? Banzai! Banzai! Banzai! Congratulations, they cried in advance of certain victory.* But more soldiers were needed. More and more men, younger boys were being sent, middle school boys in glasses like himself.

"Yoshi," O-bachan had said looking into his eyes. "Be like the tiger. He goes out strong and fights, but doesn't need to die. He returns home, maybe his foot is lame, or an eye blinded, but he returns. Your father needs you to harvest the rice. Elder brother is not well. We are lost if you don't return. I'll write to O-ji san, and ask him to find a post for you in Hong Kong. We'll never dare have a war there." Age had made Grandma's words bold, and he'd rebuked her. "Don't talk of our country like that, O-bachan! If a neighbor hears you, you'll be labeled traitor! Someone in the neighborhood association could kill you!" "Let them," she had said. "I am a worthless old woman. What good am I if I cannot earn even the rice that I eat?"

Yoshi hissed through his teeth remembering their exchange—*Just survive, Yoshi. Just survive.* The wind whipped through the gaps in the wood slats of the train car, and he grasped the coarse board to take the weight of his legs. It was in this way that he slept, his dreams taking him home. At the next stop to load coal, a rumor went round the train, unbelievably good news—*They were going to fight with a famous general who would lead them to great victory.* Everyone's spirits cheered, and, as the train started again, Yoshi looked out between the slats.

Bigger than anything he'd ever seen or imagined, unearthly in its vastness, the green flatness of middle China seemed to scream at the sky. Even the crisscrossing streams seemed to lose themselves in the grasses. There was also a brown underbelly to this savage land, for Yoshi smelled its burp in the cool wind. Organic and seething, the grassy lip of the land appeared alive, and capable of swallowing armies whole without a single cry. Like a harbinger of coming things, the smell of death blew over the grass, puckering his smooth, innocent face.

Central District *3 November 1937*

AFTER ALGY HAD LEFT that next morning, Ana went out on the streets to explore her newfound freedom and to look for a job. All up and down China, the Crown Colony was reputed to have streets lined in gold where a coolie could become rich overnight. Even Ana had imagined something similar while under Chan's roof, but here on the streets of Hong Kong she saw refugees in rags just like in China. Ana began calling on the businesses along Des Voeux Road and soon discovered no one was hiring. She had so desperately wanted to repay Algy for his kindness but was quickly disappointed. Eventually her mind drifted to Jack. *What if she saw him?* She was excited for a moment, remembering how she felt when he'd looked into her eyes. He would certainly ask where she'd been. She'd rather die than tell him.

Around noon she saw a tomato roll off a vendor's cart onto the street and grabbed it. Leaning against a wall, away from the human river of traffic, she bit into the aromatic red flesh. The ripe fruit shot hundreds of seeds into her mouth, and as she wiped her lips she could only wonder how nature could be so prolific and so cruel. Like so many seeds in a tomato doomed not to survive, many of these people who passed probably wouldn't either. Scanning the Asian faces before her she caught her own reflected in a window across the road. A flower shop.

Hurrying across the road she entered the elegant lobby off Queen's Road, smoothing her dress, and putting on her best smile. Just as she was about to speak, a white man on his way out stopped before her, and stared. Ana froze too, for she could remember his face—*his face above her in the throes of passion … A customer from Macao!*

As if on cue the man asked with a warm, curious smile, "Don't I know you?"

Overcome, Ana ran the whole way back to Algy's flat slamming the door behind her, feeling a burning shame. She cried on her bed for a while, but knew there was nothing to do about it. The other girls were still at Fausto's, still being raped by him. Her heart ached for them. She was the lucky one. She got up and began straightening the disarray on Algy's desk, eyes blurred with tears. He'd taken the day off from work to go to a business luncheon and then said he was off to a party on the Peak. Ana picked up the embossed invitation. She'd have loved to go, and the card said "dancing." But Algy was the retiring sort and last night when she'd pleaded with him to take her to this dance, he'd balked, explaining that Hong Kong was terribly provincial. "I've no way of introducing you, Ana. People would be curious, thinking I was hiding something." She put the card down and hearing a knock noticed a letter being pushed through under the door. Ana stooped over and picked it up.

China Coast Navigation was written in a strong masculine hand across the top along with the name *Jack Morgan*. Her heart skipped a beat, and she went and sat down by the window, holding the envelope in both hands against her chest. His image came to mind and obliterated her sadness, like sunlight flowing into a dark room. She passed the envelope over her cheek, smelled it, and when she could take it no more, went to the kitchen and steamed it open. It was dated last night. Although she was elated to have something he'd written, her joy faded as she read.

Algy:
I have it on good information that a Mr. Fritz Heidegger is in town looking to buy ships possibly for German War effort. We must get to him before anyone else, and sell the Havana. Call immediately—get an interview. He'll appreciate your German … do whatever it takes. Things are desperate and as you know, I'm unable to leave Macao. The firm's future depends on this—I expect to hear from you right away.

JM

P.S. I'm including a list of prices and different combinations that should interest him.

Ana re-read it and frowned … But how could she get this to Algy? He was on a beach somewhere. She paced the room, thinking—*My German is impeccable—all he needs is an appointment.* Her hand lingered on the receiver. It would be easy over the telephone. Certainly, it was a way to make it up to Algy. She would do anything to help him.

"Hong Kong Hotel?" she said to the operator a minute later. "Yes, I am looking for a Fritz Heidegger. Yes, that's right. Sorry?" she said with a quaver. "No, I'm not a secretary. No. No, it's not a solicitation." This was more difficult than she'd imagined. She bit her lip, "Tell him … Please tell him—ah—that Mrs. Jack Morgan is on the line." She felt queasy, but when she heard the room being buzzed and the man's husky voice answering, she switched to her sweetest German, knowing instinctively she was dealing with a ladies man. He told her he was astounded by her accent, and that she must be beautiful with a voice like that … and she cleared her throat. "I'm actually calling in behalf of my husband who won't be back until tomorrow. You see, we've something remarkable you might like to consider," she told him officiously. "My husband's accountant, Mr. Worthing, can bring you the paperwork. Perhaps you could look it over tomorrow at tiffin with him?"

There was a pause on the line then the voice answered her in English curtly, "I've had nussink but a lot of annoying solicitations since I've docked here, and I'll hev you know tsut I've turned every vun of zem down."

Ana felt her heart plunge but she quickly attempted a different tack and, lowering her voice, chided in her most alluring bedroom tone, "*Ahhh*—Mr. Heidegger, I believe you will regret this decision."

She heard him chuckling appreciatively. "Aha! Now tsut is sa most compelling sing I've heard, ya? Let us say I agree, but only if *you* come. What do you say?"

Ana hung up a few minutes later, thrilled with her success, but knew she must warn Algy to contact Jack straightaway and tell him about his appointment in town. Ana picked up the invitation. *She could just take a note up for Algy at the party, then leave.* Simple enough, but spotting herself in the mirror she frowned. Knocking on the door of a society event wearing a drab housecoat—even just to deliver a message—would have made her die of shame. Her folly began there, and ended with her laying out all her dresses she'd taken from Chan's and selecting a slinky black wonder with a surprising décolleté. With such an important message, Ana was certain Algy couldn't possibly mind the intrusion at the Summerhays party. But working the nighttime sing-song clubs of Shanghai, surrounded by festive debauchery and extravagant elegance, her parameters of judgment had broken down, one by one. Ana had transformed into a bird of paradise, dwelling solely in the world of gentlemen. She entirely forgot that conformity was everything in the world of women, but twirling in the beaded dress before her mirror, her only guide was her heart and the desire to escape the memory of Macao.

It was dusk when Ana stepped out to look for a rickshaw, and in the dark she blended in with the masses. Everywhere Chinese locals, exhausted by work, bumped past her on narrow unlit streets and stairways. Treading cautiously in her high heels over cobbles and down the zig-zagging steps worn smooth with age, her heart was racing with excitement. She hired the first rickshaw, "Peak House," she said, and they glided off into the dark. The name on the card sounded like gold to her. *Surely*, she thought, *these people had wondrous connections.* Perhaps Mrs. Summerhays would be a pleasant generous lady, and might assist her in obtaining employment as nanny or governess—even as companion to an elderly person, anything, she thought, to repay Algy's kindness.

The Lovers

12

Peak House *3 November 1937*

ALGY HOPPED OFF THE Peak Tram at Barker Road, shivering in the fog, and hurried along in the darkness until the manor house lights appeared through the foliage. Attendance was required at all of these work parties but Algy quailed at the thought of entering, thinking of Albert. He had already skipped work today just out of fear of seeing him again. *I will just get a drink, say hello, then hightail it.* He suddenly heard the pad of bare feet. *A rickshaw coolie!* Algy hid behind a shrub just to be sure. Over and over he pictured Albert's face as the shit bucket came off his head; the man had sworn to kill him.

"You there! Didn't see you at work today," Duffy, the company solicitor, said as he dismounted, and peered into the shrub.

"Ah, here it is!" Algy held up his rabbit's foot, flushing, attempting to ignore Duffy's look of incredulity.

On front steps, Duffy rang the bell. "You get the cable from Morgan I sent over today?"

Algy frowned. "But Jack's still on his honeymoon."

The door burst open, rhumba blaring, lights blazing. And standing in the center of the great hall, packed with guests, was the newly married Mrs. Violet Morgan, a distinctly sour expression on her face.

"Well, apparently it was a curtailed honeymoon," Duffy muttered discreetly as the butler announced them.

Algy's mouth hung open in surprise, but he immediately gave Violet wide berth and circumnavigated the room scanning for signs of Albert. As he neared the opposite side of the room, however, the front door opened, and after the butler spoke a hush passed over the crowd.

"What? Algernon? *Algernon* Worthing? Impossible!" Violet's irate voice electrified him and he froze in horror.

"He's over here." Everyone turned to stare and a space opened up around him, growing like a sand pit. Algy felt the blood rush to his head—there stood Ana—attired like Shanghai Lily. *God help us!* he thought.

"Ah, my dear brother!" As she rushed to take his arm, a cloud of delicious perfume enveloped him, and her stunning beaded dress sparkled, revealing an eyeful. Not a man in proximity could look away and Violet's eyes gleamed poisonously bright from under her sequined headband as she took in the competition.

"*Don't stop*," he hissed, and deftly steered Ana away, horrified Violet might recognize Ana from the tarmac for wearing the blue dress.

"What did you say your name was?" Violet asked, tailing them, her plummy voice sarcastic, *loud.*

"Ana, Ana Worthing." She released Algy's arm, turning to her hostess. "How do you do?"

Violet's thin red lips pursed in disgust, livid she'd been upstaged at her own party.

"I'm his half-sister actually," Ana innocently explained. "I grew up in Germany."

"So your father made the rounds, I see."

"Why, hello-hello! What have we here?" Percy raised his glasses, sizing Ana up like a man checking a horse for conformation. "Germany, did you say?" his voice round with appreciation.

Before she could answer, a sly muskrat of a man stepped up, "You know, Hitler marched into Austria yesterday, have you heard? Chancellor Schuschnigg was forced to step down and Hitler's Nazi lawyer was made chancellor. Pretty shocking, don't you think?"

Algy poked Ana in warning. *If Jack saw her he'd think Algy brought her to destroy his marriage. If Albert saw her, he'd tell everyone she was a whore!* "Ana," he whispered, with extreme discomfort.

"I was only schooled in Germany, Sir," she replied, discreetly pushing Algy away. "But I haven't been there in years." Then turning she smiled at Percy, sensing an ally in him. "Germany has many financial woes from the peace agreements. England's rich with colonies but Germany's in a precarious position just now."

"How true," Percy waved dismissively. "But enough politics."

Ana gave a warm smile. "It was so kind of you to invite my dear brother this evening."

The old man let out a laugh, "What a treasure! What a treasure! And you, Worthing's sister!" Taking her arm, he led her away. "Come have a drink and I'll introduce you to everyone. *Ana Worthing!* Imagine that!"

Algernon felt sick—people knew his father here and would know this was a blatant lie. *But how to extract her?* He raised his hand, opening his mouth—but only a squeak emerged; *Albert Chiswick had just entered the room.* Algy lowered his head and scurried between throngs of guests making a beeline for the front door. He nearly made it—but *something had attached to his sleeve!*

"My dear boy!" the lady cooed. *It was her hand.* "How long it's been! Why haven't you stopped to see me?" She was leering through bifocals looking very much like a female Wallace Beery with her extra chins and wide mouth.

"I–I've been busy," he said, trying to release himself, but the old dame held on like he was the last man on earth. Spotting Albert on the horizon Algy ducked behind her as the opening notes of a fox-trot were sounding and the floor was clearing.

"Algernon!" she spun about, still clutching. "Be so good as to dance this one, or I'll write your mother you treated me shamefully!" To his immense mortification she steered him capably out onto the empty dance floor, crushing him to her bosom, everyone watching as she wheeled him around. It was then that Albert turned his head—*and their eyes met.* Thunderstruck, Algy knew it was all over. Like a frightened colt, he snapped free—tripping over people and chairs, then catching his balance, he ran for his life, leaving Ana to fend for herself at Peak House.

The momentum took him out of the house, down the verandah steps and out into the darkness, startling the waiting rickshaw coolies. But he was flying, and the feeling of escape seemed to build upon itself. Whether it was the sound of his own footsteps on the path echoing against the cement manor walls, or whether it was really Albert following, he didn't wait to find out. All the stress of the previous months, the lies, the falsified ledgers, the animosity at work, the face of the planter and his wife, being thrown out of his flat, his poor aging mother—all of this pushed him onward, and he swerved through the darkness, a white blur, arms flailing, right onto the coolie path.

He should have known better. Even just strolling down the Peak Road it quickly becomes evident that it's something to only attempt during daylight hours. Certainly, up at the top the gently sloping road affords spectacular vistas and offers no challenge. However, one only need continue around a few hairpin bends to see a pleasant walk take an abrupt turn for the worse. Even a casual sightseer ambling at a slow pace will easily accelerate beyond the capacity to immediately halt at will. This, along with creepers, fallen branches, poisonous pit vipers, and spiders, creates a confluence of evils best avoided in the dark. *It was dark.*

Alas, Algy had started his journey at a clip and very soon, he came upon the drop and accelerated towards the next switchback. Screaming and flailing he tried to stop by grabbing at a tree trunk on the way down. At this speed it only catapulted him off in another direction like a monkey through trees and he shot through a mighty web, catching the spider with his forehead. He felt it too when it stung him. Sailing and flapping madly with his hands, he slapped at the insect and the web, while his knees tried to keep pace with his plunging torso—but he was a projectile now, hurtling downward. A flash-flood sluice designed to break streams of runoff at a rapid glance did appear to be steps. Looking down he saw they were not. His feet left solid ground, treading air, and his fall was similar to water, straight down. The fifteen-foot sluice deposited him neatly on the next lower level, groaning in a heap of leaves and debris.

It was some time before he came to his wits, and mostly it was the pain, steadily turning up, like the volume on a wireless. Sitting at the bottom of what appeared to him to be a vertical cement concertina, Algernon touched his head gingerly and found a hot pulsing knot over his left eye, attesting to his encounter with the insect. He instinctively attempted to stand, but putting weight onto his arm made him shriek with pain. This however did not stop him from crawling fitfully through the leaves in terror of snakes, all the while howling in terror.

Peak House *3 November 1937*

LEANING OVER THE BAR, Jack pressed the lever on the soda siphon wondering why Number Two Boy kept insisting it wasn't charged. He studied the mechanism. Tonight for once he was letting Percy do all the entertaining, for the honeymoon had sickened him.

"Makee no noise," the boy insisted pointing at the cartridge.

Jack nodded, adjusting it and hoping Algy had been successful in getting an appointment with the German. *If only I hadn't been stranded on Macao with no telephone.* Suddenly soda water shot out onto the table and floor. Jack slapped the boy on the back. "Makee noise now."

Jack set the spritzer down. He remembered Violet's cold eyes on him all the way back from Macao. He'd had time to think about it all day. Jack poured another stiff drink, and threw it back. Unlike other husbands, he'd prided himself on not holding her previous sexual liaisons against her. Yet she appeared to despise him; his very touch made her recoil. A line from Lawrence kept surfacing in his mind—*"I believe in being warm hearted ... especially in love, in fucking with a warm heart."* It was how he felt too. He had hoped for love in his marriage, perhaps developing with time, but that night knew it could never happen between them. *Her heart was stone cold.* Jack put the glass down. 'Till death do us part' was a contract he'd never have signed in business. Seeing guests looking for more ice, Jack went off toward the cellar, glad to have a reason to leave. He passed the kitchen and took a sharp turn down a long unlit hall. A door opened in the dark passage ahead of him and he stepped aside, making room for whoever it was.

"I'm looking for the WC," the woman said holding out a finger with a puncture. In the other hand she held a long-stemmed rose. When she looked up her glossy red lips parted in surprise.

He felt a shock in his gut just from her voice and his gaze went from her lips down, following the plunge of the décolleté where her breasts arched out over the tight curve of fabric in total disbelief. *She was alive, and standing in front of him!* His tiger was clipped there, and seeing it he felt a pang of remorse.

"You told me to keep it until we met," she said fingering it.

"Ana ... I've, I've had people looking for you ... *everywhere.*" he said, confused. "I waited ... all these months ..." *How could he tell her he'd gone and made the biggest mistake of his life?* "Where were you, for God's sake?"

She looked away.

Jack turned her chin but she resisted, then suddenly with an anguished sob her arms went around him and she hid her face against his chest. He looked down, felt her trembling against him, and the breath caught in his throat; she was like a lost child. He enclosed her in his arms, holding her to him, stroking her hair to calm her, but was aware of a million nerve endings under his skin coming to life. With every moment too, his regret grew, bruising him with pain. When her tears subsided, he whispered she was safe with him. At that, Ana looked up slowly with strangely frightened eyes. "What are you afraid of?" he murmured, then leaned over and kissed the tip of her nose. A little smile quavered on her glossy lips. He found they were soft against his, wet, and when they opened he felt a fluttering spiral of emotion. This first kiss left him breathless. The second was hot and dizzying. The third left him panting, and made him want to forget propriety, clothing, and even Peak House as they sank along the wall.

A click sounded behind them and they froze still clinging to each other. The hall light flickered—then a clattering of dishes echoed. They saw a servant pass by in the distance, then they looked back at each other, and each moment longer that their eyes held, the tenderness between them grew until it hurt. He'd never met such a mysterious, emotional lover; a woman made for loving. He stroked her face, kissed her temple, the corner of her eye, mesmerized—holding back. But as his gaze moved down to her now swollen lips, and the tip of her tongue that was barely visible he leaned in with a groan kissing deeply … It was all he could do not to go further and finally he stopped, clasped her hands in his, his breath ragged. He knew this woman could satisfy him; meet all his urges, tame him. "Ana," he said, aching for her. "I—."

"*Jack*," she interrupted, voice tremulous. She was looking at his hand—the gold band he'd put on yesterday. "You're *married?*" A long shadow passed over them and they both turned to look down the hall.

Albert Chiswick's large body filled the door frame. "Indeed he is," the voice said.

Jack turned to Ana, ignoring Albert. "Wait. When can I see you again?"

Ana backed away.

He forced her to look at him, his hand catching hers, just as the sound of staccato heels echoed in the kitchen hallway, approaching.

"Jack? *Jack Morgan*!" The voice was like shattering glass.

Ana broke free from his grasp, and ran in the opposite direction while Jack turned slowly and leveled a cold gaze at his wife, a stranger to him now.

"Just as I expected. No restraint!"

Jack pushed past Albert, and followed his wife, "Violet, dear. Are you jealous? Perhaps then you'll return my affections *this* evening …" He took her arm with violence, and made her look at him, whispering so only she could hear. *"Or will you be with your other man? The true father of your child?"*

Violet struggled and, pulling free, ran all the way from the back hall to the large dining room which had been cleared for the dancing. At the doorway, she tripped, nearly falling, and catching herself against the wall, picked up the dinner bell, sounding it madly. The music stopped. Everyone stopped. Violet Summerhays, missing a shoe, hair tumbling out on one side, announced with a raw surge of emotion, "Dinner! Dinner is served!"

As it wasn't a dinner party, guests were confused and stared openly. Violet stood flushed, gasping for breath, and was quietly removed by her amah, who had come from the kitchen when the bell rang. Guests were ushered back to the dance floor and the music began again, but people knew they'd borne witness to something deliciously scandalous at the home of the preeminent Percival Summerhays.

Peak House *3 November 1937*

RUNNING BLINDLY PAST GUESTS out into the back hallway, Ana was caught by a heavy hand.

"So, Miss *Worthing*—is *that* who you are now?"

Albert Chiswick was glaring down at her, his small eyes glittering. "You think you can fool all of them and Morgan, too? And what about me?" He shook her. "You think you can disgrace me like you did, then laugh about it?"

"I didn't mean to," Ana cried, wrenching herself away, stumbling through a dark sitting room, afraid to turn her back to him.

He followed, pointing his finger at her as he spoke. "All my life people did that to me … *humiliating me!* You thought that amusing, his dumping night soil on me? You're a cruel slut."

She backed up against French doors and found them unlocked. Outside, the ground was soft under her heels and she hurried through the garden sinking while looking back into the darkness to see if he was following. She rounded an orangery and discovering a gazebo, tried to hide behind it, and tripped, falling to the ground. She lay silent, listening.

Somewhere there was the crack of a twig, the brush of shoes over stone. Ana's eyes opened wide, as she lay frozen where she had fallen. A few moments passed, then suddenly the footsteps were right there. She looked up, wanted to scream; Albert held a gnarled stick raised over his head. She didn't cry out, instead raised her hands to ward off the blows. *But they didn't come.* Albert lowered the stick and laughed.

"Neither you, nor I, want a scene. You, for the whore you are, and I for knowing you. But let it be known, you won't rest easy. I'll be watching, day and night, and when there's no witness, I'll thrash you, don't you doubt it. Just remember these eyes," he said raising his finger to his face. "You will see them again." And then he kicked her once, then twice, and then when the flash of passion it aroused in him ignited, he beat her with the stick until it broke and his breath came ragged.

The Favor

13

Eastern China *4 November 1937*

AT TWILIGHT THE TRAIN slammed on its brakes, catching the dozing soldiers off guard. After a screeching halt, there was a long eerie silence and then the clop of a horse. Footsteps ran along the gravel outside the train and the order was given to disembark. Grabbing their packs, they hopped out into formation. "*Banzai, banzai, banzai!*" they all cheered.

Their excitement was short-lived for they were met by a squad of professional soldiers, almost ruffians, and the leader, a gray haired lieutenant astride a swaybacked mare, surveyed them with sharp cruel eyes. Abruptly, he hissed down at his aide, incredulous, "These are middle school children!"

"New recruits, Sir!" the man bowed, furiously apologizing. Even he was new. Yoshi and the soldiers who heard this squirmed inside while behind them the train pulled away stranding them there. They'd been awaiting their congratulatory welcoming speech. But this officer said nothing. No mention of the Emperor. No mention of the glory. Surely their general didn't approve of a man such as this. No one even shouted, "Congratulations on being called to the colors!" They waited, all three hundred and sixty, backs straight, heads still, ears listening, but the man looked right through them. Yoshi felt his fighting spirit quail as he became the boy from his village again. The clouds moved past the moon, and the black grasses flickered and whispered. Only the idly drifting Hinomaru, the flag of the rising sun, stood against the unfamiliar darkness reminding them suddenly that they were not villagers. The lieutenant spurred the animal so that it spun around and when the command came they all jumped in their skins.

"March! March to the thirty-fifth infantry! Six hours northwest!"

Then came the *banzais*, less vigorous at first, then wildly energized. In a body they turned about, and marched. Yoshi's eyes went down to the feet of the man ahead of him. *This leader is disappointed*, Yoshi thought in dismay and, like the rest of his group, wondered what their mission was and where their famous general would be waiting. He also wondered what they would eat that night.

Three hours later Yoshi shifted his pack as they took a small slope up to a bridge. It was a new Japanese bridge, for it carried the insignia of the men who built it. He felt proud as he marched over the wood slats, hearing the rush of water. Just as his lungs filled with pride and he threw back his load, he coughed. It was the same smell he'd noticed from the train—a sweet smell of rot, only now it was stronger. As they marched over the bridge, eager eyes scanning the horizon for signs of camp, Yoshi's gaze turned downward to the thick braided water that rushed below … *Hands, arms … faces.* He recoiled in shock. *Had he imagined it?*

Yoshi stared tensely at the back of the man's head in front of him. Thump-thump-thump vibrated the bridge and his very bones, and suddenly it was too late to look back as they stepped onto the gravel and vanished into the tall grasses. Training Commander had told them, "When there is fear, remember the spirit of war. What is the spirit of the bayonet? To kill. To kill. To kill." The words meshed in with the thump of the boots. Thump, thump, thump; already he felt better.

Mission flat, Caine Road *4 November 1937*

THE DOOR OPENED QUIETLY and Algy limped into the candlelight. Ana sat up on the sofa. "What happened to you?"

"Never mind that. Where are my pills?" he asked, eyes red with pain as he pushed past her to rifle through his drawers with his good hand. Ana found them and Algy shook out a handful of tablets, swallowing four. She was about to stop him when they were interrupted by the telephone.

"Don't answer," she warned. "It's Albert, I'm sure. It's been ringing all night since I got back from the party." They stared at it until it fell silent.

"Well, if it rings again, I'll give that bastard a piece of my mind." But he said this without any spirit. "Did he say anything to you at the party? He's determined to kill me, I'm sure."

Ana shrugged. She was starting to bruise but felt too ashamed to tell him and instead reached up and touched his forehead gently. "*Ohhh.* What happened to you here?"

Algy sighed, shaking the pills. "Took a short cut and fell off the blasted Peak." He spied the envelope. "Ah—what's that?"

"I came up to the party to give you this. It's important."

"Dash it all! Is *that* the cable? Duffy mentioned it."

"Yes. I had no choice but to come find you. How was I to know it was Jack's house?"

Algy scanned the note. "Good God! He'll think I've arranged this but I've been out all day!"

It was at that moment that the telephone rang again. Algy froze but Ana picked up the receiver, listening. Her eyes widened and she held it out to him. "*Jack,*" she whispered.

Algy blanched taking it. "Hullo-ello! What's that? Ah—the *cable* ... Ya–yes, I have it." He shooed Ana away in a state of panic, plugging his ear against her entreaty.

When he hung up a few minutes later, Ana returned. "Well?"

Algy flopped down in the armchair. "I lied. I said I have an appointment with the man."

"Not a lie. You *have* one tomorrow. That's what I was trying to tell you."

"Oh, good show, old girl!" he said rubbing his arm.

"Yes, but look at you." She gave him a hand mirror. The red lump over his eye was spreading, even his eyelid was ticking.

"Gosh. How am I to go like this? I'll be dashed if I can hold court on anything. Get me my ciggies, will you? Ah, there's an angel."

She handed him the pack. "A pity Jack can't go."

"Yes." Algy tapped one out and lit it. "He's got lunch with Madame Sun Yat-sen tomorrow. Or so he says!"

"You mean *THE* Sun Yat-sen?"

Algy nodded, puffing.

"Impressive. She's a Communist, you know. But they say she had a terrible row with her sisters and brother-in-law … *Chiang Kai-shek*."

"Oh, bother that. I can't see what *business* Jack has seeing *her*."

"Never mind. Have another cup of tea, then off to Bedfordshire. Fritz Heidegger will meet you at Wiseman's Café at 1:00 tomorrow. I think that's plenty of time for you to recuperate and make the sale. Here, take the letter and study it. His figures are—"

"Recuperate? I can hardly move without wincing, and I look like I've been in a barroom brawl."

She brought him ice wrapped in a cloth and pressed it to his forehead. "There you are. The swelling will come down." She turned out the lights. "Try to sleep." Algy abruptly sat up and reached for the whisky bottle. Ana shook her head. He was hopeless in this state and, pouring him a shot, knew she'd have to pitch in and help him tomorrow.

An hour later he was snoring peacefully when Ana took the ledgers and spread them out on the desk. She was impressed with his neatness, his clever notations, and—*forgeries*. She made a strong pot of Lapsang tea, then sat down with pencil, paper, and abacus and was startled to discover Jack owned an imaginary rubber plantation.

She shook her head wryly—*What a man.* Though she didn't know the ins and outs, by dawn she had quite a good understanding of the affair and had made her own calculations of losses and potential profits. One thing she was sure of—they mustn't sell even one of the ships. She'd have liked to have heard Jack's reasons, but imagined his payment on them was coming due, and he needed a stopgap to cover the expense. Flipping through the pages she saw that if he could hold out a little longer, he could realize profits from one more Eastern tour.

She got up and, as she stood by the window, her gaze was drawn up toward the Peak. It rose high up in verdant darkness and mists, all lights out. Ana closed the shutters and slept for a few hours, waking in time to get ready. She dressed quietly then went to stand before Algy, who was groaning on the bed. "I'm going out now," she said staring down at him. "Are you coming?" He murmured something unintelligible and Ana picked up a little flask by his bed—*Laudanum.* "You're a very big fool," she whispered, then gave him a kiss on the cheek.

Peak House *4 November 1937*

THE DAY AFTER THE scandalous party, Jack found Violet strangely ebullient when she and Percival came up to join him at the new Rolls Royce. "You drive," she said handing him the keys as if nothing had happened, then she and her father got in the back.

"Roll up the windows," Percy exclaimed. "There's sure to be a draft!"

Jack complied, then glancing at his watch imagined Algy was leaving now to meet the German. *I should be going, not Algy!* Jack was nearly sick over it, but Percy would have been suspicious if he'd skipped out on Madame Sun. He sighed. The engine started nicely and he headed out the long driveway as fa-wong boy opened the big gates onto Old Peak Road. The thought of losing one ship below cost irked Jack so much that he felt himself pressing down the accelerator hard. Percy's wedding present, the Rolls, was another foolhardy expenditure, but it was a magnificent beast and purred with power. As they glided along the top of Victoria Peak toward Magazine Gap Road, the world sparkled far below, green conical hills rising up out of the sea.

"Well, my children," Percy said after he finished pointing out the veneered interior of the Rolls. "This is a rare opportunity for you to meet the great lady herself. She was married to China's first president, Sun Yat-sen. Did you know that, dear?"

Violet shrugged. "Does she speak English? I've heard she's the ugly Soong. Her sister, May-Ling, was on the cover of *Time* Magazine. Quite the fashion plate."

"Madame Sun Yat-sen ugly?" Jack scoffed over his shoulder. "*Hardly*. I heard she attended school in Alabama and has a charming southern accent too, I believe."

"And," Percival stated, "she's well versed in politics. Her husband died in '25 trying to unify the Communists and Nationalists against outside imperialists. A rather capable woman, I'd say. Just yesterday at the barber's, I told that annoying Magistrate, 'Mark my words, if the Japs don't take over China, Madame Sun will!'"

"Imagine that," Violet said caustically. "Giving the Japs encouragement!"

"Darling, that Jap devil is as dumb as a Buick! But when I paid him with a bottle of whisky last Christmas, now *that* he understood!"

"I wouldn't be surprised if he has a Ph.D., Father, and that *you're* the foolish one. And as far as Madame Sun Yat-sen goes, I doubt this is a social call for her." She caught Jack's eye in the rearview mirror and gave him a pointed look. "Everyone *wants* something from you, Father. Wise up. I imagine she'll have you around her finger. Every one of those crafty Soong sisters married well. She got herself a president, her sister got Chiang Kai-shek, and the eldest got China's head of finance! Now that's an amazing bit of something, I'd say."

Percy shrugged. "Madame Sun certainly can't be pleased with the way her brother-in-law's running the Kwomintang. That was Sun Yat-sen's baby."

A half hour later the Rolls churned over the gravel turn into the Repulse Bay Hotel driveway. Madame Sun agreeing to come for lunch hadn't struck Jack as a social function either, and as they walked up the front steps, he noted the governor's official car parked outside, bearing the Hong Kong flag. "A little lunch, eh?" he smirked at his father-in-law as they brushed shoulders at the doorway. Percival laughed. Lately there had been widespread rumors in Hong Kong that Chiang Kai-shek's banker was in Hong Kong, printing up millions of Chinese Fa-Pi dollars for arms against the Communists, and was then shipping them back to Kwomintang headquarters in Chungking. But only hard currency could buy arms, and the loads of Fa-Pi only bought Chiang vegetables. Jack was intrigued, wondering if her meeting was connected to this. Madame Sun had been in hiding for years, watching her dead husband's work toward unification disgraced by her greedy siblings and brother-in-law, Chiang Kai-shek. The fact she'd show her face here at all was amazing.

There was a muted hubbub inside the hotel, and people who weren't invited craned their necks as far as politeness allowed. Violet suddenly perked up as she strolled across the lobby, nodding smartly to acquaintances at other tables. Sir Geoffrey Northcote, not a popular appointment in the Crown Colony, was already seated with a few couples and several taipans in the best alcove table, which had a fantastic sea view. Everyone stood up and made their introductions. Madame Sun moved to sit down opposite Jack, her back to the window, but he got a good look at her, and found her captivating. Her solemn eyes looked full of understanding, while her lips were round and petulant. It was a fascinating contradiction—and she was no pushover. Couldn't be. Madame was a feminist and the founder of the China League for Civil Rights.

There was the usual small talk over lunch, the weather, the rapidly improving local economy and tennis. Then, as they were finishing lunch, rather innocently someone mentioned high inflation in China. It was all the introduction she needed. From then on the wives present remained silent, too polite to excuse themselves, and sat eyes downcast, scandalized by a woman speaking politics.

"Come now," Madame Sun goaded, after a particularly quarrelsome exchange. "As prominent businessmen here in Hong Kong, you all must understand the need for a strong and united China."

"My point exactly," the governor said, looking about in apparent dismay at the abrupt silence of the other guests. "Ever since my arrival in Hong Kong I've felt the population here has no fear of the Japanese. That worries me greatly."

As the plates were carried away, Jack lit a cigar, weighing her attributes with admiration. He'd watched her movements and expressions carefully, listened to what she'd said to the other men—what she omitted, and how it fit with what he already knew. She was attractive but certainly didn't play that card—and he found that refreshing.

"There's not only a lack of fear," Madame Sun continued, "the American mercenaries, I believe, are working with the Japanese, who've made phenomenal promises of cash rewards when China can be carved up. Every day, arms are being shipped regardless of the dangers, with an eye to profits. You need only read the papers here; arms seizures are a regular occurrence."

Jack might have been the only American but he had no illusions about China. "Madame, if I may say so, you are mistaken if you believe it is only the Americans that are profiting from the war. You need only look to—," here he paused, wanting to say *her own family*, knowing that her brother-in-law Chiang Kai-shek was the prime mercenary, but instead said, "your Nationalist party to see where they're obtaining their ill-gotten funds. Just look at the black markets. Someone in China's becoming very rich on foreign aid that doesn't even reach your people."

It was a sore spot, but Madame wasn't put off. "I know nothing of the Kwomintang Nationalists. What I do know is that China's being torn apart; there's greed, of course, and self-interest, but I think the majority of the Chinese people understand a united China benefits everyone. Any Chinese citizen publicly found to be aiding the Japanese will suffer the wrath of the Communists. The Japanese are insidious in their corruption and will stop at nothing. You may think they'll be content with Canton, but they'll move further south very soon. If the residents in Hong Kong wait, they'll see firsthand what occupation under Japanese forces means."

"It's all well and good to have your—convictions," Percival gave a cough. "But dear lady, all *WE* can do is wait. I do think the Communists are earnest in their goals, but it's hard from a distance to know whom to believe. We do our part as Royal subjects; any trade of arms on our coastal waters is banned. You must understand, the Japanese fought against the Russians for us, and defeated them. It's very difficult to feel animosity toward them." Percival turned his head to scan a dessert cart. "That said, I spy a lovely pudding over there. Why not indulge ourselves," he said as he leaned toward the sommelier with a gesture for more drinks.

"Sir, if I may," she said, "the greatest harm coming to China is this type of attitude. The Communists and the Kwomintang Nationalists are divided in this civil war—and worse, with Japan playing both sides against one another. With a passive view like yours, this'll continue, and further divisive corruption won't be halted. It's the Japanese intent to make us fall. The world is still recovering from the Depression, and as I've returned from Berlin, I can speak with certitude; Germany, too, is rife with moral corruption. These are fertile grounds for widespread conflict. I've only come out today to pass on this information. For our part, all collaboration with the Japanese must be stopped."

The sommelier popped the cork at this moment, and the entire group stiffened at the shot. Northcote held up his glass. "I toast this round to the wise lady's words. Coming from my post in Africa I can tell you Hong Kong has a sheltered worldview. I don't represent a popular stance, but I hope to change your minds."

"Come now. What is it you're both hinting at?" the taipan of Swire said, leaning forward. "You expect a worldwide war?"

Northcote cleared his throat and sat back. "I'm saying Germany has strong ties to the Japanese. They're selling them arms, and selling to the Nationalists as well, with the proviso the guns not be used against the Japs, but only the Communists. Japan is the new imperialist power here and by driving a wedge between the warring factions they feel they can take all of China. What Madame Sun is saying is absolutely right. Sitting pretty, we stand a very good chance of being attacked. As governor, my prime responsibility is to the people here. Now, they may not want to listen to sense, I know the profits are tempting, but—" He shook his head.

"What are you suggesting?" one of the old great shipping tycoons finally erupted. "We aren't exporting weapons. We're minding our business, and it's not easy in these times!"

"Basil," he frowned, "I'm only here on my agenda. I need the people to rally behind me! I called you here because I thought you'd listen to sense and pass it on, as leaders of the community—the ladies too," he said, eyeing them. "Like it or not, I'm going to introduce mandatory conscription, and we'll have to have a plan to evacuate our women and children if things get worse. Just read the papers, the *New China Daily*, and you'll get a feel for what's coming from Tokyo."

There was a general murmur of disapproval around the table. Madame Sun spoke up, "I've only one thing to add. With Hitler arming himself to the teeth, Europe is in danger, and the Japanese know this. Who'll protect you when the Japanese time their expansionism with Hitler's own maneuvers? This is a global concern! You can no longer think of the Communists as your enemies."

"You may say so," one of the taipans interrupted, "but all our recent history says they are." All eyes looked down in discomfort.

"See here. I'm not fooled. The *New China Daily* is really Chou En-Lai's baby in disguise. We all know the Bolshie's have his ear," Basil said. "It's pure Communist propaganda."

"Yes, Basil," Jack said, attempting to temper him. "But Madame here is trying to say even the Nationalists are seeing the wisdom and starting to work again with the Communists against Japan—they're funding the newspaper as a goodwill gesture. She's asking you to consider this."

"They're fools and they'll live to regret it," Swire's man said. "Chou En-Lai's taking the route of *rapid reform* like in Russia. It's *dangerous. Revolutionary.* Heads *will* roll. And when they do, it will be as unstoppable as the French Revolution. Mark my words, it'll be bloody."

Madame Sun looked at Northcote then got up from the table. All of the men stood up and made their farewells, but when Madame shook Jack's hand she discreetly said something to him in Chinese so no one could hear.

After she departed with her bodyguard, Northcote made it very clear he was disappointed. But his vision of war with Japan had already marked him as "unfriendly to business" in the Colony and only made him appear ridiculous to everyone at the table. He sat down again gloomily, beseeching the industrialists and shipping taipans a few minutes further, but his energy had drained to the point that he could only stare from one face to the next, unable to bridge the gap of their "willful ignorance." But unlike his mind, theirs gravitated toward profit in their relentless battle for survival of the fittest. Maybe it was myopic, as he claimed, but they were *businessmen,* after all. Even Jack didn't want to fully embrace what the governor had said, but unlike those at the table, he realized that in the interest of profit, he must, going forward, include world war in his plans.

When the governor headed off for his next appointment, those who remained showed their disapproval, grumbling in low tones. Certainly, talk of Hitler had sobered everyone and caused the luncheon to end on a sour note. Percival led his daughter outside in silence, and the mood during the ride home was decidedly dampened until Violet spoke up.

"Goodness, all through tiffin I was hoping Northcote would put a sock in it and let me have a dip in the water. I even wore my swimming suit under this!"

"He's the governor, Violet," Percy snapped, "and I'll not have you speaking like that!"

"Father. Don't be so dull. No one likes him. Which reminds me, Marjorie has her beach party tomorrow. What do you think, Jack? If the weather is nice, let's make a day of it?"

He hadn't been to the beach for a long time, and instead of Violet, he thought of Ana. He could imagine her on the beach running ahead of him, turning, the sun reflecting off her sparkling wet skin, her eyes, and red lips, laughing.

"Jack! Why don't you answer me?"

"I think, Violet," Percival said, "that meeting such an important lady should have inspired thoughts other than playing on the beach. Madame Sun thinks there will be a war."

Jack looked in the rearview mirror at them in the back seat, "There *is* a war. *Already.*"

"Good Heavens," Violet said, "he's just an alarmist, and we all know these periodic 'flaps' fizzle out to nothing. Jack, what did that awful lady tell you? I see you made an impression on her siding against all of us."

"Hardly. She told me I was, 'as wise as a great fool.' Normally it's a compliment but in this case ..." He laughed. What he hadn't said was that Madame Sun had also invited him to call on her at her residence at his convenience.

"Yes, but I thought I heard her speak to you in Chinese," Violet demanded, pouting. "How could she know you'd understand?"

"How, indeed."

Percy laughed, "I wish I spoke the lingo."

"I never heard such rubbish, Father," Violet sneered. "And that won't help! According to Madame, better study Japanese!"

The Other Man

14

Hong Kong Hotel *4 November 1937*

THE GENTLEMAN AT TABLE seven happened to turn when the maître d' pointed him out to her. Catching his eye, she flashed a smile.

"Mrs. Violet Morgan? Percival *Summerhays's* daughter?" he asked, almost suspicious, a sardonic twist to his sensuous lips. "It is indeed an honor. Fritz Heidegger." Bowing stiffly he took her hand in his, "I didn't expect such a beauty." He was tanned and athletic in his bespoke suit.

Ana laughed, embarrassed by the lingering gaze, and noted ladies at other tables eyeing him appreciatively. Taking her seat beside him on the curved sofa, she removed her gloves, thankful she'd remembered to slip a cheap band on her finger.

"I look like an old man, ya?" he gestured to his sun-bleached hair, taking out a Gitane cigarette, offering her one. "The sea, as Conrad says, she is a ravishing mistress. But I am only sirty-sree … and most eligible."

She saw him glance at her ring, but the word husband never touched his lips. The rest of the conversation was in German, Fritz doing most of the talking. He spoke with eloquence and passion about Darwinism, the Fauves, and Oscar Wilde, and Ana got the distinct feeling he didn't have much opportunity to converse while on shipboard. As he theorized, she wondered what a well-read dandy could want roaming the seas managing a tough crew, storms, and pirates. But there was nothing false about him—*everything was false.* One knew exactly where one stood with a man like this.

"And now, my deah," he said, in English, "I hope you don't mind my familiarity. I make mistakes in English, you must correct me. But I sink it the language of love."

"Do you!" She laughed, and he offered her another Gitane, lighting it for her.

"You don't agree? For me—vhen I don't know exactly what I am saying, I feel—" He looked up as if in thought. "Yes, I feel free. In German I am restricted, proper. In anosah tongue it's easy to speak one's mind, you agree?"

Ana nodded, "You're naughty in English, certainly," and removed his hand, which had come to rest over hers. When he became excited he lost focus and his accent suffered, becoming heavier, but this flaw charmed her. She tried not to smile.

"Please call me Fritz," he said, "and may I—*Violet*?"

"Really, if it pleases you to speak English with me, you may. But don't imagine it will get you anywhere."

"Ah, then tell me, why is it that you come to me?"

"I come to you with a business proposition."

"But vhy me?" he asked, amused, eyeing her lips and dress as she spoke.

"I have a proposal. You, being German and, as rumor has it, in the position to buy, I thought I should come to you first. But I need a promise of utmost discretion."

He laughed, "I don't belief you. But lies coming from a lady as beautiful as you are magic to my ears."

"Lies?" Ana reddened. "I am the heiress of a large shipping concern, as you well know. I've recently come into—how shall I say—*hard times*, and need to dispose of a few vessels without anyone in Hong Kong knowing. I have a reputation to maintain."

"Is that so?" Fritz sat back, frowned, and then looked at her. "But I'm not in Hong Kong to buy ships, as rumor has it. And I am leafing for Manila, tomorrow, at noon. I have a problem vis my local kontekt who walked out on my deal. I'm not buying, I'm *selling*."

This was a crushing blow, and she looked down, feeling her eyes welling. *Why hadn't Jack made his own sale? Why leave it to poor Algy?*

"Tch, tch, tch, I didn't realize things were so bad," he said. "I know Percy Summerhays. I don't *know* Mr. Morgan. How badly does he need this?"

"I'm ashamed to beg. Even a loan perhaps?"

"No loans on ships these days, my deah. But let me think." His eyes narrowed as he studied her. "Are you discreet? This is a small place, yah? Trusting anyone here vis my kind of deal is a rhisk."

"Why do you think I came to you as opposed to someone from this town?"

He sighed and tapped a fresh Gitane on the tablecloth. "Ah, sis town—sa English," he said, disparaging. "Zey do all seir dirty work heah. Evangelizing, no? Sa drug trade ... They put sa squeeze on Germany. You see, they have it down to an art form, clean noses, clean hands at home. But take a look—sese coolies are second-class citizens in seir own country."

"Human rights, Fritz?"

He laughed. "Darlink, I'm here to ride a wave of good fortune." He took his time lighting his cigarette and strangely enough, Ana felt completely at ease in his company, watching him, letting him relax into a deeper level of confidence with her.

"The laws in sese colonies are in flux, sa political climate ... it does not go deep. What I mean is tsut sings go on heah as usual, but on sa surface, it has to look pukkah, ya?"

Ana took up her glass of wine, and traced the silk whorls on the tablecloth with her finger before she spoke, "I like risk."

When she sealed her utterance with a mischievous look, he leaned back in his seat, surveying the restaurant, "Zo! Perhaps I *can* help. But let us move to a more private location." All around the tables were filling with European businessmen taking their tiffin, and the atmosphere of the room was convivial with talk and deal making. She saw him notice how gentlemen watched her with interest from other tables. Fritz frowned, then made a slight gesture to the elevator.

"No, I won't go to your room," she said quietly. "But there is a little *dim sum* place on Stanley Street. Only Chinese merchants eat there—we'd be completely ignored—a noisy sort of privacy. I think it best, considering … I'm married."

He smiled benignly, glancing rather obviously at her ring. "As you vish."

Mission flat, Caine Road *4 November 1937*

Algy was waiting when she walked in the door several hours later. "Where've you been? Put me out of my misery. Did you do it?"

"What do you think?"

"Think? I woke up at half one and ran out of the building in a state of shock. I looked for him in the restaurant, and the front desk. Finally the maître d' was kind enough to tell me that the '*German couple*' had left!"

Ana laughed, removing her gloves, and her mock wedding band flew to the floor, making a ping. "So much for the marriage to Jack, eh?"

His jaw dropped. "What are you saying?" He leaned over and picked it up. "A curtain ring?"

"I had to complete the picture, didn't I?" She put it back on her finger, laughing and pretending to admire it.

"What picture? By Jove, you didn't!"

"I did, and your head will spin when I give you details!" She glanced at the little flask on the table top. "You can blame it all on that laudanum, you know."

"But the *numbers*, Jack's *numbers*. You used those as a guideline? You can't have gone *too* far below his price, have you?"

"I didn't *sell* him anything. Fritz isn't buying. It was only a rumor."

"Then what are these details?"

"We have an agreement." Ana pulled out a piece of paper. "His original partner here developed cold feet and if Jack will step in, and if Fritz approves of Jack, they sail at noon to Manila, two days from now."

Algy snatched it and reading down the page, looked up at her from the sofa. "But you've no right to make a contract. And look! It's signed *Mrs. Violet Morgan?* That makes it *invalid*."

"It's to your benefit to honor it. Besides, I believe it's a good copy of her signature. You had one sample of it here, in your paperwork." She shrugged, "I approximated as best I could."

Algy stared at her, stupefied.

She marched over to him, slamming her hand down on the paper, making him jump. "I've saved your lives with this! How is it that you don't see? Jack won't have to sell even *one* ship! I've brought him business that'll solve all his cash flow problems. He'll have far more in Mex than he could ever have hoped for from his own proposal, which was pretty foolish if you ask me."

"Foolish? It was legal! What do I say when he calls?"

"Well, you could tear this up, and tell him the truth. Fritz is an arms dealer, looking for a local trader to ply his goods into the China seas under a local company flag, and that you told him to shove off. And while you're at it, ask if he has any other plans."

Algy picked up his badminton racquet with his good hand and heaved a big sigh. "He doesn't have a month left to swing things along …"

"Well, I can't solve *all* his problems. He does seem to have a knack at getting into the strangest compromises. Like his marriage," she said. "Why does a man like that marry a woman he has no intention of loving? His behavior's appalling." Ana sank down into a settee. "Oh God, had I known what he was like I never—"

Algy had a peculiar look on his face, "Would have—*what*?"

"Nothing."

"Nothing? Surely, you don't mean—?"

"Albert and Violet *caught us.*"

Algy struggled to his feet in shock.

"*Kissing!* Kissing, that's all."

"Bad enough!"

"There's something else I should tell you."

"Not sure I want to know."

"Fritz asked me to travel with him, no strings attached."

"How's that? You don't even know the man! Surely you—"

"I hardly know Jack."

"That's not fair! You can't leave me just because of *him*. Just say the word and I'll give him the bum's rush into the harbor!"

"Jack?" Ana smiled, smoothing her dress out. "Fritz has none of the domestic problems that seem to define Jack's life. I need to get away for my own sanity."

"So that's what this is about. Give me my bottle. I want to sleep this off and wake up a month from now."

"Laudanum? You better not. When Jack calls, you'll need to think clearly."

"I'm sick of Jack. You see what's happened to my life? It's his fault. And don't you make a hasty decision. Give it a day."

"No."

"But why leave town? You've got me here."

She toyed with the diamond tiger, then removed it. He'd pleaded for her to wait—*yet he'd gone on and married.* "Fritz is a nice man," she said. "He makes me laugh."

"You're in love with Jack, aren't you?"

"I should give this back."

Algy threw down his racquet in disgust. "Damn it all. Keep it for now."

There was a sudden sound of a door and footsteps coming up the hall—too early for the priests to be returning. They looked at each other. When the knock came, Algy gestured for her to hide in the kitchen, then unlocked the door. A bearer handed him a giant bouquet of long-stemmed roses and a note. "This is an invitation for *Violet* Morgan." Ana hurried in and attempted to snatch the note away but he held it out of reach. "Dinner at eight?" Algy scoffed, then released it to her eager hands.

Peak House *4 November 1937*

JACK WAS STILL TALKING with Percy about their lunch with Madame Sun when Violet edged into the library, trailing her fingers along the back of the Chesterfield sofa where he sat. *How beastly he'd behaved toward her. Kissing Algernon's sister, then flirting openly with that old Madame Sun. All because of Peebles!* She came around and sat opposite him. "Jaa-aack … I don't see why you're too busy to stay for tea today. The Hamiltons will be here, and Connie's just had a new baby!" Jack looked away.

Percy was sitting in the comfortable armchair with a drink in his hand. "You wouldn't catch me at tea with the Hamiltons if I was feeling well. I feel it here," he said, holding his chest.

"What do you think, Percy?" Jack continued as if she'd never entered the room. "Will Northcote get Swire and the others on board?"

"Father," she frowned. "If only you'd chew your food! Rose has the ideal pills for indigestion. Shall I get them?"

"Why Northcote called on us is clear," Percival said reaching for his cigar. "He wants our help with his mandatory conscription and evacuation. But dash it! The man's not lived in the Far East! We know the Japs'll never come this far south; it's different in Europe with Hitler."

"It's *all* nonsense," Violet declared. "Besides, the Japanese wouldn't tolerate the food shortages and water rationing with the ridiculous numbers of refugees here."

Jack grimaced. "Hamilton's probably coming because he caught wind we saw Northcote at tiffin."

"Nonsense," Violet interjected. "I told you they came to show off the baby! Jack and I should try to have a little one of our own, too. What do you think, Jack?" She hadn't meant to say that, but was too late now.

"What?" Percy looked up, confused. "I thought you *were* expecting? We rushed your wedding and—?"

She thought quickly, "False alarm, Poppa! But we mean to have the real thing soon. Don't we, Jack?"

"Real thing?" He looked at her with undisguised anger, while Percy flushed. At that moment, however, the house boy came in announcing guests were arriving. Jack excused himself abruptly, saying he had work at the office, but he wasn't quick enough to escape Violet. She met him in his changing room.

"What are you doing?" he demanded. "This is my private room."

Violet stood before him, then kicking the door shut, undid her blouse. "I bought this new brassiere the other day. Do you like it?"

"Violet, you have guests arriving," he said, looking away to his closet of neatly pressed white shirts, his expression stony.

"Ah, not six months ago you would pant all over me for an opportunity." When he said nothing she added, "So, is it Algy's *sister* that's come between us?" She looked at her lacquered nails. "I'd tell Papa if I thought you were serious about her. Are you? But then how can you be—you've only just met."

Jack said nothing, but removed a clean suit and shirt. She caressed his shoulder, and he flinched. "What is it you said down there about a 'false alarm'?" he asked in a measured tone.

Violet shrugged, amused.

"I hope that's not true," he warned.

"And why is that?"

"Goddamnit." He spun to face her. "I married you because of it!"

"Really? But, better it be yours, no?"

"What's come over you?" he demanded furiously.

Violet looked at him, indifferent.

"You saw Percy's face down there," he said watching her carefully. "He was as shocked as I am." His voice dropped, "*Was* it Peebles?"

She laughed. "You have your secrets; I have mine." She slid out of her top and let the blouse fall off her finger. He just stared coldly. Violet felt her anger growing and undid her skirt. It dropped. She had no panties on and the look of shock on his face pleased her.

Jack threw a robe at her in disgust.

"You Jack, modest?" When he didn't respond, she furrowed her brow. "And how might one prevail upon you to—?"

"I've *kept* my promise to *your* father to marry you," he said cutting her off. "That's all I have to say on the matter." He grabbed a fresh change of clothes and headed to his bedroom. Violet followed, the robe drifting open; she liked the feeling of air on bare skin. "Weeeeellll. That explains it," she said, and leaned at his door. "You're jealous of Peebles. How childish, but sweet."

"Good God," he said, turning to look. "Put on your clothes. There are servants around." Jack shut her out but after a few minutes she slipped in undetected and watched him change through the carved Chinese screen. She was surprised how easy it was to toy with his emotions, but then bitterly recalled his impassioned embrace with the girl.

Back in her room, Rose set out a frock for her to wear at tea. "Rose," Violet asked. "What do you think? Jack and that woman. Could she be a lover from Shanghai? It didn't seem like *strangers* kissing."

"Him not taidza. Master makee laughee inside him mouth. You folo gir'! He catchee hab-time! Him play-play, pulim! What for? Wifu no do bed-business Macao side, eh!"

"I doubt he's laughing to himself as you say. Besides, you said holding back the bed-thing was *smart*. That it makes them want it more."

"*Hai-yah!* For un marry gir'! You *WIFU* now! Plopelty b'long man, eh? Triple Goddess!"

China Coast Navigation & Co. *4 November 1937*

There was a tentative knock on his office door and Jack looked up and saw Algy standing, arm in a sling. "Bloody hell. What's that on your forehead?"

"I had an *incident* …" he said, indignant.

"Ah, the old banana peel?"

"That's gratitude."

Jack suddenly sat up. "Good God! You saw the *German*—like that?"

"I see you've a deep interest my well-being," Algy said, easing himself down in a chair. "I've sprained my blasted arm too!"

Jack went to shut the door. "So? Did he agree?"

"First of all, your information on Fritz was wrong. He wasn't in town buying."

"What?"

"No. *Not* buying."

"Oh." Jack picked up his tennis racquet and plopped down in the wing chair, deflated.

"But he's willing to do a deal."

"Like what?" Jack asked leaning back, irritated. "A loan?"

"Noooo …"

"I need a drink," Jack groaned. "Let's go to Rosie's. We can talk there."

Out on the noisy praya along Connaught Road, Algy continued, "Actually Fritz has German arms manufactured in Hamburg for export. The Chinese don't have the solid coin to pay for it, so there's an intermediary and …"

"Surely, you're joking."

"You sent me to him, remember?"

"Yes, but—you didn't agree to anything, did you?" he asked squinting in the light.

Algy handed Jack the paper as a queue of dock workers bumped past carrying heavy sacks of millet on their backs.

"But—! Who signed this? You?" Jack waved the paper at him.

"That's not important. We can tear it up, or deny Violet ever saw the man."

"*Violet? She* was *there*?"

"No, no, no. Never mind. Let go of my arm. You can turn it down. It's unimportant." Algy tried to snatch the paper back.

"What the bollocks were you thinking?" Jack demanded holding it at arm's length, while several lorries went by loaded with rattling crates. They walked up along the pier's edge then headed inland.

"Oh, bosh. If you get caught, you'd only be reprimanded, that's all."

"Are you an idiot? You know this intermediary?" he lowered his voice. "I'm sure it's the Japs. And Fritz is probably in with one of these triads dealing for the Kwomintang with Jap money. I am willing to bet anything that there's a clause that the weapons are only for the civil war against the Communists."

"I don't know why you're so overstimulated. It's only a minor offense. Who cares who shoots whom?"

"Because Algy, this deal would put us between three warring camps; anyone could back out, and kill us. Don't you see that?" They paused by road works where a chain of Hakka women in black moved dirt out of a deep pit, hoisting it up in bamboo baskets.

"All I see is you're hurling abuse at me again," Algy said whisking away the paper. He was balling it up to throw it over when Jack grabbed his wrist in a pinion grasp that made Algy cry out loud, "My arm, my arm!!!"

Coolies near them laughed, pointing. "*Chee-sing gweilo!*"

"I'll give them '*chee-sing*', Jack said, taking the paper. "I need to think this over; after all, you didn't sell my ships. And no one will give loans anymore. I might have to take it."

"Oh! So—now I'm not such an idiot, am I? Fine. The ship leaves day after tomorrow. If you get on well with him, you need to be off to Manila to square the rest of the deal with another party. There, now it's all in your court and I wash my hands of it. Go away, and boil your head, for all I care."

Jack gave him a withering look. "I want the details."

"There's nothing more to say, though there is a third component in Shanghai," Algy added as they walked up toward Wellington street, the dirty cement hot underfoot.

"Where's Ana?" Jack asked abruptly.

"Ah, you refer to my *sister*. Moving to Germany."

"Germany?" Jack stopped still. It was the last thing he'd expected to hear.

Algy darted between two vehicles, but it took Jack only seconds to stalk across the road and restrain him. "You little worm. Germany's at war. What aren't you telling me?"

"I–I think she's found a man—a *friend*."

He studied Algy's face. They were standing outside Rosie's but Jack barred Algy's way in. "That's not possible."

"It is, actually."

"Don't lie."

"Not a lie." He pulled his arm free. "But, I don't see that it impacts you in any way." He pushed on the door to the pub, edging his way in. Servicemen were drinking beers and arguing, a few others had Rosie's pretty China girls in their arms on the dance floor. The mambo was loud.

"She's probably upset with me," Jack muttered, as they bumped past a serviceman molding a taxi dancer to his body. She was wiggling an erect finger on his shoulder much to the amusement of those watching.

"Everything is always about you," Algy grumbled, as they sat down at a table sticky from beer.

They ordered gin and bitters, and Jack sat quietly, remembering Ana and their wet kisses; desire pulled at his loins. "Where can I find her?"

"What? Oh." Algy shrugged. "She knows Fritz. I saw them together." He looked about disinterestedly. "They're both Germans after all. Maybe they went to school together."

"What? Are you telling me Ana set this up? But why?"

"I—she did it as a favor for you. And don't look at me like that."

"A favor? An *illegal* deal? That's no favor! And now, *suddenly*—she's *leaving*?"

"Yes. Yes, she is," Algy said smoothing an eyebrow. "And I've had about enough of this."

Jack felt dumbfounded. "But, then he's her *lover*, has been all along. It's why I couldn't find her all these months—like the detective surmised."

"Lower your voice," Algy muttered as a waitress set down their drinks tray.

Jack watched her walk off, eyes on her slim hips, then took out a cigar and pinched the end off. "So—wait!" He suddenly turned to stare at Algy. "Is this Ana's *favor* for Fritz? That's it, isn't it!"

Algy shrugged and took up his glass. "You're going a bit far, old chap. And you don't have to take the deal, you know."

Jack snorted, then looked up, rolling the smoke in his mouth then letting go a thick cloud. "I'm afraid I have to. They've thrown down the gauntlet, haven't they?"

"There's no gauntlet," Algy said. "It's all in your head."

Jack set his jaw. "We'll see." He took a long drink.

"They didn't set you up."

"We'll see."

"But Jack—*you* sent *me* to see *him*."

Jack shrugged, watching a serviceman's hand groping a taxi dancer's ass as they danced slowly past the table. Celibacy was no good for his nerves. And that was what his marriage was turning out to be. He drained the rest of his drink, then glancing around the room licked his lips nervously and said, "There's something else I need to talk about." He looked down. "It's Violet."

A Misunderstanding

15

Eastern China *4 November 1937*

He was only a few days travel out of Tokyo marching under a full moon across endless fields; already Japan was a mere fleck somewhere beyond the East China Sea. He *was* in China to kill, but he didn't even know where he was. *Somewhere in China* ... It was strange that the Chinese spelled "China" with characters meaning "center of the world." He'd always thought the center was where he lived, his town hall, then Tokyo. All this travel and thinking turned him inside out and upside down. Yoshi pushed his glasses up his nose and wondered when the fighting would begin. All he wanted was to go home.

It was well after midnight when Yoshi and his fellow recruits marched into camp. No greeting came from soldiers sitting around small fires, but a few turned their heads away from the flames to stare at the new arrivals. Instead of feeling welcome, Yoshi wanted to sink into himself, especially when he confronted the blackness in their eyes, that low cunning look of the inari—ancient shape shifter, the fox. *Could it be true? Or had the war done this to them?*

I must transfer, he thought. *I must! I'll write to uncle. Being alive in Hong Kong was better than being buried in Yasukuni.* He headed toward the nearest trees to relieve himself and stumbled off over rough-trodden grass toward a most hideous stench. At first he thought it was the latrine, that of two hundred soldiers, but after he undid his trousers and his stream of piss arched into the darkness, he noted the funny sound. *A spray of water hitting a taut surface.* Leaning forward he saw he was urinating into the open eye of a dead soldier. In fact, everywhere about him there were paralyzed forms ... but a few moved. "O-mizu! O-mizu!" came the febrile cry for water in the dim moonlight.

Yoshi ran back to the camp, forgetting to button his trousers, pointing.

The soldiers glared. "Didn't your mother teach you to put on Western pants, inakamono?"

Yoshi flushed, "I need to get water for them. Where can I get some?"

The soldiers exchanged glances. "They have cholera, I wouldn't get too close."

"But, they're Japanese!"

One soldier finally pointed to men coming uphill with buckets from the river.

Yoshi stared. "But, they told us in Tokyo to boil the water."

A hunched silhouette of a man with his back to him, turned from the fire to look at him with yellow eyes. "Beat it, ina-fu," he whispered.

Yoshi stood unmoving, frightened by his language. *Why had he called me a comfort whore?* The other men also turned their backs, resuming an eerie, silent vigil of the fire.

Yoshi turned to find his company, tumbling over himself in the rush to return, but once in their midst he noticed he still couldn't get rid of the stench in his nostrils. Yoshi ate his dinner, gulping down the rice balls with two hands wondering if the other recruits had heard the voices of the dying men. If they didn't know it that night, at dawn, they all knew. Young boys rising speechless from their new bedding could see it just a hundred meters off—*the river.* Worse than what he'd seen from the bridge … *hundreds of bodies, Chinese, Japanese, limbs, torsos, all in stages of rot, swollen purple or green, rafts of human detritus, both armies, clinging to one another as they drifted past camp. And we drank this water last night …*

"March!" The order sent a jolt through their bodies. "March. The Chinese are retreating!" They stood up packing their things, afraid to talk, and followed the experienced soldiers. Yoshi looked straight ahead, but his heart was marching south toward the British Colony.

Lyndhurst Terrace *4 November 1937*

THE CHINESE GIRLS AT Rosie's looked like the ones on packs of Ruby Queen Cigarettes—permanent curls, flushed high cheeks, and red smiling lips. Rosie's was a strictly play-play-yes, fuckee-no joint, catering to randy, rowdy British servicemen on shore leave. No one local or from their firm would come here. "Violet?" Algy asked with a smirk. "Really? Surely you're not going to blame Violet on your nasty state of affairs." Jack ignored him and ordered another round. Algy shrugged. "Well, I can't imagine why you're in a lather over *Ana's* motivations." Jack seemed already drunk to him. "Perhaps it's too much ginger on your part."

"A bit indecent of you," he snarled, but without any force.

A waitress with knock-out legs and a pearly smile set down their second round, then leaned over their table. "You wanchee suckee-suck?" she asked, lips glistening. Her gaze lingered on Jack, who declined the offer with a slow wink.

"You know what?" Algy said, as she moved off. "You're just too pigheaded to admit you *need* this deal and *owe* Ana for it."

"*Owe her*? It's really none of your business."

"Maybe, but your callous disregard of your marital status turned Ana against you."

"I don't care," Jack said, looking into his glass, seeming at a loss.

"Then why the devil did you marry? You had the job. What more could you want?"

"*It was not what I wanted, damnit!*" He slammed his fist down quietly, then whispered, "She told Percy she was pregnant."

"Bollocks! You're lying and you are drunk."

"I *am* drunk. But I *never* did it with her. *It must have been Peebles.*"

Algy's jaw dropped; then regaining his composure said, "Ah. Jack the cuckold. You told me the same lie when you were drunk at your wedding. I told you not to marry her."

"Look, you were probably right that time. But now I'm serious. There is more to it." He looked about uncomfortably. "Do you remember that little hat girl at the French milliner's?"

"Er–what?" Algy pulled at his collar. "That rather nice looking French gal?" he grimaced, sucking through his teeth. "Crippled though. Life dealt her a cruel blow, I'd say … Don't tell me, *you*—?"

"Little Nadine from Hanoi. *No—I didn't do that,*" he said with disgust. "She was a child—sixteen. *No.* It all started because I needed a special gift for Violet—but I can't make sense of it. Rose discovered a specialty milliner and gave me a swatch of fabric. They constructed a hat to match. It was such a big hit with her that I kept it up. Violet, however, kept insisting also on knowing where these mystery hats were from. The more I hid my source, the more determined she became."

"I'd have said, Tootle-pip, see you later!"

"Yes, well, Violet expected presents on every occasion so I wasn't about to reveal my secret." Jack took out his wallet and paid as a group of raucous Jack Tars, fresh off the boat, burst in the door.

Jack and Algy walked back along Stanley Street. "Do you remember, Nadine used a horrible bamboo staff like a coolie," Jack said. "A little over a year ago I bought her a lovely glass walking stick, with silver rabbits inlaid down its length. When Nadine saw it her eyes filled with tears! I don't think anyone ever gave her a present before. A month later when I returned from a trip, and stopped by to pick up the latest hat, she wasn't there. I waited, and the boss came out from behind the curtains and showed me the paper. *She'd killed herself!* When I went home, distraught over the news, Violet went into a jealous rage, accusing me of having been *lovers* with Nadine."

Algy stopped and scratched his head. "But, what's this have to do with anything?"

"I'm trying to tell you," Jack said in a low voice. "I think it was a bold-faced lie. I can't explain it, but I've been getting the feeling Violet had a hand in it."

"*Her death?* But how?"

"You see, that night I cornered her. Asked how she even knew who the girl was. I'd never talked about Nadine. She was forced to confess she'd found out where I got the hats, wormed it out of her amah. Then she'd gone down there to Queen's Road and spied us through the window, having tea and laughing."

"And?"

"And in a jealous fit she admitted she made up a rumor involving the son of the Chinese herbalist. The story gathered unexpected momentum involving his furious parents, and ended up with all the locals shouting at poor Nadine that a Chinese wouldn't take a gweilo, much less a cast-off like her! Violet told me Nadine must have thrown herself under the Peak Tram as a result."

"And you've known this for a year! Why the blazes bring it up now?" Algy flicked his cigarette butt away. "Couldn't you have run the company without taking on a ball and chain?" Jack looked miserable and Algy sighed. "Well, don't take it hard, old boy. You wouldn't be the first to marry for po-zish!"

"There's more to this Violet's not telling."

"Based on what?" Algy shrugged. "It's not like she pushed the girl off the platform." They crossed the street back over to Connaught Road and came to stand by Queen's pier.

"I can't put a finger on it," he said looking out over the dark water. "Sometimes I catch her staring very hard at absolutely nothing, totally oblivious to anything I say. I wonder that she's not right up there … There's *more* to Violet than meets the eye."

"I'll say!" Algy made an exaggerated sign of the cross saying, "Tiara, brooch, earring, earring! That's all there is to *that* mercenary."

"You're not listening."

"Oh I am. But this has only come up since Ana returned, hasn't it. You just want permission to play the field again, ditch the wife?" Algy felt he struck a chord, for Jack's jaws clenched angrily as he lit his cigar, his eyes looking away. "Jack, you were a bloody fool to marry, and now you're concocting a murder or insanity clause just to be free of the whole thing. You see how this looks, don't you?"

Jack was stubbornly silent, then erupted. "You know," he said, his voice harsh with bitterness, "I've decided, since Ana brought this deal to the table, *she* needs to be along on the trip to Manila … to see it through."

"You're pulling my leg!" Algy said, afraid for Ana. She was a delicate thing, needing protection.

"No. I want to see her and her lover Fritz together. You tell her," Jack said, furious. "I'm calling her bluff. She's setting me up. That detective was right. She couldn't have hid out here in Hong Kong all these months alone; she's had *Fritz* all along."

"Ana? But Fritz only just *got* into town."

"I won't play a fool to these women any longer. You see what they've done to me? You arrange for her to be on that ship tomorrow or no deal."

Algy stared in disbelief. "Oh. You've got it bad, don't you?" Jack turned away as if he didn't hear. "Why, you're so soppy over her you don't know if you're coming or going." Jack flung his cigar down and crossed the dark empty street. "Jack!" Jack kept on walking. "There's no way out of your marriage, old boy. You're stuck, hats, murder and all!"

Bela Vista Hotel, Macao *5 November 1937*

FAUSTO AMBLED HEAVILY DOWN the slope from the Golden Hind, wiping traces of café crème from his mustache. Passing the Café du Monde, he waved at the clientele smoking cheroots and playing cards under the awnings who called him to his usual seat. He tipped his hat. "Not today, I have business." He was thinking of the mysterious cable he'd received the night before. *Could that German tart really be hiding in Hong Kong*?

The humidity hadn't lifted off the low-lying island yet and Fausto kept mopping himself with his handkerchief as he moved past the stately homes of Macao, under the acacia vines, and up the Rua Comendador Kou Ho Neng to the Bela Vista, where he hoped to gain further understanding.

"Can I help you?" the receptionist asked.

Fausto propped himself against the desk. "I have found the gold pocket watch of one of your clients," he lied. "It was recovered in my establishment. He was staying here, and I thought you might have his home address. A 'Mr. Worthing.'"

The clerk flipped through some pages and said, "Ah, the wedding party." He scribbled something down on a paper, and then passed it to Fausto, who pocketed it without looking.

Once outside Fausto took a rickshaw to the old Chinese quarter, streaming past the vivid hues of the street market, past schools and incense shops, to descend at the corner of de Lanterna, where he hobbled off and removed his sweat-creased suit jacket. As he pushed open a begrimed shop door, a bell tinkled, and squinting in the darkness, he sniffed, his mustache twitching from the smell of fresh lacquer and mold. The shop was nearly impassable from furniture piled to the ceiling, and he called out for his friend, Isidrio Chang, importer of Asiatic antiquities—and women. Hearing nothing, he mopped his brow, then sidled between dusty stacked camphor chests, Ming chairs, and carved screens, at last pulling open a sliding panel.

He was taken aback, however, for upon entering the bright lit room he found himself facing a white man taking tea with Isidrio.

"Ah," his friend exclaimed, standing up from the table, "this is the gentleman I was speaking of. The one and only Fausto Rodrigues, proprietor of the Golden Hind. Meet Van Leiden, here."

The Dutchman, flushed from the sap of European beef, stood up to shake his hand and Fausto said, "You are a newcomer to the Far East, I see."

"But, how do you know?" the man stammered.

He was just the man European women scorned: thin, bad posture, no confidence. This type often came East to snatch away native girls, whose esteem of the white race blinded them to merit. Fausto growled at the amah in the far corner, "Get me a drink."

Rebuffed, Van Leiden looked to Chang for support.

"Fausto," Chang interceded, "my new friend here is a journalist, traveling the world's pleasure centers and obtaining an education." He took a puff of his long pipe and said, "In Port Said, he was told that Macao was one of the centers of a worldwide white slave ring, an octopus, you said, did you not?"

"I did, but this is purely on the up and up, Mr. Rodrigues," he said, trying to improve upon the introduction he had received, noting the distance Fausto put between them.

"You are writing a very dirty novel, my friend, and you should be the first to admit it," Chang said.

"I need to talk to you, Isidrio," Fausto said. "Alone."

At a signal from Chang, Van Leiden thanked his host for the tea, and left the shop, but not without mentioning that it would be a great honor to call on Fausto in the near future—if possible. Chang waved him off, his eyes now cold, his smile patient. He locked the shop door, then shuffled back in his slippers to the room that served as his kitchen, and headquarters.

"Someone cabled me—that client of ours, Chiswick. The one bathed in shit. He says he's seen our German gal in the company of an Englishman in Hong Kong."

Chang's eyes flashed. "Ah! Then, you shouldn't have dismissed my new friend. We could use a good-looking white chap to lure her back."

"He's a journalist. He may actually print what he sees."

Chang waved him off. "A lazy one. A few puffs of the poppy, and he'll lose interest."

"You've told him our business?"

"Everyone here knows what we do," Chang said. "He was quite interested. Why not send him to look for the girl? She doesn't know him. It would be a good cover. Think of it, my friend, and come have a smoke." Fausto sat down begrudgingly and took out the crumpled piece of paper from his pocket, smoothing it out on the table.

Algernon Worthing, China Coast Navigation Co. Hong Kong, Telephone 22113

Chang took a wet chopper from the kitchen sink, and dried it on a dirty rag. "If he crosses us, he can be reduced to ten thousand pieces of grub for my famous Shanghai blue hens." He opened the sliding door to the inner courtyard and gazed appreciatively at the stacked cages of silky white hens with blue skin around their eyes. Chang's mother, a tiny woman tottering on bound feet, was feeding them at that moment and Fausto watched as they pecked madly at the mince swill in their troughs.

Peninsula & Oriental Steamship *6 November 1937*

From the gangway, looking up, Ana could see the outline of the three men against the sky, waiting for her. When at last she arrived up on deck, Jack wasn't there, but Fritz's eyes sparkled and he greeted her with a kiss. Behind him, Algy was pacing, disconcerted.

"Is there a problem?"

"Now tsut you're here, sere is no problem," Fritz said. Algy excused himself.

Ana watched him leave. "I thought I saw all of you here?"

"Are you referring to your *husband?*" Fritz laughed uproariously. "Your Jack was particularly interested in sa fakt tsut you two were married! You should have seen his face! I said, 'Your vife, Violet speaks lovely German,' and he about fell ovahboard."

Ana looked away mortified. "Do I have a cabin? I need to lie down. I wasn't planning on coming."

Fritz immediately took her valise, and led her to her stateroom, but when he opened the door, all she saw were roses, dozens of them. She turned to look at him, bewildered.

He smiled. "For you."

"But Algy only just now told me to come join you."

"I work quick. Flowers are easy, I sent a boy for sem sis mo'nink. But sis," he said hiding something behind his back, "I retrieved from my safe. I had it wis me last night. Look," he whipped out a jeweler's box. "No strings attached."

"Isn't that rather impulsive?"

"Come, don't be a spoilsport." He opened it and flashed before her a large diamond, which he slipped onto her finger. "Much bettah san tsut ozah sing!"

Ana looked at her hand, admiring it, and then finally taking it off said, "We haven't discussed anything like this."

"You accepted sa ticket out of Hong Kong," he countered.

"I just needed to get away."

"We bos know you are not Mrs. Morgan. You already confessed tsut, my deah."

Ana sighed, looking up at him in dismay.

"You're breaking my heart. Sink of it as payment for sa deal? Come. Wear it tonight." He took her hand in his.

"It is the largest stone I've seen."

"Four carats. Put it on. You may find you like it."

Emerald cut. She looked at it, and slid it back on, holding her hand out. It flashed like a search light. "Are we going on to Shanghai?"

He nodded with a hint of a smile.

"I hope to find my brother there. And to look up my friends."

"And why not? Now, let's go on deck so I can show you off. But your eyes are full of tears." He leaned closer and gave her a lingering kiss, then another one. "Tsut's bettah, my deah."

Peninsula & Oriental Steamship *6 November 1937*

THE WIND WAS PICKING up and the ship rolled over the waves, heading northeast. Most of the first-class passengers had filed past to the dining room, yet Ana was still absent. "Why is she late?" Jack scowled. He was eager to see how she was with the German, hoping his suspicion was wrong.

"There she is." Algy pointed. "With Fritz."

Ana wore a white dress that ruffled noisily in the wind, but watching her, Jack noticed upon seeing him she abruptly hid her hand behind her. "Good evening," he said pointedly. Fritz was cavalier as usual, but Ana didn't even look at him. Jack turned to Fritz, "If you don't mind, can I speak to her for a moment? It's why I insisted she come along."

Fritz shrugged, "Fine by me! Come, Worthing." He put his hand on Algy's shoulder. "We're in time for hors d'œuvres."

Jack led Ana to the railing. Night was falling and the deck was deserted. "Look at me," he said staring at the side of her face, but when she refused to look at him, he grabbed her wrist raising up her hand. "Payment, is that it?" he asked clutching her fingers. "I should tip you overboard for what you've done to me."

"And what exactly is that, Jack?" she accused hotly. "I've helped you get a deal so you wouldn't have to sell your ships. What's wrong with you? You've a lovely wife, a big home on the Peak … Why so miserable?"

Her words lashed at the very heart of him, deliberately cruel, and he held her hand tightly. "Is that what you really think? Or is this a game?" His voice was husky, low. "Because, I don't play games." He leaned over and pressed a kiss to her lips, gentle and warm, testing her. But she turned away, backing onto the railing, her look inscrutable. Saying nothing more, he turned and went in to dinner, sitting down at their table. Ana came in a moment later and sat down by the German. She never looked his way, even once. Fritz went on, oblivious, his laughter and his conversation infuriating. Worse still, everyone seemed to notice the happy couple, remarking on how adorable they were. Jack touched nothing on his plate, but drank heavily.

If he had to put it down to one thing, it was the ring—that, and listening to Fritz's plans, his half-baked philosophies on the world. When the dinner ended, all the diners excused themselves, couple by couple, and soon the room was empty except for the staff clearing away the tables. Jack ordered another gin and bitters, then went out on deck.

The wind had calmed down so everyone had come out to enjoy the night sky and live music. Couples were dancing or lingering along the railing, holding hands, pointing at stars. Jack saw Fritz take Ana in his arms. A waltz was playing and after three graceful turns, the two of them flew by Jack, the German crying out in surprise, "You almost tripped us Morgan!" On the next turn he said, "But, your vife, she dances divinely!"

The next time they passed him, Jack's fist flew out and met Fritz fully and solidly in the face.

Passage to Manila

16

Peninsula & Oriental Steamship *6 November 1937*

JUST BEHIND HIM, A woman gasped, "The man's out cold! And this in first class!"

Algy could hear further shock and outrage but, not being one for vulgar displays, he moved farther down the rail and sniffed, looking out over the sea. He wondered if he could truly bear up under the strain of Jack's jealous behavior. *And things had started off so well!* Only last night Fritz and Jack were knee-deep in plans to squeeze the Axis's global juggernaut for their own profit. That it had come down to this fracas so quickly was a remarkable shame.

Their scheme had been a shell game extraordinaire: Jack would purchase motorized junks that would pick up German weapons off Macao, then transport them to Hong Kong under cover of night. There, they would be stamped with Hong Kong export labels and shipped out to Manila where they would be relabeled as papayas, bananas, and durian, and stamped "Manila." They'd be reloaded for Shanghai at the back of the container, with the fruit at the front as decoy in case of inspection. Algy flicked his cigarette butt over the rail—his thoughts interrupted by a loud groan, then another. He gave a quick look behind him. A score of shocked passengers had encircled Fritz, while several men appreciative of the diversion reenacted the right hook that had laid Fritz out. When Ana gestured to him, Algy pushed his way through.

"Please," she whispered over her shoulder. "Go see about Jack."

He stared at her impassively, then heaved a great sigh.

On the lower deck he stopped at Jack's door and found it unlocked. Inside, the room was dark and Jack was lying on the bed, staring at the ceiling. Algy shook his head. "I suppose you know that you've won this round; he's flat out, unconscious."

Jack growled, "I didn't win anything."

"Well, you scored points with the lads in third class. That should gratify you," Algy said lighting a cigarette and taking a seat.

"What's *she* doing?"

"Well, *she's* taking care of Fritz, that's what. And I suggest you go tell him you're sorry while there's still time. We need this deal."

Jack sat up rubbing his head. "Tell her to leave. I want her off at Manila." Then he startled Algy by getting up himself and heading out the room and down the corridor. At Fritz's door Algy caught up, restraining him.

"Wait. Stop. You're won't do anything regrettable, will you?"

Jack ignored him and knocked. There was the sound of music being turned down, and after a few moments there were footsteps on the carpet and Ana's face appeared behind the door. Jack stiffened, but pushed past without a word. Fritz was lying on a Recamier, a cold compress on his eye. Algy grimaced, expecting the worst, but when nothing occurred he entered. The stateroom was most luxurious, all in tufted velvet and illumined by glowing amber sconces. An open terrace revealed moonlight on the sea.

"Ach, you old blightah!" Fritz grinned. "Don't mind if I don't get up. I know when I've been licked. You got me when I wasn't expecting it."

Algy noted the midnight blue smoking jacket with the gold chevron patterned ascot that matched Fritz's eyes, complementing his tan. *Rather nice,* he thought. He sat down without being asked and helped himself to a bonbon from the butler's tray. There was an open champagne bottle nested in ice, a humidor, and a soothing French dance tune coming from the radio, tuned to a program beamed out of Hanoi—an altogether desirable setting, Algy thought a little jealously as he swallowed the creamy chocolate. *I wouldn't mind being this fellow's lapdog,* he thought, amused. *Jack was so cheap.*

"I came to apologize," Jack said looking down. "I'm—I'm still a bit drunk."

Algy leaned back with an appreciative sigh and plucked another from the ruffled paper, a cherry liqueur, and chewed quickly, relieved there was no breach in cordial relations.

"It only hurts ven I move," Fritz laughed, pressing the ice to his head. "Here, old boy." He toed the ottoman with his slippered foot, pushing it toward Jack. "Take a cigar, and hev a seat." He showed himself the real sportsman, while Jack looked shabby indeed. "Listen, Morgan, I'm the vun to blame. I took it too far, old boy."

Jack's jaws were clenching from all the "old boys," and Algy saw him bristle further when Ana took her seat by the German and adjusted the compress on his head. "I'm not myself," Jack said abruptly looking toward the door. "You'll have to excuse me."

Algy was shocked by the swift departure, and the two on the sofa exchanged glances as the door shut.

"He's a moody chap," Fritz said, pouring himself some champagne with one hand.

Ana had a worried look on her face. "Is there something I can do?"

Algy had wanted to tell her she'd done enough, but thought better of it as he bit into a nougat crème. "Ana, maybe you could come to my room a moment?"

"Fritz, do you mind?" she asked. The man was genial and waved them off.

Ana took Algy's arm and they walked down the corridor, satin gown fluttering delightfully. He smelled her perfume. "Ah, *Miss Dior!*" He sighed. "Mother's *favorite.*"

"Fritz gave it to me." Ana smiled, then flashed a diamond. "This too."

Algy gulped, taking her hand in his to look. "Quite the booty, old girl. Does Jack know?"

"What's he to do with it? He's disgraceful, married, and carries on like a sailor. Tonight has clinched it for me." They entered Algy's room, and Ana sat down leaning comfortably back. "This whole experience makes it that much easier to leave Hong Kong with Fritz."

"And cast me off? You're so ... *so American*."

"*American*?"

"Yes, like Jack. Bold, unprincipled. No stick-to-itiveness." He removed his tie, impatiently jerking at it.

"What've I done?"

"You're leaving us, for that ... *that German!*" he said, flinging the tie and then his jacket onto the bed.

"Ah, and the Germans offend you as well! Is there anyone the English *don't* despise?"

"Oh, Ana," he cried, exasperated. "I can't *see* you with *him*." He flounced down onto the tub thinking he'd love to take either off her hands. Fritz was really dashing, and quite athletic.

"Look here. Why do you want me to stay? Because of Jack? As some sort of concubine?" Her eyes brimmed.

"Tsk, tsk. You're not being very pukkah, just now," he chided, but the waterworks began.

"I don't care," she sobbed. "I'm *Russian*, not *English*. I don't want to *be* English. I wonder at the *English* wanting to be English!"

"Right-ho." He got up, fetched a fresh cigarette and lighting it, blew smoke rings up at the ceiling. These outbursts were not his forte. "Why not give it time?" When she continued sniffling without response he added, "Jack's a well-meaning bastard, despite appearances."

"I don't care. Fritz knows *about Macao*—likes me *as I am*."

"But look what you've done to poor old Jack. If he keeps drinking like this they'll be serving him up in aspic like a sturgeon, decorated in cucumber slices."

"Don't be silly. Pour me a drink." She came to sit beside him. "Jack's married and …"

"And Fritz is a mere school-boy to Jack, and you know it. Besides, Jack *needs* you. And as far as his marriage—he was pushed into it."

"Pushed? She's carrying his child!"

"What? No, no," he waved. "Not *his*—but, I didn't say that. Listen, he's decent, Ana. The fool was ready to throw it all away for you—the firm, everything. Well, at least until you showed up with Fritz. Wasn't his knock-out punch proof of his feelings for you?"

She was silent.

"Come on. Give Fritz the old heave-ho."

"But, Jack doesn't know about *Macao*—doesn't even know I'm Russian. Or that my brother's a heroin addict. And my friends in Shanghai—they're all close to Chou En-Lai. Tanya's husband is one of his Communist advisors."

"Oh pish posh! Jack doesn't give a hoot about politics or Boslhies. Believe me, if you'd only seen how he was when you were missing all those months. He even paid a detective to look for you. Listen, I've never been in love. I certainly wouldn't cast it aside. Isn't Jack what you want?"

"*Want*? My brother wanted opium. A lot of good it did him."

Algy lit a cigarette watching his own reflection in the porthole window. Like a mirror, it didn't show the other side of things. "Oh, stop being so dashed sensible," he said letting out a cloud of smoke and took out a handful of chocolates stowed in his pocket.

"That's half the box! You stole those from Fritz!"

"Ichi for the michi! Algy grinned. "You know, *Japanese*. One for the road. Have one, baby, on me."

Peninsula & Oriental Steamship *7 November 1937*

THE CABIN LIGHTS WERE out and he stood leaning against the porthole watching foaming whitecaps curl over black waves for a long time. When he heard the rapping on his door Jack glanced at the luminous watch dial, wondering what Ana was doing with Fritz. He thought of Fritz's stateroom, full of life and music. It jarred that they, *that Ana* could be so happy. The rapping sounded louder and he went and unlocked the door.

"I came to see how you were." It was Algy in his pajamas and robe.

"How *I* am? I'm a goddamned *idiot* to do this deal, so don't ask how I am!" He went to lie down on his bed. "Did you see how that *fool* was dressed? He looked like a canary with that ascot and silk jacket."

"Ah, the arbiter of taste, are you?" Algy sat down and lit a cigarette. "Listen, good news. I've persuaded Ana to stay. When we dock in Manila tomorrow Fritz will head back to Hong Kong alone. You'll do the rest yourself. I've got the contact information for you here—a Kwomintang agent."

Jack sat up. "She's used goods as far as I'm concerned."

Algy turned white. "You bloody dog!"

"And she's a coaster."

Algy stood up, trembling and pointed toward the hall. "She's in there right now telling Fritz she's not going with him because of you!"

"That's rich. But, she'll not play me like that. I'll meet the contact in Manila, but she can get off there and be on her way to wherever she's going next. I've a hunch our big Shanghai client is head of the Green Gang."

"Big Ear Tu? No, I don't see that. Fritz is above board."

Jack went to the mirror and checked his stubble, then picked up an open bottle of gin from the table and poured the remainder into his glass. "Why do you think Fritz's contact before us backed out?"

"So. Is that it? Minutes ago you're insane with envy, and now it's business again? And why are you still drinking? You look ghastly. The girl loves you, but if I were her, I wouldn't leave Fritz for you. You're rude and have no sense of style. Just look at you, sleeping in your clothes."

Jack turned, pointing at Algy with the empty bottle. "You forget, all I know is we found her in a sing-song club, and she's already got a rock on her hand the size of a golf ball. A payoff for the deal? Delivering me to my death? I've been a fool. I should've just paid her, got what I was after, and been done with it instead of ..." Jack turned away and drained his glass for relief.

"She's so much better than you, you've no idea."

"Oh, I've an idea all right. Just make sure she's gone when I get back."

Manila *7 November 1937*

Before dawn the ship docked in Manila and by the time the sun cracked the horizon, Jack was already on the back of a motorcycle, briefcase between himself and the Filipino driver. Rumbling over the dirt roads of Makati, they left the city, flying out over open fields, between rice paddies, road grit in their teeth. Even Fritz had warned it was unwise to go without him, but Jack didn't care. The roar of the motor drowned out thoughts of Ana and when the sun rose high, hammering down, nothing really mattered. Certainly, he couldn't bear the sight of the German a moment longer, for he kept imagining Ana in bed with him. *Who else had she tricked?*

After another hour the motorbike slowed to a halt, and the driver pointed out over a great mirror of water that stretched to the horizon. "Dis bad plaes," he said squinting toward a grass hut on stilts perched in the middle of the water. There was no road, just a raised narrow mud footpath leading across the water toward it. A dense column of smoke was rising behind it.

"Go on," Jack said.

The driver eyeballed the path like a tight-wire, then gunned the motor. The path crumbled, right and left. Green rice shoots and silvery water zipped past. The driver didn't slow for a moment. They flew past a naked woman and child bathing below, and farther along a snarling dog leaped out of the water taking up chase, only to fall back in. On the verandah two men stood up as the motorcycle approached, rifles cocked, aimed at Jack's head.

When the driver cut the engine an immense silence was revealed. The air was heavy, the sun was grilling hot, and out back the bonfire was snapping. On the deck the guns jerked upwards; Jack understood, and raised his arms over his head. An unsettling odor of burned human hair was coming from the fire. Behind him he heard the sound of the dog scrambling out of the water. Sweat began to trickle down his face and body as a third man came out, staring down at him. He gestured to come up. Jack nodded, and the sunbaked treads creaked as he climbed upwards slowly to face the muzzles. On the top step he was patted down, then allowed to take out the seal Fritz had given him. After a long moment, the gun barrels lowered.

"Ato Barrandas," the guard called out.

A thin, dark-skinned man of Chinese descent emerged from the hut, blinking, looking as if he'd been ill. He wore spectacles, neat white trousers, but was bare-chested and bony. "Show me the papers," he said weakly, lowering his red eyes, gesturing Jack to follow.

"Sure," Jack said, handing them over. "You'll see …"

The man held up his hand for silence. Taking the papers inside Ato sat down at a table and spent a good ten minutes looking them over, adjusting his glasses, holding the paper to the light, and checking for the company watermark. Finally he took out a scrap of paper, and wrote something down. Handing it to Jack he nodded.

Jack scanned it. "The Chung Wai Bank?"

"Yes. Do you know the third party?"

"I've an idea now."

The man went to sit on a dirty straw floor mat that was made up as a bed. He lay down, closing his eyes, and continued speaking. "The buyer is Big Ear Tu. In a country of guanxi he has more power than anyone, even Chiang Kai-shek himself."

Jack frowned.

"He poisoned me two months ago. Thought I'd tricked him. But it was someone from the Shanghai Merchants Association." He turned his head to look at Jack from the floor. "Afraid?" He attempted a laugh, but it came as a sharp breath that jerked his withered chest. "You'll be eating your own kidneys. You know … this is a deal … for the Kwomintang." He gasped and swallowed hard. "You, you can't have Communist contacts—not even casually. It's—" He left off finishing this, and stared at the ceiling for some time. "Transgression," he whispered and the word hung in the air.

"I don't know any Communists," Jack said, shifting his weight, then suddenly recalled lunch with Madame Sun.

Ato pointed to an assistant who had been squatting in the corner with a revolver and the man jumped up, bringing a folded paper to Jack. "This list of contacts will cover for you when your ships dock in Manila. They'll arrange the crates and labels and local produce. The name at the top is the contact here. Military Police." Ato grinned weakly. "He is on our side." He stared as Jack looked over the names. "You must be a desperate man, Jack Morgan. But, you will be well paid." He laughed and coughed, then sat up spitting blood into a dirty rag. "If you live." He pointed to the door. Jack nodded and walked out into the sun's heat.

The ride back to the boat was oppressive. The driver sped over dirt roads pockmarked with large drops as the clouds opened, and by the time he'd reached the docks, they had been thoroughly rained on and dried off. He was stiff and mud-caked as he hurried up the gangplank, and he'd not been a minute too soon. On the upper deck he watched the coast pulling away and couldn't help thinking of her dark hair, and the way a loose strand curled up to the corner of her mouth, the way it framed her big green eyes. When Manila was just a shrinking speck on the horizon, he turned to go to his room, a knot in his chest. He hadn't been able to forget their stolen kisses or the feel of her soft yielding body in his hands as she'd clung to him at Peak House; she obviously knew how to please men. *She knew how to please him.*

China Coast Navigation & Co. *8 November 1937*

VAN LEIDEN ENTERED THE elegant building on Pedder Street and asked the receptionist for Mr. Algernon Worthing. She informed him he was out on business but divulged his home address when Van Leiden showed her the empty box he'd wrapped prettily. "A gift," he'd said with a wink. A few minutes later Van Leiden was walking up the steep incline on Ice House Street congratulating himself on his ploy. He turned right at Wyndham, passed the carpet shops, then got lost on Chancery Lane. By the time he'd reached the address on Caine Road he was dripping from the heat and removed his jacket. There was only a Catholic mission to be seen and he looked about, dismayed. Finally he knocked on a red peeling door. A few minutes later a cross old nun came out.

"I'm here to deliver a package," he said quickly glancing at the number. "A Miss Ana. I don't know her last name."

The nun snorted. "This is a gentlemen's residence. There are no *women* here." She tried to shut the door but he stuck his foot inside.

"Tell me then, is there an Algernon Worthing?" he asked, and then to irritate her lied, "I believe his lady friend whom he lives with sings at the Jade Flower."

The nun was aghast and attempted to slam the door.

"If you notice, Sister, I haven't removed my foot. But," he said handing the gift through the gap in the door, "I'm sure Ana would like to receive this. Just leave it outside Mr. Worthing's flat if you think it safe."

She snatched it from his hand, then looked down at his foot. Van Leiden laughed, removed it, then strolled back down the hill. As soon as he'd got the prostitute back to them, Isidrio and Fausto would know he was trustworthy and let him in on the business. Back in Central District, Van Leiden entered the Hong Kong Hotel and taking a seat at the bar scribbled out a cable for Macao. *It should be easy to get the girl,* he penned. *I found Worthing's flat.* Then he walked over to the concierge and slapped a few coins onto the counter. "I need this to go out—*now*."

Central China *8 November 1937*

Yoshi didn't know when his fighting spirit started to die, but more than a thousand miles away from O-bachan's cooking his spirit had become as heavy as his pack. The pillars of Yasukuni shrine should have braced his heart, but in truth they didn't. He'd sent a request for a transfer to Hong Kong hundreds of miles back. *And he'd been so hopeful.* But every step into China had changed him. He was not the innocent village boy any longer. *I can't go to Yasukuni now, Yumi-chan,* he thought aloud. His sister would think him a disgrace if she knew. He was certain of it.

He blamed the commander for his first murder, for that was what it was. An innocent villager. He remembered her face, staring up at him in terror. The girl had rosy cheeks, almond-shaped eyes, and a pretty mouth. Around her neck she wore a necklace of tiny blue cloisonné butterflies. She was the last one alive in the village they came into. Troops ahead of them had raped her and left her to die. *Kill her*, Yoshi's commander barked. Her eyes moved back and forth between the two men and it seemed her thoughts became words in his mind. *Save me. Save me. Save me, please.* Commander was watching. Yoshi had his finger on the trigger. He thought how she looked like his little sister, then squeezed the trigger.

So many killings came after that first one—and each death slightly less personal. Yoshi thought it hadn't been bad shooting people he couldn't see, spraying buildings and shrubs—*but the prisoners.* These he faced head-on. He read their expressions; felt the weight of their hearts in his own. He remembered every face of every person he shot like that, at close range. His commander was always saying—Three all! Meaning, burn all, seize all, kill all. *Anyway, it really was true,* Yoshi thought as he marched away from the dead. *Couldn't afford to feed prisoners. Even our own wounded suffered.* He'd left friends behind without legs to fend for themselves, and those with cholera they let starve. Walking across China he lost his soul to excuses. Valleys, rice paddies, dusty fields, burned villages—there were corpses as plentiful as buttercups. He dreamed over and over that just around the next bend his own village would suddenly come into view and he would drop his gun and his pack and run to his family. O-bachan would be resting on the porch, Mother would be pressing pickled daikon into wood vats, Father would be drying fish in the sun. Other times he'd imagine he'd come upon his family and his own men would start shooting—and just like here in China they would be peppered with bullets, falling without reason, spinning like autumn leaves to the dark grass. *Three all*, he whispered. *Three all . . .* He looked up at the sun dizzy with hunger. *Please let my transfer go through, please,* he begged.

17

Peninsula & Oriental Steamship *8 November 1937*

The foghorn sounded as it finally escaped the clinging haze into open sea, leaving behind the low buildings and coconut palms of Manila's shoreline. In his cabin, Jack showered off the road dust, the tepid droplets trickling over his skin. *How he yearned for a cold shower.* He could feel the ship move underfoot, and closed his eyes under the slow rain, feeling an enormous emptiness growing inside. Afterward he put on a clean suit and headed down the corridor toward the dining hall. Smells of sour milkfish soup and coconut sticky rice were rising up from below deck in a thick cloud of steam and Jack felt sweat begin to trickle down his back. For the first time he felt sick of the tropics, sick of everything. *How he longed for a simple honest plate of grits.*

He was the first diner to be seated and emptied a drink as waiters filled the long buffet with covered silver platters, plunking vases with purple sprays of orchids onto tables. Sitting there observing the slow progression of the elaborate table-setting ritual, he smoldered. Tipping back his drink, he imagined her naked beneath him, as his lips and tongue tasted, nipping, drinking in—while she laughed, sighed, and …

"Another drink, Mr. Morgan?" The waiter hovered, smiling.

Jack looked up, nodded and then attempting to set his mind back on track, thought of the arms deal. *It would secure Percy's legacy, but what about me?* The firm was nothing but a loose association of employees, desks, paperwork and a client list. There were the ships, of course—beautiful and hulking—but nothing you could curl up in bed with. No, there was nothing like Ana. Her insidious wiles had captured his imagination.

As the diners began to enter, he heard Algy, but he wasn't prepared to hear the silvery laugh. It was like a chill from a wind chime and made him sit up. *His whole body throbbed at the sound.* Ana hadn't seen him and was smiling, simply radiant in white. He watched as her every step toward him brought a stab of pain, and delight. His eyes ran over her body; desire and dismay quilted an erratic pattern in his heart.

She stood before him, a little frightened, and Jack looked into her eyes. His heart was pounding.

"As you wished, Ana has come back," Algy said in a bold-faced lie. "So I think you should at least get up, Jack. *Jack?* Aren't you going to say something? Fritz has gone back to Hong Kong."

His eyes continued to bore into her. Ana turned pale and Algy put his hand out to stop her from leaving.

"Let's all just have a nice meal," Algy insisted and they both sat down facing Jack.

Algy was prattling on, filling in the spaces with small talk, but Jack and Ana ate in silence, avoiding further eye contact. Jack stabbed at the prawns on his plate pleased that she wasn't wearing the ring. He decided he'd sit out the meal on principle, and not utter one word, but then the captain came over and clapped him on the back, asking about Percival. Eventually he brought up the Japanese. "Their Imperial Army is completely in charge in Shanghai. Be warned, my friend. I tell all my passengers this." They spoke for some time and when the captain was about to leave, Algy interrupted, wringing his hands, asking if it was still safe in the International Settlement.

"The real battles are beyond the Jap supply lines, and the going's tough for them," the captain said with a laugh and a wink as he walked off. "As for yourself, keep your fingers crossed and don't venture past the barbed wire."

After an interlude, Jack found it in him to speak again. "So, Ana." he remarked. "Here we are together again. Yet, I don't know the least little thing about you."

"And you should!" Algy brightened up. "Ana has had a very interesting life. She's of noble descent and speaks five languages. As you know, she can sing like a dove and cook too."

"Is that a fact," Jack sneered.

"Yes," Algy said, excited. "She makes amazing crepes, and you know, before she went to Germany she actually studied with the same tutors that worked for the Romanovs. Can you believe it?"

Jack glanced at her. "*You're not German*?"

"No," she said cautiously.

"Russian's her first language," Algy boasted. "Her father was a general and—"

Jack snorted in disbelief.

Ana smiled prettily, raising her eyebrows.

"Is this true?" he asked her.

She nodded. "Why?"

Jack folded up his napkin and quietly got up and left the hall. In the narrow corridor he heard Algy hurrying behind him and stopped.

"Jack? Jack! What's the matter?"

"When we dock, you are to take Ana across the river. Put her on the Blue Line for Hong Kong. She's *not* to stay in Shanghai under *any* circumstance, understand?" Algy stepped back, confused. "*Not under any circumstance*," Jack demanded, furious. "I'll be waiting for you at the Cathay. Don't let anyone on shore see you together."

"But why?"

"Your blunder may have cost us our lives. Now, get out of my sight."

Caine Road *9 November 1937*

Ridiculous! Van Leiden wiped his face, re-read the cable, then crumpled it up in dismay and walked back up the slope. *Fausto expected him to break into the flat just to verify the girl lived there?* Coming to a stop across the way, he shielded his eyes from the sun as he scanned the missionary flats. Sure enough, the old nun was out front again, sweeping along the street with her grass broom. He sighed, throwing down his half-smoked kretek.

"Say, Sister," he said ambling across the street toward her. "I thought you said this is a full house. The place looks empty."

The witch kept sweeping.

"What about this couple I'm after? You know, Mr. Worthing. Is he still on his business trip? He's no missionary, you know. He take the girl with him?" The woman moved off and he pointed up at the windows. "You got keys to their flat? You'll find her, or her clothes. Go check." Getting no response, he said angrily, "Show me a *man* who has no desires, and I'll show you a liar!"

The nun's eyes gleamed angrily as she turned back into the building, slamming the door behind her. But Van Leiden heard the distinct jangle of keys. He chuckled. A half hour later, however, the door opened. Van Leiden, squatting on the curb across the street, stood up. The nun and an old Chinese man were laboring with an open crate, maneuvering it out onto the pavement. There were more behind this one.

Van Leiden strolled across the road and picked through the items ... A woman's dress, a man's suit, a wrap with sequins, a set of pots and pans. "What are you doing?" he asked, as the nun came out again.

She handed him his gift package. "You can give it to her in person. Now leave. I've called the police."

The door slammed and the bolt clicked. *Kutwijf!* he spat out. He'd only wanted to irk the old bitch, but now it appeared he'd gotten Worthing and his whore evicted ... Van Leiden paced by the crates, wondering what to tell Fausto, but before he could deliberate further, a tall Indian constable in uniform approached him, turbaned, with a cultivated handlebar mustache draped over his ears.

"You, there! Is this rubbish yours? State your name and address, Sir." The constable was holding a pad of paper and a pencil, and considering him gravely as a crowd gathered. "Speak up!"

Thinking quickly, Van Leiden pointed, shouting, "Stop, thief!" The constable turned his head in time to observe stealthy hands pilfering shirts and slacks, and cracked his swagger stick sending the beggars off. Van Leiden took the opportunity to disappear.

Shanghai *11 November 1937*

THE STEAMER WAS MOVING slowly down the Whangpoo River as they approached the Shanghai docks while Ana repacked her bags. "My coming along to Shanghai was a big mistake. Jack's furious, isn't he?"

"No worry. He's under pressure. Not to mention jealous. Here, let me pay your ticket back to Hong Kong. You can wait for me there."

"But, I'm to leave—*now*?"

"Jack's idea," Algy said over his shoulder. "Come see the blockade," he said as the gray predawn landscape moved past the porthole in slow motion, dismal, war-torn, with sunken hulks left and right.

"Maybe I should stay in Shanghai if he feels like that."

Algy turned around. "What? Don't you like Hong Kong?"

She went to apply her lipstick in the long mirror. "I have to look for my brother here. He's always in the back of my mind." Ana straightened her dress. "This frock is really démodé, so Hong Kong."

"Ana, this is not the gay town it once was. It's being run by the Japanese and triads. You heard the captain."

"But my friends will think I'm shabby. And what will Mischa say?"

"Your brother's an addict. He doesn't care how you're dressed, and he doesn't want help. Besides, Jack said you absolutely must leave today for Hong Kong. The Blue Funnel leaves at three."

"Is that so!" she said putting down her hairbrush. "He says go, and I drop everything? And why is that?"

"For your safety."

"*Hardly.*"

"Ana, if I could roll you in a carpet and throw you on board the next steamer out, I would. People are getting shot. And worse, what if you see Chan?!"

She laughed, giving him a peck on the cheek. "My friend Tanya will take me in. He can't abduct me in civilized company! I'll find her at the Palace Hotel. She's always there with her husband. I knew them well before Mischa got me stuck singing at the Jade Gate with his debt."

"I see, I'm fighting a losing battle," Algy sighed. "Right then, let's make a pact. I'll arrange for you to remain on board till evening. Jack and I have meetings all over town today and if we run into you, after I promised you'd leave, it would put the kibosh on things. Here. This is enough cash to get you and your brother back to Hong Kong. Now, how long do you think it will take to find him?"

"I don't know, but my Russian friends are sure to know where he is."

He raised his brow. "Didn't think any were still around."

"Yes. I told you. Tanya and her husband, Komrad Diamant. He's very important."

"Egad! That man's got a target on his forehead. Even I know he's been advising the Communists. I'd be surprised the Kwomintang hasn't killed him."

"Algy, look, we're almost here," she said hurrying to the porthole as the motors reversed.

He touched her arm, "Promise me you won't come near our hotel. Look at me. Promise?"

"The Cathay?" She gave him a flirtatious smile. "*Promise.*"

After repeated good-byes, she lounged in her stateroom, then finally fell asleep. When she awoke, the room was dark and the sun had set. The steward was knocking on her door, and told her they would depart for Vladivostok in a half hour.

Ana hurried to gather her things then caught her reflection in the mirror. Fifteen minutes later a couple of deckhands turned to look as she passed, giving a low whistle; she had changed her clothes and knew she looked divine. A porter carried her bags down, loading them onto a rickshaw. Ana hopped on happily, and they were off down the dark street; it didn't take long to notice the changes. Ana pulled her wrap over her shoulders in concern, wondering why the street lamps were out. Buildings seemed oddly vacant, windows gaping, and figures huddled in the shadows, while gunshots popped in the distance. If her rickshaw boy dropped her off here she'd be killed. Further up they passed the American Consulate but it was gray and dismal, steeped in a strange eeriness. Ana hurried her boy, clutching her purse to her chest and when two autos raced up Szechuen Road they narrowly missed her rickshaw. "Hurry, hurry!" she cried out almost in tears. At the Palace Hotel she heaved a sigh of relief and nearly ran inside.

Live jazz was coming from the bar area, and her step quickened across the marble lobby. It was such a difference to walk into a place with money in her pocket, new silk stockings, and a dress that actually belonged to her and not a sing-song club. She passed into the large salon and glanced at the band that played the in days before she worked at Chan's. *Yes, same old players as before.* She looked about the room. *Tanya's husband, Komrad Diamant, was not at his usual table.*

"How many in your party, Mademoiselle?" the waiter asked.

"Have you seen Mr. Diamant this evening?"

The man blinked. "Shanghai Communists not so welcome." He tipped his head toward the crowd. "Jazz is very popular in Tokyo. These days we're occupied by the 'jazzanese' army," he said laughing, moving away from her, nodding at a couple just arriving. "Mr. Nakamura San, good evening. Your usual table?"

Ana was startled. It was subtle, but obvious if you looked. *All the tables where the usual westerners had sat were actually occupied by Japanese, many in uniform.* Ana walked back to the main lobby, and made her way to the concierge counter, leaning against it feeling a little weak. Even worse, she felt too scantily dressed.

"Madame, can I help you?"

"Yes, yes. I was to meet Mr. Diamant. You do *know* him?"

"Of course. But Europeans who've remained in Shanghai have left us for the Cathay."

Ana went to sit on the large sofa in the center of the room, watching as guests arrived and departed. Her hands worked the edge of her purse and she could plainly see there were absolutely no Europeans about. She heard footsteps approaching and looked up, expecting the concierge with good news, but a handsome Japanese officer stood at attention before her.

Ana's smile froze as he bowed slightly, "Would you care to accompany me for a drink?"

She fumbled with her purse, trying to stand up, and he helped her to her feet. "I–I'm so sorry," she said hurrying off, and called for her luggage and a rickshaw. The Cathay Hotel was only a long block away but now she was afraid. *What if Tanya had left Shanghai?* Her rickshaw driver hurried along and Ana's heart was racing as they dodged potholes. Her fear grew with every bump and when the coolie lowered the shafts in front of the Cathay, Ana realized Algy had been right to insist she leave. But now it was too late—and here she was at the Cathay where he'd explicitly told her not to go. *But Tanya will be here. We can leave together quickly.*

Ana sent in her bag then looked around the street. Her last sight of Wong burning in the car flashed with ghostly immediacy. She hurried in through the door but found she was instinctively drawn to where she'd last seen Vassily. The ceiling was repaired. The bar stools were occupied. Only the expansive mirror was gone, and a large hunt painting was in its place above the bar. It was then that she heard her name. "Ana, *Ana!*"

She looked left and right bewildered until she spotted him waving at her. It *was* Komrad Diamant! She burst into a big smile and he waved her over.

Ana flew across the lobby, holding back tears, as he held his arms open for her. They embraced joyfully but she sensed a tension in him. "Oh, Ana," he said in his deep, Russian voice. "How good to see you are well." Then taking her aside, he said, "It's not safe here. Haven't you heard?" His brows furrowed, and his kind eyes searched hers. She did not want to hear this, did not want him to let go of her hands; she closed her eyes for a moment.

"Heard what?" she asked.

"All of us must go. Why are you still here?"

"But what do you mean?" she asked, distressed by his tone.

"I am leaving tonight. Tanja has left already a month ago. It's not safe for any Russians here. I know you are not a member of the party, but the Kwomintang has gotten very strong in Shanghai. My man who was to meet me has not shown up. I fear the worst. It seems the United Front is in name only. Chiang Kai-shek has tricked us!"

She looked into his eyes, her voice trembling. "Komrad, have you seen Mischa?"

"Mischa?" He looked surprised. "I have only come into Shanghai today by train. I cannot imagine he's still here. I thought that—"

"What?"

"But Ana. He left a long time ago with the Chinese gal."

Ana stood disconsolate, staring as if into a huge void.

He nodded at a man standing by the exit, then told her, "I must go."

There was nothing to do. It was as if the floor had opened up under her.

"Ana." His warm palm was heavy on her shoulder, "You're all right?"

"Yes, yes, Komrad."

He pressed her hand gently to his lips. "I hope we meet again, my dear."

"Please," she whispered, feeling tears smarting as he kissed her, "hug your Tanya for me."

Diamant's genteel charm was so soothing, so reminiscent of her father. She watched him striding away with nostalgic longing—even though he was a *Bolshevik*, he reminded her of summer nights at the family dacha, playing with her sisters and Mischa, listening to her father's friends singing old Volga songs. Politics meant nothing to her now that Old Russia was no more, and she felt tears starting as she waved again, rather pointlessly as the door had already closed behind him.

Stumbling back through the lobby, not knowing where to turn, she went to stand by the elevators but had no reason to be there. Then she remembered her bags. *But where will I go?* Ana turned toward the bell station, when a hand reached out and grabbed her arm very, very hard, and didn't let go.

Central China *9 November 1937*

YOSHI'S EYES KEPT COMBING the skies for the rare occasion a parachute might drop with crates of supplies. Orders were to confiscate food and weapons from the peasants, and that would have been fine had the villages not been smoking ruins devoid of life. Hearing the Japanese were arriving, the hungry Chinese set fire to everything in advance, destroying even their precious rice crops. It was desperation on both sides—merely a question of who would starve first. He imagined he'd march days even if just for a whiff of rice crackers and soy sauce toasting over a flame, or better still—the sticky, smoky scent of O-dango, chewy rice balls dipped in hot runny molasses sold at the train stations!

There were corpses everywhere. Had to step over them. Maggots were the only things in this war that weren't hungry. *If I were a maggot, this would be heaven.* The idea made him laugh aloud and the soldier marching by him muttered, *You're crazy, Sakura*—but did so without heart. *No one had heart on an empty stomach.* They'd started off eating dried shiitake and dried tofu, but there were days now they'd eaten only grass. Some of the boys drifted away at night hoping to escape, but it was everywhere. It was all they had to return to. War was their mother, father, and country. It was march, march, march. But somewhere there had to be an end to this road. He'd seen the end for a friend the night before, the boy—for they were both still young—twisted in agony, eyes wide, teeth bared in a last groan. *Is this where I'm marching to? A hundred li into China just to find some hovel under a tree where I can lie down forever?*

The next day in camp Yoshi was sitting in a half lotus position one morning, cleaning a wound with a piece of newsprint, thinking things over.

"You're Sergeant Sakura, aren't you Sir?" the young messenger asked.

Yoshi couldn't help noticing his neck, the throbbing blood vessel—a place he'd buried countless bayonets without thinking.

"You have mail, Sir!" the boy said, thrusting forth an envelope and immediately rushing off.

He looked at the faded cover—it was the very envelope he'd sent out months ago to his uncle asking for a transfer. Yoshi stood up and began to laugh; stumbling backward he began to cry, he was laughing so hard. *How many nights did I lie awake hoping this letter would save me?* The thought doubled him over with laughter until he was gasping. When a passing friend asked him to share the humor, Yoshi waved the letter. "Jodan da yo! A joke!"

His friend took it and exclaimed, "Bakayarro! No wonder, you asshole! You wrote *China* right here at the bottom! Hong Kong is just Hong Kong! This must have traveled the expanse of China and come right back like a pigeon! But why send it to Hong Kong?"

"It's not important now." Yoshi looked away. "Leave me alone."

The Monkey's Cousin

18

French Concession, Shanghai *9 November 1937*

At the far end of Rue Moliere, Jack got out of the car and removed Fritz's note from his breast pocket. *Were they lost, or was this Tu's?* He stared at a wall topped by broken bottles and barbed wire then checked the numbers painted on the curb. It *was* the correct address, but there seemed to be no entrance. Jack stepped back into the street noting a wide pagoda roof shrouded in ancient plane trees. Lances of sunlight touched here and there, sifting down between leaves and shadows, revealing other structures. The compound occupied an entire block. He glanced down the street toward Algy, who was already questioning a guard outside a large corrugated gate. "This has to be it," Jack called out to their driver, pointing to the manor house. "You wait for us here." The man had been completely useless ever since they mentioned the infamous Tu.

"My no stap here. Tu, he kilman!" the chauffeur squawked, fear visible in his eyes. The engine was running as if he were about to lift his foot off the clutch and leave. "My no tellee lie," he said pointing to his ear. "Just now—*hearum gan! Boom!*"

"Never mind the gun. You wait. This is business, savvy?" But the driver shook his head, *no*. "Goddamnit!" Jack swore and ripping out his wallet waved a wad of Fa-Pi bills at the man. Too late; it was a terrible loss of face and Jack knew it.

"Plaes nogut. You no kam bek!" the man said taking the money.

"Even so, you waitum here," Jack said pointing to the curb. He sighed and glanced at his watch, then stalked back across the road. As he did, he detected a movement up in a third-floor casement window; *a gun was following him.* He moved in closer to the wall out of sight and when he reached the gate discovered the armed guard was insulting Algy in the vernacular. Jack stepped up, answering him in Chinese—that as there were no girls to bugger, could he be offering his sister's services? Before the guard could recover, Jack shoved Fritz's paper in his face. The tactic appeared to work, for after inspecting it, the man unlocked the imposing gate and let them pass.

As the gate swung open, an ancient stone garden opened up like a jewel box before them. Sharp, sponge-textured stones gnarled skyward by an arched bridge where ruffled lotus leaves rose elegantly from a still black pool. They had heard at their hotel that Tu had won this place at a game of Fan Tan the week before. It was amazing. A whizzing noise caught their attention. On the other side of the bridge they spied two servants in baggy black trousers and white jackets beating a shackled monkey with a thin whip. Jack kept walking, noting a possible escape route, and spotted several Rolls Royces parked in a queue beyond a low garden wall. As they mounted the front steps, another guard scanned his paper, then opened the front door. Jack could hear Algy running to join him.

"Jack," Algy cried out, breathless, bumping into him as they entered a marble vestibule. "I–I didn't know monkeys could scream."

"Shut up," Jack whispered, but he needn't have been cautious, for they were being ignored. Armed guards were marching noisily up the stairs, Mausers flapping at their sides as they carried pine boxes to the upper levels, depleting stacks in the vestibule as more were brought in from outside.

"I say, this is as busy as Waterloo station," Algy said.

In front of them was a curving staircase, and to the left an impressive pair of wooden doors that might have led to a library. The guard who'd let them in didn't leave his post outside the door, and they sat down puzzled, wondering if they'd be announced.

"I offered to buy the monkey, you know," Algy whispered. Both their eyes suddenly moved to the crack of light under the pair of library doors. Abruptly one opened, and a pale bespectacled man came out. Closing it behind him very carefully, he turned to face them. His eyes widened. He'd obviously not expected to see white men in the hall and did his best to rush for the front door.

"Why, T.V. Soong!" Jack called out and leapt up, crossing the room with his best cocktail party smile, and stretched out his hand for the famous man—blocking his way out. "What an honor!" It was startling to him that Soong, the financial wizard behind Chiang Kai-shek's revolution, was here, at Tu's. Soong, easily recognizable from the newspapers, had a curved sensual mouth, and round tortoise-frame glasses that gave a fashionable, studious air to the bespoke pinstripe suit. Trapped, he gave a smirk of acknowledgment, pausing, but ready to fly.

"I've heard so much about you from my father-in-law, Percival Summerhays," Jack continued, noting that the door whence Soong had come from had not properly latched, and a crack gave view of movement in the room beyond.

Soong licked his lips nervously, eyes looking for a way out, and was obviously not pleased with the association with Tu. "Ah, so that's who you are." Soong looked puzzled for a moment, "American, though, from your accent." His eyes darted over at Algy.

"Yes," Jack nodded, observing the Harvard-educated man. "And your accent as well."

Soong chuckled, turning toward the outer door. "Those bloody British," he said, hand on the knob and a foot outside already.

"Tell me," Jack said detaining him, "what do you think, how long will it take China to shake the Japs?"

The man laughed, relieved Jack was letting him play politician. "Give them three months. They'll be bankrupt, and we'll win, hands down." He was about to turn away again when Jack touched his arm.

"Yes, but where will China get the funds if this lasts longer? In the light of rampant inflation, Fa-Pi dollars are worthless."

Soong laughed heartily, but his nostrils bristled at Jack's audacity. "China needs no finances," he stated grandly. "It imports arms on credit." He then excused himself with a smirk, and walked out the front door.

He wasn't fast enough for Algy—who, already annoyed by the expression of anti-British sentiment, stood up and pointed accusingly. "What about that monkey outside?"

Soong, on the outer steps, paused in the sunshine, and turned. Then a great smile split his dour expression. Behind him, the monkey's head had parted ways with its body by way of a rope and chopper. Algy swooned at the sight on the stone path, while Soong said, "That? That's a *Communist* monkey," then hurried down the path out of sight. The guard closed the door behind him.

Standing in the vestibule, Jack could only wonder. Would Soong have made the comment on importation on credit had he known he and Algy were selling arms? "You do realize who that was," he said.

"I don't care. It's bloody hot in here."

"But the connection. Don't you see?" Jack sat back down and turned to look at Algy. "China's principal economic reformer has just walked out of a triad home as if it were his own." Algy was daintily pressing a perfumed handkerchief to his temple, and Jack felt a frisson of annoyance pass over him. "It *means* that Chiang Kai-shek *must have realized* the only way to unify a country this enormous was to use the *organized crime network already here.*"

"How's that?"

"Don't you see? China has thousands of miles of disunited territories each ruled by a warlord trying to kill off all the others—you can't unify that. But all along the Yangtze River there are five million addicts with a well-established distribution system for heroin, morphine, and other opiates. Put it together. He's grafting the new China to the deeply established root of organized crime."

Algy shrugged. "I can't listen to you gassing on until I've had my tea."

Jack grabbed his wrist and twisted it to get his attention. Algy stifled a yelp and Jack ordered him to ask the guard for the WC and see what they were unloading. Algy blanched, but did as he was told—and a guard pointed the way upstairs. As Algy disappeared to the second floor, Jack's thoughts were interrupted by raucous laughter that suddenly boomed from his left. He turned and saw the door had crept open and a shaft of light outlined its prodigious height. From somewhere a draft pulled, and the crack grew in width, enabling Jack to see in. The distant face of a young girl, no more than twelve, stood facing Jack, eyes downcast. She was holding a tray. *Someone, out of sight, was pelting little stones at a silk shoe on that tray*. Jack leaned to look—when there was a sudden draft again, and the door slammed shut. Inside, the voices stopped and there was a shuffle of slippered feet. A Chinaman, dressed as a servant-cum-scholar, stuck his head out and abruptly addressed Jack with a lovely Etonian quaver. "Ah, you are here. Come in, come in. We had a little—ah, little delay."

Jack looked about for Algy, then not seeing him, quickly crossed the marble vestibule and stepped inside.

Immediately, he was blinded by late afternoon sunlight glaring in through a large bay window—but the preponderance of the room was unlit, dark and stinking of—*could it be*? *Creosote?* A litter of spat pumpkin seed hulls crunched underfoot and Jack entered slowly, blinking, aware first of a table tenanted with human forms on the dark side of the space. Not knowing what to do, he stood awaiting invitation, observing the young girl motionless, head bowed, outlined with sunshine. His eyes followed her gaze down to the tiled floor where the shock of one un-bandaged, tiny broken foot folded in half under itself greeted his eyes. It was bleeding slightly. Her other foot, shod, was more like a hoof, and tucked into a pointy red and gold slipper. He'd never seen a bound foot without its covering, but hid his shock. He looked back up into the shadowy side of the room, and at the table, an octopus of arms and heads, trying to discern the features in the darkness. There was an abrupt rustle, and the man closest stood quickly and turned to face him.

He had to be an addict; his skin was ashen and eyes dead as a shark's eyes. He had small shoulders and long swinging lifeless arms, and he wore a long, dirty blue gown that finished off with pointed European boots. But it was by his ears alone that Jack knew him.

"Have a seat," Big Eared Tu said in Chinese, and the Etonian interpreted simultaneously. Tu gestured for the slipper game to continue and Jack took the empty chair. This time, unlike his gaffe with Chan, Jack decided he would keep to English and the "ignorant foreign devil" protocol. "You know the game of raft, don't you?" Tu said jutting his chin. One eyelid seemed to be stuck in a long continuous wink. "That fellow there has succeeded in tossing lotus seeds into the shoe, see? Now he wins the honor of a drink of wine." Jack watched as the man raised the girl's other slipper, making an elaborate ritual of sniffing, then drank, while the others burst into laughter. The sight of bound feet naked were said to be highly erotic to the Chinese male, a lotus of sorts. One of the figures at the table didn't participate in the game but sat watching Jack with an unflinching stare. Jack wanted to turn his head and look the rude observer in the eye, but instead he looked hard at Tu.

"So, you are the American who dares do business with Tu," the Etonian said.

"I don't fear Tu; it's the British government that's my concern. I'm breaking the law selling arms to you."

"The law?" Tu's voice echoed, first in Chinese, then in translation. The men at the table stopped to look. "The laws in Hong Kong are a very *fine* net, too tight. Holes are necessary for people to breathe," Tu said staring. "But you are right not to trust the government. Unlike politicians, I'm an honest man."

"What are you saying?" Jack asked, pushing his chair back, so that he could eventually get a look at the man burning a hole in him on his right. As he did, his chair legs shrieked on the marble floor and Tu looked down smiling, interpreting Jack's action in some inscrutable way.

"I'm saying I trust no one." He looked up with a spark at last in his eyes. "Just here, in my own city, the Shanghai Merchants Association tried to have me killed. *They're all Communists!* We've gotten rid of all Russian influence, those *filthy* Bolsheviks, and have purged the city of its drug pushers." By habit, he repeatedly checked the perimeter of the room, darting a glance here and there. It was unsettling. "We need to protect the new China, a child in the womb. Politicians talk honesty, but when they need muscle they come to Tu to do whatever it takes to silence their foes. But with me, you see? We have this open friendly conversation now on guns. No need for lies!" The men playing raft kept tossing seeds at the tray, but without interest, taking their turns more and more slowly, their ears attuned sharply to what was said. The girl hobbled about the table on her ruined feet, circling the table, but each time as she skipped the man to Jack's right, it seemed the tension grew among the others.

"Well, I have no ties to Bolsheviks." Jack's words echoed in English then Chinese. "I can give you no more proof than the fact that I've trusted you and have come into your house with a clear conscience."

Tu grunted, raising his palm. "I will buy your weapons at cut rate. I'll take one shipload every fortnight. Much of this has already been negotiated with your German." He picked up a locked gold teapot and drank from the narrow curved spout, obviously afraid of being poisoned. "You'll grow rich from my contract."

Jack smiled, but added, "I must warn you these weapons cannot be used against the Japanese. It's the only condition I must abide by on my side, with the supplier."

Tu laughed and his eyes flickered over the room. "Obviously you don't understand. China has no fear of the small cousins. They're not the real enemy."

"Fine. The terms are half up front and the rest on delivery. My contact here will act on my behalf."

Tu slammed his hand on the table and shouted. When he stopped, Jack watched intently as his words were magically transformed into polite Etonian English. "Money is not always a clean interest," the translator said, quavering as Tu pointed. "See this man that you've noticed staring at you?" All of the players stopped still. Tu's dead eyes had suddenly awoken again and locked onto Jack's as if in dare. Jack, glad to comply, turned to face the man at his side.

The eyes were wide open, as if in supplication, and the mouth dripped ever so slowly, a rivulet of blood. The forehead of the bearded Caucasian was peppered with black powder around a thumb-sized hole. Jack quickly looked back at Tu with a grin, "Ah ha! So, *THIS* is the monkey's cousin!"

Tu's eyes widened, and then he began to laugh wildly. The other men joined in as well and the room was racked again with crazed mirth. Suddenly, Tu stood up. "Ah! You'll do fine. Soong said he knows of your chairman, *Summerhays*. You must have seen Soong leaving, no? But you realize. I have eyes everywhere. If I hear you've even brushed sleeves with a Communist in your sleep you'll join your ancestors tomorrow." Tu signaled at the translator, who took out a business card and handed it to Jack. Again, his eyes zig-zagged the perimeter of the room as he spoke. "That name on the card is my associate, Harbor Master Chen. He speaks English, French, Russian. All the shipments will be finalized through him, his office. I'll have him call you at your hotel."

Jack was already being escorted to the door, but he paused. "It is company *policy* not to accept anything but *hard* currency. Gold or Mex." He took out an envelope and handed it to the translator.

"You insult me, Mr. *Summerhays*," he said with a hint of sarcasm. "I thought you were interested in our fight for democracy, for freedom." He snatched the envelope. "That man at the table was a Bolshevik. We've rounded up all of them now."

"My name is *Morgan*. And no one in the region is here on a charity mission. Not even you, Sir. Not even the Bolsheviks," Jack added, annoyed. "And I can't run a business on credit."

"Ah, a comedian. You need this deal more than I do! *Mr. Summerhays*," he said again deliberately. "I have my informants in Hong Kong. Don't think I don't."

After an uncomfortable good-bye, the door closed behind him and Jack, standing in the vestibule, faced Algy, who immediately sprang up. "Where the devil have you been?"

Jack pulled him along quickly past the guard who waited for them to exit the residence and they hurried down the front steps.

"It looks like they're supplying the whole of Shanghai with opium and machine gun shells in there," Algy muttered excitedly. "I say, let go of me, will you?"

"Keep it down."

"But it's an English lorry they've hijacked," he said pointing back. "From the window by the loo I saw armed Japs sitting by the cab smoking. There were bullet holes in the doors."

Jack relinquished his grasp halfway across the courtyard, and they stood where the monkey had lain, a dark wet spot on the stone. "Look back now," Jack said, and Algy gazed toward the open library window. Tu stood outlined in it, a formidable figure who suddenly pulled the curtains shut.

Algy gave a low whistle. "Just watch it, Jack old boy. You think your charm will keep you from taking a purler, but I wouldn't bet on it."

The guard at the gate unlatched the bolt and seconds later they were standing out in the relative safety of the street. The sun was beginning to dip.

"You realize we're alive because he let us go?"

"Right ho! And Tu's a good egg too."

"I'll give you good egg. Tu's wealth is estimated at a cool 40 million US!"

"I'm not sure dollars amount to anything if they're Fa-Pi dollars! And by the way, our car is nowhere to be seen."

Jack continued down the block toward the corner, then finally slowed to a stop. The driver *was* gone.

"I *told* you he wouldn't wait."

"You know, I've just about had it with you. I've swung a corker of a deal in there on my own, *and* I've gotten us out alive."

"Ah, my heartiest congratulations, Sir! I've had plenty of time to think things over sitting in that hot vestibule as well. Your problem is that you only think of yourself. I don't mind for myself, but you disgraced Ana with your selfish behavior at tiffin yesterday. I can only say I'm glad there are still a few Russians left in town she can turn to."

"Ana's here?" Jack went silent for a moment, coloring furiously.

Algy flushed, suddenly uncomfortable under his gaze.

Jack shook his head. "You're an imbecile!" Disgusted, he turned and began walking briskly down the road.

"And why's that?" Algy demanded, hurrying behind. "She's not under your command."

Jack stopped, and faced him. "Do you think I just make things up for my amusement?"

Algy shrugged.

"That gunshot our driver heard—*?* Back at Tu's table I saw the former Russian advisor to the Communist Chou En-Lai. He was sitting there like Whistler's mother—*but with a hole in the head!*"

"Lovely, but Ana's a *WHITE* Russian, *not* a Communist."

"As if Tu would care! He's deeply paranoid—and, if we're fished up bloated in the strait one day, I wouldn't be surprised. He's got a strong foothold in Hong Kong. I suspect he's moving his finances there because the war is making business difficult here, even for him."

The sun had set by the time they walked into the lobby at the Cathay Hotel. Algy was unusually submissive, and meekly asked, "Jack, what if Ana had roundabout connections—you know, to some—*some Communists*? Would *we* be—*implicated?*"

Jack stared in disbelief. "I don't want to hear anything more from you."

Algy escaped to his room without another word and Jack entered the Horse and Hounds Bar, pulling up a stool and waiting to be served. As the minutes ticked by, Jack felt himself scintillating with anger, staring at the boys behind the counter who were apparently placing bets on something across the lobby.

"Ah. Mr. Morgan! How can I help you?" one finally asked.

"Gin and bitters," he barked. "And while you're at it, get me a detailed map with the Whangpoo godowns." A page came back with the map a few minutes later and handed it to Jack, but then continued in an animated conversation with the bartender and another man chopping ice. Curious, Jack finally turned to look at what had captivated them. "Boy," he said, giving a piercing look through the big window and pointed into the lobby. "That man over there—with the beard?"

The busboy set down a dishrag, "Yes, Mass-itah?"

As he said this the man turned completely around and Jack saw a woman on his arm—*Ana*. He felt his mouth drop. *She will kill me yet,* he thought.

"You refer to that man—with the pretty lady?" the boy asked. "He is the famous Komrad Diamant. Longtime resident, famous. We are not certain he will get out of Shanghai. We take bets just now," he said with a grin, and then giggling smugly at his colleagues held up his hand, fingers wide. "Five. Five to one."

"For his survival?"

"Oh yes," the man answered. "He will die. No more Communists in Shanghai."

Jack was still reeling in dismay and stepped away from the bar. He could see her perfectly, those red lips and laughing eyes as the Russian leaned over and kissed her on the mouth—*a lingering kiss.* The action elicited a shock in him but before he knew what was happening, a Chinese rushed in from the outside and hurried the Russian out a side door. Ana now stood alone, smiling, oblivious. *Obviously she'd just had a liaison with this man too!* The notion curled in the pit of his stomach, building into rage as he stalked across the lobby toward her.

He couldn't remember asking her to come upstairs. Perhaps he'd asked her for a drink and she'd agreed, for she'd followed him up. They'd talked, exchanging idle words, but Jack could only think of the face of the dead man back at Tu's, drooling blood. He didn't recall much of what he'd said but remembered her holding a glass, and her surprise, it falling—and the shattering sound on the tile floor of his balcony. Maybe he'd said she was a coaster, a floozy, but a look of surprise came over her, even dismay. She was a good actress, he told her so—his fingers pressing deep into her flesh as he led her to his bed.

She didn't run away, not even as he peeled the tight dress upward over her hips, letting loose her breasts, breasts that other men had touched. It was as if she didn't care. *Or did she?* Stroking her nakedness with his own, it infuriated, hurt him. Rolling over her, he kissed her everywhere, kissing where other men had been. *The Russian, the German … who else?* The thought drove him mad. He wanted her to want him, need him like he did her. She lay passive, turning her face from his yet everywhere he touched her, her skin was hot against his, igniting his desire and his anger—*coy, she wanted this.* He heard her tell him quietly, *Please stop, Jack. Not like this, not like this.* He entered her with a thick groan and her cries for him to stop only added to the rhythm with which he bore all he had into her, a vessel for all his unspoken rage, lust, and even more, his despair. The motion, the repetition, was setting him free but he may as well have been battering his own head against a wall, for though she did fight him, it was also with him, for she held on tight, and when the final clenching hold came, both were one, knotted in spirit. Jack knew he was lost.

"Oh why, Jack," she whispered. "Why?"

Her tearful voice and tight hold caught him, bringing him back, reeling down from space and broke him. Choking and gasping, he knew he'd found himself—*his place was with her.* He fell over, spent, empty of mind and soul, and she held him and he her. And he knew he'd never be anything without Ana. It was then he heard and felt her shuddering cries, first soft, then audible. Jack felt a sudden, responding and powerful ache in his own heart, and almost cried out. It had not been her choice—like *this. He'd been wrong, so, so wrong.* He grasped her hand, but she drew away, rejecting him.

She rose and pulled clothing over her nakedness, crying in agony or shame, he didn't know which. He himself did nothing but lie in the dark, immobile, from the distance of a vast chasm, clinging to the last vestiges of self. The knowledge that he'd pushed himself on her, undesired, unwanted, was devastating, almost as much as his feeling of betrayal. Her mad flirting with others, her plans to leave with Fritz, the diamond on her finger—and even this Russian.

When Ana shut the door the sound broke him, the wood meeting wood, the metal finding its place with a click; it was a seal on his heart that bruised, and tears singed his eyes as he lay still, unmoving, moved. He called out her name in vain. The sound hung in the darkness above him, dangling in the silence. *Too late, too late.*

JARDINE

Hong Kong *1997*

Auntie Tam rang early Sunday. "You come quick," she whispered.

Believing the worst, I dashed over breathless, ashamed for fighting with him last time. He was lying on a chaise longue in his smoking jacket with a Chinese comforter that he must have just pulled up. No, he wasn't dead. Not even close. There was a cloud of cigar smoke hanging about the room. When he saw I'd noticed it, he tried not to grin and said in pidgin, "Long time no see, Missie."

Auntie came bustling over, "He dress for you, look all fancy but never mind, he die soon. He say iron dis, clean dis, what for? Pooh! I say, she no care. You wanchee tea?" I followed her to the kitchen where she opened a white baker's box. "You gone almost *whole* week! No good!" she clucked, giving me a sharp eye while putting a custard tartlet on a plate. "Here, just bought."

"Before or after you called me?" I asked, letting her know I knew her game.

"You too smar', give me trouble. Go, go, go." She shooed me out of her kitchen.

Chomping on the custard, and enjoying the pleasantly greasy crust, I went in to see him. "So, you're feeling worse?" There was no mention of my last visit, that I'd accused him of lying and that I'd stormed out. But he didn't know his dying yellow rose was still on my windowsill.

"Oddly enough," he said raising an eyebrow, scanning my tartan mini-skirt and black punk boots, "I'm suddenly feeling better."

"I bet." I flung open the curtains and a block of light from the street fell into the darkness he lived in. When I turned to face him, the red swirls in the Persian carpets had come to life, and his blue eyes twinkled. Here was the man who got away with everything.

"I haven't had all those curtains open in years," he remarked sitting up.

I glared, but felt myself caving. I couldn't help liking him.

"You're not still upset, are you?" he asked, boyish charm at work.

"About your big lie?" I sat down, taking another bite of tart. "I'd *never* have known you were *Jack*." I shrugged, thinking of what he'd done to Ana, and felt kind of disgusted.

"But, you wanted to know everything, so I told you."

"Yes, disguised as Algy. But Ana forgave Jack. I mean, *you*—apparently, and Violet *wanted* you back. So why pretend you're someone else to me?"

"Jardine. I didn't want you to hate me, never see me again. There's been too much of that."

"*Hate*?" I closed my eyes, thinking it through. I sighed finally. "So, you really are my—*my grandfather?*"

He nodded.

"So I'm American—English—? Do you know about the Chinese part?"

"Burmese," he corrected.

Burmese? I stared, mouth gaping as if I'd been struck.

"You know," Jack said, suddenly looking out the window and pointing. "Those dentists downstairs had a pole right there that dangled hundreds of strings of customers' pulled teeth. I'd forgotten about that. They used to click in the breeze."

I excused myself and went to the kitchen to help get tea. "Why's he talking about teeth? Did he have a stroke?" I asked feeling dizzy and freaking out from what he'd just told me. I stood there with Tam, numb all over. *I wasn't Chinese? Burmese? I didn't even speak Burmese!*

She laughed at me as the kettle steamed vigorously, and behind her through the tiny window I saw the wink of blue from Victoria Harbor. "Teeth? Mebe he say, I wanchee tell you somtin', but you need pull har'," she said jerking at the air.

I thought she was joking, but couldn't tell because these old-generation ladies had crazy ideas drifting like butterflies—to be interpreted with the wind, the rain, how they stood in relation to chi. I switched to Cantonese and after a few minutes somehow felt calmer, Chinese again.

I went back in, putting down the tea tray. He lit up his cigar, smug and aloof, Jack Morgan all over again; it was all on his terms. "You know, I've been thinking," he said with a piercing glance. "You're still modern Chinese. All your claptrap about being an orphan, socially ostracized. It's just excuses."

"Huh?"

"Jardine," he said cautioning, "nursing all these feelings of injustice only breeds hate. It's a germ in your system; it grows, takes over. Like my cancer." He took a puff of the cigar watching me through the smoke, almost smiling. "In my case its name is Violet."

"What?" I asked, incredulous. "You don't get me at all—I just found out I'm not even Chinese!"

"Oh, you're Chinese all right. But the Chinese are in an identity crisis of their own. *Like you.*"

"Oh, give me a break."

"I am. You're fractured. But so is China. History's taken your people through so many wide bends. With Mao and the Communists you denounced the past and killed sixty million teachers, merchants—*innocent lives*. Before that? Dynastic rule brought brilliant culture and art, but also extreme cruelty for the peasant class. Just try and piece it together. You get a fractured identity—a break in continuity. And isn't that what an orphan is?"

"You're too cerebral. Our culture *is* integrated, it's *got* continuity. Look at Chinese fashion. I mean, there's the Shanghai Tang stuff with the high slits and collars—in fabulous colors. Then there's the modern stuff, all deconstructed in black and gray ... Not that you'd know about fashion."

"Shanghai Tang fashions? Those are just Mao suits in fruity colors. You're making my point, Jardine. There's no solid modern Chinese identity yet."

I was annoyed and took more tea. I liked modern China—*and old China*, right next to each other. Like girls in mini-dresses, high heels, and Chanel bag knockoffs, shouting on cell phones while shopping for eels in wet market.

"Everyone's got trouble with integration," he said. "For nations, it seems easier to have reversals, like the Communists' 'Cultural' Revolution—*killing* half the citizens rather than *bridging* the gap, growing, moving forward and making the hard choices. The noble savage of yesterday is today's oppressed, and tomorrow, the next Mao."

"But you're saying oppression and emancipation are like a reversible pullover. That one side isn't better than the other! You're wrong! History's moving forward, not up and down."

He laughed. "Sorry?"

"Progress!" I shouted, pissed off.

He pretended to have a flea in his ear. "Progress? That's an illusion. Every country's a predator, every system a living breathing thing that needs to eat, even *you*. You can stop eating meat, but who's going to protect a humble stalk of broccoli from your gnashing teeth? Socialists and Fascists prey on the small businessman, Communists prey on the hopes and dreams of their subjects, Capitalists on the aggrieved worker, and in all these systems money follows either ability or corruption. To live is to eat. It can be symbiotic, or murderous, but it's not going to change."

"So what's to stop me from strangling you?"

"Society and culture, illusions of nicety—they stick a smiley face on things."

"You're depressing."

"I'm just trying to tell you, you don't need to fit into any club. Be yourself."

"But who's that? I have no roots, I told you."

"Prejudices you mean. Honestly, those dentist signs with rotted teeth really looked savage when I first came out East. But as years went by and I met so many different people, I realized that my prejudices weren't truisms, especially when other people made statements that offended *me*. Cultures are like that. Their edges are tender; where they interface there's pain—and their logic only works at home."

I stared down at my black nail polish, wondering where he was going with this, and peeled off a loose chip as he spoke.

He seemed puzzled for moment, then said, "You think those ghastly black fingernails are *you*?"

"Sure," I said, snide and satisfied. "I like punk *culture*."

"Fine. But consider this. I once saw a servant washing his feet in Violet's priceless Wedgwood soup tureen out back. Not malice, just a bowl, right?"

I laughed. "Form is function, that's Chinese."

"Or, just maybe this servant thought we white folks butchered our meat at the table, sawing away with knives and forks like Cro-Magnons. Maybe he felt superior. Chopsticks, after all, *are* the Chinese solution to hacking up bone and gristle at the table in plain view. That's culture, you see? Different ways of getting food to your mouth *then claiming it's the only way*—then judging others from this vantage point."

"You're reading into it. He was just washing his feet."

"They still call us foreign devils, don't they?"

I flushed.

"Your black nails and these silly military boots—that's your way of rejecting conformists, saying your subculture's superior to the style of dullards in pinstripes. Isn't it? But you're conforming to your group."

"I guess."

"There's no difference between you—don't you see? Culture is arbitrary. It's primitive man clinging to something, anything, in a world of numbers and violent flux."

"So there's no identity?"

"It's not the life preserver you seem to be hoping for."

I stared at him blankly. Really, this was not what I wanted to hear. He'd already cut me adrift with the Burmese surprise.

"You're distinguishing by race, by *being* Chinese or *not* being Chinese, but you needn't, you could use language, class, religion ... even your silly punk clothing. People live in a near-constant state of near delusion, caught up in their society, their times, their politics, and their silly 'educated' opinions."

"But look at Europe; everyone seems fine and not oppressed in, say, Sweden."

"No one but the next Einstein. The creative thinkers—*they're the ones* sacrificed for the common good."

"But this is the modern *world*; we're trying to bring everyone up to the same level."

"*Down to, down to.* Modern man is no better off; he only thinks he is because he has television and gadgets, can shit in a flush pot, and see the world—*still a savage, though.* Not much can make a dent in that thick skull full of fairy tales. I call ignorance a social lubricant. It works well, generally, unless there's a real conflict and everyone wakes up to reality. Then you have your flux, riots culling the population. You think your progressives are superior, advanced because they kiss the feet of science—thinking you can avoid this savagery in your blood; but you can't see what's ahead of you. You know the old joke: progressives always cry out, impatiently, 'Rush forward!' But the reactionaries are already ahead of them, and seeing the coming explosion shout, 'No-no! Go back!'"

"Yes, ha ha. I know where this is going. You're blaming the bomb on the progressives."

The fat round red tip glowed as he smoked. He was watching me steadily, then he rolled the smoke in his mouth, and let out two puffs. "Hiroshima. Nagasaki. The twin daughters of progress."

I crossed my arms watching the two clouds disperse in the room.

He leaned back to look at me. "I date the end of the nineteenth century with the West tinkering with nuclear fusion around '38, Hitler's rise, and then with the Japs kicking us whites out of Asia. A confluence of evil." He smiled, shrugging. "Or progress." He looked down and, removing his wallet, took out a picture and placed a very worn photo gently on my palm. It was as light as a cigar ash. "This is *your* mother, *my* Bella. Born into all that. *She*—was my *whole* life."

A baby of two years looked up at me. *Mother?* It was a direct punch to my belly and I felt my thoughts skew off course—everything stopped, but for my tears.

"I had everything a man could want, but rotten luck came with it too."

My eyes came to back to rest on him, a halo of blurry light. I blinked. His blue eyes were full of tears.

"Divorce was unthinkable and I'd given my word to Percy so I couldn't jump ship. Besides, Hong Kong was so promising! You couldn't imagine it was all about to end and a lot of us would die."

"Promising?" I gulped back emotions as I looked down at my mum.

"Hong Kong was humming! The *rest* of the world was in collapse. I guess the timing was all wrong, but my God, the output was amazing—shoes, cement, paint, batteries. Then the West called for war supplies, so we cranked out transistors, gas masks, helmets, you name it. Our new electric plant in Hum Hong was cranking out 60MW. We were on the cusp of great things!"

"I don't understand. Either it was the end of the world or some kind of Hong Kong industrial revolution?"

"Yes," he muttered.

"What?"

"I don't know—it was terrible. As if something great, about to be born, was crushed at the first gulp of air. Germany was eating up Europe and Japan was eating up China. Churchill couldn't fight on both these fronts, so he conceded to Japan's barbarous takeovers.

That left us alone out here in the South China Sea, drifting on life support.

"So—there was nowhere to hide?"

"That's about it. The Japs were battling their way down to our back door while the Nationalists and the Communists were killing each other. You have to grant a lot to the Communists; they fought for China, while Chiang Kai-shek fought for himself. He had FDR duped, eating out of his hand. But imagine, if we'd backed the Communists, things might not have gone so bad. The Japs would have had a harder fight—might never have made it down here to us, and maybe we'd never have dropped the bomb. Then maybe in turn, we would've had the clout to avert the Cultural Revolution." He shrugged, then shook his head. "But our little Bella, our baby girl was born right as the world was poised to tear apart. You have so much hope for a new baby—so much hope."

I clenched my teeth. I didn't want this story to end up bad—something that would haunt me forever. I stared at Mum's baby face, those shining eyes, wondering what could have happened. "You said her name was Bella?"

An irrepressible smile spread over his face. "We named her after our Italian midwife, the nun. Oh, our Bella—what a miracle. She was the smartest, fastest, most beautiful baby. And she amazed me—I felt so responsible, so humbled. I *learned* things." He spread his hands wide. "*Love*," he said, laughing.

As I watched him I could tell he was seeing a little person before him, like a film, her tottering, then walking, then running into his arms. It was Jack Morgan, unguarded.

"We were so busy with our little Bella we didn't see the sun blot out. In March the next year they forced every able-bodied man to register; by September, England had declared war on Germany. The next year, the men were outfitted with tropical marching uniforms and put into compulsory service. Mostly, we just paraded around swinging our arms and waving flags in Statue Square. By 1940, Germany was bombing London. France had fallen. What home was there to return to?"

"America?" I suggested weakly, but he didn't seem to hear.

"On December 8, 1941, the planes came, dive-bombing Central …" His voice cracked. "Fires burned, people lay dying, others were confused in the noise and smoke. We were a rag-tag army. Our weapons were rationed; only half the men had rifles, and there was only one Thompson submachine gun per section. Our shells were rationed too." He stared at me. "A country has a duty to protect its citizens, but Churchill left us out here to die."

I was quiet as he pulled himself back from the past; I could see this telling was exacting a toll, and he looked away. I went to the kitchen to refresh the teapot. What was the point in all his grief kept in so long. Why? My own throat ached like a tight cord was tying it off. I thought of his cancer, and then of my Mum, his Bella. We'd both lost.

It was some time before I went back in and sat down. He didn't help himself to the tea. He had no interest.

"Tell me the rest," I said.

"I can only tell this once," he said exhausted. "You want a history, a past, I'll give it to you. But there's a price."

"Yes, but there's a *price* of not knowing my past, too. I'm the product of your colony, not white—not yellow. So yes, we had a civil war, but it was a *Chinese* war. The West stuck its nose into our business. What's the legacy of the West but anger and resentment, everywhere you go? How do you explain that?" He reached for my hand, hopeful, but I pulled away, afraid. "It's all I know," I said, and stared out the window.

"But—you *are* the legacy, you blur *all* the lines," he said, his voice tender. "Jardine, my dear," he said, eyes softening. "You're part me, part Bella, part future—you're the new Asia—full of hopes, and you're beautiful."

My lower lip was trembling. No one had called me that; no one had loved me either. I gritted my teeth against the desperate need to belong to someone, something. *This man loved me. I saw it, felt it, and yet …* I didn't want to give in to him like all the others had; I didn't want to love a man with a foot in the grave.

"Jardine, you *must* know. I've kept my life on hold all this time, just hoping Bella would return, hoping that terrible hole in me would be filled." He stood there, watching me as I stared resolutely out the window, hardening my heart.

"Then where is Algy?" I demanded, turning around. "The Mr. Worthing you *pretended* to be."

He didn't move, but I felt the internal shock in him, saw it in his eyes when he quietly said, "My dear, Algy took his life."

Book Three

1938

Hear Albert

19

China Coast Navigation & Co. *23 February 1938*

Things changed after Old Summerhays stepped aside, and it was said Jack Morgan ran a tight ship from the old man's cracked leather wing chair. No, Percy stayed up at Peak House now under strict orders, taking no visitors—Albert hadn't been able to see him for months, and outsiders speculated he'd been pushed out by Morgan. At the firm, the official word was he was taking a rest-cure, that he'd had a bout of influenza which had progressed, afflicting his lungs and one of his heart valves. *Poppycock*, Albert would say, but had to bite his tongue so as not to say more, for one couldn't go about casting aspersions on a white man's character in British Hong Kong—*but how he wanted to.*

As things stood, Albert, titular head of accounting, had gone from landing bum in the butter under the old man to having three outstanding warnings under Jack. Heartless people laughed. They had resented his "in" with Percy—their fathers had been mates in King George's Navy. Either way, clerical errors and misplaced files under the old chairman hadn't been cause for dismissal—not until

Jack took over. Only last week rumor had it that someone might precipitate Albert's departure by "losing things for him." All this went through Albert's mind as he gingerly shook out the clipping from the envelope he'd just received with the morning post. Putting on his glasses Albert unfolded it, hands trembling. There was a sudden rap at the door. He looked up and quickly tucked the paper away.

"Taipan wanchee see you top side," Jack's messenger boy announced sticking his head in.

Albert nodded, feigning good cheer until the boy shoved off, then took a swig of the Remy Martin in his drawer. *What could that blackguard want now?* As things stood, his digestion was spoiled, his nerves were on edge, and he was a sneeze away from sacked. Case in point: Jack had had no qualms about canning that worthless milksop Worthing after a falling out in Shanghai—*and they'd been on good terms!* Albert took out the clipping from the *North China Daily* again, smoothing it out. It was photo of several people grinning with the infamous criminal, Big Ear Tu, at a Shanghai nightclub. Sure enough, Percy's son-in-law was there—gin and bitters in hand. The print below read: "Investing in China. Tu Yue-sheng raises much needed capital for the railways in disrepair from aerial bombings." It was damning—but was it enough to ruin him? *Yet Morgan was forcing his hand.* Albert cringed. *I must tread a thin line—for Percy loves his son-in-law.* Looking up at the wall clock, he reached for the telephone and dialed Peak House. It was a gamble, but it must be done.

Hanging up a few minutes later he hurried upstairs to the boardroom, a creeping smile on his lips—*he'd gotten a private meeting with the old man!*

Knocking tentatively, he entered the boardroom. Jack Morgan stood with his back to him, outlined by a spectacular view of the harbor, and spoke without even turning around. "We're leasing out an enormous godown in Sheung Wan but for two months I haven't received a plugged Mex for it. Albert, how do you expect I collect payment with a misplaced contract?" He turned suddenly. "Look at this!" He tossed a sheaf of paper across the table. "Over $10,000 lost in revenue on the Wolseley account. That's *your* negligence." Jack glared at him for a moment, then snapped, "You've a week to set both things in order or face dismissal." Jack picked up a brown-stained document. "And by the way, try to avoid using company papers as your personal tea coasters."

"Not to worry, Sir, I'll arrange an inspection of all the files today." Then, grandly obsequious, he snatched away the offending paper. "I'll have this retyped, Sir."

An hour later Albert's rickshaw came to a halt at 10 Old Peak Road. *If exposing the Java deal didn't do it, the picture in his pocket give a toehold against the man.* Breathing heavily in the humidity, he headed for the shaded entrance of the club, crushing fallen pink blossoms of the bauhinia tree underfoot as he walked.

Percival had already taken a table on the verandah and was engrossed in the *South China Morning Post* when Albert pulled out a chair. The old man set down the paper with great irritation. "Albert, you realize my daughter was listening in on the telephone when we spoke? Iced tea is all I'm allowed, confound it!"

"Absolute rot! But, I see you're not wholly restricted to invalid food," Albert said, eyeing the remains of steak and gravy on Percy's plate. He selected a luncheon plate for himself as the cart came by.

"Not when I do the ordering!" He had kindly blue eyes that had of late clouded. "I must say, I was keen to leave the house when you called. Can't do it often, mind you."

"Percy," Albert said, shaking the napkin out and tucking it under his chin, "I think we need to talk about the progress on the China deal."

"Oh, that." He frowned, pulling at his collar. "It's the one thing I'm thankful for—Jack handles all the unpleasantness now. You ready for a drink? The doctor says I'm 'yellow all the way to the gills,' but I'll not start drinking water at my age. Thins the blood!"

"But surely, being imprisoned on the Peak away from your own firm can't be right. It's downright cruel, I should say." Percy drained his scotch and soda then set the glass down considering Albert's appeal, then abruptly focused on a wedge of cheddar. Alarmed he'd not stirred Percy's sense of outrage, Albert added, "You're healthy as a horse, old boy, but what's a horse without his work? Useless! Even a turn in the paddocks would suffice!"

The man put down his fork. "Ah. It's good of you to call on me, Albert, to cheer me with a social call. You know, had you waited another day, we'd have missed one another, and who knows, by the time I get back I might be dead."

"But—but what are you speaking of?'

"It's this God-awful heat, you know. Violet has decided to send me to Chung King for fresh air."

"Chung King!" Albert felt stymied.

Percival prodded the pale Cheshire with his fork, then skipped over it, plunging into a ripe Stilton. "The plane leaves tomorrow," he said raising a greenish, waxy hunk to his mouth. "Violet says it should be amusing." He chewed, glancing at his watch. "Jack's picking me up in an hour, so I needn't return in the heat."

Jack? Albert's eye darted to his own wristwatch, then grimaced. "All the way to Chung King? I'd think you'd prefer to set the company on good footing before your—before your time comes as it does for us all."

"Oh, Jack has things well in hand."

"Well then," Albert cleared his throat, shocked by the indifference. "I want you to know, I've come for a specific reason. Being a devoted employee for nearly twenty years, I *worry a great deal* on *your* behalf, and …"

The old man coughed, turning bright red from the neck up, and struggled to catch his breath. Albert waited nervously until Percy finally barked impatiently, "Yes, yes, go on, my man!" He raised his glass to his lips, "You were saying?"

"*Right.* Look, I feel I need to ask you about the Shanghai deal Jack is working on. Seems there's been much travel but—" Albert paused, hands spread wide, with a weighty look.

"Profits? Are you asking about profits?" Percy raised the newspaper, shaking it at him. "This is where they're going!"

"No, *no*. Not *those* profits," Albert said trying to steer the subject back to Jack.

"What else is there? Listen." Percy pushed his spectacles up his nose. "Here, listen. 'Japanese military and naval action is simply large scale banditry against—against foreign interests in the areas they have occupied.'" As he read aloud, another shipping tycoon, wiry as an Airedale, passed the table and stopped to interject, "Percy, it isn't cricket!"

"Ah, Hollis!" Percy spluttered, putting his heavy arm out to the vacant chair.

Hollis set down his tennis racquet. "The thing to consider," Hollis said, pulling out a chair, "is the Japs aren't going to back down. Not until we do something."

"But what to do? Our hands are tied. They were our allies. You can't just reprimand them."

Albert wanted to shake the table in aggravation.

"Percy, they're engaged in a full-scale war in China," Hollis frothed. "And blast it, it should be declared a war! I'm not interested in this Sino-Japanese development hocus-pocus. It's simply a scam to get what can be got, and they've taken more than their share. Shipping revenues are down, and they aren't honoring foreign treaty rights. I can't get my steamers into Nanking, or Wuhu, and Canton is up in the air, open one day and closed the next. I can't stay in business like that."

Albert cleared his throat. "Gentlemen, as I was saying, these problems are—"

"Hear, hear!" another man said, running up the steps from the grass court. "No one can."

"Ah, Smivvy, come, strap on the nose bag."

Smith dragged a chair across the tiles. "What I want to know is why the damned Chinese are dealing with the Japs on one side and bombing them on the other? Boy! Gin and bitters, here."

"Ah, the prize question." Percy hooted, putting away another piece of cheese, eating faster with more agitation, and drinking more whisky and soda than lubrication demanded. "I read the Japs' customs return for last month," he added, pulling his collar. "Fourteen percent on import, and seventeen percent on export. That's more than blooming double what we and the Americans combined get!" He paused to look over the pudding tray as it came by and pointed while the other men settled into their chairs. Albert felt his career inching away from him.

"I thought you were on a restricted regimen," Hollis said eyeing Percy's pudding as the waiter ladled hot custard over it.

Percy checked his watch. "Thirty minutes before my son-in-law arrives and the table is cleared off. All I'll have is a cup of tea before me and look the saint, what?" He guffawed and this brought another coughing fit. First he turned red, and holding up a hand he waved off their concern, but the coughing continued past the point of comfort, and his ears tinged blue.

Hollis's laugh died early on, and he kept an eye on the older man. When Percy stopped coughing, and people at the other tables had looked away, Hollis continued quietly. "I keep thinking the Chinese are cut up over Woodrow Wilson. They fought on our side then expected us to tell the Japs to get the blazes out of Manchuria. Fair's fair! But Wilson was scared the Japs would boycott his League of Nations, so he told 'em to stay. Now the Chinese won't trust the Americans, or us. In their eyes we're as bad as the Japs. I'd say we're in a pickle."

"As bad as the Japs? We're worse, we're damned fools," Percy said looking at his watch. He downed two final bites then signaled the waiter to clear away the evidence.

"Listen, the Chinese factions don't trust each other anyway! How can we trust them?" Smith interjected as Percy's plates were removed. "You never know who you're dealing with or what side the bread's buttered on with the Communists or the Kwomintang."

The other man slapped his hand down on the table. "Both, I reckon. The fools in the US are shelling out millions for the China Relief Fund, and it's ending up in Chiang's private budget and not with the really needy. Meanwhile, the Russians are betting on the Communists, and Japan is hedging her bets paying out both parties to fight each other." Here the conversation dwindled as what he'd said sank in.

Albert snatched the opportunity. "And yet," he said slyly, "there are some who are turning a profit from all this confusion."

"Profit?" Hollis exploded. "Just tell me how! We haven't been able to dock anywhere on the China coast with any sort of regularity since the Japs took over Shanghai. Business needs consistency!"

"Well," Albert prodded further, "has anyone thought of branching out into other sorts of business?"

They all looked at him blankly.

"Rubber, for one thing. CCN's turning a remarkable profit in Java."

Hollis was dumbstruck. "In rubber?"

Albert couldn't have planned it better.

Smith guffawed, "You've got to be a blasted idiot thinking there's profit in rubber."

"There could be. Japan's eating up rubber for her war effort," Albert said. "And Germany will be needing it."

"Bollocks! Everyone's out of *that* business for now," Hollis said with force. "Synthetic rubber's the way of the future. Percy, where'd you get this fool?"

"Nonetheless," Albert said smugly, pushing Hollis's button again. "We're turning a remarkable profit. Percival knows all about it."

Percival had been listening to this last part of the conversation with a quiet disgrace.

"No, no. It's true." Albert added the finishing touch, "We're making a fortune in rubber and I'm willing to bet that we're the only firm on the coast turning a profit *because* of it. And if there's a second world war ..."

"With all due respect—*NO ONE* is making profits! We're not offloading anything, anywhere! No delivery, nothing!" Hollis said. "Now how the blazes is there profit in that? And rubber? Confound it." He put his fist down. "Rubber is *dead!* And there will *be* no world war!"

Albert smugly tipped back his glass congratulating himself that Percy's friends had gotten his point across for him. Now it would take very little to point out that Jack's ledgers *had* to be fakes. As the last bit of tonic pleasantly chilled his palate and sunshine came through his upturned glass, he was startled by the sound of a chair falling backward. Putting down the glass, he looked up in time to see Hollis standing up with his mouth dropped open, eyes staring at the ground. Albert blinked. Where Percival had once sat there was now an obvious gap. Mystified, he stood up himself and only then fathomed that his crowning achievement of argument had been wasted.

"He's having an attack of apoplexy," Smith shouted, "Get help!" There was a great clatter of cutlery and dishes as people at the surrounding tables gasped and stood up.

China Coast Navigation & Co. *28 February 1938*

SOMETHING BIG AND WHITE pipped him on the side of the head, and Algy dropped his pencil. Reaching down he discovered it was a paper airplane and quickly balled it up.

Jack laughed, heading to the door, ducking as the wad whizzed back past him. "Come on, I want to show you something," he said over his shoulder.

Outside on Connaught Road, Algy followed Jack to the Rolls parked at the edge of the pier.

"Why so glum today?" Jack asked suddenly, as they got in and he steered the car onto the transport ferry for Kowloon.

"Divestitures, ships for sale, trucks purchased. I'm so busy lying on paper my eyes are crossed. Your vision of the future is a tad too fantastic for me. Stop! Look out! You very near drove off the edge!" The ferry rocked under sudden swells.

"Algy, that Burma Road's made me more money in a month than all Percy's ships have made the past year. And I've only one convoy running." Jack pulled the parking brake and gestured toward the hills on Kowloon side, "There's the future, my friend: China!"

"Indeed, a tad optimistic. But tell me about the large transfer of cash I noticed," Algy said suspicious. "Where did those funds go?"

Jack gave a smirk. "Let's have a martini at the Peninsula, and then I'll show you."

An hour later Algy was startled to see they were slowing down at the Kai Tak runway just as one of the ancient British military planes limped toward takeoff. Jaded and annoyed as he was by Jack, he couldn't hold back a gasp when he entered a hangar several minutes later. Three enormous silver airplanes stood in front of him surrounded by a whirr of activity.

"Three new Douglas DC-3 Dakotas," Jack said as men hauled crates past them. "The most versatile transport aircraft in the world. Just in from California. We're going to crack open the Japanese grip on trade with these! What do you think? No blockading these gals!"

"But!" Algy reeled. "You don't mean— ?"

"No one'll touch our profits when these begin their routes Monday."

"But even our military doesn't have something as extravagant as this. Come to your senses. Return them before it's too late."

"Bollocks!" Jack said, striding off.

Algy scratched his head, amazed at the staggering amount of supplies being unloaded by trucks at the back of the hangar. All earmarked for China, he supposed. "Airplanes aren't proven," he said running after Jack. "You've a mania for everything modern, but we ship by sea. It's how we *made* our money." When he looked around a pile of crates, he saw Jack had already climbed into a cockpit and was waving down, smiling.

Central China *28 February 1938*

THE MESSENGER SHOOK HIS arm. "Sergeant Sakura, you're wanted at the commander's tent."

Yoshi felt his bowels turn liquid at the thought of the man, and sat up quickly. *Da-me, da yo! Not good,* he thought.

The commander was sitting cross-legged at his field desk, and after perfunctory bows, Yoshi's eyes picked out the small paper with the official red seal in his superior's hands. "You have impressed someone, Sakura. This is an order for your immediate transfer."

Yoshi's eyes widened in disbelief.

"*Kempetei.* Elite Intelligence Division."

Yoshi didn't understand. He made three little rapid nervous bows. "Please, I didn't hear you, Sir." *Was it a cruel joke?*

"Oita! Kono yogore! You're to turn in your kit, and take the next train out. You're reporting to your next post undercover. A Chinese peasant."

Yoshi didn't want to ask where they were sending him, but his fears mounted when the commander said, "You've given me a lot of trouble. Go to the gunner's tent and hand in your rifle. There are worthier men than you that will hold it. *Hitotsu yaki o irete yaru beki da!*"

Teach me something? Yoshi was confused with this rude manner in which he was treated, but bit his tongue. It would be the last time.

The man pointed to the other tent and Yoshi had no choice but to bow his way out backward. At the entrance he saw that he was expected. Two gunners waited and followed him in. They closed the tent flap and in the dim light, he saw the medic who told him to stick out his tongue. At first Yoshi clenched his jaws and saw the men at his side move their hands down to their weapons. He had no choice. Yoshi watched as the tongs came toward his tongue. At least the sword was sharp. He didn't scream in pain, but closed his eyes very tight.

The commander was standing over him as Yoshi fell to the ground writhing. "You're to be posted in Hong Kong! Let's make sure you don't disgrace your colors." He paused as Yoshi spit blood, then hissed. "*You?* Kempetei? I don't know how you're getting out of here. I made sure your request never left camp." He stood looking down at him with disgust. "At least you won't be able to talk. *Bakayaroo!*"

The next morning Yoshi was in a fever, his clothes were gone and he found himself dressed in some dead peasant's clothing. "See that our own boys don't kill you!" was the farewell. He was loaded onto a train with his official transfer, and after five hours of trying to sleep on the floor and being kicked by his own soldiers he crawled away into a coal wagon, where he lay shivering in pain, watching the night sky as the train travelled south. In his agony and fevered state he drifted in and out of sleep, but as he awoke now and then he stared up at the moon and saw his beloved O-bachan's face, hovering among the clouds.

Yoshi, I will write to honorable Uncle, O-ji san. He will send for you so you don't have to fight. Our small nation will never dare to attack the British in Hong Kong. You will be safe, Yoshi-chan, and you will return to work the family fields again. In his delirium he felt O-bachan's wrinkled old hand on his shoulder but no one was there. A tear slid out of Yoshi's eye, and he turned his head away from the light.

Dangerous Inroads

20

Canossa Hospital *18 March 1938*

Everyone was amazed that the heavy club lunch hadn't killed Summerhays. Albert shrugged, *good joss.* Peering into the hospital rooms, looking for the correct number, he couldn't help but think the old man could have died salaaming Jack and never known he'd been betrayed. *Damned lucky for me,* he thought as he sidestepped the sign—*Family visitation only.* This was his last chance to burst the old man's bubble and he knew it, but today he was better prepared. Jack's secretary, Nancy, had unwittingly given him a vital piece of the puzzle.

A few months ago he'd slipped into Jack's office unobserved and had come upon the oddest thing—*a map of China marked up in red ink.* This hadn't been a map of the *sea* or the China coast as would be fitting CCN's chairman, but an *INLAND* map, and the lines—they were China's key *rail* lines; the Pin-Han, and the Lung-Hai! *Was this why Jack was always traveling on business? But why? It was an enigma.* Albert's hand had run down the north-south line to the juncture point circled in red, Cheng Chow, a seedy village notorious for prostitution, crime, and opium dens which exploited the convenience of the rail axis—frequented by trainloads of soldiers. Further afield there were more curious marks—red crosses miles from civilization. It had been a stunning discovery—yet he couldn't find the connection. Still couldn't—but he was closer, though—for it all seemed to dovetail with what Nancy had mentioned only yesterday.

Jack had just stepped out when Albert caught her in her office setting down the telephone in tears. With minimal prodding he'd discovered a tenacious client, Tang, regularly gave her hell over a Shanghai contact, Mr. Tu. Gushing with sympathy, Albert took Nancy to lunch, where she inadvertently mentioned some odd train stocks on the company portfolio and how she had found it difficult scheduling Jack's China trips. Albert bought her a posy for her troubles, and that night dug out the train stocks hidden in plain view.

Coming to Percy's door, Albert tapped his pocket where he had the photo of Jack and Tu *and* the train stocks; this time he was ready for justice. Raising his hand to knock, he paused, and hearing voices leaned to the keyhole.

"Well, he's not your father!" There was an abrupt silence. "Jack, I need to speak to Father—*alone*."

Albert heard approaching footsteps and hurried away in time as Jack exited the room and took the lift down the hall. As the doors closed, Albert rushed out of hiding to listen.

"Violet! I didn't want to go to China. And if I want a drink I'll damn well have one."

"But what about the firm?"

"It's his problem now. I'm not interested."

"But, Father," she whinged. "That's all you ever *cared* for. Your *legacy* is in question."

"Damn it, girl. Just leave me be. The firm can blow up for all I care. I'm dying! You hear me? Stop lying about it."

Albert didn't have the heart to listen further and headed toward the stairwell. In fact, he was so dismayed, he sank down onto the top step. *Dying? Dying!*

He groaned. *What use was it then? What use! If I'm to get real justice, I'll need to wring it from Jack himself!* He smoked a cigarette in the stairwell, his hatred focusing on Jack, imagining him dead, and throwing rocks at his head. *I can't shoot the bastard myself,* he thought, *or attack him with a chopper in an alley. I'm not Big Ear Tu.* Albert thought a moment, dejected, then sat up, startled. Throwing down his cigarette, he ran out of Canossa Hospital, and flagging the first rickshaw, headed to the nearest private telephone booth. It took a half hour until the operator got a good connection to the Shanghai Race club.

"Bob, you wanker," he shouted with tears in his eyes. "Yes, yes, it's me. I need another favor. Yes, the photo of Tu was on the money. But I need more. I want you to dispatch a telegram to Morgan. No. It needs to come from the Cheng Chow area. *Cheng Chow!* You've a friend somewhere out there, Shang-Kwe, isn't it? I said, *SHANG-KWE!* That's right. Have him send it to Morgan direct. I want it to say the following. You have a pencil? Good. *Departed Shanghai for Canton. Stop. Delivery problems. Stop. Awaiting your arrival. Stop. Monday night meet me Cheng Chow Station. Stop. Tang*—Got that?"

After that, he had the operator dial Shanghai again, but this time it was the number he'd taken from Nancy's desk. "Yes, is Mr. Tang there?" He waited for some time and then a very English-sounding man came to the receiver. Putting on his best Irish waterfront accent Albert said, "I dunno wot you t'ink, Sorr, but a Yank in Cheng Chow's sellin' you out good'n propah. May's well cot your bollocks off fohr I 'eard 'e's tellin' the filt'y Japs where to bomb your thrain supply banks. 'E's done so wi' mine, fohr I'm a tinder-hearted fool wid no judgemint for min's sowls. But, go'n an' see fohr y'sel'. 'E'll be there Mond'y next, and you'll know wot's wot, I reckon. Aye, the 'ead of a bullet twood not be waysted on that bhoy, twood be a right *invistment!*" When he'd hung up he grinned. That Tang chap had been in a tizzy, but he'd gotten the message all right. They would send someone out to that dung heap looking for a Yank, and they'd find the only white man for miles, Jack, wandering about with no reason to be there. And what was one more dead white man on the dung heap of this war? *Nothing to nobody! Now that was justice!*

Peninsula Hotel *18 March 1938*

Isidrio Chang tapped his long pipe emptying it at the base of a palm, then subtly gestured to the far end of the lobby with his slender finger. "You, go back where we came from and pick up the little white paper I dropped, see? Go, go!"

Van Leiden didn't like being made a fool of; his ears went hot as he stalked off in search of the paper, his gaze passing over countless well-heeled patrons, until it came to a halt at the white scrap. Reaching down, he was too late, as a lobby boy in a pillbox hat picked it up.

"Yours, Mass-itah?" the smiling face asked.

Van Leiden snatched at it while his eyes strayed to the real object of his efforts. There, at the nearest table, he saw a couple dawdling over tea. Trying not to stare, he took in the profile of the woman, and lingered, hoping she'd turn her head. The man with her was one of those pasty English types, raised on boiled cabbage. *Ah, there.* She looked his way. *It had to be her.* She had large eyes and a big bust. Van Leiden pocketed the paper and turned on his heel. Out on Salisbury Road he gave Fausto a confident nod. "I congratulate you on your selection."

Chang laughed, while Fausto chaffed. "She appeals to you?"

"Marlene Dietrich, with a heart of gold! Am I right?"

"This isn't the business of hearts. I want her back," Fausto said. "It's now a point of honor. I have clients asking for her repeatedly."

"And that fop she's with?"

"Not such a fop as yourself!" Fausto said. "We only spotted her now by accident, you fool!"

Chang held up his palm for silence. "They were evicted from the mission flat. We lost their trail because of you," he accused. "But because of their bad fortune, we have found them again."

"Enough," Fausto sighed. "If this lackey of yours wants to continue to work for us, tell him what he's to do." Turning to the street, he hailed a rickshaw, but when the boy named a preposterous sum, Fausto bristled. "For that price you could ride *me*, you idiot!" The grinning coolie was not quick enough to avoid the fat man's swing, and the fist cuffed him full in the face so that he fell backward onto the cobbles. There was an outburst of laughter from other coolies while Fausto marched off to the next rickshaw. Van Leiden turned to Chang for explanation.

"You. Go follow those two," Chang said curtly. "And don't come back without the new address, understand? We need her back in Macao. It's a matter of face now. Fausto will not rest till it's done."

Lower Peel Street *19 March 1938*

THAT DAY, AS SHE gathered up her piecework for the charitable English ladies at the Helena May Club, the morning post arrived. Running late, Ana took a letter addressed to her, noting that the pale blue envelope had no return address but was written in a familiar Russian script. It must be from Tanya, she thought happily and decided she'd read it after she'd dropped off her piecework. Tanya was the one person she'd hoped to keep in touch with and she wanted to enjoy her letter at her leisure.

At the Helena May, Ana collected the modest payment for her piecework. It was the club's contribution to white women who'd hit hard times in the Far East—and she was grateful for it, though a little ashamed too. But ever since Algy had lost his job with Jack over her and the Shanghai muddle, things had been very difficult for them. Finding a bench in Statue Square, Ana sat down and eagerly tore open the letter, expecting news of the war. Inside, however, she found a short note from a stranger. "Your brother, Mischa Vukovna, was killed in a Nationalist anti-Communist raid. He was in the company of …" Ana tucked the letter into her purse.

The heat that blazed up off the pavement was comforting at first, but as she walked it grew stronger and stronger. She removed her hat, and gloves, and began to move quickly. Perhaps because she hadn't eaten that morning, or at noon, or perhaps the sun—but Ana felt her vision failing her. Dark starry gaps floated in the periphery so that more and more of the street and the people vanished in a blur of darkness. The coolies bumped her, voices shouted rudely. She was running blindly, the entire scene before her blurring from her tears. At Queen's Road her foot missed the sidewalk.

China Coast Navigation & Co. — *19 March 1938*

SITTING IN THE BOARDROOM high above Queen's Road, Jack shook his head as he read the telegram again. *More trouble with the trains.* Because of this he'd have to head back into China right away. Jack scanned a wall map and then he looked at the date on the telegram. *Too late to call—Tang would be somewhere on the road, perhaps in Canton by now.* Jack looked at his watch. There was little time to spare. He stood up reluctantly, turning to look out over Victoria Harbor. Directly across the water he could see the clock tower at the Canton Kowloon Rail terminus. As one of the few remaining inroads to China, it too was breaking down. The Japanese stranglehold was cutting off all entry points, one by one. For the past two months there had been continual delays, and after Tu's cut of the profits, the trains ceased being worthwhile—especially now that he had begun flying the Burma hump. Jack sighed and decided he'd have to go, if only to finally sever ties with Tu. "Nancy," he said, sticking his head out the door, "telephone Kai Tak airfield. I need to get into Cheng Chow. Charter a plane, chop-chop. And call up to the house. I'll need a suitcase packed and chauffeured down."

A half hour later there was a knock on his door. Nancy frowned in warning, "I have Kai Tak on the line for you."

"What's the problem?" he barked into the receiver.

"Charter an airplane? To Cheng Chow?" The man on the line laughed. "You fly over Jap lines that way, mate. Nice way to get stuffed! Our lads may be daredevils, but they're not crazy. The Communists' Eighth Army is reported to be in dire straits out there—the Japs are gaining on them. But I can help you if you're quick about it. I know a pilot going into Suchow with medical supplies. You can catch a train from there. Hurry up. He leaves in two hours."

As soon as he hung up, Nancy interrupted him. "Mr. Morgan. Shouldn't I verify this meeting? I just don't feel right about it. Besides, you have so many meetings scheduled for tomorrow."

"Reschedule, Nancy, and I'll thank you not to worry on my behalf."

"I could try Tu's office at the Chung Wai Bank?"

"No." Jack grabbed his suitcase on the way out, eager to get this last meeting over with. "I'll be back in a week. Tell Violet, and check in on Percy every day." He had just enough time to pick up a box of provisions and rushed on foot to the Hong Kong Hotel, his mind full of worries. If he stopped his business by rail, it left everything up to his planes. Percival would have been thunderstruck at the mere notion of *trains*—but cargo planes would put Percy into orbit. Hurrying along, Jack frowned when he was forced to a halt on the narrow pavement. A big crowd was thronging, a woman had fallen, and he could see a lady's shoe. Jack didn't pause to look closer but circumvented the huddle of spectators by stepping onto the street.

At Wiseman's, Jack picked up a box of provisions, and twelve hours later the plane landed; he stepped out onto an improvised grass airfield in the dead of night.

China. He didn't need to see, he could tell instantly he was there—smelled it, the soil, the fields all fertilized by human excrement. He waited for his ride into town, slapping at mosquitoes, wishing he'd brought a torch to see. Behind him the Yellow River bogged, luminescent in moonlight, and from the shore in the obscurity he saw a skinny white dog running. It sidled by his legs playfully, something dangling from its mouth. Jack leaned over stroking its smooth head. "What's that you got, old boy?" He looked closer.

Little half-moons, slender digits, the fingers of a human child. Jack stepped away, his stomach churning, and he vomited behind a tree, bracing himself against its rough bark. Like sweet and sour, hot and cold, good and evil, everything came together here—uncensored. There were no euphemisms. All around, birth sprang from death in China in a naturally luxuriant way, without illusions—and it was this that had drawn him to it—what he loved about China. It was real—magical and terrifying.

"Going to Cheng Chow, are you?" A torch glared into his face behind the tree and Jack squinted, throwing his handkerchief away. The man, a priest, apologized, and shone the light over at the plane's cargo being removed and loaded onto a waiting truck. He introduced himself as the new medic for the Eighth Army. His name was John, and the crates were his medical supplies. "I'm heading west too," he said. "And I've just been listening to a wireless dispatch. You better come along and help me load. We've twenty minutes to get to the station. Another train won't be by for days."

Driving over unpaved unlit roads at fifty miles an hour with a headlamp burned out and supplies bouncing around was unsettling. Worse, now and then dogs, trees, and lone stragglers would appear out of nowhere—a frozen image of terror caught in the headlamp. The truck would swerve to avoid impact, and then the blindfold of darkness was upon them again. When at last they were deposited at the crowded station, Jack found himself shaken and standing in the blackout darkness of a post aerial raid guarding medical supplies while John went to find a carrier. In the distance Jack could hear bombs dropping. He tried to get his bearings in the darkness, smelling tar, burning coal—and fear. Hundreds of refugees and soldiers brushed past unseen, but the obscurity around him had a density to it—people's anxieties and swirling thoughts were almost palpable. Suddenly, John came racing back with his torch, car boy and cart in tow. "I found our train! Hurry!"

Their overloaded cart squealed behind them as they ran down a long platform, passing through clouds of steam, searching in the darkness for their first-class car. Finding it, their car boy quickly handed all the medical supplies in through a window, and none too soon, for the steam engine hissed, the whistle sounded, and the train jerked twice. Inside, Jack sat back relieved, then noticed that people on the platform suddenly began scrambling onto the rooftop even as the train began to pull away. They were gaining speed. Slowly air began to flow in through open windows, lifting first at the cotton curtains, and then the pungent odor of urine from the water closet began to waft as the door flung open with a rush.

"Why so many riding the roof here?"

"The price is right," John said taking out a flask, pouring Jack some hot Jasmine tea. "Besides, up there they can see the bombers coming; they've a better chance at getting off than we do."

"Any hits lately?"

"They normally aim at bridges, but two trains collided last week trying to outrun Jap planes." He topped off Jack's tea as the engine picked up speed, clattering over the points, but the interior lights never came on. The Japs were too near.

Jack looked out the window as the nightscape streamed by under a cloud-covered moon, the endless fields of red sorghum taking on a purplish-black hue. Across from him, the missionary opened his Bible and Jack turned his thoughts to the Burma project. *I could put in an order for several more American-made Ford trucks.* He took out a pencil and paper and jotted down the figures. The scope of the Burma Road thrilled his imagination. Constructed across the border with China, it had been hacked out of sheer rock by desperation alone. He imagined himself flying over the expansive landmass following a lone ribbon of road from darkest Burma and crawling east, a growing lifeline in a vast virgin territory. He could imagine the steady chip-chip-chip of the tools on stone, the voices of the hill tribes put to work, and the dense silence of the trees as the men cut out the 715 miles from Mandalay to Kunming. In his mind's eye he swooped upward over nameless uninhabited mountains of China spreading out below as far as the eye could see. His thoughts came back to Ana—*her face.* He could see it over the trees; in the darker regions he saw her eyes and in the folds of the hills remembered what he had done. His throat clenched up with regret. And then he remembered Percy lying in the hospital bed, his voice choked with remorse. *"I won't die in harness, Jack. To blazes with everything. I just want to live."* The train was stopping and his mind came back to the present. His own life was falling apart and the last thing he wanted was this train ride to see Tu.

Jack peered out the window, and as his eyes adjusted he saw miles of waving grass transforming into soldiers lining a platform. John was sleeping soundly as troops boarded, the train rocking with their added weight. Before he could see their faces, uniforms, and rifles, he could smell them—their body heat, their wounds, their breath, their exhaustion. There was nothing but standing room and there was an air of death in the cabin. John awoke and said quietly, "Don't lean too close, lice don't fly, but trachoma is rife." Countless soldiers stood smiling down at them, though without hope. They were miles from any family and certain never to lay eyes on them again. *Who could imagine what propelled them forward? Perhaps hunger?* Hours later the train stopped in a dank place, barren like the underside of a rock. *No station, no signs of life.* The men poured out, descending into the black land as into a grave.

"Surprised, are you?" the missionary asked reading his thoughts. "They fight selflessly for China as if they were paid a decent wage—as if there were a future." He shook his head. "No supplies, no food, they jam dirty rags into gaping wounds and off they go! The public isn't even grateful because the soldiers must steal whatever they eat. Bitter, isn't it?"

Jack nodded, silent, and as the miles of darkness streamed past, he felt every step was taking him farther and farther from where he wanted to be. He remembered Percy's feverish, desperate rambling at the hospital, his voice calling for the young seamstress he should have married.

"Elisabeth. She's a good woman. Jack—but it's too late for me! It's too late. I've done it all wrong!"

The air moved freely through the car now that the hundreds of bodies were gone, and Jack breathed in deep, but the scent of death and sadness lingered. The missionary sat up and shared some sweet bean buns, bowing his head, saying a prayer aloud as Jack bit into his. "What are you hoping for out here?" Jack asked, bitterly. "Converts?" He'd lost his own faith in God.

The missionary scratched at an ugly rash on his neck. "I thought so at first. But the peasants don't have time. Only loafers come to us, take the food and don't hear a word we preach. So I've just been working alongside them. They're not the most honest people I've met, but as we've brought Christianity on the same ships that carried opium, you can't blame them for calling us devils, either." He stretched his bony arms and looked relaxed, almost content. Not much more flesh on him than on these soldiers. "I took a few classes in field medicine, and here I am. They've no antiseptics, no surgical instruments. And I do talk about Jesus to them but I think the talk and work is really for my own benefit."

"Don't you worry about getting killed all alone out here?"

"Alone?" The man looked at him thoughtfully. "God is here. It's the human heart I worry about."

Jack laughed, irritated. "So, I have a black heart?" He leaned over picking up a coin he'd dropped.

"Oh, the darkness is born in all of us—along with the light. The trick is to never *feed* your darkness—or you'll find you've a devil you can't control." His words hung in the sudden wild rush of air that beat against the sides of the train. It was a moment before Jack realized they had stopped and another train had sped past them. "Ah, the cause of our delay. Chiang Kai-shek's armored car. That's American Famine Relief money at work." He sighed. "So, what's your business out in the wilds? Drugs, prostitution?"

Jack was taken aback by the cynicism. "No. I'm heading out to meet a business partner. It seems the trains are becoming too unreliable. I'm considering pulling out entirely."

"Good plan. The Japs are twenty miles north of Cheng Chow, flying over all the time and dropping their bombs. It's been deserted for months."

"That's odd. I was supposed to meet my contact at the Hotel of Flowery Peace."

"Direct hit by aerial torpedo last month. Nothing there, the station's gone as well. Your man out here didn't know?"

Tu was the first man to be apprised about that sort of thing. Jack suddenly remembered Ato Barrandas slowly dying outside Manila and felt a chill pass over him.

"We're coming to a station now. I don't know which, though."

The train was slowing again and they passed the acetylene flares of food vendors. Jack and the priest stepped out onto to the platform to inquire where they were, but the station was a smoking ruin, the water tower passing moonlight through it like a sieve. They went back inside, taking their seats.

John was staring intently. "What are you going to do?"

"Well, I think I'm going to have a sudden change in plans before the night's through."

"Quitting before they 'quit' you?"

"You're far sharper about worldly things than I'd have imagined," Jack said flipping the silver coin he'd found into the air, disgusted, bored, and a little afraid.

"You disdain that lowly coin you're flipping, yet it would keep a coolie fed a whole week." He gazed at him closely. "You know, I've found that people always take extremes; they're complete materialists—or else they live up in a cave, mortifying the flesh." He tapped his temple. "Your cave's up here, Jack. You're an idealist."

"Hardly," Jack said. "I run a top shipping firm in Hong Kong."

"A taipan? Hah! Still, an idealist."

"How's that possible?"

John smiled mysteriously. "People are my job." He tapped Jack on the knee. "You're just conflicted. I was once too. Then I met a Japanese monk on pilgrimage who said, 'Keep your position, John, keep your position. All of society depends on social order and each person fulfilling his job dutifully.' I thought he was referring to my *meditation posture,* but no. He meant that even the rich taipan must keep his position; just as the lowest untouchable worker in a charnel house who carries corpses to the pyre must also keep his position. Both are vital for society to work smoothly."

Jack stood up to stretch, walking back and forth in the compartment. "Why Buddha? You're Catholic."

"One God—a hundred names."

Jack squinted at him, irritated. "That's sacrilegious."

The priest shrugged. "People cling to holy books but only worship the book itself. Buddha knew this would happen and said, don't worship the *finger* that points the way! Don't get caught up in the physical trappings of your religion and its culture. People thump their Bibles but forget all about our Creator. That's why I'm out here."

Jack looked at him suspiciously. "They know about these views at the home office?"

"I'm loyal to my faith, but frankly, I'm also far enough away from the velvet hammer."

Jack laughed. "You're crazy, or you've been in China too long."

"Maybe. But we're living in dangerous times. All around us history, science, and education are being manipulated by political forces hungry for power. Germany, Japan—entire countries are taking the wrong turn in history. Violence is being touted as the route to liberation. Imagine the folly!"

"You mean like this hell that's happening in China right now? That's *your* Buddha, no? And dash it, why stop there. Look at Europe, that's a *Christian* mess for you."

"Ahhhhh. Stuck on the finger! Get it?"

"*No.*" Jack shook his head, and then leaned over to look out the window. You always ran across these missionaries in the East. *The remotest hovel in some village, and sure enough, one of them comes out blinking, Bible in hand.* "What about you and your black robe and white collar? Isn't that being stuck on the trappings? Same as the pointing finger, no?"

"It's my 'position.' I'm keeping it. I'm a Catholic priest, that's all."

"A lot of help you are."

"Jack, people everywhere are questioning themselves, their gods, their lives; good and evil. We're at that point—does humanity survive or fall into the abyss? It makes us all think when we're confronted by this colossal front of wholesale slaughter."

Jack thought of the Chinese soldiers. "I'm only questioning my *job*."

"Ah, then you *must* fail."

He looked out the window again, frustrated. Outside on the platform two men were arguing by a station lantern in a strange dialect, gesturing wildly, pointing one way, then another, while a crowd of passengers had slowly gotten off and now also participated in the debate. They hadn't moved for the last hour. John stepped out while Jack waited, unable to get comfortable, but closing his eyes. *I'm wasting my time here, my life …* He thought of Ana. *It's her I want to see again … And why can't I?* This last thought startled him. He looked down at his gold wedding band.

The missionary returned. "Looks like they're bombing up ahead."

"Then are we heading back to Suchow?"

"It seems we've been cut off from behind, though you can never be sure. Maybe the bridge is gone, maybe not. They say the Japs flew to the west." Just then the whistle shrieked and a moment later the train jerked and began creeping along. Again, passengers on the platform began scrambling back up, being hoisted by urging hands and voices already on the roof. Inside, all the lights were extinguished. Passengers craned their heads against the windows, looking up at the sky. "The glare of the stoke hole is a good target from above," John said. "Be ready to jump off."

They were going to make a dash for it, this became clear, and John rechecked his medical supplies, pushing the boxes tight as the engine picked up speed. Jack sat hard into his seat as the clattering of the rails became a hammering roar, and there was nothing to do but hold on as the train bucked left and right, knocking items about the car. All eyes combed the brightening horizon for evidence of planes, and for some twenty minutes they hurtled across the plain until finally their grip on the seats relaxed. The train slowed a little, and they took this as a positive sign. It appeared to be steady enough to have tea but just as John tipped out the remainder into their cups, the train abruptly hit the brakes. Hot brew flew over their slacks, but the burn didn't hold their attention. *It was an air raid.*

The silver gleam appeared first as a speck in the pink light of dawn—a tiny airborne craft—flickering, growing in size. The violent screeching of the brakes was all around, and the train was still sliding on at a tremendous rate. Everyone watched as the Japanese aircraft approached, bracing for the final halt, and even before it came and they had fully stopped, people began dropping off the train roof, while inside bodies jammed out the doors. Jack and the priest joined the flow of passengers spewing out over the field as the planes came whizzing down low.

Rolling onto his back Jack saw the red ensign of the first as it swooped over the stranded train and instead of dropping a bomb it passed overhead with a tremendous roar.

"A Mitsubishi Zero," John said from the long grass beside him. "What a bird!" A second and third plane dove past and then looping back up came for another pass, reconnoitered, then were gone. It was obvious the train wasn't the target today. All the passengers boarded again, and as it was now full daylight, out came the pumpkin seeds, hard-boiled eggs, and tea. Groups moved between the cars and much joking and buffoonery filled the air after the morning's tense adventure.

Jack didn't waste time inquiring about the next stop, Shang-kui, and was told he could get a train back toward Suchow from there. When the train finally stopped at his station, it was midmorning. He left his provisions for the missionary and disembarked into a muddy hovel with the well wishes of his traveling companion, "Remember all I said! Love and pray from the heart! You will be heard!"

Sliding along the wet path at the station, Jack gritted his teeth in annoyance at the parting words. His life was falling apart, and of all things, he'd been forced to share a cramped compartment with a priest for twenty-four hours! He shook his head in dismay as he walked and found things didn't improve. The adjoining rest house was packed with wounded soldiers waiting with passive desperation in their dark eyes. He left that building, feeling terrible for them, and stood by the tracks alone, and at a loss. Another structure had been burned across the way, and it still smoked. There was a stone hut beside that, but there was no other sign of life. Jack looked at his watch. He had eight hours to go and began pacing the length of the platform. He passed a Missing Persons wall with pages and pages of Chinese script pasted up with names, some with pictures of smiling faces, forlorn now in their peeling wet state. He paced back the other way and caught sight of his own face in a piece of chrome metal nailed to a station wall. The man he saw looked hard, defeated—*Father coming home from the mines with his long angry silences.* Jack felt dumbstruck. He'd lost a bit of weight since Shanghai, and his hair had grayed. He hardly recognized the man he'd become in the decade since he'd come East and had lain cut open on deck at the mercy of strangers. *Poor Percy—he saved me, but now he is dying.* His heart hurt at the thought of it.

Jack paced the deserted station yard another half hour, his feet wet with mud, then glanced at his watch when he heard a sound. Across the tracks a Chinese with a stethoscope had emerged from the stone hut and looked up at the sky, arms red with blood up to the elbows. Only the two of them stood on that lonely expanse of railroad, fifteen feet apart and worlds away from anywhere civilized. Jack watched intently as the man took out a cigarette and lighted it while squinting at a point in the distance. Jack could almost hear the cigarette paper burn, they were so close, and he nodded, but the man looked right through him—no acknowledgment at all.

Jack Morgan was *always* noticed, by his presence alone, his energy, even by those who *didn't* know him. *I send important supplies into these remote regions. I'm the chairman of China Coast Navigation … Peak House … the Jockey Club …* His justifications of self-worth, one by one, whisked away like smoke on the platform. His social self of Hong Kong, taipan, the thing he'd built up over these years meant nothing here. *Was Percy right? Did it all really mean nothing?* Jack went back and looked at himself in the chrome. He stood back. It was unsettling. He already had Father's dry look of disappointment. Jack touched his jaw, frowned … then turned and walked across the tracks.

He dropped his duffel bag by the hut door and entered. Immediately, and without an exchange of words he was put to work in the grizzly task of washing dirt out of wounds. A good five hours passed when he was finally called to attention by the doctor. "Look—this one," the man said in halting English. Jack was startled and came over to look. "They cut his tongue," the doctor explained, prying open the jaws.

It was gruesome, a knobby red stub. The man made a guttural cry. "Are these Communists or—or Kwomintang?" Jack asked, appalled by the cruelty required to carry out the act.

The doctor shrugged, indifferent to blame. "Both sides same, Chinese. And their greeting to me, *Wo-men ch'ih k'oo*, also same."

Jack stared at the shaking bundle of human flesh wondering if it would live. *We eat bitterness*, the doctor had said; it was the Chinese wartime greeting. Jack's heart went out to them, yet he was not sure he liked the particularly cold eyes that were leveled at him by the patient. He looked closer and noticed the peasant had something written on his filthy shirt front. Jack pointed out two very familiar Chinese characters written in blood. "Does this say what I think it does?"

The doctor laughed uproariously, "Yes! Hong Kong! *Hong Kong!* Can you believe it? Our patient has a sense of humor! He needs a hospital, not Hong Kong."

Jack looked in the man's eyes, seeing fear and pain. "I'll take you," Jack said to the man in Chinese. *There was distrust in those eyes, even anger.* "Hong Kong," Jack said again, and the peasant nodded silently with no change in expression.

Shang-kui, China *21 March 1938*

THE ACHE IN HIS mouth was bigger than his own head, throbbing, unbearable, and everything he looked at was muffled in pain. He could hardly focus but he had to. The gaijin in the dim hut was saying something, looking at his shirt. Yoshi was afraid and inched away on the dirt floor, then groaned because he'd moved his head wrong. The Chinese doctor looked up, then came over and pushed some pills between his lips. Yoshi tried to swallow but they stuck in his throat. The white man came over and stooping down, forced him to drink tea. Yoshi swallowed, but it burned the stub in his mouth so badly he nearly passed out. The gaijin staring at him looked concerned. He was muscular, hair covered his arms where he'd rolled up his sleeves, and he was a giant in the small space, radiating heat. This was the first foreign devil he'd ever seen and it was frightening looking into those colorless eyes.

A train whistle woke him and before he knew what was happening, the gaijin had hoisted him and was carrying him out like a sack of rice. They were climbing into a train car and he felt himself set down on a soft cushion. The pain from the motion flashed in his head outlining every tooth in his jaws like lightning. *If I'm to die now, let it be. Let me die now.* He came to again, eyes tearing, but could see a first-class train compartment with antimacassars on seat backs. Curtains were blowing. The foreign devil was sitting across from him. Yoshi wanted to die. The man leaned forward and forced hot medicinal tea on him. The first sip burned so bad he lost consciousness. When he came to, the man pushed the cup toward him again and didn't let up. Each time he awoke there was more tea. Yoshi was confused. For some time he began to think he was at home. He tried to call out, "O-bachan!" but the room was different from home, dark and swaying, clacking. He could see O-bachan's misty face smiling at him. "Drink, Yoshi-chan," she urged.

When he awoke again he was in a clean room full of light. A woman in black was standing over him and the gaijin was there. He smiled down at Yoshi, showing teeth. The two were talking in a lateral language when a Chinese doctor came over and felt his forehead. *The hand was cool.* Yoshi closed his eyes. His pain had dulled into a white cloud and he was floating a little. Someone was squeezing his hand. Yoshi opened his eyes half expecting O-bachan. It was the foreign devil trying to talk to him in Chinese. The Doctor came over, and shouted in Chinese as if Yoshi were a mental defective. Then taking Yoshi's hand he spelled the kanji—*Hong Kong*—on Yoshi's palm with his index finger. *It couldn't be!* Yoshi blinked and looked to the window in surprise—*Hong Kong?* He looked back at the men in shock, then realized his action was an admission he'd understood.

Then the doctor and the gaijin burst out laughing, clapping each other on the back—then the white man took out a meishi card and left it on the bedside table.

One week later Yoshi Sakura was discharged and stood outside the hospital on a sunny hillside with the foreign devil's name-card in his hand. The war in China seemed a century ago, but he wondered if it might follow him here to this paradise. *Why else was Uncle here, but to kill?* Yoshi began to walk, looking left and right. Everything here in Hong Kong was new, exciting. People wore fancy clothes and the girls were so pretty! Yoshi thought he was in heaven. Even the buildings were taller! And he could smell delicious food from all the vendors' carts—sweet, sour, fermented. His stomach began to growl. Somewhere on these streets he thought he would spot a fellow Japanese who could help him find his uncle. But what would he say to O-ji san? *That a foreign devil had brought him?* Yoshi hissed through his teeth in dismay. *His debt to this foreigner was ominous.* Yoshi squinted again at the foreign script on the card then pushed it deep into his pocket. Strolling down the road he repeated the name to himself the way the nurse had pronounced it—*Jyaa-ku Mo-ganu.* Jyaa-ku. *We will meet again Jyaaku,* he thought uneasily, then abruptly stopped in his tracks.

Tied outside an official building was a black horse. Memories of Kyoka, his boss, and his beloved Kamakura besieged him as he went up to the animal. Just then a soldier rushed out of the building. Untying the horse, the uniformed man mounted the gelding on the left side and trotted off. Yoshi froze. *On which side do foreign devils mount? In Japan we mount on the right!* The ghost had been *correct* again! He began to sweat, and feeling dizzy sat down on the curb. He'd lost his tongue, his family, and now, what if the ghost came again and threw her centipede on Hong Kong? In front and behind, voices and footsteps of the living swept past like the wind. *Everything has been foreseen! Life and death, nothing is sacred.*

A Visit from the Past

21

Des Voeux Road *19 March 1938*

THEY WERE STARING DOWN at her, a circle of heads blocking out dazzling light. Ana blinked. Her skin was burning and she realized she was lying on hot pavement surrounded by strangers. As she hurried to stand, picking up the shoe that had come off, a gentleman took hold of her arm, helping her along.

"Are you seeing anyone for your condition?" he asked in a low voice, handing her a calling card. *Dr. Black—Red Cross Hospital.*

Ana colored in shame, hiding her face. "If–if you call me a rickshaw I'd be grateful, doctor." He helped her mount, and as it jolted off over the cobbles she realized that if he had noticed her condition, soon everyone would.

All these months she'd tried her best, tried to starve herself so as to lose this child; it hadn't worked. Now she couldn't even cry. She had nothing left, no reserve of emotion. *And Mischa, dead.* Somehow, after the initial shock, it didn't surprise. He'd died a thousand times in her mind; opium was his love. *Guilt, that's all she felt.* At her street corner she paid the coolie and walked toward home through muggy heat smelling of noontime cooking as tears streamed down her face. Everywhere, greasy juices dripped from dangling ducks, coils of red innards spiraled, crimson squid, steaming vats of gray noodle water—all that, and a growing despair pursued her up the long stairs, past her apartment, past the top landing toward the roof, and up a metal ladder. At the top, she leaned breathlessly against the trap door, sobbing her heart out—when suddenly it flew upward revealing a clean rectangle of blue sky. A little moth flew up into all that blue and vanished. *Maybe it was my soul,* she thought, *leaving this horrid world.*

Hearing a sound, Ana looked back down, blinking. Below, lying in the square of light that had fallen inward she noticed two emaciated vagrants on the floor below. One reached out a hand to her while the other one, coughing, took hold of the lowest rung. It seemed there was no way to escape misery. She had a few coins—*No need of them now.* Ana tossed her purse down to them then walked across the roof and leaned over, the tips of her shoes just over the edge. *All she had to do was let go.* The view straight down into a dark shaft between tenements seemed to pull dizzyingly at her. Five stories below, those stone steps with dull hard edges would crack her head like an egg, rusty iron terraces on the way down would tear off a limb. Ana grabbed hold of a swaying clothesline, afraid to jump off. She was thinking of her child. *It was his too.*

"What are you doing?" The accusing voice boomed across the hot tarry roof and in three long strides a hand jerked her away from the edge. "Did those bums steal your money? Did they hurt you? I saw your purse and—"

Ana couldn't do more than shake her head as Algy brought her safely down to their flat and sat her down. "Ana? Listen to me! My dearest. I have some thumping good news! Here. Dry your eyes! You won't need to sew anymore. That's right, I've quit my horrid job! Ah-hah! I thought that would get your attention!"

"B–but why?" she asked, looking up from the handkerchief.

"Bad times have come to an end, my dear," he said gesturing with a fresh cigarette. "Yes! Your Jack, I saw him in town all maudlin and rummy like a half-boiled pudding. Said he was just back from an inland trip to China. And you know, he was so glad to see me, he insisted we go for tiffin."

"How do you mean half-boiled? Is he ill?"

Algy shrugged, lighting his cigarette and puffing excitedly. "Just old and tired, but that's not the point. He's rich! And he credits his success to your gun deal!"

"I don't believe it."

"You must. He's asked me to work for him again and begged to know where you were."

"You didn't tell him!"

"Didn't breathe a word." Algy blew a cloud up at the ceiling.

"And, did you take the job?"

"Did I? I said, 'Jack, I'd rather be kicked to death by an ass than work for you again.'"

"No!"

"Silly goose! I took it, but at twice the pay."

Ana sank back and he rushed to her side.

"What is it? You look pale! What you were doing on the roof? When I saw your purse in the hands of those beggars, you know I imagined the worst."

"And what's that?"

"What?" He stared, dumbfounded. "Well, kidnapped, that's what! I thought of that horrid man you described."

"Fausto. *No.*" Ana pulled the letter from her pocket and handed it to him.

He quickly scanned it. "Oh, Ana," he said taking her hand. "Tell me everything. We'll go through this together."

Unable to hold her secret longer she stammered, "It's not just Mischa, I'm *pregnant.*"

Algy sat back, dumbfounded. "Well, it can't be me!"

Ana, who felt tears starting, suddenly laughed.

Algy swallowed nervously. "Not Fritz?"

"Not Fritz."

Algy leapt out of his seat. "Tell me who, and I'll kill him!" Then he stopped still. "No! Not him!" He stared while Ana began to cry under this scrutiny.

"*Jack?* But why didn't you *tell* me?"

"I want you to promise. *Promise you won't tell.*"

"*Absolutely not!* Make him pay. He *can* pay! Besides—he's *asking* for you! You can't expect me to lie indefinitely." He stared at her. "Anyway, he's determined to find you."

"Believe me, that will pass."

Algy smoothed his eyebrow, then suddenly shouted, "Oy!" and grabbed hold of her.

"Algy! What's come over you?"

"Just this, my dear—*imagine,* Algernon Worthing to be a father! Now that is a shock—even to me!"

"Have you gone mad?"

"Ra—*ther!* Come," he twirled her around. "A little mambo always makes the heart glad."

Peak House *2 April 1938*

JACK SAT IN THE library, thinking. *All this furniture, a staff of twenty-five, the gardens, the bills, the ailing old man in bed; it was all on his shoulders.* Then there was Violet. She sat across from him reading, twirling a finger in her hair, with one eye on him, in a studied attitude of feline languor. He looked away. For some reason he couldn't get that stone hut out of his mind, washing wounds for hours in semi-darkness, steeped in the smells—blood, excrement, and pus. He'd certainly learned what was real. And when he'd finally heard his train chuffing into the station, he'd been ashamed to leave. He'd taken the mute peasant along, but that doctor had remained.

Her touch startled him, and he moved away, getting up to find a cigar.

"So. What do you think, Jack? I'm waiting," Violet purred, following him, placing her hands on his shoulders. Let's plan a date when I'm not at a social, and you're not at work."

"Sorry? Oh, you don't schedule … *that.*"

"Why, Jack! Are you blushing? You are! Think of it, Father would love to have one running about the place."

"One what? It's not a dog. And you, you can't even get dressed without help."

"You do say the oddest things. We have staff. I presume that fits the bill."

"I presume," he said shutting the humidor with a snap. "Though it can't be accomplished by separate lodgings."

"Meaning?"

"Whenever I have showed an interest in sex—"

Violet stood up in a rush. "Don't say that *WORD* in my presence."

He picked up the newspaper angrily. "*Sex*," he said.

Violet stared. "You," she snarled with disgust. "You're speaking of nothing but gratification of your lower urges!"

"No, Violet!" He slapped the newspaper down. "I fulfill all your material needs and you've a duty to me which you've neglected.."

"And what of our wedding night? And your *hideous behavior!*"

Jack leaned back in the tub chair and lit his cigar, puffing till the end glowed. "My behavior? After what you'd said and done with Peebles?"

"All I expect is a child! I have that right. It's *your* duty."

"I could take a lover, you know."

Violet's face went pale.

"Do you have any inkling of what I go through to keep you on the Peak, with your staff, your European tailored dresses, your parties? We're in a global crisis—and you tell me to do my *duty*?"

"Oh darling, for goodness sake! You're blowing it all out of proportion."

He felt her at his back again and he turned suddenly, and clenched her hand so tightly that she gasped. "You find me offensive, is that it? In the most intimate moments, I fail you?"

"I don't want to argue. Everyone says we have the ideal marriage." He let go and she came around, reached for his shirt buttons, toying with them, her voice at once childish yet purring. "We only need a child. It would make Percy so happy and it would complete the picture."

Jack removed her hands from his shirt, but she slid onto his lap. Outside the window only the dripping foliage was visible through the steamy fog—a green, tropical gloom. "Are you happy, Violet?" he suddenly asked. Her skin in shadow was dark, olive and lavender, and when she smiled uncomfortably her teeth were gray.

"Of course."

"Really happy?" he asked quietly.

"Everyone says what a lovely couple we are. Just wait until they hear I'm expecting."

"Is that all you want from life?"

"What silly questions." She took his hand, and led him upstairs. "Naturally, I expect parties, jewelry, trips abroad. That sort of thing. And, of course a child."

He felt a strange disconnected feeling taking over him as she pulled the bedroom drapes shut. When he mounted her, he closed his eyes. When he opened them, he still felt nothing, though he'd done his duty. He lay still in bed afterward remembering soldiers' faces, gaunt, in pain, and then later, his train trying to outrun Jap planes in the darkness. It all melded together into a strange reality that made him wonder—*What am I doing here?*

Violet got up and went to the bath, "No matter. Perhaps this once, and we'll be lucky and won't have to do it again. I'm in estrus."

"What? *Oh.*" He was silent a moment. "Listen, I'm leaving on business tomorrow. Two weeks and …"

She put on a robe and shut the lavatory door.

Gage Street Market *2 April 1938*

FAUSTO CLUTCHED THE ADDRESS in his hands as he sat in the back seat, sweating, excited, and slightly on edge. He couldn't afford for this to go wrong. Ana's absence these months had proven a growing embarrassment with his European clients—and he hadn't been able to reveal that she'd run away. If he said she was busy, the customer felt unimportant. If he said she was sick, they worried about disease. Hiding his chagrin, he'd chatter jovially, "Old boy, breasts come in different sizes like potatoes. I have many on offer." *But how it galled him!* Fausto looked out the car window now at the Hong Kong street scene. He'd be dragging her down the steps minutes from now; and if all went as planned, he'd be teaching her what's what by nightfall. "Hurry up," he said leaning forward.

The driver was finding it difficult to maneuver down Gage Street, narrow as it was. A bicycle loaded with caged humming birds, sandals, and feather dusters bumped past his window, while two coolies hefting a basket between two bamboo poles, carrying a pig, set it down in front of the car. Fausto mopped his brow as the chauffeur hit the horn.

"You, driver!" He rapped again impatiently, his breath misting the glass partition. "I'll go on foot. Wait for me there, and park as close to the door as possible." He got out and made his way up the incline toward an antique shop where Van Leiden waited, watching the flat.

"Ah, here you are," he said to the Dutchman sitting in the window behind a screen. "Is she there now?"

"She's alone. That fop she lives with has been gone on business for two weeks. But, I've been wondering, how do you expect to persuade her to leave with you?"

"No worries. I'll wait until the amah goes out. You said around noon, I believe?"

"Yes, yes. Every day she goes out. But I don't think it will be any easier a job convincing her and—"

"Put it out of your mind. Ah, look. My driver! Go, sit inside the car, and motion to me here when the domestic leaves the flat. I'll take care of the rest. When I come out with the girl, open the door straightaway—and be ready to pull her in."

Fausto watched Van Leiden walk back to the automobile, then began his wait. Just when he thought he would pass out from heat, he got the signal. *Amah had left.* Fausto pulled his hat brim down and stepped out into the traffic.

Lower Peel Street *2 April 1938*

IF ANA HAD LOOKED out of her window at that very moment, she'd have spotted Fausto in his white suit beetling through the crowd, but she was preparing Algy's shirt for work the next day, making sure the iron was good and hot. He'd been gone for fifteen days now, and she'd been impatient to see him. She checked the clock again then nibbled on a slice of fruit that she'd fanned out prettily on a saucer. Just an hour or so and he'd be home. Ana dampened a handkerchief and, putting it on the shirt, pressed the iron down, listening to the hiss of steam—and felt her baby kick. *Seven months already.* Setting the iron back on the trivet she rubbed her stomach gently, then hearing a noise on the landing, turned around. Wiping her hands on her apron, she raised the latch and opened the door. Fausto stood about to knock.

Ana shammed the door, but it bounced off his foot and he hurled himself into the room, knocking her against a wall. In seconds she was pinned against his body. Ana kicked and twisted in vain, but he had her in a tight body lock and was deftly fastening her wrists together. Then, with a sudden kick, he sent her tumbling to the floor in the direction of the sofa.

As she fell, her shoulder and side took the brunt of the shock. Gasping, she peered up from the floor as he approached, and hid her belly from a possible kick. Fausto's brow dripped profusely and he paused to look around casually, his breath whistling out of his nostrils. "Not doing badly, eh?" He casually removed a revolver and pointed it at her. "Now. I'll ask you nice. Get up. Off the floor." With his other hand he helped himself to a slice of dragon fruit. Ana stood up cautiously and his eyes went straight down to her belly in shock.

For a second she was triumphant at his dismay. "Not what your customers want, is it?"

Approaching, he frowned. "Easily fixed—I have many prostitutes like—"

Ana lunged away, dodging the ironing board, but Fausto grabbed hold of her hair, yanking her to him. He didn't notice her hands. Tied together, she'd still managed to grab the scalding iron—and now she spun around, pressing it against the thin fabric of his shirt. She could smell the burn. Fausto let out a shriek of pain sending the iron crashing to the floor, but still, he held on. Hauling her behind him by her hair, pain and rage propelled him out the door and down the stairs like a half-mad bull. Ana kicked and screamed all the way, but Fausto hardly seemed to hear.

On a lower landing, an old Chinese man was coming up the stairs. Fausto shoved and the man fell, tripping halfway down the flight ahead of them. Pulling Ana along behind, Fausto approached the fallen man, and began to step over him. As he did, Ana saw the Chinese raise his leg up neatly between Fausto's—and the next moment they were tumbling, hurtling through the railing with a loud crack. They went over together, the checked floor tile rushing up at them. *Everything went black.*

Ana sat up woozily on something soft, and looking down, her eyes focused on red and black and white. It was blood. Blood was puddling on the black and white tiles; it was everywhere. Ana braced herself and found she was on top of Fausto, who'd apparently broken her fall. He was lying on his side, moaning. Getting her balance, she quickly got up to hide as he began to revive. Watching from under the stairs, she saw him roll over onto all fours and groan. The old Chinese was shouting curses from upstairs, but Fausto didn't seem to hear as he crawled very slowly to the stairs and grabbed for the newel post. Hand over hand, he pulled himself up while slipping in blood that was gushing from his head. At last, he slid away toward the front door dragging a leg behind him. Ana crawled out of hiding but as she stood up the room began to spin.

Queen's Pier *2 April 1938*

The Blue Funnel steamer had eased into port before twilight, three hours late, and the delay only added to his anxiety. Algy pushed to the front of the other passengers to see what was holding them up, hoping he could get away before Jack saw him. The disembarkation gate had not yet been lifted, and he shifted his valise and umbrella, waiting. Up ahead, towering above Hong Kong like a great wall, Victoria Peak stretched east and west, hiding the dipping sun. He glanced at his watch nervously. In a week the arms and medical supplies would be offloaded into Rangoon and their trucks would be heading back into China with Vietnamese rice. Percy's accounts would be bursting with profits—but he couldn't get excited about that. *Not when he was to be a father!* He was also fed up with Jack's obsession with Ana. Ever since he'd been back from China he'd been mooning about like a love-sick puppy saying he couldn't sleep. It made Algy want to throw up. Suddenly a whistle sounded and the crew flew into action, lowering the gangway. Relieved, Algy hurried down ahead of everyone, and although the praya was warm underfoot, the town was already steeped in cool swirling breezes and long shadows the color of the sea. He shouted for a rickshaw.

"All right, what aren't you telling me?" Jack demanded, grabbing his arm. "Dashing off without me?"

Algy didn't turn around, and instead waved a coolie over.

"But I want to celebrate the Rangoon deal—how about dinner?"

It had taken all his effort not to shout, *I'm having a baby!* But it *was* Jack's, after all. That thought really capped his pleasure. "Look, I'm sorry, but I'm dying for a bath, and a proper tea." He mounted the rickshaw, and feeling a bit cruel said, "You need to go to Peak House. You made that choice, now live with it." The coolie hoisted the shafts and grunted as he heaved into motion.

He left Jack behind in the dense evening crowds guiltily, but the feeling soon passed. *After all, what he'd done to Ana was appalling.*

At the corner of Gage and Peel, the coolie stopped, breathing hard, letting him off. Algy took his gear and hurried up the steps. Ana would have something for him to eat, and they would sit by the window looking out over the rooftops toward the glinting water and dream their dreams of a family. His accounts were settled; he had a growing deposit at the Hong Kong and Shanghai Bank. *What could be better?* As he made his way up the last flight of stairs, he was thinking of boy names when something rushed from the darkness at him—*the amah.* She was completely insensible with hysteria and began dragging him by the arm into their flat. "Where's Ana?" he demanded, then shouted, "Ana? Ana!" The door was open, lights out, and everything was in state of smash.

There was a faint rustle in the corner of the room by the bed. But he could see nothing. Algy stumbled across the room, falling against a table leg, and cried out as he tripped over the ironing board. Raising himself he saw something lying on the daybed, shivering. "Ana, is that you?" His hands found hers and cold fingers held onto his. "*Ana, Ana,*" he gasped, crying over her, seeing her face suddenly in the moonlight. Bruises, dried blood, her face, her arms—all battered. Her eyes were glassy, unblinking in her chalky face. "But what's happened here?" he demanded of the amah, who scuttled away from him, fearing a blow. There were no answers, and as he grasped the situation he cried, "The baby, Ana! The baby!" She didn't move.

He was told it would take an hour for the doctor to get to Lower Peel from the Red Cross godown in Wan-Chai. As he waited, Algy switched on the lights and put the room in order while trying to get Ana to drink some tea. He sent the amah downstairs to wait for the doctor, and then went to sit by her side, holding her hand. "Who did this?" he asked again, squeezing her hand. "You know the doctor will ask. He'll send a constable here to file a report. *Ana?*"

This last bit of reasoning seemed to affect her for she turned her eyes to him, and got one faint word out, "Fausto—"

"What's happening here?" a voice suddenly demanded.

Algy leapt up seeing the doctor and rushed him. "She's here—she's here. What do you think? Will she be all right?"

"Out of my way. Boil some water."

Clutching the doctor by the arm Algy cried, "W–why? Is it to come now?"

The doctor growled taking out a rubber hose and tying it about Ana's arm. "For my tea, man—and make it strong, I've had a long day."

When he returned with the tea tray, the doctor looked up. "Are you the father?"

Algy blanched, cups rattling.

"Then make yourself scarce. I'll need the amah. I can't tell you anything until I've examined the patient further."

Algy sent the amah to the doctor's side, and then pulled the partition across the room and sat down at the kitchen table, crying silently. He would have prayed but was sure God wouldn't forgive him for calling on Him only in his hour of need. He then thought of his mother in England. Too far away to help. Certainly, had she been here, she'd have been shocked to an early grave by these sinful circumstances—his living with an unwed pregnant woman assaulted by a pimp and her only son pretending to be the father! His eyes went to the telephone. *This was all Jack's fault.* He stood up and paced the room, wringing his hands. Yet, Jack always knew what to do. Algy dabbed his face with his scented handkerchief. *At least the doctor was here.* When the amah returned to the kitchen for towels, he restrained her. "How did this happen?" he whispered. He did not release her until she let out a torrent of explanations in pidgin—insisting Ana hadn't wanted a doctor, and a neighbor had brought over a special concoction from the herbalist down the block. Algy smelled the remedy she held up and to her horror, poured it down the drain. "No mumbo jumbo!" he said, then collapsed, despairing, at the kitchen table.

"Keep it down in there," the doctor called out.

Amah gave Algy a poisonous look, and leaning close accused, "Trouble come from move! *Three time!*" she hissed so the doctor wouldn't hear. "This flat, that flat! Pregnant woman mas stap one place! Missie catchee baby Shanghai side. Nedum stay put!" She continued blathering on about bad joss while Algy tried not to listen.

An hour later the doctor tapped him on the shoulder and Algy was startled to his feet.

"She appears out of danger. But watch her. This is my number should you need me tonight. I've given her an injection to make her sleep."

"And what of the child?"

"You'll need to give her these four times a day. Fill the prescription at the chemist in the morning. As far as the child—" He looked up with an exhausted face. "I don't know. The fall was quite a jolt and she is bruised internally. Common sense says expect a miscarriage—but who knows? *Tell her nothing.* She may very well come out fine."

Algy watched him hurry off down the stairs and went back into his flat and closed the door quietly. *And tomorrow I must go to work with Jack and pretend I know nothing. Pretend I haven't a care in the world.* Algy went over to the bed and saw that she was sleeping gently, and turning out the lights went back to sit by her side, setting the number of the doctor in front of him.

Unpleasant Discovery

22

Jordan Path, Kowloon *8 April 1938*

THE SMELL OF BURNING toast brought Albert rushing into the kitchen where he discovered his house boy dozing at the kitchen table, face pressed into the *South China Morning Post,* lip open and drooling slightly. "Tat-sui! Get up! The toast is on fire!" Albert jerked the topmost paper out from under the boy's chin, upsetting a cup of tea onto other correspondence. He was about to give the boy a wallop when his eyes came to rest on a small piece of news highlighted by a drop of tea acting as a lens.

"Well, if I'm not pissed as a fart!" Albert gasped, blotting away the liquid. Finding his spectacles he read the article, stunned. He'd been feeling ominously unlucky as of late, for Jack had gone into China the previous month but had returned without a scratch. However this—*this was the nail in his coffin! God's will!* Percy had rallied and been brought home from the hospital a week ago and now Albert raced for the telephone, dialed Peak House.

"Yes, yes. I need to speak to Mr. Summerhays. It's urgent." He clung to the receiver, eyeing the article. "Yes!" he shouted with relief when he heard Percival's tired voice some long minutes later. "So very sorry to disturb your breakfast, old chap. Uh, no, no, this is a *very private matter.* Can we meet somewhere—now? Sorry? Oh. Right. Well—if you *can't* leave the house. Yes, yes, I'll bring whisky—cigars too?"

Minutes later he flew out of his flat across from the Gun Barracks and in an hour he was up on the Peak in the shadow of the great house. Sticking close to the tall shrubbery and out of range of the upper verandah, he kept low under the hedge, carrying the paper sack of contraband under his arm. Wide rings of perspiration were seeping through his jacket when he finally reached the gap in the hedge and glanced up at Peak House. Seeing no one, he made a dash for it.

"I don't have the keys," Percy apologized from the front seat of the Rolls in the garage. "Otherwise, I'd have you drive me to a cat house." He sat with inert hands, but there was a flicker of sarcasm in his sunken eyes.

"Aha! To Lyndhurst terrace!" Albert grunted with fondness as he slid into the seat, but he was startled by the change in the old man. "Here." He handed over the sack, then removed that morning's copy of the *South China Morning Post.* "You seen this yet?" he asked, pointing to the bottom of the far column.

Percy raised his glasses, and read it twice. "Impossible. It's a lie."

"But it says the planter killed himself for failing to sell his plantation. The very one you purchased a year ago!

Percy pushed the paper aside furiously. "There must be a mistake."

Albert took out the photo of Jack and Tu. "Then this should tip the scale."

Percy took the photo, squinting at the fine print. "Jack investing in the railway? Bosh! This could have been a random shot at a bar."

"Or not," Albert said quietly, taking out the railway stocks. "Tu is not a random sort of chap. Neither is Jack."

Percy stared at the stocks, breathing hard; for once he looked defeated.

"In your interest, may I suggest we verify this Java deal first before you take this further?"

Percy glanced at him, his face cold. His hand went to the doorknob, and rested there for a moment; then he turned back to look at Albert. "You take the next ship to Java, and I want a full report. In the meantime, I'm calling my solicitor."

"And not a word to Jack," Albert said getting out.

Percy shook his head, no, his eyes strangely watery. "Albert. He's the son I never had."

Lower Peel Street *9 April 1938*

ANA HAD A LATE breakfast while her amah went off to wet market, and she scanned the advertisements in the fashion section of the paper, a hand on her belly. Algy had been very fussy over her but, apart from a few bruises, she was doing remarkably well. A whole week had passed since her fall and yesterday she'd left the flat for the first time—to her doctor's Wan-Chai office. He'd pronounced her recovery amazing. Ana looked down. *Baby kicking again!* This brought a smile to her face. She looked back at the paper and a pretty illustration of infants' jumpers caught her eye. *They'd just arrived at Lane Crawford's and were on sale only today.* She looked out the window. Algy had told her not to go out without him, but as he was at work he hardly needed to know. *It was lovely outside.* Ana stood up and stretched. *There seemed no reason she couldn't take a rickshaw to Central and back.* She smiled as she remembered how Algy constantly complained about having to lie to Jack about her whereabouts. He begged Ana to let him confess. She remained steadfast—however, the knowledge that Jack still desired her brought immense hope and Ana began to soften towards him. She recalled how his eyes had lit up each time he'd looked at her. These same eyes were imprinting themselves inside her, on *their* child. *He may want a future with her—he may even leave his wife.* The more she thought about him these days, the more she believed he *should* be in her life—for the baby's sake and her own.

Outside, the hurly burly of the streets was exhilarating, and when her rickshaw deposited her on Queen's Road, her spirits lifted. Ana strolled along to Lane Crawford's department store and smiled when the uniformed boy opened the door for her. Inside, ceiling fans cooled her as she passed through the café filled with ladies and gentlemen and instead headed straight to the children's section, where the sale sign attracted much attention. At her request the clerk removed the advertised jumpers from the glass counter and spread them out for her to choose.

"It's all I have left, Madame. All the new mothers are coming in today."

Ana took out her fan, feeling especially hot and tired suddenly. "May I sit down for a moment?" She was shown to a chair several feet away where she relaxed while another clerk went to fetch her a glass of water. As she waited, she decided the yellow one was prettiest.

"I 'avent seen you before, Madame. You newly arrived?"

Ana nodded, and thanked her for the water, taking a sip.

"When are you due?"

"September."

"Ah, so soon! That'll be 'ard on you, Madame. With August ahead of you! When I 'ad me first I said, never ag'in a baby in the fall! Me man said the same, 'e don't want me sufferin' so with the next!" She smiled, then seeing she had customers excused herself.

Ana sat quietly wondering. *Even the shop girl had a husband.* She felt the baby kick, hurrying its way into the world, and smiled. It was energetic and busy like its father. A shrill laugh startled her and she looked up. Two very well dressed ladies had stopped at the counter. One of them was fingering the jumpers while the other was holding up a christening gown.

"Ned says our next absolutely *must* be a girl. What about you?"

The other lady picked up the yellow jumper. "At this price, I'll take these three, yellow, peach, and white."

"Three! Violet Morgan, you didn't tell me you were expecting!"

"Go ahead, wrap them up!" She turned to the other woman. "The first, you know, will be a boy, *Percival*, after Father."

"Just a moment," the clerk said, and looking over at Ana asked, "Are you finished with these, Madame?" Ana nodded quickly, hiding her face.

"*That* person is buying these?" the supercilious voice asked.

"No, Madame, I'm wrapping them for you now."

Ana busied herself with her fan and peered into her purse, hiding her face.

The two women walked off with the chit to pay the cashier while the clerk wrapped each little outfit in clouds of white tissue. Ana watched. Each beautiful little outfit would go to Jack's *real* child. Suddenly she felt all her joy rendered vulgar, *indecent*. She'd been wrong about Jack. *She could never tell him.*

"I still have a similar one left in green, Madame, would you care to see it?" the girl said as Ana placed the empty glass on the counter. She couldn't find words to answer, but hurried out onto Queen's Road, choked with regret.

Batavia, Indonesia *13 April 1938*

ALBERT'S STEAMER DOCKED IN the Dutch town full of low whitewashed buildings, and let off its first- and second-class passengers off into the sweltering heat. Albert was among those, and finding his friend late, paced back and forth on the praya watching nubile Javanese girls in sarongs pass by. He took off his white jacket, gasping in the heat. Eventually the steamer began disembarking hundreds of indentured coolies from the bowels of the ship, all headed inland by rail for the vast rubber estates. Finding himself swamped by the growing crowd, he was relieved to spot the white Aston Martin driving up.

"So, Manfred," he said, his shirt sticking to him as he pulled himself into the front seat, "forget your excuses of lateness. Tell me what I want to hear."

Manfred gave him a searing look and swerved out onto the road, passing through the Amsterdam Arch. "If you'd come out sooner, Chiswick, that man would not be dead today."

"Look out, you sod!" Albert shouted, bracing as a donkey cart cut them off.

Manfred swerved into the opposite lane, leaving startled pedestrians in his wake. "You're hoping to get an advance for this bit of horseplay, aren't you?"

Albert sank into his seat, irritated that Manfred was behaving as if the blame lay with him. "I'll cut you in on it if it pays out," he said, eyeing native women doubled over scrubbing clothes in the roadside canals. Others walked along the edge of the dusty road in brown and white batik, balancing laundry baskets on their heads; so close he could have reached out and pinched one.

"Pay raise or not," Manfred said, "this tragedy could've been averted. I knew him. Really, a sterling chap."

There was nothing to add to this line of thought so Albert just stared out the window as they left town and entered the jungle. In his mind he reworked variations on scenes from his future life at Peak House with Jack cut out of the picture until a few hours later they turned off the road. It was a planter's house, with whitewash showing under jungle lianas thick as pythons.

"You say the woman is still here?" Albert asked, looking around as he stepped out of the roadster onto a gravel drive waist high in weeds. A snake swished brazenly across their path and insects twittered madly. Albert took a deep breath of the heavy air while Manfred went ahead and knocked heavily on the front door. It crept open, and they entered, curious. Already the forest was encroaching—spider webs hung like party streamers, small lizards on the ceiling did push-ups, and the floor was covered with small animal droppings. Nothing of value remained save a long case clock which stood silent in the kitchen. Manfred called out in the dialect, but his voice echoed eerily. Albert was becoming more dejected by the minute.

What to report to Percy? He'd been hoping to tell of children, hungry and waiting for their father, and a white Dutch woman surrounded by hostile natives.

"Over here," Manfred said from out back. He was pointing at a crouching figure of a thin, bedraggled native woman who didn't respond to Manfred's questions. "His wife."

Albert gasped, "A *native*?"

"They had *seven* children."

"Intentionally?"

Manfred shrugged rolling his eyes.

"But why won't she talk?" he asked, annoyed.

Manfred led him back to the road through a garden. "She's grieving. She's human, you know."

"Then why are you leaving her out back like a dog? And where are those children? Where's the furniture? What's happened here?"

Manfred got into the automobile and sat behind the wheel. "This woman is waiting for her own death, I imagine. I'm sure she thinks we're bankers coming to collect. But you needn't worry about the children. They're back in their kampong, reabsorbed into the broader family unit. What I'm interested in is the story you'll tell back in Hong Kong," he said with suspicion as he pulled out onto the dirt road.

A grieving wife waiting to die, and a litter of children thrown to the mercy of some kampong sounded bad. But the fact that the estate was never even purchased would leave all sorts of ugly questions in the old man's mind. *It couldn't be better.* Tomorrow he'd go to a solicitor and a notary and have all this put to paper for Percy. "What's the place selling for now? I imagine it could be had on the cheap."

Manfred chewed on his kretek, then gave the one finger victory salute.

Albert shrugged. Manfred's moralizing made him sick. *I'll be fucked if I care,* he thought as they gathered speed and he looked out the window. Parallel lines of infinite rubber trees played havoc with his eyes. He was going to have a delicious rijstaffel for dinner at his hotel that night and a bottle of Martel and ice afterward. For once, things were going well. He thought of Peak House's green sweeping lawns and imagined standing on them looking out over Victoria harbor. He could almost taste victory.

Sudden Death

23

China Coast Navigation & Co. *17 April 1938*

A WEEK AFTER THEIR cargo planes made their first flight in through Chung King, Jack and Algy were looking over profits when Jack's secretary put her head in his office. "Mr. Morgan." There was a warning note in her voice that gave him pause. "You're wanted at the house. It's Percy himself, but he didn't elaborate," she said looking uncomfortable.

Jack nodded to Algy. "Take over from here. I'm going up to see what's what. Probably an argument with Violet." The old man had been out of sorts for the past week, curt and aloof. Jack imagined he was in pain and tried to comfort him, spending his free time reading aloud at his bedside—something Violet wouldn't do.

The driver took the short route up through the noontime crowd and when they finally pulled onto the drive, Jack could see Percy smoking a cigar on the verandah.

Alarmed to see him out of bed, Jack stepped out. "I thought the doctor said—."

Percy stood up, his face reddening as Jack came up the stairs. "Don't you tell me what to do, young man!" he snapped, cutting him off. "You've a lot of explaining to do. Violet's out, and I've sent the servants away—so I'll not mince words." Percy grabbed a copy of the *South China Morning Post* from a wicker table and handed it over. "Well?"

Jack scanned it, unable to anticipate what the drama could be about.

"Goddamnit! That! There!" Percy choked out, pointing.

The notice was only a few lines long but upon reading it Jack blanched. *The planter—dead?* He was so startled he said nothing. He knew he'd arranged a loan for the man, so why he'd killed himself was beyond comprehension.

"Rubber is out, is that it?" Percival barked, his blue eyes bulging as he stepped back to suck on his cigar. "Well?"

"I didn't buy the estate."

This unexpected admission sent Percy into a coughing fit, "How—how dare you!"

Jack looked about to see if he could get a servant to calm Percy, and noticed a mixed drink on the side table. "Let me get you some cold water instead."

Percy pushed past him and snatched the drink, downing it in one go. "Don't patronize me," he spluttered. "This—this man killed himself because of you! Why'd you lie? By Jove, why? Who the hell are you?" he demanded, pointing with his cigar.

Jack felt himself go rigid at the abuse. "I'm the man you hired to turn your failed enterprise around. And, if you recall, you said you liked my cheek, that I had guts."

"Yes, my very words. Little did I think they'd be thrown back at me like this." He was shaking his head, looking weary, and finally he just sat down.

Jack took a seat as well, thinking the doctor would be livid that Percy was at the bottle again.

"You don't appear to be in the least bit disgraced. Where are your morals?"

"I did what I thought best."

"That's it?" The flush of anger returned. "And my money!"

"If you look at the bank statements, you'll see multiples of your initial investment."

Percy leaped up, turning white. "But, you lied! That man's dead because of your greed and deceit!" He suddenly grabbed Jack by the lapel, shaking him. "Speak up, you!"

Jack attempted to back away, "You said I could manage half of the profits from my French Indochina rice deal. I took you at your word, but when I returned from Shanghai, you changed your mind without warning—deciding to invest that money in a failing rubber business. I already had an order out for three ships. Understand my frustrations, if you will." Percy let go, speechless, his face seeming to bubble with restraint. "I think you should sit down again so that we can discuss this quietly," Jack said, hoping the tirade was over.

"*Quietly?*" Percy pointed with the cigar, firing up again. "You're a bloody *LIAR*."

"Yes, I lied, and that's inexcusable. But you've made decisions that have nearly ruined us more than once."

"I *BUILT* this firm. I can *DESTROY* it— if *I SO WISH*."

"Percy, I approved a loan for that planter so he wouldn't have to sell to you. He'd be able to stay on and remain working the land. I don't know what went wrong on that end."

"You made a loan—*AGAINST* my purchase offer?" Percy coughed. "*AGAINST* my bidding?" His eyes were round with incredulity. "God, I trusted you!"

"And yet you asked me to do things that would sabotage the firm." Jack glanced down toward the harbor and pointed. "It may be full of ships, but ours is the only firm making profits. Did you ever ask how? No? I've wanted to show you but you didn't care. I wanted you to rejoice—to rebuild the firm *with* me but you were *indifferent!*"

"You went too far. I don't care about the rest." He turned and walked toward the open bottle on the side table.

Jack followed. "Just look at the bank balance! I've not even drawn a salary for the last year. I've done it for you!"

"Young man, you'll find you get old mighty fast," he said pouring another whisky. "And I've lived long enough for my daughter to disappoint me, and now for you to betray me. What's left but drink?"

"Please don't," Jack said taking the bottle and holding it away. "The doc—"

"How *dare* you?" Percy growled, eyes following the liquor as he snatched at the air and dropped his cigar. "Give! *Give* me my bottle!" Jack held it at arm's length from the old man, whose blue eyes were the only cool spot of color in his face. "You ruined me! You and my ungrateful daughter!" In a sudden fit of rage he grabbed Jack with one hand and knocked the bottle with the other, sending it crashing. "Now look what you've done! You've ruined me!" Percy suddenly lurched, and taking Jack by the neck, choked him with rage. "You liar! *Liar!*" the old man spat uncontrollably, but with those words Jack felt the pressure suddenly release. Percy fell straight back onto the wooden floor of the verandah with the thud of a rotted tree, his heels kicking a tattoo into the floor as he frothed.

"Percy! Percy!" Jack leaped to his side. "Percy! Please forgive me! I didn't understand you. Please!" The old man's countenance was frozen. He wasn't breathing. Jack rushed up and down the verandah for help, but the entire house was empty; he didn't know what to do. Running back, he took out a handkerchief and wetting it in the liquor that remained in the glass, wiped his forehead. The man's eyes flickered for a moment as he looked up into this world for a last time. "Jack," he said with sudden warmth in his eyes, "my son," and then he died.

Peak House *17 April 1938*

UP ON THE ROOF with heaps of wet laundry in baskets, clothespins in her mouth, Rose looked up, hearing a sound. Peering over the edge down through the trees, she spotted Mr. Morgan getting out of the Studebaker. *A bit early*—she thought, then, taking a pin, secured a heavy sheet on the line. How her hands ached from all the wringing and hanging. Too much yin! The herbalist told her to brew thunder god vine tea with hare's ear but she'd forgotten. She sat down on a low stool and took out her pipe. News from China had it that thousands upon thousands of people had drowned. She struck a match and puffed. *Could it be true that Chiang Kai-shek had thought it wise to flood the Yellow River? Would it really forestall the Japanese, who were moving south?* All night the staff had argued in the kitchen over the consequences. "We'll have masses of refugees, again, they'll come over the border and take all the jobs." This had been the view of Young Wang, who was highly regarded in the household. Old Wang had conversely, like her, been worried about souls buried alive in all that water. *All those unmarked graves! They'll seek revenge on Chiang and chase him out of China! They'll come back ten times stronger to avenge their wrongful deaths. And if the Japanese forge the mud? If they take Canton, what will happen to Hong Kong?* Questions ran through her mind like the eight winds and ten directions. *I must find Old Wang,* she thought. *He'll settle my worries.*

Hurrying through the house, she noticed no servants about, and down in the kitchen found it deserted, lights off. Rose stood still for a moment, and then realized something must be very wrong, for only twice in the entire time she lived there had all the servants been dismissed. Once, when the lady of the house had died, and once again when Violet and Percival had their big fight because Percy wanted a new wife. Yet—*she heard a voice, an angry voice.* Rose shivered, and hurried toward the front rooms, careful not to make a sound. They were speaking too quickly for her to understand. Hurrying through the front parlor, she peered through the wooden louvers.

Percy was holding up a newspaper and she saw Jack push it aside and point angrily to the alcohol. Rose cringed—*Just don't take away his bottle,* she thought. Percy was grabbing the newspaper in his fist. *Too much excitement. Perhaps they were arguing over the flood in China?* She heard him shout the word "liar" several times. When the old man turned red as lychee, she hid. When the thud came, she wasn't surprised. She heard Jack shouting, "Help," his voice straining, as if it to break. *If I go now*—she thought wringing her hands—*he'll know I was watching.* Instead, she hid behind the curtains, weeping in fright. She remained until the ambulance carried the body away and Jack, red-faced and choking back tears, departed with them. Old Master was dead this time. *She could feel it.*

Rose crept out onto the verandah. The place was oddly quiet under the spreading trees, and the very air itself seemed to shimmer with their dark, expelled anger. A hundred poison arrows suddenly assailed her chi. *Hai-yah!* She brushed and swatted at her arms and legs as if attacked by bees and hurried inside, rushing up to her room at the top. There, the sight of the small red temple above her bed calmed her, and she bowed in obeisance. Then, quickly reaching for two packs of incense, she hurried back down. It took her a few moments to light the joss, and she puffed on the sticks until dense smoke rose up from the red flaming tips. Quickly, she waved it about in the air where the two men had fought, then proceeded to wash herself with the smoke, brushing off their bad chi. Then Rose went to the bottom of the steps and pushed the smoking joss into the ground on both sides so the sanctifying smoke unfurled upward and in through the house. Next, her eyes traversed the expanse of the terrace, seeking out misplaced items. A glass, a broken bottle—she swept up, put the glass away, then thought what to tell Violet. Like the very smoke that filtered back through the house, Rose's words, too, were always subtly chosen and woven through Violet's logic, patiently guiding her with an unseen hand. It amused her how the British lived here on Chinese land, eating Chinese sweat, believing themselves impermeable—yet even stone gives way to the soft persuasion of water and even this rigid culture which ruled over yellow man now would break under the weight of its own pride one day. As she stood thinking, her eyes came to rest on the copy of the *South China Morning Post—the cause of the quarrel?* There was nothing on that front page to tell her which words had caused this falling out, nothing except a tea stain at the bottom. She inspected it and noted a few fibers of the paper were broken in an attempt to save the print. Pleased, she folded the paper carefully, took it to her room, and hid it deep down in a large ceramic storage urn filled with raw rice—her insurance policy against dark days of hunger sure to come.

St. Michael's Cemetery *20 April 1938*

THE MOURNERS HAD LONG gone and Jack watched as the priest in black strode away on the dusty green hillside. "Don't you think we should leave?" he asked.

Violet said nothing, staring at the fresh earth. Rail thin and also in black, she stood motionless over her father's grave; only her dense veil moved with the breeze. Now and then, fragmented views of her face were visible—an eyeball, then a corner of her mouth—then it all vanished again in distorted folds of blackness. Somehow, without the push of her intense personality, when he saw her like this, silent and fragmented, she seemed utterly mad. He looked quickly away at the grave marker, wanting to distract himself from the dawning realization that his wife was very ill.

"Percival Summerhays, July 5, 1863–April 17, 1938," he read. And then in the next line, "Slainte Mhor," a nod to his love of drink, something Percy had put in his will a long while ago in happier times. Reading these words aloud made his throat tight. *Warm, big hearted Percy—gone—yet how he needed him now.* He felt tears choking him and took Violet's hand in his. "I know you miss him," he said. She didn't flinch, but held for a moment with gloved fingers, then suddenly—a streak of black flew past like a swimmer at the crack of the starter gun—Violet had launched herself onto the mound of fresh soil and was on all fours, *digging.*

It took a moment to come to his senses, but yes, she *was* digging. "Good God! Violet," he cried. "Stop!" She didn't heed him at all, but as Jack pulled on her shoulder, her motions went wild so that dirt clods flew everywhere. "*VIOLET!*" he said, jerking her back onto the grass so she lost her veil. She squatted, blinking in the light, and he saw she was holding something. He took it from her gently. A jeweler's box—and a ring inside blinked in the daylight—an engagement ring. He looked at her questioningly, and she vaguely pointed to the dirt. Jack felt a confused sadness. "You want *HIM* to have it?" When she didn't answer he said, "All right. Go ahead."

She dropped to her knees and began digging, her purse over her wrist, her nylons laddering, her underwear visible. He turned away overwhelmed with his own grief and guilt over Percy's death and didn't know what to do. Giving her a moment in private he finally returned. "Come now, let's go back," he said, holding back tears. Violet didn't protest, but stood up and walked beside him with her purse hugged to her chest. "Was this a ring Percy gave you?" She didn't answer. "I've never seen you wearing it," he said. It did strike him as odd.

Violet gave him the minutest smile and continued at his side, silent, self-contained, covered in dirt, her dress askew. The hair on his neck stood up; perhaps it was the smell of the grave, perhaps the look in her eye. *She smiled again. God help me,* he thought looking away.

After dinner that evening he went to the library. Violet followed.

"Jack, we must start a family." Her tone was flat.

He was so startled, he laughed. "Now?" She gave him a strange glassy look, and he shrugged. "Anything you want. But I'm going to read awhile."

"No, Jack. I do mean now."

"But, it's been a trying day." He looked out the window. "What's that burning out back?"

"Your clothes, I believe."

He sat up, "What?" *She almost looked pleased.*

"Chinese tradition. All the clothing of the mourners is burned after the funeral. I hope you weren't wearing anything you particularly liked. Your shoes. I threw them in too."

Jack stared. "Right, then." He went back to reading, but Violet didn't leave.

"It's what Percy wanted," she said staring at him with narrowed eyes.

"Really, darling." He smiled, but was thinking of her madness. She came up to his chair and began undoing his shirt buttons. He watched her face, trying to understand what was in her mind as she worked her way down to his belt. "All right, let's go upstairs." *It had to be the grief,* he thought, *somehow distorting her reactions.* Upstairs Violet vanished into her dressing room while Jack waited. After some time he got up see to what the delay could be. He heard some rustling in her closet and thinking to cheer her, playfully peered round saying, *Boo!*

Violet shrieked in terror and pushed something reflective under a heap of shoes. Startled by her reaction, he went back to the bed and, hearing her following him, wondered what she could have hidden.

"Ja-aaack," she cooed, turning kittenish, and when she came back to bed he noticed she was carrying her handbag. Violet slid her hand along his back, in a caress. "I want you to make me a little *Percival*. Imagine if he were to be conceived on the same day Poppa was buried!"

The thought unnerved him, but he said nothing, staring into her face. She moved against him, naked in the shadow of the room, and when she got on top he didn't resist the cool smoothness of her skin, and the flap of her breasts above him. Very soon he was mounting her, and minutes later, gasping as he came, he opened his eyes.

"You do your duty?" she asked clinically, her gaze flat again.

He nodded, turning his head away, feeling a chill. Violet removed herself and went into the bathroom, locking the door behind her. As he lay on the bed waiting for her to come out, he looked on his chest and noticed something dark. Sitting up he saw fingerprints all over his body. *What?* His hands went down to touch the marks. *Soil! Smudges of soil!* He leapt up and looked to the side of the bed where he'd seen her put something. *There*, by the bedside lamp, *he saw it.* Leaning down he picked up the little jeweler's box he'd held that morning. Inside, it was gritty. *She had filled it with soil from the grave!* Jack looked over the bed, and to his growing disgust saw the soil from the cemetery. And her purse too, spewing dirt! *Soil marked his skin, was ground into the bed cover, it was everywhere and it smelled like cold damp rot. God help us*, he said, his voice breaking. *Oh Percy*, he cried.

The Five Percent Solution

24

Chater House Square *23 April 1938*

Sunlight blazed outside on the praya, and the distant voices of the wharf coolies could be heard above the streets. Here, inside the oak-paneled room, under the sanctity of English law and beneath a portrait of the King, the spirit of the East remained at bay as the solicitor read Percy's lengthy will. "To my second cousin I also leave a stipend of—" The man droned on while Albert studied the crowd. Violet was her arch, aristocratic self, yet she was wearing a poisonously bright print dress and seemed unnaturally gay as she nudged a friend at her side, who also appeared flushed and giddy. In contrast, Jack, oddly enough, sat several people over, dressed in black, very somber, head bowed. Albert couldn't help but wonder if a rift had come between the lovers. He shrugged, however, and looked down at his own trembling hands, and congratulated himself for laying off the bottle last night. *If only Percy had done right by him!* It would be the crowning point in Albert's career. But he'd need to be sober. He looked over at Violet again, who snickered aloud suddenly. Or had it been a *hiccough?* Undignified, nonetheless.

The solicitor cleared his throat at the interruption, then continued. "To my daughter I also leave the piano as well as ..."

Albert sighed as the man continued to tick off minutiae having no bearing upon himself. Albert had done the work, gone to Java, and laid out the notarized information before the big man himself. The suspense was now killing him. The solicitor turned the page.

Moving closer to the edge of the seat, he eyed Jack, who appeared to have no interest in the proceedings, but sat deep in thought, gloomy. *He was a good actor, that man, feigning grief! I'd give him the bum's rush off Queen's Pier, I would.* Albert sneered with disapprobation, then abruptly sat up. *What? Had he missed it?* Eyes wide, he looked about the room like a startled hen, as did the others who were suddenly sitting upright too. The solicitor stopped reading.

"Excuse me, would you repeat that part?" Violet asked tenuously, her eyes wide.

The solicitor didn't question which part, for there was the slightest hint of satisfaction in his eyes, and he began again.

"The company, which has been under the supervision of my son-in-law, Jack Morgan, for the past ten years, shall be divided in the following manner. Forty-seven and a half shares interest go equally to the above mentioned, and to my daughter, Violet. The remaining five percent share vote goes to Albert Chiswick.

There was a murmur in the room, and people nodded at Albert, respectfully. The reading of the will then continued undisputed, undisturbed, but upon Jack's face there was a sudden dawning that Albert couldn't fail to perceive. *Jack Morgan was not sure how to take the news. Well, neither was Albert.* Forty-seven, forty-seven, and five percent. *But, what the bollocks for?*

It wasn't until after he'd wandered nearly all the way home when it struck him. "Cor Blimey, it's brilliant!" Albert turned about on the pavement, and headed into the first pub. "Matey," he said to the bartender, "the sun shines out my arse! A triple scotch! And for all these loafers—drinks on me!"

Peak House *23 April 1938*

FA-WONG BOY LAUGHED AS Rose walked stiffly down the driveway at Peak House in Madame's cast off clothing, and pointed her out to cook's apprentice. "Olo Auntie, day off! Supposey catchee one piece ha-sze-man!"

"No bubbery, you!" she scolded, then, tucking the newspaper into her large straw grocery bag, clamped her arm as a precautionary measure against thievery. Violet and Jack had gone on to the reading of Old Master's will, but Rose had more important business in town. She took the Peak Tram down, watching the dizzying vista of Wan-Chai rising up from below. At St. Joseph's she grabbed the first rickshaw and alighted a half hour later at Man Mo temple. She knew with a bed emptied in the house, the balance of power was upset and a new order would attempt to form. Before it could, she must uncover the secret to Percy's newspaper—whatever she could glean would guide her henceforth. For certain, hers was a grave responsibility, and she felt its weighty burden as she hurried along the road in the midday sun.

Green glazed roof tiles sparkled on the squat building that sat like a new tooth in a cankerous stretch of establishments on the back end of Hollywood Road. Rose entered the dark temple. *Mo,* she prayed, *protect us from the coming war. Give us enough rice, so we can stand against the Japanese.* She bowed her stiff back as she passed the Eight Immortals guarding the temple, nodded at the sacred brass deer who'd granted her longevity, gave a small donation, bowed, then took in the red glow of the main altar, breathing deep the heavy acrid incense to purify her body. This done, she bypassed Pao Kung, for she didn't believe in Justice, not while China was in the hands of foreign devils, and took up a chim, shaking the metal canister obtaining her lucky number. Next door at the Litt Shin Kung Temple, she approached the soothsayer.

"What does Kuan Yin say?" she asked, looking the old man in the eyes.

He looked at her carefully. "The rabbit always has three exits to his burrow."

Disappointed with this fortune she headed up Ladder Street and entered a dark hallway that smelled of stale grease and night soil. The door on the top floor was painted red, and she knocked loudly several times. She was related to these people very loosely, as they all came from the same village on the mainland.

"Come in, Elder Sister," the young man said, letting her in. Three Chinese children were sleeping on straw floor mats, and stepping over them she went to the terrace. At a table covered with newspaper, a cousin was cracking watermelon seeds, chewing the meat inside to buttery softness then feeding it to a fat white baby who grinned back at her.

"Your day off?" Rose asked in English looking at the white child.

"Hai-yah, my Madam talkee, 'Takum lik-lik Kum-bo.' My tinkee dis time no can do. My talkee, 'Madam, dis day off!'"

"Hav got wa-tah topside, but good heart!" Rose sympathized, tweaking little Campbell's ear. She took out a box of sweet bean cakes, and switching to Cantonese, offered them, "These aren't very good, an unworthy gift, I hope you take them."

The younger man called her back in and they sat down on an unmade camp bed, where he offered her tea. After a formal chat about China and the rising price of rice and coal, Rose drained the teacup. Then, apologizing for taking his time, she took out the newspaper and handed it over with both hands.

"Elder Sister, how much do you pay me?" he asked respectfully, scanning the small article. "I read it fast, but my education took many years of suffering."

They struck a price; he poured her more tea, then got down to work. After a minute or two of grimaces and nodding, he held a finger up, indicating he was ready. "Island far 'way," he pontificated like a schoolmaster, embellishing for effect. "Man kills self, five children and wife with chopper when business fail. Shame and disgrace on family. He sell property, but deal go bad. Debt come back to house with bad chi, make him run amok and die. You satisfy?" he added.

She marveled at his English, then asked him to repeat the information, not knowing how to fit this into her knowledge of the situation. Shaking her head, she finally got up and, taking the paper, tucked it into her bag. *The Master of the house was a serious, hardworking man. Why,* she mused, *had the Old Master called Jack a liar, and why had these distant murders upset the two men?* Rose knew Percy easily parted ways with his money, so to anger him one needed to cross a different line. As she headed back home she reworked several possible versions, but the one that felt right disturbed her most.

Master Jack had absconded with Percy's money to buy a concubine—the wife of another man who found out, killed her, then killed himself. She shook her head over the terrible blunder. Many times Rose had observed white people in arguments losing face needlessly over small points. Percy, being white, had viewed Jack's lie as unpardonable, and had left him no way out. A Chinese would have understood—a lie could be a considerate way of describing the truth so no person would be injured, and forced to take desperate measures to rectify face. Either way, it didn't bode well for Violet. Now Percy was dead over a few silly words, and Jack was alive to take on a new concubine. Rose abruptly recalled her fortune back at the temple. *In this light it made sense!* Jack did have many exits at Peak House. *He was the rabbit—playing both sides of logic, East and West—and running out between.* Rose tucked the paper away, pleased with herself and her interpretation. *No doubt this would come in handy.* Pointing to a coolie, she gave the address, then adding in pidgin, "Chop-chop! No daw-dling, you!"

Chater House Square *23 April 1938*

In the hall outside the solicitor's office, Jack cornered Algy, drawing him into an alcove to speak quietly. "What the blazes do I do?"

Algernon frowned. "You mean, Violet and her friends?" He cast a glance toward the lift where they stood chatting. "Do they usually drink this much? I found them all unbearable at brunch."

"What? No—*the bloody five percent,"* Jack said. "I was supposed to get the swing vote! Where the devil did Albert come from?"

"Ah, right, the five percent. Won't mean too much in the end, though."

"Don't be too sure," Jack said with a quick look over his shoulder. "This was Percy's revenge."

"*Revenge?*" Algy looked blank. "What on earth for?"

"The rubber estate."

"Impossible. There couldn't have been time."

There was a click and they both looked up. The solicitor was locking up his office, and Jack abruptly turned to the man—an old friend of Percival's. "Excuse me but, when was this final version of the will drawn up?"

"One week before Percival died." The man gave a frigid stare. "And now, begging your pardon, I have a meeting."

Jack and Algy exchanged glances.

"Oh, Jaaaack!" Violet called out from the end of the hall—laughing. "Jack, what do you think? Do you likey taxi-dance girley? Let's have a male opinion here." She was pointing to a native girl in a high slit cheongsam who passed by in the custody of an officer.

"Leave him alone," Pippa's husband, Will, hushed her as Jack approached, taking her by the elbow.

"I will *not!*" Violet pouted. "Besides, Jack's afraid about the will."

"Ooooo, scary biscuits!" Pippa giggled.

"No," Violet said, "he's upset because *I have half the company.* That's what it is, Jacky Dear! You don't want to *sharrrrre, fifty-fifty!*"

Will cut in, "*Not* fifty-fifty."

Pippa laughed. "See, men split hairs. Whattyoucallimgot only got *FIVE LOUSY POINTS!*"

"But don't you see?" Will added tersely, "Violet has greater control. It's more than fifty-fifty; if she doesn't agree how things are being run, she can side up with old Albert and vote Jack down!" He laughed. "Isn't that so, Jack?"

Jack was silent.

"*Jaaaaack*, tell me it *isn't* so?" she said wobbly with drink. "You mean *I* could *unnnnndoo anything—YOU do*—at the firm if I obtain *Albert's* approval?" She stared at him, toying with her necklace seductively. "Come now, can it be *truuuue? Jacky*—I *deserrrrrve* an answer."

He stared. "Don't you think you've had enough to drink? This is not a party, Violet. We're in a government building—and your father has just died."

Violet suddenly shrieked with laughter. "Pippa darling, I'm going to pee!"

Algy Breaks His Word

25

Jordan Path, Kowloon *12 August 1938*

The typhoon was stalling over the South China Sea and rain was blowing against the windows. Hearing lightning crackle, Albert awoke dazed and squinted at the alarm clock. *It hadn't gone off!* He rang his bell angrily and the servant came hurrying in, inquiring about breakfast. "Not now!" Albert snapped. "Get my clothes, you fool! I need a gift! A gift!" He pushed on his slippers and tore off the calendar page for the previous day, chucking it on the floor. "I have a vital assignation on the Peak," he said. "My good suit, please." As the boy hurried off he wondered how many months it had been since the funeral—*three? Almost four*—and *still, Jack hadn't begun to treat him as partner.* "'Five percent of what?'" Jack had retorted when Albert had finally demanded a cut of profits. "You see as well as I, ships aren't moving. Perhaps you want a cut of the losses?"

Albert peeled off his pajama top and rummaged about the flat, opening cigar boxes, looking among old coins, elastic bands, pencils, and dirty pictures. Jack couldn't sack him now that he was a titular partner, but remaining in his windowless office was humiliating;

the clerks laughed callously about his big "promotion" and Albert endured the humiliation. Having pinned his hopes on Jack being fair minded, Albert had forgotten the one important thing. *He didn't need Jack. He already had the five percent.* Yesterday, having realized this sorry fact, he'd gone and picked up the telephone and rung Violet.

Reaching under sheaves of paper on his desk, then searching under his bed, he retrieved a dead mouse, excoriated his boy, then fished out *just the thing.* Dressing with care, he tucked it into his pocket and rushed out into the rain, cheered enough in fact to give a twirl to his umbrella.

At the appointed time he panted up the steps to Peak House. A servant let him in and Albert waited patiently, dripping in the hall under Percy's 1910 dusty tiger trophy with the snarling yellowed fangs. Hearing the tap of heels on the marble floor his ears perked up. "Violet," he said when she came around the corner, "how lovely. Percy would have been delighted to see you as I do now."

This did something to soften the hardness, but only slightly. "Yes?" she queried. "On the telephone—you said you had something to give me." He could see everything about his person evoked disdain in her and it was as if she expected him to just hand her the aforementioned gift and simply toddle off.

He began rummaging through his pockets. "Ah, here it is!"

"Ooooo," she said leaning away, "What on earth is that?"

He held it up for her to consider.

"Gracious! A hairy chicken foot with toenails! Why bring *this* to me?"

"Yes, yes. It's rather ugly when described this way. It's a *grouse* foot, my lass. See, it has a silver clasp on the back and goes like this, let me show you." He pinned it on himself. When she didn't warm to it, he finally said, "Violet. This is a Scottish tradition! And you, not knowing!"

"And what tradition is that?"

Albert couldn't imagine why or how the Scots had come up with it and not being Scottish himself, secretly agreed it was ludicrous.

"Ah, that Percy's daughter should ask me! Do you realize he gave this to me some twelve years ago?"

Violet's interest was piqued and she leaned tentatively, taking a new look.

"Yes, for good service. You see, it's not an object of monetary value," he said quickly removing it and stepping across the space between them. "May I?" he said, holding it to her silk dress. She didn't protest, and as he plunged the thick silver pin through the delicate fabric it made a large hole before it hung properly. "Go, go to the mirror. Magnificent, isn't it?"

Violet was a bit thrown, but did as he said, her finger touching the tawny down on the leg.

"That very thing belonged to your dear departed mother," he lied, watching her face.

She abruptly turned, shock registering. "My—my *mother*? But why—*to you*."

"You don't remember, my dear, but I knew her well," he said.

She gestured to the Chesterfield in the library, mystified, and they sat down.

Perhaps, because it was so soon after her father's death, he now found it easy to manipulate her conversation, and shortly thereafter, Violet even ordered tea.

"I must say, it's odd Father didn't have you up to the house more."

"My dear," he said leaning back. "In the early years there was much candle burning." Violet didn't bat an eye, and thus emboldened he added, "As he's seen fit to make me partner in the family business with a five percent vote, I'm hoping to renew my friendship with you, the beloved daughter of my dearest departed friend. I'm older and wiser in the ways of the world so I hope you can lean on me whenever you're in trouble."

"*Trouble?* What sort of trouble?"

"Tsk, I don't mean *real* trouble," he frowned with self-importance. "You see, there is a famous Greek, was it Socrates, or maybe Aristotle, I can't recall, who said a woman needs three men. The first, to marry and provide status and the requisite material things of life. The second, as her soul companion, a philosopher of sorts. And the third, a lover. I hope you see me as your confidante," he said, leaving the distinction unclear.

Violet gave him a chilly look. "Don't get carried away."

He laughed heartily to cover his embarrassment. "My dear, you can't expect everything from a husband. Didn't Percy ever tell you this? Well, he should've. But there are things a father can't tell a child. You see, Violet. You're smart. I know you aren't taken in by clever words."

"You fool! Are you coming up here in the midday hours to make love to me while my husband's away?"

"Ah! Then you've seen through me," he sighed. "But we do share an interest, my dear, a link."

"I'm no fool. Are you actually attempting to suggest overthrowing my *husband*?"

"Not at all, not at all. I came here to re-establish old ties, to share with you my sympathies over your loss! I'm not interested in Jack, to be honest." He studied her carefully, then got up to walk around the room, inspecting the paintings. "But," he said, turning to face her, "the other day I ran across an interesting file. Did Percy ever mention diversifying into the Kowloon Canton Railway?"

"Never!" Violet stood up, frowning.

Albert shrugged. "I only mention it to verify my understanding of Percival's intentions. I want to remain true to his designs for the future."

"Then you must know," she said standing by the door, "Father never wanted to shift away from shipping—even though he did have an interest in rubber."

"Indeed, but I wonder, did Jack and your father always see eye to eye on this? Just a passing notion, here."

She suddenly laughed. "They did have a dust off once!"

"Is that a fact!"

"Not coming to blows," she said. "Just a row over rubber. Jack perceives himself to be a pioneer of things moderne, but entre nous, you don't start off in a new direction just because it *suits* you."

"Ah! Please, come sit down beside me. *There now.* We see eye to eye, my dear. Though remember this—it never does to scold a husband—they can be brutes! No, I say, hire a good cook, and provide him with the *entertainment* he desires." He winked. "Anything else my dear, come to Uncle Albert."

"He *is* a brute," she said quietly, and somewhat bitter.

He eyed her sharply. *Married life had not put a bloom in her cheek.* He took up his hat. "Call on me at any time—and may I suggest, keep your tongue over this meeting."

After their meeting, Albert stepped outside into the chilly Peak air and opened his umbrella. Making his way along the damp road toward the tram station, he shuffled through an ankle-deep fog that seemed to crawl and ooze at this elevation. *How isolated she was,* he thought looking about at the forest, *to live here among cliffs and clouds.* It struck him as a Willow Patterned loneliness. Soon he was engulfed in a thick fog himself and the tapping rain began, and by the time he reached the station it was a roaring downpour. Standing under the shelter, he watched the rain blending with the air. The Chinese said it was yin and yang comingling, and they stayed out of the rain, but he liked that idea. *Rather poetic,* he said quietly.

Victoria Central Market *12 August 1938*

WALKING PAST FLY-COVERED MEAT and cold slippery eels, and hearing the persistent whack of meat cleavers, Ana paused at a wide pool of bloody water as a painful contraction made her cringe. Smells of the wet market merged—durian, blood, rotted onions, the whiff off a fetid drain. She gulped hard. The doctor hadn't mentioned the baby could come early, but she headed for the exit, pushing her way through shoppers and baskets in another wave of nausea. Breaking though the tangle of people she stepped out the East Gate. Cool rain tapped her face and she leaned against the edifice, gasping for a breath of clean air as the fog wrapped around her. Sprinkles of mist filled her eyes with freshness. *A typhoon.* She let out a sigh of relief and the claustrophobia vanished with the pain. Ana remained against the wall for some time as the rain grew stronger, and started when a hand clutched her arm.

Amah's expression of concern surprised her. "Missie, you womit?" Ana nodded weakly and they left at once for home. The bumpy rickshaw ride made her wince repeatedly, but it wasn't until they were walking up the stairs that her water broke.

"Hurry, Auntie! Open the door. We must send for Algy straight away!"

The old amah was fumbling with the keys, and when she turned to Ana and saw her, she gasped—and catching the railing, *Amah dropped the keys.* Both leaned over watching them tumbling through space, sparkling, falling past four levels all the way down to the ground floor. "Hai-yah! Bad joss, bad joss!" Amah wailed.

Lower Peel *12 August 1938*

"THE BABY IS COMING," Ana whispered when Algy entered an hour later. She was lying down, ominously pale.

Algy was soaked, hair plastered to his head like streamers; his shoes bubbled, and puddles grew where he stood. He felt panic rising. "B-but *where* is the doctor?"

"The typhoon," she smiled wryly. "Haven't located him. You're dripping, you know."

"Ana, this is serious." He squeaked across the floor.

She looked at his shoes. "Don't you think you should change?

"I'm going to call the hospital."

"There's nothing they can do. The nurse said I should send for this list at the chemist. They're rationing bandages, cotton even."

"How so?"

"Everything's being kept back in England for the war effort."

"Then give me the list," he said, picking up the telephone. "But I won't accept this negligence!" He rang the operator and finally got the hospital. "Yes, my—my *sister*'s having a baby, it's an emergency!

On Lower Peel—by Gage Street. Can you get a doctor? Yes, yes. We did call earlier. Yes. *Ana*. Ana Worthing." He gulped. "Sorry? A different name? Vukovna, right." He wiped his face. "Well, no matter. For goodness sake, where's her doctor?"

"Excuse me, Sir," the head nurse told him. "Childbirth is *NOT* considered an emergency. We'll send you a doctor if he arrives; if not, the midwife."

"But—but there could be *issues*," he whispered.

"Sir, our midwives have been doing this for twenty years."

Hurrying over to the chemist a few minutes later, he realized Dr. Black had never told Ana there were possible complications. As the order was being filled, he stared at the floor, overwhelmed by the smell of disinfectants and medicines. *And I called her my sister! I should have said wife! Why didn't I? Am I so afraid of scandal?* He paid his bill and ran out, noting only halfway down the street that his hands were empty. Drenched through and through, he scurried back into shop, his suit plastered like a rag on him, and found the clerk was already holding his sack up at the counter, smiling oddly and staring.

"Chee-sing gweilo!" he shouted at them before they could humiliate him. The native clerks were gob smacked a moment—then all burst out into raucous laughter. *Bugger them all*, he thought running back home. Sniffling, he let himself into the flat and immediately went to Ana's side. She wasn't doing well, he thought, seeing how she gritted her teeth and turned her head away, but after a minute she appeared fine again.

"My God, Ana, I can't take this!" he cried out grabbing at his head, then sighing as he sat down at her side. "Hasn't that doctor called?"

The door opened behind them and their amah let in a nun. "The doctor is beezy," she announced. "He 'as a senta me 'ere inna his place. I am Sister Bella." Then, turning to the amah she barked out orders which sent the woman scurrying. "Are you necessary here?" she asked absently, looking at Algy.

Piqued by her condescending attitude, he mimicked, "Pliss, I would like a word with a you inna de oder room," thinking his Italian imitation was spot-on.

The nun glared and Ana looked up from the bed, appalled.

"Sorry!" Algy gulped, but she did follow him to the other room. He then whispered, "Didn't you talk to the doctor? He told me her baby could die."

"You're a big trouble, I cana see. You are not even the fader. Go over there," she said, fanning her hand loosely, shooing him away. "And do nota make this worse with your stupid jokes." Before he could interrupt her, she cut him off. "I'll let you know if you are wanted. It coulda take all night. And, can I heva your watch?" she asked. Algy removed it and handed it to her, feeling completely doomed, and sat down in the kitchen, his face in his hands.

Sometime later, the nun entered, her wire glasses steamed up. "The baby 'as a wrong pozition. I willa 'ev to move it or it cannota come out. You may not want to stay." Ana was groaning in the other room.

Repositioning? Algy got up and paced the room, then burst into tears. The midwife didn't waste time coming back out.

"You are *NOT* 'elping one bit. Who are you, if nota the fader?"

Algy didn't know what to say. His blood pressure was through the roof. He just knew it.

"Where *is* the fader? He shoulda be 'ere! This isa 'is responsibility."

"Ana does not want him here, he—"

"Basta!" the nun snapped. "I 'ave a very difficult delivery here. I need alla da help I canna get. Ifa the fader of thata child cares one bit, you bringa him here. Neither she, or da child, might live. It is a confusion inside," she said twirling her hand in the air like an egg mixer. "Find him. I don't a need a biga monkey likea you crying. Go!"

"*Algy.* Algy?" Ana's voice came from the other room.

He found her deathly pale. "What is it, my dear?" Ana burst into tears and he held her hand not knowing what to say.

The nurse gestured to him with a jerk of her head to get out as she went to the bedside. "My dear Ana. There will bea no problem ifa you 'elp. Understan' me? "

Algy shut the flat door quietly, then bolted down the wet stairs and slipped in the unlit lobby, bumping into a camp bed by the exit. A homeless family woke up, staring at him. "Sorry!" he shouted.

Hurrying outside he found the street ankle deep in rushing water. He couldn't call Jack—*Ana would kill him.* Between the crashes of lightning and thunder, he could hear her distant screams. *How wretched,* he muttered, wringing his hands. In the doorway of his building a Chinese man and his wife now stood holding a sleeping child, a family on the edge of starvation. They were watching him and suddenly he saw himself through their eyes—a pitiful white man, standing in a downpour. A man with no blood ties, a man like all these white devils who comes to suck up the money and, like many, dies, unfulfilled, an arrow shot far from its bow, wildly missing its mark. His own blood might, like that of so many English before him, be spilled on this rock so far from home, and no one would care. Algy could no longer see or hear through the warm river of rain, but just stood there, feeling it wash over him, feeling utterly alone as he cried. Through his tears he saw a blue light. It was a pub down the street. Inside he pulled up a bar stool and as he sat down he noticed a telephone sitting squarely in front of him.

Peak House *12 August 1938*

Tonight they were alone at home, and Jack, nursing a third drink after dinner, looked out at the rain. He had been on edge all evening and didn't know why. It could have been the telephone. He heard it ringing in the hall yet again and sighed. *Violet's partying friends.*

Even though it was August, all the fireplaces and stoves in Peak House were lit against the damp, which unchecked would rot every piece of leather, silk, fabric, and wood with a green leprosy, letting off a tickling stench of mold. Jack stood up and poked a log back into the fire, then threw himself down on the length of the sofa and lay still as if a rock had been placed down on his soul. *Rot. I'll rot like everything here.* He heard her voice again from dinner that evening, running a loop in his head.

"But don't you agree, Jack, there's something prestigious about shipping, don't you think? I wonder, if you hadn't started off with Father, might you have considered *trains*?"

Jack had been cutting his steak. "Nothing wrong with trains."

"Whatever do you mean?" she'd demanded, her crazy eyes glittering as she fished for some revelation. *Could she know about Tu? Impossible.*

"Shipping's about making connections—so you can eat apples from Vermont, sip China tea, and sniff perfume from Grasse. It's a network of arteries, timetables. All of it, the cranes, trucks, airplanes, wharves—it's all just shipping to me, one and the same."

"But there's no *honor* in trains," she said licking her lips, eyes flashing; disappointment ran thick in her veins. "I've seen how packed they are going in and out of China. *Filth! Full of refugees.* I wouldn't set *foot* on one, and I'd never have my *family name* on such a business."

Violet hadn't become pregnant the previous month, and he knew what that meant. Lying still in the library now, waiting for dawn, he gazed at the ceiling. The phone rang again. He heard the tap of her shoes. *There*, he thought, *like clockwork.* She would come, sit down beside him on the sofa, take a sip of his drink, then begin to undo his shirt.

The door clicked. "Jack," she said coming into the room. "What are you doing lying in such a state of dishabille? What will the servants think?"

Jack slowly sat up, the shrill edge to her voice dancing about his brain. He didn't want to look at her.

"Boy. Come in here. Fluff those cushions and put his shoes outside. Where are your carpet slippers, Jack?" She sat down opposite, quiet for a while, her diamond necklace flickering in the lamplight.

"It that your gossiping friends ringing all this time?" he asked, irate.

She raised her brows with a little vinegary sneer. "A call came for *you* some time ago."

Jack sat forward. "At *this* hour?"

"I was busy with the staff—they're doing all the silver polishing. Imagine, I caught one of the boys polishing *filigree* with *gravel* from the drive!"

"Well, who was it? On the phone, I mean."

"What? Oh." She shrugged with an oblique knowing look. "Just that sniveling homosexual you spend so much time with."

Jack felt himself coloring, but refused to rise to the jibe. "But Violet. It's nearly midnight. Was there was no message? It's unlike him."

She smiled, "God knows, he's an impudent fool. I didn't bother to pick up again. He's got some nerve ringing here."

"Then that's been him *all* this time?"

Violet sneered. "Perhaps for an *assignation?*"

The first connection didn't go through. Jack clicked the brass hook anxiously and finally got the dial tone back. "Operator," he said, "Can you try this number again?"

She came into the hall behind him, listening. "For goodness sake. Why bother?"

The connection came through with a crackle. "Ja-ck? Is that you?"

The note of panic in Algy's voice sent an odd shiver through him. "Yes, what's wrong?"

"Where've you been? I've been calli—" There was thunder overhead and cut out the rest of his words but Jack heard the fear.

Violet linked her cool arm through his and whispered breathily, "*No. You are not going!*"

"Algy! *WHAT IS IT?*" Jack asked, forcefully unlinking his arm. "*I'm having trouble hearing.*"

She cornered him against the wall and began to undo his buttons. "You promised. Jaaaa-ack. *Tonight,*" Violet said with a sinful smile, but her eyes were hard. "What is it with you?" she murmured through her teeth, more like a low growl. "Joined at the hip, are you?"

"Please … the … me!" the voice quailed on the line and then in the midst of a flash of lightning said, "You are—*Ana …ying!*"

"For goodness sake, Violet! *I CAN'T HEAR!* Algy? *ALGY!*" In all that rain and thunder, he was sure he'd misunderstood and now the line was dead. Jack found himself feverishly re-buttoning his shirt, unable to think straight; *Algy had said her name!* He brushed Violet aside and taking the car keys, ran out into the rain while she shouted after him.

A half hour later he found Algy, sitting on the landing to his flat, sobbing.

"Damnit! What is it?"

Algy pointed upstairs. "Top floor," he said.

Jack ran all the way up, pushing open the door, panting. Inside, in a bedroom an old nun sat on a low stool with her back to him, and lying face to the wall was a sight that made his heart turn. "Ana?" he gasped. "Is that you?"

The old woman turned around, "Ah! So *you're* the fader."

It was a declarative statement that stabbed him to his very marrow. "*Yes!*" he said, before he even knew what he'd uttered. The nun motioned him to come away for a moment.

"She is exhaustion," she said in a low voice on the other side of the screen. "I hev turned da child around inna da womb, but if it does nota come soon, it will die."

"Can't I see her? *Please.*"

"I do nota know where you 'ave been, but if you are responsible man, you will bring her back. The child, I will take care."

A weak voice cried out for water. Amah handed him a glass, and Jack came around the screen with the nun. "Ana," he whispered.

The face wrung with pain and sadness changed before his very eyes, and the recognition that passed between them was unlike anything he had ever known.

"Jack." Her voice stretched into a smile at his touch.

"Yes, it is me. I'm here," he gasped, leaning to kiss her hand.

She grimaced, biting her lip. "It's not—*not* going to *die*, is it?"

"Ana, no, you—"

The nun pushed him aside as Ana writhed again. "Go 'elpa da amah with da pot of wohter." Jack did as he was told but when he returned the nun said, "It is better det a man not see dis. You have done your job. Go outside. I willa call you when we are finish."

Ana was gritting her teeth, her forehead glistening, but her eyes followed him. "Jack?" She held out her hand and he reached out to her. *His tiger charm. It was there—in her palm.*

He squeezed her hand. "I was a fool, Ana," he whispered hoarsely, his voice thick with emotion. "But I'll be with you always. Our child too. I'll not disappoint you again, not ever."

He was shown out by Ana's forceful little amah, who had no stomach for romance. Pushing him out onto the stairwell, she said, "You men, Chinee, foreign devil, same-same, like shit in bucket. Bery good you come."

The door slammed behind him and Jack laughed with a surge of gladness—in one hour his life had completely changed. He found Algy sitting on the cold damp landing in complete dejection moaning that Ana might die. But Jack refused to think the worst and sat down on the steps to wait, praying fervently for her and his child to live. Not once did he even *think* of Violet, or Peak House, or the promise he'd just made—and what it would take to keep.

JARDINE

Hong Kong *1997*

THE WORLD SMELLED CLEAN from here. I was standing on the rooftop of Grandfather's building between clotheslines that dipped heavy with upside-down shirts flapping arms, slacks walking, sheets snapping. Shielding my eyes from the glare off the harbor, I looked toward Central District. Jammed between mountain and sea, it was a sparkling geode chock-full of skyscrapers. Among all these structures, my favorites were the Hong Kong Shanghai Bank—it looked like Darth Vader's death star. Even newer, the Bank of China was a worm from Dune with poison chopstick antennae. I looked over at the dated Jardine Matheson's structure, colonial great-grandfather of them all, its every window round. Because its founders started the Opium War, we Chinese called it "building of a thousand assholes." But there they were—all gleaming and relatively new buildings, yet the old uneasy relationship between East and West, Britain and China, was cast in *them*—in metal, stone, and glass, for all to see and remember—or try to forget or forgive.

"Once upon a time," I said wistfully, "there was a little island out to sea from China, where foreign devils found safe harbor for opium ships and—" Auntie huffed, clothespins in her mouth. She was hanging a wet bra and her high-waisted Marks and Spencer undies. "And," I said with a grin, knowing I was irritating her, "they all lived happily ever after. Happy endings are best, don't you think? Hong Kong's rich now. Why not just forget the past?"

"Hai-yah!" she ripped out the last clip from her mouth. "You born yesterday! You see Hong Kong rich today, but Hong Kong not always skyscrapah here, there. Not always rich. Hong Kong orphan, like you! Got nobody, eh?"

"So when did it change?"

She started hanging stockings. "1960."

"Really?"

"So many problem," she said turning to me. "China not stable, then Hong Kong not stable. Like parent and chil', same." She came over with the now empty basket and sat down beside me on the edge of the building. "You orphan, don't have old generation tell you truth."

"Yeah, I know, people kneeling on glass," I said. "Kow-towing against the cement street till they split their heads open." Instantly I regretted it. Tam looked hurt.

"People die to come for chance! Run 'way from Mao!" she said angry. "And when government in China get angry with British, they make life hard in Hong Kong. Many strike. All worker sudd'ly go back to China—nobody here! No business! Other time Communist poison gweilo bread in bakery! And you know plague?" she asked getting more and more excited. "Many time thousand people sick and die here. Too crowded. Now cemetery crowded. No food—everything grow China side, see? Then Communist, they have worker union, they have 'm'bargo, go take *ALL* money out of English bank! So many problem but British steal Hong Kong, so China never happy, ah? It big problem with Hong Kong, see?" She shook her head. "No good. Can't fix"

"But why 1960?" I asked.

"Silly goose! World war finish! China close door and Hong Kong take US dollar! Hong Kong people work hard for cheap money. Easy get rich if you have luck, ah?" She shook her finger, laughing at my ignorance, yet a little dismayed too. I didn't know why she spoke in broken English to me rather than Chinese, but it didn't shame her in the least. Auntie had inner confidence sparkling from her eyes like I never would. She pointed to my eyes. "See, I have tattoo eyelinah!" She pointed to hers. "Don't buy makeup. Save money! Save time! Ah?"

She laughed at me. I looked at her eyeliner and noticed it was true, the line was perfect every day and I told her so. "When did you come here?" I asked, "You have family in Hong Kong?"

"Hai-yah! I'm Hong Konger! My family fishermen, maybe pirate too!" She laughed, but then her face grew still for a moment, almost sad.

"You married?" I asked slowly.

She waved her hand at me, exasperated. "I sma't modern gir'! Stay singou!" Then she said, "You know saying, eh? Woman marry out side direction, garbage water t'rown from house? Not me!" She stood up slowly. "You wantche tea?"

I followed her back down the concrete steps to the flat. "How about the old man? When did you meet my grandfather?" I asked in our language, feeling closer to her, wanting her to know that.

She opened the door. "That long time 'go," she answered then switched to Cantonese. "My name was Tam Ming-Chun, but I took a Western name when I came here. Tammy, sounds like family name, Tam. I left my fishing village when I was just a girl." She explained she'd gone to train for nursing and met Jack when he came to a children's home in Kowloon looking for a lost baby in 1941.

She said this over the kitchen table to me, carefully, watching my face. Her Chinese voice was very pretty, high-pitched and girlish when she spoke, but also sad. "I'd gone to help a missionary lady who was running the Fanling Babies Home. It was a terrible day, you see. We'd just received a call from a friend of Mildred Dibden, the lady running the place, warning that the Japanese were near. We were up on Kowloon side in the New Territories closer to the border. Mildred and I, and about seventeen other nurses, quickly got the eldest children into a lorry.

"When we shut them in the back of that dark truck," she said, "the children were crying and scared and no one knew what was going to happen. Only thirty-four got out and we still had fifty-four babies left behind. I went back inside to check on a sick baby when I noticed a handsome English soldier in the nursery with Mildred. He was walking from bed to bed looking at the faces. Mildred was telling him that we didn't have white babies. She hurried off to see if she might find another lorry for the rest, when he came to look at the baby in my arms.

"I remember his face like today. Like a film star, but tired. He was heading to the front, and wanted to know if we had food for all the children and warned *THEY* were coming. I told him I didn't care. Those *TURNIP HEADS* wouldn't hurt our babies—but of course I didn't know. He gave me his name card and told me to contact him on Hong Kong side if I ever saw a white baby girl, three years old. She'd been missing a week already and he'd been going to orphanages and hospitals looking and asking for help. I didn't know what to say, but as he left he added, 'If you need anything for these babies, get word to me, I'll help you.' I didn't *think* I'd see him again.

"Then the Japanese came. A few of us had been outside hoping the first lorry might return, but instead the turnip heads came marching down the road at us. The soldiers must have seen there were women inside and broke in. Mildred was carrying a baby when they kicked the door down so they grabbed a nurse, throwing her onto a bed to rape her. Still carrying the baby, Mildred ran to stop them but they smashed her across the face with a rifle—then—" Auntie's face went hard trying to keep the pieces in. "They stomped a baby, killing it, then raped all of us. *Even me.*"

"You don—you don't have to tell—" I said, feeling overwhelmed.

"No, I'll say this," she said, placing her hand over mine. "Later, I had a Japanese baby. I drank a special tea when I was six months pregnant." She squeezed my hand. "It fell out of me into the toilet and I saw it dying in there. I was just *sixteen*." Tears ran down her old cheeks but she kept looking at me. "You see, the baby didn't ask me to be its mother, but still it was innocent like me. At night I still lie in the dark and remember it drowning. *My only baby, a little boy.*"

I watched her agonized eyes, realizing all the sadness people held back inside—you'd never know passing them on the streets of Hong Kong. My mother might have been missing, but each one of those babies in that orphanage had been displaced—they'd be grownups now. I wondered if all of Hong Kong was like that, a city of displaced, damaged people, working, saving, obsessing about getting rich—distracting their sadness with hyperactivity and noise. I looked at Auntie who was now scanning the morning paper.

"Hai-yah! Look! Look stock ma'ket!" she said in English, eyes moist with tears. "I sell this and now, double!"

I smiled. English was good for that, distancing oneself from emotion. "How is it you work for Jack? Did you find my mother among all those babies?"

She sighed and got up and began washing dishes, her back to me. "There are other sides to problem, ah? I was nurse, you 'member? Ana sick, so he hire me. Soon after, Japanese take him to Stanley Prison—*four years*."

"But how'd he survive?"

She laughed turning around. "He like Chang Kow-lao," she said, comparing him to one of the eight immortals. "He hundred year old! Drink poison—*not die!* Go one way—*face other!*"

I thought of what I remembered of the old man Chang. He was supposed to be a shape shifter, and white, the color of death, and could turn into a white bat, or he could appear to die and be reborn. He would ride on a white donkey, backward, and for the Chinese this meant he was simultaneously moving into the future but looking into the past. Chang Kow-lao had mastered life's changes, moving between the living and dead and back again, fearlessly. I thought about my grandfather. It did seem like he had tricked life, and yet not. She was making up a tea tray. "Here, take this to the old doorman downstairs," she said.

I nodded and carried it down. He was snoozing but, when I set it down, he started, his eyes shooting open like he'd seen a ghost. "Jio san!" I said, and ran back upstairs giggling.

Grandfather had been taking a nap and was awake now, looking at another photograph of my mum. "Come sit by me," he said showing it. "Isn't she lovely? I thought of her as my last chance. To make good for once."

I wanted to ask him, *But how do you lose a child?* I couldn't—for I thought of Auntie. *There were many ways to lose a child.* I looked at the photo. Even as a baby, I recognized that smile. *That was my smile too.*

"Just before her third birthday," he said. "Then she was gone. Not even a final '*Good-bye, Poppa*.'"

Listening to him, I felt my emotions choking me and realized I was one of those Hong Kong people eating my sorrow, just to keep it down.

"She was born in August 1938, sign of the tiger. Like me," he added proudly. "That was when the Japanese bombed the border at Lu Wo, closing it off. Then later, when we were busy expecting her first teeth, teaching her to walk, to run, we were so happy, so alive, we didn't notice how ominous things had become. A quarter of a million refugees had retreated onto Hong Kong Island by then, and we had trouble feeding everyone. People in Mid-Levels were coming down with cholera and smallpox. Ana was so worried she didn't allow Bella outside much early on. By her first birthday Bella was saying, 'Poppa-Poppa,' all the time throwing her baby arms around my neck. That was around September in 1939, when Germany declared war." He sighed. "Here in Hong Kong the government interred all our German friends on Stone Cutters Island, and then decided to requisition private ships and aircraft as needed. I was scared; it was all I had left. Then, by 1940, after a siege of a British settlement in Tianjin, the Crown caved in. England was forced to sign an agreement that they wouldn't take action against the Japanese in the future. *It was the ultimate loss of face—but they signed it.* People at the top saw what was coming, and a thousand of the British women and children were evacuated to Australia by force. But it wasn't popular—everyone was bitter about it and said it was completely unnecessary."

"Did Ana leave?"

"She got around it by volunteering in the Nurses Auxiliary—you know, bandaging, bedpans, and blood pressure."

"But what about your planes? Did you lose them?"

"Nearly. I was conscripted in November of '41 and stationed in the Northern Territories with the Rajputs and the Punjabis. We'd be the first in combat if the Japanese came over land—*which they did*."

"Did Chinese join up?"

"Some volunteered. We had Chinese orderlies, drivers, and translators. But that's a tricky question," he said looking at me. "We couldn't trust them. The triads were a fifth column, conspiring with the Japanese to slaughter every white person before the Japanese invaded so as to avoid Chinese casualties. We didn't dare arm anyone. Anyway, with the way the Brits treated them, many Chinese had animosity for us. Some were downright glad when the Japs packed us all off to Stanley Fort Prison. The locals lined the streets and watched us whites publicly humiliated after the surrender. We were forced to march down Des Voeux Road with just the clothes on our backs. We didn't know if we were to be killed once we reached the prison. The Chinese just stared—retribution I guess."

"I can't believe the Chinese wouldn't have wanted to fight off the Japanese. I mean it was their home too."

"Yes. Some formed a guerilla movement and gave their lives fighting alongside us, valiantly. But there was a lot of apathy; the Chinese refugees here were already kicked around and betrayed by every side—Mao, Chiang Kai-shek. The civil war was still going full bore, and the Japs were driving people from their homes southward. Those that escaped back into China didn't have it easy either. A lot of them joined the Communists and later when the Red Guard got going, many people ended up turning in their own neighbors and family in desperation. It's not always easy trusting a Chinese business partner with that background."

Auntie Tam brought out some tea, but I couldn't speak from shock; What did he say? *Hard to trust the Chinese? Is that what he'd just said?*

"When you *see* bad things," he went on, "when you *do* bad things, as in war, you get to explore the realms of the human heart and see what it's made of. We're all capable of the same atrocities. I think if you can at least admit your evil side, you can be forewarned, you can fight it—that inner devil. Otherwise, you get a country like Germany, nice ordinary folks who slide into their satanic role in history just because they don't know how far they can go."

"The inner *devil?"* I asked, sarcastic.

"Your dark side," he said with an impatient wave of his cigar. "Ordinary people who haven't tested their limits and haven't done any soul searching will judge others, exclaim loudly that in the same circumstances they would keep their ethics and remain outstanding citizens. But trust me, once your heart has been stretched like the Chinese, it may not snap back."

"You can say that—but what about the Japanese! Look at them!"

Jack laughed, taking a few puffs. "The Japanese soldiers were *subjects* of the Emperor—they had to do as they were told or die. I can see you don't understand that—you're judging them from your perspective, today. But you see, as a *citizen* you have *choice, personal responsibility*—they didn't. They were made into pawns. The government was all powerful back then with no constitution to keep it in check. Today government is dangling entitlements, like carrots, trying to lure the public back under their control, abolish rights. See? You can lose your freedom like that—piecemeal—and wake up in the dark ages again. No war will ever be the last, my dear. We are fighting our human nature. All of us. Don't you see that?"

"You think I'm an idiot or something!"

"No, just asleep, like most. I'm not telling this to make you feel bad or guilty. I want you to remember what's in your blood. During those seventeen days we were fighting off Japs, your Chinese refugees here were all starving, waiting for the next meal. Hordes queued up outside Victoria's Central market for a tiny ration, and then the Jap planes came swooping down from overhead, firing into them with machine guns. Can you imagine? Dozens of people in the line fell down dead, *but no one stepped out of line.* You'd have to go through a lot to be that stoic not to scram. Those poor people were whittled down to nothing. Now, I'll tell you what the Japanese did to them. I think it was in '42 and Isogai was our new 'governor.' He knew he couldn't feed all these refugees, so about three quarters of a million Chinese were forcefully repatriated across the border—at bayonet point. Those who'd seen the atrocities across the border in China absolutely refused to leave Hong Kong. So the Japs just tied these people up in barbed wire then pushed them into the harbor to drown."

"But then how can you say you don't trust the Chinese?" I nearly shouted. "What about the Japanese—what you just told me!"

"The Japs? I trust them," he said looking at me with a dare in his eyes.

I glared at him, "That's racist."

"The Japs never were colonized," he said, then heaved a sigh. "It makes a big difference. Not to mention their past. China tortured its peasant class for thousands of years. The Japs have a similar feudal background, but they had the Samurai, like the knights; they had a code of honor. You both 'save face,' but they—"

"But they killed and raped, and did things like nobody else! You *KNOW* that!"

"I *know* they're the same as you and me."

"They followed orders! Is that honor?"

"Survival is a natural instinct and protecting yourself is, too. That was the Japanese take. They believed they were doing a favor to all Asia, kicking white Imperialists out."

"I don't understand. You were in their internment camp, Auntie told me. You of all people should be sick of war—not defending it."

"I'm not defending anyone. If only everyone were sick of war! But see, I learned something from the Japs. You do one of them a favor and they owe you for life. It kept me alive in Stanley Prison when everyone else was dying of starvation. It's called obligation, *giri*—the glue of Japanese society. The Chinese focus is on connections—*guaxni*—get it? Who can get me what I need? *See the difference?* The Chinese are natural survivors, while the Japs unite to win, as a group. Mankind will take one of these routes, and the future will depend upon it. Guanxi or giri, that'll be the choice."

"I don't understand." What I wanted to say was that I didn't want to hate his old gweilo guts. And I felt that hate creeping in, coloring everything I saw. I clenched my teeth. "I don't want to hear more."

"Listen, when I was in China, do you remember I found a very sick Chinese soldier? I brought him back to Hong Kong with me. He turned out to be the Japanese nephew of the barber who became commander of Stanley Fort Prison. Yoshi turned up to warn me just before the invasion, and after the takeover, he worked for the Japanese Governor Isogai as his groom at St. John's Church where they stabled their horses. Yes, horses crapping in church! Isogai liked to ride around Hong Kong Island for exercise and Yoshi was so good with the animals he became very trusted—possibly also because of his connections or because he had no tongue. He would pass information to me at Stanley, and would bring me and my friends food at great personal risk."

"I don't care about some Japanese guy. You said you don't trust Chinese people; then why do you live here?

"Why?" His voice was calm, tender, like a balm. "I love the Chinese. They're hardworking, energetic, and positive. And it's the only life I've known for sixty years." He reached over and placed his hand over mine. "Everything I know and love is here."

I stared at his arthritic hand then looked into his eyes. "Sixty years *is* forever."

"Waiting for Bella has been forever."

I stared at him, frowning. He seemed a shape shifter, good one moment, horrid the next, "You know," I said, "all my life I thought of my Mum as mine alone to lose, but there you were—*a gweilo*—just a few blocks away from me thinking of *her too*. It's hard to get."

He took my hand in his. "In you, in your blood, the whole conflict—East and West is made one—made into something beautiful."

"Oh, Grandfather, why? Why is it always politics? I hope Ana wasn't like that too."

He laughed, his blue eyes sparkling. "Your grandmother thought with her heart, and she mocked me constantly. And I'd tell her I'd love her forever and always—hoping she'd say it back to me."

"Didn't she?"

"No. She'd say it was just words, and that she'd stay with me until I learned to love Violet, even just a little bit. And I'd say, 'Then that *is* forever, darling, because I'll always hate her.'"

I frowned, a little uncertain. Auntie brought me tea and we listened to the Victrola while he rested, closing his eyes for a moment. I watched birds skitting past his French windows where Auntie had placed the new bird feeder. Back in the orphanage I had had budgies once—a rare privilege. I felt so connected to them—they were mine and as close to as family as I'd get. But one day, my blue one escaped. Every day he returned to my window to peer in at his friend inside, singing and scolding, tapping against the glass. My heart broke watching it. A week passed and I finally opened the cage so the other one could join its friend. But it wouldn't, it stayed, and Blue died outside, waiting. I wondered what Grandfather was waiting for.

"You know, Jardine," he said, eyes flickering open, "Ana became an orphan too. When she was ten in St. Petersburg, Lenin came into power." He reached for his cup and I topped it off. His blue eyes locked onto mine. Jack Morgan again—*taipan*—he took the tea and my heart did a little flip. "It was 1917," he said with the faintest smile, then looked away, aging again. "Lenin confiscated private property, nationalized land, industry, banks, transportation. Since her family was associated with the Romanovs, they were thrown into prison. She and her brother were able to escape but he became separated from her on a train and didn't make it out of Russia. Eventually, he escaped to Mongolia, then Shanghai." Grandfather put down the cup and stared out the window.

"I'm surprised," I said, finally. "I thought only Chinese people told these kinds of stories."

He shrugged. "There's no monopoly on suffering."

"What are you looking at?" I asked.

"Those birds. Never saw them before." He looked back at me.

"I gave that feeder to Tam," I said as I poured myself hot tea.

"That's just going to bring rats."

"Chinese say rats are good luck. You have to have food to have rats," I said with a teasing smile. "Tell me, why did Ana come East?"

"Well," he sighed. "She spent some years in Germany. Working, studying, living with her governess's family—but you know Germany was in the midst of its progressive upheaval. Their socialist agenda was to improve the world with science and eugenics. It sounded great but the result was the slaughter of six million people. Ana had to get away. Can you see the pattern? Like with Hitler in Europe, out here, Mao's Red Guard cleared the way for him in '49 to do the same thing, only here Mao killed *sixty million* people. Ten times what Hitler did. This is why *all* government officials need constant vigilance—like maximum security prisoners."

"I don't see the pattern, other than the struggle for power and innocent people dying."

"No? Look at Americans, they've been tricked. They've given their government free rein too—in exchange for self-gratification. They've traded freedom for free love, dope, electronics, and handbags—all trinketry. The progressives are on the loose again. They'll delete the genetically flawed and the elderly this time. Ah! I see you're rolling your eyes. Last time they got rid of Jews, homosexuals, and Slavs while civilized people turned their heads the other way. Humans are capable of anything, mostly great hypocrisy. All of these leaders had *two* sides, Mao and Hitler both. They were big-talking humanists—they could charm your pants off with one side of the mouth, while calling for the execution of innocents with the other. Why, I've even seen tourists with Mao T-shirts! Why not wear Hitler on your shirt, too? Young people are shallow—they go for the wrapping without wondering what's underneath."

"But, Grandfather, I don't care about politics or history. I *am* like those American kids you've complained about. I like electronics, and I love shopping at the mall at Pacific Place, riding the chrome escalators and seeing all four stories of glass shop windows and the new designs on the mannequins. I eat fast food. So maybe I'm a little American, too?"

Jack re-lit his cigar and looked at me smiling. "You also dance like Ana, you know." He laughed. "It's the little Russian in you coming out. Put on the Victrola again."

"But, what about Ana? What she said. Where do Violet, love, and forgiveness fit in? You're always picking sides. I think she was trying to get you past that."

He blew out a smoke cloud, staring me down, "that record there," he commanded.

I got up and read the label by the Ink Spots. "This thing? 'I don't want to set the world on fire?'" He nodded. I wound the crank wondering how someone could be so in love, and so angry all in one.

"The last time I saw my lovely Ana, this song was playing. I can still see her big green eyes looking into mine. She loved me with all my faults. But Jardine, I didn't deserve a love as big as that."

What *did* he deserve? I was quiet, wondering. Here he was, an old man with nothing but time to think over all his spent choices, and reshuffle his wisdom and prejudices into new options and combinations. I started to think what he was saying about Chinese people being stretched—that he was really talking about himself and how he lost my mother. *EXCUSES.*

"Jardine. You see that bent old man in the lobby downstairs?"

I looked up startled. "Huh?"

"That's Mr. Yoshi Sakura. He says you remind him of Bella."

I felt like my insides were tearing. "Why would you say that?"

He shrugged. "We have tea every morning here at this table, he and I. We smoke and listen to jazz records." He laughed when he saw my dismay and suddenly held up his hands and made some intricate gestures.

"What's that?"

"Yoshi taught me a little sign language over the years. I can also cuss rather eloquently," he said, his blue eyes twinkling.

"But—what did you just sign?"

He lifted his cigar to his lips. "To wonder is to begin to understand, my dear. Now, let's have a toast with our tea. There's a bottle hidden in there," he said pointing at a very tall standing vase.

I reached down, fishing it out while checking over my shoulder for Tam. "And what shall we drink to?"

"Oh, pick an assassin. Che Guevara, why not!"

I shrugged, pouring more brandy in his porcelain cup. He was like an ocean, and I just a pebble dropped in ... I couldn't see the shores. I wondered if Ana could see her way around him. How old would she be? Seventy? I didn't dare ask; he was drinking down a lot of sadness with his Darjeeling.

"Well?" He looked over at me suddenly, feigning happiness. "Bottom's up, Toots!"

Book Four

1941

IDEAL HUSBAND

26

Robinson Road *15 March, 1941*

ANA SET DOWN A fresh copy of the *South China Morning Post* and turned the page. Every issue brought more bad news from Europe—*Rommel driving British troops back and taking over Libya—the United States beginning to lend military equipment to England without payment.* This last bit of news, the paper said, was just one step short of war. Ana pushed the paper away and pulled the towel off her head, shaking loose her damp hair. She hadn't seen Jack for over a week.

"Bella, Bella darling?" she called.

Amah came in. "Bella finishee chow-chow, Madame."

"Thank you," Ana said reaching for a comb. "She can stay with me until her poppa comes. They're still doing military maneuvers over on the Gindrinker's line and he can't stop here too long or Violet will complain."

Amah laughed, wagging her finger. "Mass-itah wanchee see Madam! Tiger-dog, no can stop," she said giggling because the astrology signs Ana and Jack had were the best pairing there could be in the Chinese Zodiac. "Long time marry!" she said as Ana combed out Bella's hair. "She got Mass-itah face. Same-same!"

"Where's Poppa? I want Poppa!"

Ana kissed her daughter's plump cheek and carried her out onto the terrace while Bella fingered Ana's tiger charm.

"Mine!" Bella said, trying to pull it off.

"Not yet. One day, when you're a big girl."

Bella began to cry sleepily, and shushing her, Ana rocked her, looking out over the darkening rooftops. Individual outlines became indistinguishable with nightfall. Below on street level she heard the shuffle of footsteps, but soon she couldn't see who or what it was. Things were changing so quickly, yet on the surface they remained the same. A year and a half ago every passport agency had been jammed with people trying to leave Hong Kong. A man on a corner in Central shouted over and over, *War! We are at war with Germany!* His words gave her chills even today. She still had a copy of that issue of the *South China Morning Post. 3 September, 1939.* The world hadn't ended, but in the West the front lines were inching through Poland toward France—while here the front steadily crept downward through China. People had nowhere to run.

Ana pressed her lips on her baby's soft hair, frightened for her, but the sudden ring of the doorbell made Bella squeal, and Ana let her down to go greet her father. He tossed her in the air to much laughter and delight, until Amah took away her charge. Jack then eased himself into the sofa and Ana brought him a whisky and soda, sitting down beside him. He leaned over giving her a lingering kiss.

"I don't like this subterfuge," he said resting a hand on her thigh possessively. "I hate going up to Peak House."

"I was hoping you'd say how much you've missed me."

He gave a wolfish smirk. "I'd think you'd be jealous of her"

"Of Violet? Oh Jack, pity her, poor thing. She's got a profound yearning to be a mother. As far as living with her, you must until we know what we'll do. *Patience.*" He lit up a cigar, looking at her with his icy hot eyes, taking in her silk gown. Ana picked up her needlepoint, pretending she didn't notice. "There is going to be a ship coming to take the wives and children next week, those that have agreed to leave. Do you really think the government can force all of us to evacuate? If our men are staying, why should just European women and children leave?"

Bella came running into their conversation. "Poppa, Poppa, I want a piggy ride!" She stood holding onto his knees, jumping up and down.

"Not now my love," he said stroking her golden curls and giving her a big hug. Satisfied, she went to sit on the floor, playing with a balsa plane, making engine noises. Jack smoked, watching her play, then in a lowered voice said, "It may be a good plan for you both to go. I know men who are marrying their Chinese girlfriends to get them British passports … If they're all leaving, you should too." He put his arm around her, "Well?"

Her needle followed the pattern slowly and carefully. "I won't, Jack." His face was tan from the marches and drills up in the New Territories, and he still had sweat and dust from the road on him. She kissed the corner of his mouth and felt the slow passion that burned in him run through her own body.

"This was so complicated," he said in a husky voice. "Every night in camp I'm thinking of you here over on Hong Kong side, but I'm stuck with a bunch of guys with indigestion out in the Kowloon hills. Hugh brings liquor and does the Highland fling and the other Scotsmen imitate the bagpipes. It's a sad affair." They laughed together, while Amah took Bella for her bath. "I'll be there to kiss you goodnight, Sugar," Jack said as Bella threw kisses all the way out of the room. Then he said to Ana, "Remember that day on the beach?" He stood up and led her to the bedroom and shut the door quietly. "Why don't we go again, the three of us this time?"

In the darkness Ana caressed his neck, tracing the sunburn line, loving the salty tang of his skin, but she felt sadness too. "And if we're seen?" she asked. How strong her man was, and yet in the Northern Territories he was only flesh and blood. Was his body going to stop the Japanese bullets? Jack ripped off his khaki shirt and singlet and she began to explore his chest, nuzzling and kissing while her hands undid his slacks. She could already hear Jack panting and his hands were running over her body. How different this was when there was love ... And yet, with love came the pain and fear of loss.

Afterward they dressed in silence. "Each time I leave you is harder and harder," he said kissing her tears. Ana held him to her tightly, feeling the slow steady beat of his heart. "I really want you to think about leaving Hong Kong with Bella." He put a finger over her lips to silence her. "I opened a firm under her name last month," he said standing back to buckle his belt and straighten his shirt. "It's wise to be prepared."

"But I don't want Violet's money," she whispered following him to Bella's room. She was sleeping, arms wrapped around a stuffed bear. He leaned over and kissed her cheek and forehead, then left the room.

"It's not *her* money," he said as he stepped out of the flat, turning to look at her through the door. "You *know* that. Besides, could you have loved me, poor and uncivilized with nothing?" He raised her chin, looking into her eyes.

"Nothing but your looks?" She tried to shut the door but he put his foot in and, laughing, pried it back open. "Ana, come with me to the beach tomorrow and bring Bella. I'll pick you up, say nine?" He gave her a quick kiss. "You won't regret it. *Trust me.*"

The Helena May *15 March 1941*

ACROSS FROM HER, PIPPA sat bouncing baby Thomas on her lap. Mother and child simply glowed. Yet Pippa was unaware of her beauty, even Violet could see that as Pippa laughed, flushed, chiding the little boy that she'd had in less than a year of marriage. Violet had experienced all of Pippa's stages of pregnancy vicariously—until that hollowness inside had begun its clamoring, like a gong in an empty space. Unbearable! *Unbearable!* Jack hadn't given her a child, and whenever they had sex she hated *it*, hating him, coming to believe he was getting something for nothing.

"Everyone was so jealous when you married Jack," Pippa said interrupting her thoughts. "Just think how beautiful your children will be," she said, obviously trying to be kind.

Everyone pitied her not having a child, and Violet could barely listen from disgust and jealousy. All she could think of was the baby room at home, filled with clothes and furniture—and no child. Pippa was standing up, talking and gesturing toward the loo, her plump face radiant as she awaited some answer.

"Sorry? Oh, right. I'll hold Thomas while you go." Violet held out her arms for the baby in swaddling clothes. "I may as well get into practice," she said looking at Pippa slyly. "I think I'm really pregnant, this time,"

Was that a sneer that flashed over Pippa's face? Pippa excused herself with a superior little flounce and Violet found herself alone with little Thomas in the grand public room of the Helena May. Not pregnant, no hope of it. Above her, the ceiling fans stirred the air, and all the wicker tables and chairs sat vacant.

A range of feelings coursed through her at that moment—strange, uncontrollable feelings. Holding the fat creature in her thin arms, she watched its head wobble. So much bursting roundness under her hard fingertips! A waxy pupae. It was looking into her eyes, evaluating her somehow. *You, Violet, are the barren one*—it seemed to say. She flinched at the unspoken accusation, holding to him tightly, and two hot tears squeezed out from her eyes. "I'm not barren," she heard herself whisper sharply.

The baby squealed from her pincer hold, his face reddening. Violet removed a layer of swaddling and he began to kick and hit her in the chest. Startled, Violet felt the baby slip down her body; she almost dropped him, catching him only by an elbow and knee. She clutched at him, pulling him hard against her. The child began twisting as if fighting the nearness of Violet's body, as if despising her touch. She pulled him to her all the tighter, trying to squash the efforts out of those limbs, but only made it worse. Finding he couldn't move, Thomas burst into loud, hacking sobs, and standing in that empty long room, with only the portrait of the Queen to supervise her, Violet covered his mouth. *Shut up—you!* The gasping, choking under her hand became frenzied and abruptly the kitchen amah stuck her head in saying something.

"You wanchee I help?" she repeated.

Violet shuddered. "Get back in there. I can manage, you fool." The woman vanished through the French doors, then Violet shook him, squeezing the fat upper arms tight, as tight as she could, and he screamed in still higher octaves, his face a violent red blotch with a big black hole in the middle. She felt her fingernails dig into the rich flesh, voluptuously, and somehow the noise jelled in her mind, a satisfying aria—the pinching, the screaming—rising, rising, rising, rising together in pitch until they merged in a single note—yes. And the shrill, tremulous emotion she'd long harbored without release shuddered through her limbs, as Violet closed her eyes.

She couldn't hear anything else and the curtains billowing in off the verandah drew her as if in a dream. She carried the gasping, trembling thing, raising it up in her fatigued arms, until she heard her name from far away. Instantly she lowered the child.

"Violet!" Pippa rushed at her snatching away the baby. "What's happened here? He's naked! Thomas, you poor little thing." She kissed him feverishly and his face mended into harmony like a shattered plate assuming its former perfection.

Hateful disdain wrung her heart. She'd wanted him to like *her*, had wanted him to *prefer* her to its mother. She glared at it. *Horrid, horrid, thing.*

"I must go," Pippa said, frightened.

"But we've only just arrived," Violet protested anxiously. "They'll be bringing out our drinks shortly." It was so like her to blow this out of proportion.

"Never mind," Pippa said over her shoulder gathering her things.

Violet found her head splitting so she could hardly speak. Later, after her solitary lunch, she stepped out into the sunshine on Garden Road, holding to the doorway, bracing herself. Somehow she felt caught, and tried to rework the details. *I was only showing the baby the view of the Peak Tram. The Peak Tram! That was why I was holding it up. On the terrace. That was why, that was why. I wasn't going to throw it over! How ridiculous.*

Violet spent the remainder of the day at her vanity, combing her hair, puzzled that the more she combed the more it seemed to fall out. She went to lie down, and then after some time absently ran her fingers through her hair. Again the thought came to her. Frustrated, she got up and went to the mirror, looked—then sat down to inspect. *It was so troubling.* She peered closer, closer, then began pulling hairs, one by one, to test their durability of course. A few hurt, but some she pulled without effort. This maddened her, seeming to prove she was indeed about to lose her hair. By seven that evening, when Jack appeared home from the office, she had a patch the size of a sovereign plucked bare.

"Violet? Are you not well?"

"Why do say that?"

"It's just … you're wearing your *kimono*." He seemed nervous. "I don't mind … it's pretty. You can wear it to dinner, as long as there is no company. Is there?" He was tanned and healthy as a horse, though of late his hair had grayed. But there was something that offended—a satisfaction, a smooth confidence to his walk.

Auntie Rose came into the dining room followed by cook boy carrying a silver platter. She halted, staring at the kimono, and almost tripped the boy behind her. "Come topside, change clothing. Not plopah."

Violet coolly observed her amah, then Jack. They seemed to be communicating something secretly with their eyes. "Ooo!" she said, shaking her head. "I can't bear this. He is *my* husband, Rose."

Rose backed out of the room blushing, while Jack announced, "Violet is in fancy dress tonight. I forgot to come in costume." He closed the door. "You look lovely, my dear."

She felt ice in her veins as she watched his performance. "You have some nerve. 'I've forgotten to dress,' you say. You've forgotten much, much more. I put myself before you for three years! Nothing! No heir! How do you think that looks?"

Jack stared down at his plate as the boy came back in with another platter. "Just leave it there on the buffet," he said quietly.

Violet stared at her own plate, then knocked it to the floor.

"Violet? What's happened?" He came around the table, but she shrieked when he tried to take her hand.

"No!" Standing up and grasping a fork in her fist, she jabbed at the air between them, "No! I'm the one—it's I who has the bloodline!"

He was crimson and clenching his jaws but sat down and began picking through a stack of mail at the table.

"So, now you *ignore* me?" Violet felt rage bubbling up. "Look at you! A poor boy from what, Kentucky? That I should even *know* of such a place! And yet, you want to take over. You're nothing. You never will be. Yes, you just keep on reading, you fool!"

Jack began cutting his steak methodically and finally he looked up after a few bites. "I've just noticed here," he pointed to the text with his knife, "Douglas MacArthur says the Japanese will never join the Axis. They think that the Hawaiian Islands are overprotected and the Japanese could never threaten US power in the pacific."

He was pointing with his knife! She threw her fork down and stormed out of the room, then abruptly came back in. Pulling her kimono wide and revealing her naked body to him, she said, "What you see here is not for you. I will take it elsewhere. I *will* have children with a *man* who's *not* infertile. You've realized that, haven't you! It's *you*, Jack, *not* me!"

He put down the journal, his expression inscrutable.

She wanted to hurt him, yet was having no effect. "Didn't anyone teach you how to hold your knife?" she snarled. "I may as well have married fa-wong boy from Swatow, for all your knowledge of etiquette."

Jack picked up his drink and finished it, then poured another one in complete silence.

"You bastard!" she hissed. "You don't care about anything!"

There was a dreadful coldness that came over his face that frightened her, and she rushed forward, kimono flapping open. "O *Jaa–aaack.* I didn't *mean* it. You are not angry? You silly boy." She touched him, caressed his face, but he sat stonily, jaws clenched.

"I bet you saw Pippa today, didn't you?" he finally said.

"Pippa?" She was taken aback. "Yes, and what of it?" *Had Pippa called him?*

He put down his glass, "I've noticed this—ever since Pippa became pregnant you—"

There was a violent slap and before she even knew what she had done, Violet was stalking out of the room, her right hand throbbing painfully. *What if she tells the whole town?* Violet ran up the stairs and found by the second floor landing she was feeling her scalp, feeling for the gaps. *Was that a weak root?* She pulled, testing it until it came out. *Why would he say that? I don't care about Pippa's baby. I was showing it the view. That's all. I wasn't going to drop it.* In her bedroom she leaned forward for a closer look in the glass. *What if Pippa told? What if she'd told Jack? What if she tells everyone?* Violet let out a long, thin wail of despair. *Feelings were so troublesome. That they were rats—I would drown them!* She clenched her jawas and clutching at her hair, swallowed her thoughts and cries, but pulled so hard that tears came, silently running down her face.

Rumor

27

Wyndham Street *1 August 1941*

"They are too foolish to know what is coming to them," O-ji san said when Yoshi visited his salon on Des Voeux Road. He said this right out loud in Japanese as English clients were leaning back, lathered up on his barber chairs. The Japanese in Hong Kong all agreed—since the English hadn't kicked them out, the British Empire was now only a paper tiger. Still, the white people here didn't seem to know they were living on borrowed time.

Yesterday, Honorable Uncle announced America had cut off all oil supplies to Japan. Yoshi had remained silent thinking it over. *Only three months' oil left for all Japan.* It was very bad news. *We must now fight to the death. The Americans have forced it upon us.* Visions of battles in China came to him in shades of black and gray, splashed in blood. Japan had no way out but war. *Why did America want war?*

O-ji san's job, information gathering, was simple for a man with a degree in chemistry from Japan's best university. He graduated from Todai with honors, yet the white people often treated him like an ignorant child. He got his revenge, though. The past two governors, military officers, and top brass from the Hong Kong Jockey club, all sat in his salon chairs with hot towels on their faces and talked without discretion, believing they were in the company of an ignorant yellow dog. O-ji san spoke German, Cantonese, and English; had an excellent memory; and kept detailed accounts of relevant conversations. These, he sent to Tokyo, while duplicates went to Lieutenant-General Sakai, who was strategizing the takeover of Hong Kong and was already camped at the border, mapping out final details. Yoshi's job was to take all additional intelligence to General Sakai, but the trip to the northern border was treacherous. Disguised as a Chinese peasant, Yoshi knew his own troops might shoot him by mistake. Rolling up his futon, he sighed, then took out the peasant clothing. *It would be a long hike to Sha Tau Kok—just into China.*

As he walked toward Central, he went over the list of Japanese spies he'd memorized. Several worked as dockhands at godowns run by the main British firms. He also had waiters at all the best hotels to visit, and then finally the massage parlors; Miss Takamura's he'd save for last. She would hand over her paperwork, then allow him to peer through a wall at bed exercise going on in another room. Today she greeted him cheerfully when he arrived, gave him a rice ball and sent him to the back. Leaning against the peeling wallpaper, and eating his umeboshi o-nigri slowly, he watched a customer stretched out on a cot, his hands on a girl's head. He could hear him murmuring in English, all kinds of words Yoshi didn't know. The girl with the long black hair bobbed at his waist for a while, then moved up his body slowly, and then finally sat on him with a squeal. There she began to bounce up and down on the man, punctuating his groans which were coming faster and faster. After several trips to Takamura San's, English to Yoshi had come to mean love in a lateral language. Foreign and exciting—even their *letters* lay down when written! Not like Japanese, stiff and upright, up and down.

Afterward, feeling his heart beating faster, he would head north, hiking through villages, sliding down empty ravines, but his thoughts would be dragging him backward like pulled hair, to the brothel. All that fighting he'd done in China—yet he was still a virgin. O-ji san always told him women were the weaker sex for a reason; God made them rapable. Yoshi flushed at the thought. He'd never raped, but he'd seen it. He'd also seen the faces of Chinese girls being raped. Heard the screams, then after, their dead inert faces. *He wanted nothing to do with it.* Rape was not sex or love in his opinion, not since he'd seen Miss Takamura's girls in action; they were always giggling, or moaning prettily. He trudged over hard ground in his bare feet, hoping this would all be over soon, but somehow he couldn't see an end to it. *He was sick, so sick of death, of violence.* War just kept spilling like black oil, farther and farther in all directions. He sighed, closing his eyes under the intense noonday sun. *You couldn't touch war without blackening the soul.* Sweat trickled down his face as he walked towards China, his bitterness growing.

The Helena May — *1 August, 1941*

NO ONE HAD CALLED on her since her incident with Pippa and her boy Thomas some five months ago. *Did they all know? She was so lonely it hurt.* The formal invitation to lunch though was a life preserver thrown her way—and she *was* slipping. Violet knew she was. Slipping toward a strange, dark maelstrom, feeling it catch at her, spin her. Still, as she held the invitation in her hand, she heard Father's voice in her head—*Don't trust them, don't go.* She ignored it. *They have forgiven me,* she whispered.

Auntie Rose did her hair and helped her dress that morning and it felt like the old days again, when Father was still alive. Her best friends, Claire, Connie, Pippa, and Marjorie, were meeting her at the Helena May.

And suddenly, here she was, among them. Several times during the meal she looked around the bustling room and caught herself smiling. *I'm turning the corner,* she thought gaily. *The dark spell is over. This is just what I need to set me right again. And soon I will have a child too.*

The dining salon was full of expatriate wives fanning themselves, but the heat did little to dampen the lively gossip, and the clatter and ping of teacups and cutlery lent cheery high notes to the murmur of voices.

"Violet? *Violet!*"

She looked at them, startled. Her friends exchanged glances; Pippa looked down in her tea.

Connie set down her cup and tipped her head to the side playfully, "We were saying—have you heard the latest?" Turning to Pippa, Connie smiled, all coy. "Didn't you tell us your cousin Nan has just become engaged?"

Violet looked around curiously. Everyone seemed uncomfortable. "How nice," she said cautiously. "Anyone we know?"

They all looked down, but she noted Connie's sugary voice had an edge to it. "Why—*your friend Peebles*."

"Peebles?" Violet sat back. "But Pippa, surely it can't be true. Did *you* introduce them?"

Connie cleared her throat. "Violet. You're a swell person, but it isn't right to single out *Pippa*."

"But *she introduced* them!" Violet exclaimed. "Didn't you!" She felt her breath quicken and it made her cough painfully. Everyone watched with tight little smiles. Violet picked up her cup, taking a few choking gulps.

"You used to cough like this at school," Connie smirked, daggers in her eyes. "When you didn't want to take your math's exam."

There was laughter at the table, and Marjorie said, "You better now, Violet? That's good."

"I hear the wedding will be as soon as possible," Connie said, then gave a stage whisper, "Nan's got *a LITTLE SURPRISE*."

Violet looked down in despair, her hand going to her throat unconsciously.

"Constance Morant!" Pippa scolded. "Nan will be livid!"

"Oh, bother. We all know about it," Claire said inspecting her nail lacquer. "Is their new home to be Somerset House?"

"Yes, they're going to refurbish it," Marjorie said, "though I wouldn't want to live in the New Territories with a little one on the way."

"Peebles likes to ride," Violet said in a low voice, looking up. "It's a lovely place. The hunt is there too."

"I don't much care," Claire said. "Having children does wonders for a marriage, but I can take or *leave* a *horse*." She shrugged, "Anyhow, we all have our problems, don't we? Personally, I'll have to get another nanny if I get pregnant again this year. Three toddlers are already so trying."

Violet pushed the empty teacup away, wondering if she should leave.

"You're taking this news about Peebles rather oddly," Marjorie noted cautiously. "You're married; he was just your plaything. Why should it matter now?"

Violet picked at her handkerchief, her voice catching. "He proposed to me, Marjorie. *Three times*."

"That may be," Connie cooed, "but he proposed to Nan last!" They all laughed. "Peebles's child is due in six months. But say, I heard you went on a buying spree for baby clothes. Are you expecting *again*, Violet?"

She stared at the faces around the table.

"Leave her alone, Connie. See how bothered she is?"

"Violet dear, why are you fussing with your hair?" Connie asked, amused.

Claire picked up a tea sandwich, and took a sharp little bite. "If this is how you feel, why did you turn Peebles down? We warned you Jack would be hard to hold."

Violet swallowed hard. Pippa wouldn't even look up at her. *This was her doing.*

Marjorie folded her napkin carefully. "You see, we only mention this so it wouldn't surprise you coming from another source. As a favor."

"A favor? Pippa, you haven't called me back once. And you Connie, why are you bringing Jack into this? And you Marjorie? Why?"

Connie leaned across the table. "Violet, there's no need to get so loud about it." Her big patronizing voice carried, and ladies at the surrounding tables began listening with interest. "If we thought things weren't well under *control* we wouldn't have *joked*."

"Joked?" Violet's voice went up an octave.

The others exchanged embarrassed looks, while Connie put on her broad, feel-good smile. "We thought you *knew*, and as *your friends* we *wanted* you to *know* what was being *said*." She shrugged. "If you can't appreciate that—"

"It's all lies! You're all jealous! You, Claire, have had your eyes on Jack from the beginning. And Connie, you've always wanted a house higher up on the Peak—but have I ever said, 'Too bad she lives in the Mid-Levels in a small flat with the Pharisees and the French, because her husband works for a second-rate firm?' No. I've been decent, inviting you to all my parties, yet since Father died you never invite me back and you barely look in my direction when you see me in public. And Pippa," Violet felt her throat tighten. "Why haven't you come to visit? I've left so many messages."

Connie sneered self-righteously. "Pippa'll *never* tell, but I will. You *hurt* little Thomas. When Pippa got home she found marks all over his poor little body. The doctor told her it was no disease, he'd been pinched and squeezed and shaken. You did it, Violet. You're not right in the head."

"Me? That child was sick when she gave it to me. All in a fever! Pippa?" She looked at her friend. "Did you really say this?"

Pippa didn't look up.

"Her doctor did. We're only telling you because you're forever pestering us to get together and we've all decided not to see you any more on account of little Thomas."

"*Thomas?* You're all liars," Violet said pushing the cups aside in a clatter. "You want Jack! And we all know Connie thought she had him that summer, then lost him to me! Now she's out for blood. The rest of you—"

"Violet Summerhays, you're mental, and it's probably why Jack's having an affair. Everyone's talking about it, so I'd shut up if I were you."

Violet stood, her chair falling back in a crash. "Pippa? How dare you! Tell me, why does little Thomas have jet black hair? Didn't you confess Marjorie's husband fancied you? That you met him at Kowloon side in the Nathan Hotel?"

The entire room full of women she had known for the past twenty years had gone so silent she could hear the wuf-wuf-wuf of the overhead fans. Looking left and right at all those eyes she felt they were pelting her with stones. Marjorie burst into tears and someone somewhere began to titter—until they all began to laugh, deafening her. Violet felt her mind going blank as she covered her ears, but suddenly she became aware that a hand was clutching her shoulder. The laughter cut off abruptly as she turned around; the head of the club and a gentleman stood behind her.

"Come now, dear," the man whispered, pulling her toward the door. There was something suspect about his quiet cooing voice and the steely undertone. Wriggling her arm from his grasp, Violet suddenly pulled away, her purse swinging wildly as she ran, striking the registration book and the framed photograph of the Queen from the entrance table to the floor. There was a loud deafening smash and Violet ran out into the harsh sunlight on Garden Road crying, "*Poppa! Poppa!*"

China Coast Navigation & Co. *1 August 1941*

It was an exceedingly hot morning and the clerks were taking their time over tea break. Albert stood outside the staff lounge checking notices on the bulletin board when his ears pricked up.

"And he never has tiffin at the club anymore," a muffled voice said from inside. Albert leaned closer to hear.

"Blimey, don't you know? He's got a corker of a flat for her. She's quite the looker."

"George, mark my words, your bloody big mouth will get you sacked one day."

Albert stepped in, and folding a copy of the racing times chucked it down on the staff room table where the clerks were sprawled and blowing smoke rings. "Up you go now, you achin' bleeders!" he blandished. "You look like a bunch of whores on a picnic. Get back to work!" As they filed out of the room past him, Albert collared George as he passed and asked in a low voice, "Who were you talking about, my friend?"

George looked nervous but finally muttered, "The boss, Sir."

Albert frowned to disguise his smile, then thanked George to mind his business. But as he walked off down the hall, he uttered a Hail Mary.

The next day Albert waited outside at tiffin to see if Jack left the building—and sure enough, that blighter George had been right. Jack took a rickshaw right past the club, and continued up toward Lyndhurst Terrace.

Albert himself had spent countless nights on Lyndhurst Terrace, the local stop for women and song, and thought, *Good for him*, believing Jack would go for a toss and Albert could then order his own rickshaw back to town. *One couldn't blame a man for that!* But when the rickshaw ahead of him turned up Wellington Road instead, Albert's eyes popped. When Jack's coolie stopped by flower stalls for lilies, then continued up onto Glenealy, he knew he was onto something. Passing the Botanical Garden they ended up on Robinson Road. Albert dismissed his own rickshaw a block away and gave a low appreciative whistle. *An expensive area to keep a mistress*—he thought, stepping into the building Jack had entered. He ran his finger down the roster and started when he saw the name, Ana. *Her Again! Well I'll be damned.* He scribbled her full name in his little black book. *V-u-k-o-v-n-a.*

Back at the office he sat down and thought about what he now knew, doodling and studying the name. She wasn't Algy's sister, for certain. No. He got up, shuffling down the hall to the main files, and looked under V. *Nothing.* He tried another set of files on another floor and again came up empty and vexed—but in a good way. He sat down again, chewing his lip for a moment, then sat up. It was crazy, but he ambled downstairs to the shipping department and asked for the telephone list of agents in charge of letting godowns, and started calling. After a half hour his zeal was flagging. "Yes," he repeated, "I'm looking to reach a firm letting space from you, Vukovna. That's right." And then he spelled out the name. It took twelve more tries but on the last, and most improbably distant godown, the clerk seemed familiar with the name. *And yet Hung Hom Bay was not a place China Coast Navigation had any business!*

"Yes," the voice said. "We've let an entire godown to the firm. But you have the name wrong, Sir. Vukovna is the holder, the name of the firm is Bella Pacific."

"And—and can I trouble you for the contact number?"

The man told him to wait a moment and then came back with, "28685."

Albert scrawled the number across the desk top. *Jack's direct office line!*

A half hour later Albert had crossed the harbor and was sailing along Salisbury Road in a taxi, heading for a very, very odd location

Repulse Bay *2 August 1941*

THE WIDE STRETCH OF sand glimmered empty and white like a place in his dreams, filled with his baby's laughter. "Poppa!" Bella shrieked joyfully, running to him from the splash of waves, her body glistening.

"Jack, we've already been here for two hours," Ana intruded, concern in her voice. "Someone might—" her voice trailed off as she saw him kiss Bella tenderly.

"My little sea goddess!" he said, painfully proud of the little girl.

"Amah says I'm tiger, like Poppa!"

"Number One tiger, that's you!" he laughed, tickling her.

Bella squealed, throwing her arms around his neck, and Jack kept tickling her until she burst into mad shrieks of delight.

"Jack," Ana's voice pressured. "It's a very hot day. Anyone might come down from the hotel."

"I want my time with Daddy's girl too, you know," he said jealously, and taking out a sheet of paper squinted, folding it carefully. Bella stood up, her cool hand pressed to his bare shoulder like a small wet leaf as she watched him make an airplane.

Ana's voice came to him like a quiet refrain. "She looks just like you."

"Is that so, Bella?"

She nodded, stoically. "Amah say, same-same."

Jack laughed, ruffling her hair. "Do you know what this is?"

Bella clapped. "Mitsubishi Zero."

"Jack! What're you teaching her?"

He got up and taking Bella to the water's edge said, "Ready?" The plane shot right up and out into the sky and Bella jumped up and down until he lifted her onto his shoulders. The breeze lifted the plane high into the sun where it did a loop and then went swooping down parallel to the water, gliding on air as if nothing could stop it and its paper body would never touch water and dissolve. Jack stood on tiptoes watching as it kept going and going, but the downturn eventually came and the little plane clipped a white cap and vanished.

"I can make another, Bella," he said. But he didn't have any more paper. "When we get home, we can throw airplanes from the terrace! Won't you like that?"

"I want one now!"

Ana pointed toward a line of mat sheds. "Go look there, Bella. There might be paper lying about."

The child ran off to the first mat shed, then paused at the dark entrance turning to look back. Jack waved, and she went in. They waited until Bella showed her face again, shaking her head—*no paper*. Then she dashed off to the next mat shed. Ana started to get up but Jack stopped her. There was a wisp of cloud that hung over the bay, but the rest of the sky was wide open blue, like good luck or happiness.

"Stay," he said taking her hand, squinting in the warm sunlight. "She needs some independence."

"*Jack—*"

He leaned into her, kissing until she laughed. "Are you repelling my advances?"

"Mmmmm, don't know." She rested her face on his chest, her finger tracing the scar over his sternum then turning her head, asked, "Can you see her?"

"There's nothing but mat sheds, and our little girl," he said giving her ear a little kiss. "We're too far down from the hotel."

"What is she doing?" Ana tried to sit up.

"She–she's flapping her arms, running about, like an airplane or bird." He sighed, not letting go, and felt Ana's arms go around his body, felt her cool wet suit against his hot skin. "I'll always love you, you know." He pressed a kiss to her lips and she responded warmly, leaving him breathless.

"Jack," she whispered against his mouth, half mocking, half seductive, "don't say *always*."

He let go and she sat back. Ana baffled him and he wondered how in her eyes he felt at once powerful and a master of all situations and yet on the edge of complete loss. He rolled over and sat up, looking at the waves sweeping up and fizzling over the sand. It was Ana who was the true master of their relationship, for it was from her that all life came, from her the child, from her an incredible sense of wonder at life. He didn't want to reveal his insecurity to her. "You know, I've something special I want to show you both, on the way home today," he said.

"Jack?" He heard the concern in her voice. "Someone's talking to her. Look. By the parking lot."

He turned around immediately. He couldn't identify the brunette in the red bathing costume; she had her back to the sea. Ana pulled her own into place and hurried to her child as Jack stood up, uncertain. He saw the woman reaching for Bella, and felt a stab of panic as the hand touched his daughter. Ana hurried across the sand and finally grabbed Bella, then stood by the woman, talking. Ever so slowly the woman in red turned toward Jack and like a prick of a pin, their eyes met across the sand. *Connie.* Jack began to walk away toward the water, faster and faster until he'd run into the waves and was swimming farther and farther out to sea—trying to forget those accusing eyes.

Mother and daughter were walking along the beach following his path. They were carrying their beach towels and waving at him. Slowly he began his return. The water was cool in the depths, and calmed him, but as he neared the shallows, and stood, wading in to them, he couldn't help but look. *Connie was gone.*

In the car on the way back he didn't speak. *It was his fault, his fault he didn't listen and leave sooner.* "I want to show you something," he said finally, driving back toward town. "In case something should happen to me. I've–I've started to plan for you." Bella was asleep in Ana's arms and Jack looked over at them as he took a bend in the road.

"The woman asked if you were Jack Morgan."

The words chilled him, but he said nothing. Sometime later, Jack turned the car into the parking lot beside the enormous windowless godown. "Leave Bella in the car," he directed. "It'll only be a minute."

The sun was just overhead as they crossed the burning gray concrete. Jack took a key from his pocket and they entered through a side door. It was pitch black, and he switched on a light.

Ana gasped. "Jack! Is this—?"

"Come," he said, pleased, and took her hand in his. At the front of the Douglas DC-3 he pointed up to the name in red script at the nose. *Bella Pacific.*

Ana was speechless.

"There are two more," he announced bursting with pride, "but they're on a mission to Cheng Du. This one's being repaired. I just wanted you to know that my promise to you is good."

"Jack," she demanded looking in his eyes. "Are these Percy's?"

"No," he said forcefully. "They were bought *entirely* from *my profits.* I've paid back every cent I owed. I've started my own firm, in Bella's name." Tears glistened in her eyes and he pulled her close. "I should've done this earlier as it is." He kissed the top of her head, holding her tight in his arms as they stood under an enormous propeller. "If America enters the war—the walls will be falling all around us. I'm hoping we can leave."

"What will happen to us? Jack? I'm afraid."

He was, too, remembering what he'd seen in China, and he shivered in the heat. That interminable train ride with the priest and their late night talk came back as he thought about the coming war. *Evil has descended, here, all around us, taking possession of the land and the people.* Jack closed his eyes a moment. *You don't agree with me, Jack, but to disbelieve in evil is to open the door to it.*

"Jack, darling, what's the matter?"

He looked at her. "Nothing. Let's get Bella." He turned out the lights and locked the hangar, recalling the priest whispering from the darkness of the train car. *Don't you believe in pure evil, Jack? I was there. In Nanking—not so far from your Hong Kong. I was witness when the Japs came marching in—42,000 men, women, and children—the Japanese slaughtered—unmentionable—unmentionable. Even the unborn were cut out and killed—*

"Jack?"

Bella was playing at the wheel of their car, and began to wave in the bright sunlight.

The human soul, it's capable of anything. Great things, and things so terrible you would never imagine. Jack jerked open the car door, angry. *I've seen it with these eyes, ordinary men becoming animals. Evil happens by degrees, subtly, until it's upon you—and like the rain, it touches everyone—*

"Bella! Come sit in Mummy's lap," Ana said getting into the car.

He got in and slammed the door, then glancing back across the empty tarmac toward the sea and then toward China. It was a beautiful day.

Cherry Brandy

28

Peak House *18 October 1941*

The fall evenings brought cooling winds to the border with China, and the sole entry points to Hong Kong—Lo Wu, Man Kam Tau, and Sha Tau Kok—had been captured and blockaded. Refugees, who'd fled the entire length of China, despaired when they discovered these last inroads heavily manned by the enemy. Hungry and waiting, they watched as Japanese soldiers hoisted rifles, positioned machine guns, moved sandbags—hoping for a chance to run for it. Now and then some desperate soul would try, and he'd be gunned down on the road like a dog. The Japanese too, however, were beginning to crack under the pressure and began taking potshots at villagers on the British side just for daring to carry live chickens or ducks in their line of vision. The tension was only increasing.

Jack leafed through the morning paper apprising himself of these recent killings and wondered about retaliation. He scanned the article then halted at the final line; *British reaction nonexistent.*

"*Jack? Ja-aack* I'm *taa-lking* to you. Could you stop by Wiseman's—we need some liquor," Violet said over her toast and soft-boiled egg.

She was wearing a turban of some concoction with a large sapphire brooch pinned on like a third eye—something she must have seen in a Gloria Swanson film. Jack looked down, "Uh, right," he grunted in response, keeping the newspaper as a divider. If she'd been spoiled and self-indulgent with Percy around, she had now taken it to new heights. He'd noticed of late that she seemed to share telepathic communiqués with an imaginary Cecil B. De Mille somewhere out of his field of vision, and didn't know if she did it because she thought it intriguing, or if something had altered in her mind. He consoled himself, had she truly gone off the deep end, she couldn't be so bloody *sane* the rest of the time.

"I *know* it is not *imporrrrtant* to *you*," she frowned, tapping the table, "but I need to keep my *standing* here. We must have all the mixers, Rose's lime juice, and more cherry brandy."

Jack lowered the paper. "How can you be so cavalier? Innocent people are being shot up on the border and the government's doing nothing."

"The *government?* Why should they? The Japanese are *flooded* out on the borders. *Jaaaack,* they have *DISCARDED* their *PANTS!*" She looked to the side, rolling her eyes as if someone were there. "They're in *no* position to attack, they've no access to their own supplies up north." She nervously fingered the turban, pushing in a strand of hair.

"And who tells you this?" he asked, wondering if she'd been drinking.

"Cook boy," she said, dipping a toast soldier into her egg yolk and pursing her lips.

The very action somehow sickened him. "I see," he said carefully, her logic or lack of it intriguing him to question her further, testing her mind. "But if you reason they've no supplies, then don't you suppose the British-held side will appear dearer, thus endanger us further?"

"If things are falling apa—" she began, then paused, toast in midair. "Do you *think* this *SEX-ual?* My *eating* the *yolk?"*

He knew better than to pursue this. "No. You were saying?"

"I was saying, if things are falling apart, how is it I have *no* trouble obtaining champagne, olives, and caviar in town?"

"But, haven't you noticed all the trees have been cut down for firewood along the road into town? People can't afford coal to cook their food."

"It's those refugees. They're lucky we allow them to *stay.* Your problem is that you always think it's time to *thump* the *table.*" She readjusted her turban. "But no one's going to tolerate government meddling, especially after forced evacuations. Most of the club ladies are off to Australia, and it's bloody hard to find partners for tennis and whist. To top it off, husbands who've stayed behind are out *philandering!* I've heard that every Saturday night at Wiseman's there are some thirty men vying for the few ugly women remaining."

"And how does that impact you?" he asked with irritation.

"Me?" she spluttered. "*Some* of the men are *married.*"

"Oh, right," he said scanning the articles, sipping his coffee. He'd heard from Algy that she was often at Wiseman's herself, flirting, those nights when she wasn't throwing a party at home for random strangers—the only ones these days who'd come.

"Did you know," she said licking a drop of yolk from her finger, "they expect volunteers to do *bedpans* for *sooo-ldiers?* I'll not be conscripted. And I'll not leave Peak House."

"No, I expect you wouldn't," he said, raising his copy of the *South China Morning Post*, reading that the government seemed to either ignore Japanese infractions or take grand, ineffectual stances, such as stringing barbed wire along beaches, that were unlikely to stop any invasion. "But you may have to leave." He tapped the article. "It talks here of the evacuation plan. All of Kowloon is to be moved to Hong Kong side, and the people in Central are to shift higher up the Peak."

"And where will the Peakites go? To Aberdeen? Shall we be displaced from our mansions to live in sampans like common fishermen? It's preposterous."

"Indeed."

"I do agree, however, if we *are* besieged, we *could* support ourselves with rooftop gardens. I read that in the paper. Quite a clever thought, that."

Jack imagined the massacres north of the border, the smoking ruins left behind the battle zones. There was no farming; there wasn't a blade of grass. "It says here," he couldn't resist adding, "that they are questioning whether we could subsist on cattle set loose on the hills with a few herdsmen to guard them."

"Oooooo. I don't think cows like hills, Jack," she said in all seriousness.

"Well, they have no problem in Switzerland. Maybe we could manufacture chocolate?" He dabbed his mouth with the napkin. Her madness seemed to come and go like a fever or a headache.

She gave him a withering glance and muttered something to the empty chair beside her about reforming her husband's humor.

"Aren't you worried that they're slaughtering people just north of here?"

Her plummy lips pursed into a frown. "You mean the *Chinese?* Their civil war's hardly our business. But then you are new to the Far East."

"Right then," he said standing up, glad to be escaping. "I'll be home late." Unfortunately, a house boy stopped him.

"Mass-itah! One piecee lobbah man kutim white house ou-sy, fall down! Missie, muchee smellum tlee kutim!"

They followed him outside where the servants had tackled the robber sawing down the gazebo and were perched on him behind a pile of broken lattice and uprooted shrubs.

Violet let out a howl of dismay, and moved about her gardens, bending to mourn her rose bushes. "Kindling? My precious roses!"

"Fetch a constable," Jack said to the boy, then looked at his wife. Her mental state, out there in the open—suddenly filled in the blank for him. Everything was theatrics. True, she was ill, but only because her role as wife, as society matron, as woman, was too small and had pinched and deformed her in all the wrong places—taking a larger-than-life, creative person and making a devious, corrupt, even perverse specimen out of her. Now nothing lovable remained, only a clever self-obsessed mind forced to find its own solitary diversion. He didn't know what to do; there was no pill for megalomania.

Rose stood by quietly taking in the scene beside him, and when Jack turned away she followed.

The voice behind them came meowing from the garden, echoing off the decorative stones. "Don't you CAAAARRE?"

Jack turned, and speaking in a low voice said, "Don't *you* care? How do you expect coolies to boil their rice? They need kindling."

Violet laughed. "Coolies? Is that what you said?"

"You know, Violet, de Mille stopped filming about an hour ago."

"A joke! More *humor!*" She clapped grandly looking about at an imaginary audience. She didn't care if the servants didn't understand her; she was her own audience.

Jack looked at Rose. Her dark eyes glittered, even though her face was impassive. He knew what she was thinking. He turned away, but moments later as he was passing through the house on his way out to the Rolls, she opened the front door for him. "Watch her, Rose."

She bowed her head. "Yes, Mass-itah."

Moments later as his car turned down the driveway, Violet ran out in front of the vehicle. He came to an abrupt halt, dreading what further scene might follow.

"I'm having a party this evening, remember?" she said, coming around and looking in. "Get the cherry brandy at Wiseman's. Dinner is at eight, then dancing afterward. I've invited lots of guests."

"Another ostentatious to-do? And for whom? We don't know these people."

"It's your *job* to be here," she answered with scorn. "You can't produce *children*; the least you can do is *show up!* Pippa has little Thomas, what do I have? *Nothing!*" she growled up close, liquor on her breath.

"That's rather quick off the mark. I was only thinking of our budget."

"Budget? You're driving Father's Rolls!"

"You're lucky I don't trade it for something modest."

"I pity you, Jack Morgan. You're not half the man Father was—*Not half!* And that I should be stuck with you! You're a *FAILURE* of a man! *A failure!* I could have had *any* man in Hong Kong if I so pleased, yet I'm—"

"Be my guest, have them all," he muttered, then putting his foot down on the accelerator, tore off across the gravel, sickened by her narcissism.

At the office, he closed the door behind him and unrolled his maps of China and Southeast Asia, trying to put Violet out of his mind. There were battle lines color coded for the Communist front, the Nationalists, and the Japanese. With the fall of France to Germany, Indochina had become Japanese overnight, bloodlessly. A large safe haven for his planes and lorries was now lost. It had been a profitable exit port for the large quantities of raw antimony and tungsten that he was still able to get out of Yunnan for the steel and armament industry in America. Jack began taking calls from his pilots who'd just landed and took notes on their observations. By tiffin he headed to Ana's flat, picking up a brandy for Violet on the way. It seemed he had less and less time with Ana and Bella, and furthermore, he had compulsory military service the next morning.

Beginning tomorrow he'd be spending a week hacking through the rock and dirt while the Sergeant-Major of the Middlesex Regiment shouted, "No malingering! Dig! Dig, you sons of bitches!" And they would dig in their sweaty khaki drill, and puttees, the cockneys cursing now and then, breaking into their favorite rude songs. The tools were inadequate, the conditions miserable, and the whole experience firmly brought his Kentucky coal mines back full force, leaving him exhausted, and thinking of the strange pointless lives men lead in all corners of the world.

The Pedder Street clock was ringing out the noon hour when he arrived at Ana's flat. Jack was surprised to see Doctor Black just leaving, and discovered Amah bathing Bella with cool wet compresses.

Ana's voice sounded pinched. "Oh Jack. She's got a high fever."

"How is my little girl?" he said with a smile, feeling Bella's hot little head.

"Poppa," she said quietly with big serious eyes, then began to cry.

"Make her drink some of this. She'll do it for you, Jack."

He didn't return to work as planned, but instead sat with Bella, putting fresh ice into her compresses. By evening they'd run out, and Jack sent the boy for more ice. He then went out onto the terrace for a calming smoke.

As his eyes adjusted he noticed moonlight illuminating small, half-naked boys with shaved heads who were in the grass down across the street. Carrying long bobbing bamboo poles with birdlime smeared on the ends, they were catching cicadas. His gaze stopped at a child hiding in the long grass. The other boys who passed under the lamplight below looked hungry, bones etched on their bare backs, but still, they had a sense of wonderment as they put captured insects into tiny cages. Jack looked up at the night sky and blew out a long cloud of smoke. He'd sat on a porch in Kentucky eons ago just like these boys, barefoot and hungry, and had contemplated the same stars, entire winking galaxies set in rich blackness. Nothing else had mattered. Hearing a sound directly below, he looked over the railing and caught the attention of the eldest boy. Digging in his pocket, Jack lowered change to him in a basket.

Back in the flat, Ana was disconsolate. "What if it's influenza?"

"Children get these fevers all the time," he said quietly, but knew the cemetery was filled with dead children. "Look what I got for her," he said holding up the cicada in the tiny cage.

"An insect?" she asked exasperated. "Oh Jack. Put it by her bed, then."

"It'll chirp to her after I've gone tonight."

"You better leave. You're late. Here, take a torch," she said and then handed him Violet's cherry brandy. "Bella's feeling better already." He left, passing cook boy returning with ice.

Down on the street, the children had gone, but one was still hiding in the long grass. Jack waved to him and, when the boy didn't move, Jack went over with the torch. The eyes were rolled up, teeth bared between dry gums, and dead little fingers clutched a small cage.

"Ana," he said, coming back into the flat, "I'm going to stay tonight. I don't care what Violet says." He put down the bottle of brandy, and took off his shirt. Bella was in the bathroom screaming her lungs out as Amah put her down into the tub of cold water. Jack went to Bella's room and flung the cicada cage off the terrace and then came in and took his turn holding and swabbing the red flushed child.

Peak House *18 October 1941*

VIOLET CHECKED THE TIME as she came out of the changing room, wrapped in a towel. "Well? Did he call while I was in the bath?"

Rose was tidying the bedroom and answered in Chinese. "Shouldn't you be getting dressed? Your guests will be arriving at any moment."

"Have them ring the office again." When Amah didn't move, Violet shouted, "Go!"

"We've called three times."

"Then call again!"

Rose didn't move. "I pay the temple great sums of my money to make you well and—"

"Don't you dare say I'm unwell! And I told you speak English."

"Ink-e-li pubric side," Rose said. "This not pubric." Then she continued again, in Cantonese. "I am here at your honorable father's request. Don't think he left this world without giving me instruction. I'm sorry you've gone too long like a wild dog, running this way and that. Your husband is weak, he must strike you like one strikes the young dog, before it becomes wild and runs through the village after chickens and the people take a stick and kill it. You've lost all the small gifts of charm that kept the world at your feet. Now you lose everything, your beauty, your friends. Why, I ask? Why does she run like an unchained dog? Why does she cut at her own flesh, when she has food and shelter?"

Violet sat quietly and didn't flinch when Rose began to brush her hair.

When she emerged some time later, guests had already begun to arrive and the big house was full of music and light. *Jack hadn't returned.* Inside she felt herself shriveling away. *Her womb was dying.* She could feel it. *My bloodline!* Desperate, Violet returned the smile of the young attractive American in military attire whose unabashed lack of finesse made her laugh and agree to dance with him. He stepped on her white shoes three times as he whirled her about. "I don't know these old tunes, honey. The whole darned place is pretty much behind the times."

"There are some jazz recordings there, if you like," she said feeling her pulse quicken at the thought of how angry Jack would be to see her now. They went out on the terrace and danced in the dark, his hands groping her body with an urgency that reminded her of Jack's parting words—*Go ahead.*

The song came to a stop and he released her. "You think they got any cherry brandy here?" He went to search through the bottles, "Gin, whisky, tonic, more whisky. Liqueur, port— Hey, boy," he said to the servant, "You got brandy, but no cherry brandy. Can you dig up one for me?"

The servant's eyes went to his mistress, and then back to the man. Finally he said, "Ma'm, there's no cherry brandy."

Violet stood staring at the serviceman. "We've sent for some. Come, let's dance, Harvey, or Bob, is it?"

"Mike. Who's the owner of this joint anyway?"

"*The Empress Dowager!*" she said, peevish.

He looked at her, uncertain.

What a simpleton. "You may call me Ci-Xi. The Emperor has abdicated!"

"Hey, you're crackers."

"Follow me," she said grandly and swept through the crowd of people. "And take a few bottles," she said pointing to the ice chest.

"Champagne? Baby," he whooped, "you know how to throw a swell party!" He followed her upstairs, past the crowd in the reception room, past the two couples dancing slowly in the foyer, and up the winding stairs, past Percy's father's long case clock.

"You want to have some fun?" Violet asked, smirking. She'd just love to see Jack's face—him catching her in a clinch with a common soldier.

"You betchya; fun is my middle name."

"Mr. Fun, I rather like it—sounds Chinese. I've never taken a Chinese lover, you know."

"You are an odd one, baby! Where we going?"

Violet laughed and paused at her bedroom, when the door at the end of the hall caught her eye; Jack's room. *Better still. "In flagrante delicto!"* she said leading the soldier by the hand.

"Huh?"

"Never mind, Mr. Fun, just pour me a drink. Hurry. I'm ever so *thirsty!*" He removed his tie and loosened the top buttons, then sprawled out on Jack's bed. She felt her heart beating in anticipation as he filled both glasses. They downed these quickly; Violet put her glass out for more and emptied that, the last drops trickling down her throat. "Fun, *darrrrling.* Make yourself comfortable, I'll be *right* back." She felt an incredible sense of freedom—Papa gone, Jack abdicated. *I can be whoever I want! I don't need them at all.*

Hurrying to her bedroom, she stripped off her clothes and put on her kimono and her fanciest high heels. Just as she was going to run back to Jack's bedroom she remembered something. In her closet she rummaged on the floor and slipped the glass walking stick into a hidden pocket.

Mr. Fun was sitting back on the bed, and had already finished most of the first bottle. "Say, that's some outfit! Looks Chinese."

The noise from the party downstairs filled the air between them with merriment, like bubbles that tickled her tongue and blew away the clouds in her head. "You ever do it with a French girl?" she asked, secretly touching the cane as he answered.

"Nope." He filled the glass, his face already red.

"*Ahhhh.* You said the right thing, Mr. Fun." She opened her robe.

"Wow. You move fast." Not taking his eyes off her nakedness, he began to unbutton his clothes and kicked off his khaki drill trousers.

He was a fast lover, but Violet didn't care. All the while she held to the piece of glass walking stick for protection, a weapon, or for luck, for charm, or for something she didn't have and wanted—and he thumped her. It was working, she rubbed the silver rabbit on the cane as he was riding her faster and faster to the finish.

"What?" He stopped. "Why are you grinning? You laughing at something?" He stared down at her, annoyed, his brow cocked. Violet looked at the glass walking stick in her hand and his eyes went to it. "What's that? Gimme that—now!"

"*DON'T!*" Violet shrilled, hiding it behind her back. "*Don't touch it!*"

Mr. Fun flipped her around in one easy jerk and clasped both of her hands in one of his at the small of her back. Terrified, Violet tried to writhe away, but her fingers were crushed by his big hand, along with the piece of glass walking stick in them. His free hand jerked her hips up to his, from behind, like a dog, and his thing slipped around missing, ramming painfully—then suddenly was in, pinning her in place so she couldn't move against, nor away, only *his* way. Pushing her face deeper into the pillow by segments, each thrust further and further muffled her wild, excited cries, so at last she couldn't breathe, and Violet thought her spine would snap. Feeling his balance shifting, shifting back, she felt Mr. Fun arching, rolling his back his head—and suddenly she twisted away with force, angry that he'd had his way with her.

As *it* came out, there was a deep groan from him, a kind of dismay, and out over on the bed the white seed drew its jerking arc. One … two … three. There went her baby. She felt suddenly empty, and whimpered. *I shouldn't have done that!* Yet some catlike instinct had compelled her, some catlike hatred of the man's power over her. *Hatred-hatred!*

"Look what you've done!" he scowled. Then he opened his hand to see what she had tried so hard to wrest from him. "A piece of colored glass? Jesus, you're an odd one." He tossed it behind him and it shattered on the marble floor.

Pieces of colored glass. A stain on the bed. He was pulling up his trousers. Violet stared.

"No!" she wailed "I want a child."

"Dumb broad—*no one told you to move!* Next time play possum, like you're meant," he said shrugging. He took a final swig of the second bottle and put it noisily down on the table where it wobbled and fell with a crash. Already his steps were uneven and he seemed to sway as he walked.

"I want you to give me a child." It seemed the words hung in the air like a lonely fly. Buzzzz—her empty womb was calling. The big house was silent. "Possum?" She frowned. "You mean *Pussum, the endearment ...* "

"Take a rain check, baby!" he laughed. He was standing in the middle of the room, teetering and looking for his tie and heading for the door. Violet got up and rushed at him.

"Don't go!" She held to his arms. "Please! Please?" He tried to move away and she slid down his body, clinging to his legs. This Mr. Fun, he was strong from hard physical labor and kicked her off. Violet fell back, then seeing a sparkle, crawled across the floor to find that section of glass. When she stood up, Fun was gone. Violet felt tears running down her face and lay down on the bed.

Sometime later she got up and looked at the time. *Two thirty a.m.? Have I slept?* She got up and walked through the empty halls of Peak House. It was dark. There was a sound behind her and she turned to see Rose holding her kimono up for her to put on.

"Where is everyone?"

"Party finish."

"Where's Jack? He has to bring the cherry brandy." She could feel Rose's hands on her, leading her to her bath, which was already waiting. She stepped into the water and sank into the perfumed depths, when she heard the tread of feet. *Jack!* She leaped from the water and pulling her robe on, hurried down the hall. Throwing open his bedroom door she found all the lights on. Four servants were cleaning the room in a mad panic. *No trace left of her escapade.* She ran to touch the bed cover. *Changed.* Violet screamed and took a shoe from the closet and began to wave it at them. Rose rushed into the room.

"Violet, sit down."

Violet couldn't hear any more. Everything she'd attempted to achieve that evening was gone, erased, just like her attempt at a child. Even her attempt to insult Jack—*gone.*

There was a large mirror in Jack's room and it showed her a woman who stopped her in her tracks. *Me?* She touched the hair, all wild in wisps, makeup running. Little bald patches. She held up the shoe in her hand, and coming close she struck the hateful woman full in the face—again and again, then ran off down the hall before the staff could stop her.

Every large silver pane showed her that strange woman again and again—and each time she hit the face dead center. As she hurried off, hands everywhere tried to restrain her, but she didn't quit until every mirror on the second floor was broken and she lay on the ground with the servants in a ring about her, breathing hard and staring down at the Mistress of Peak House.

"Release me. I am Ci Xi," she said looking up at them quietly. "Last Empress Dowager."

"She long time dead," house boy said with a grin.

Violet scowled, but a tear ran down her face. "You're plotting, plotting against me."

Violet's Lover

29

Lower Albert Road *22 October 1941*

How he had admired her, years ago, when her smooth bobbed hair had glimmered red and gold and she'd talked, all inspired—about eurhythmics, then had danced across the dappled Peak House lawn. Now he looked away, ashamed for her, for she was altered, somehow.

"But what truly galled was that Jack thought he could *deceive* me!" Violet said, staring, her perturbed eyes digging for facts.

"Is that so!" Albert said topping off her drink, trying to be noncommittal while puzzling over why she'd called on him.

She nodded, taking in his humble furnishings and the dirty tea things. "You're doing very well for yourself, I see. But surely, you're not drinking from transfer ware! That's for servants."

"The blue and white?" He touched the offending teacup. "I'm rather fond of the willow pattern." It had been his mother's, and she had been head cook in a large house in Surrey.

Violet scoffed, shrugging her shoulders.

"Anyhow, it's not quite the Peak, this flat, but it's a big step. I'll always revere your dear father for this great opportunity."

"My father?" she asked incredulous. "My *father* would have done much *more* for you. You were circumvented by Worthing! Now you've only *this* to show for yourself because of my conniving *husband and that pederast.*"

Albert cleared his throat. "Let bygones be bygones. He has, after all, kept up his side of the bargain." He threw a quick glance her way. "But, of course, he does have *you.*"

"Why, Albert!" she said, then broke off abruptly—and he turned his head to see what had troubled her. She seemed to be staring at a mirror in the other room. Mystified, he went and shut the door, whereupon she immediately relaxed.

"Right." He rubbed his jaw. *Had she gone off the rail?* "So, ah, what brings you here today?"

She looked at him, biting her lip a moment. "Albert. I have a suspicion Jack is seeing someone."

"You do?" He cleared his throat, startled. "Ah, well. Most men—most have a vice or two, I'd say."

She frowned. "I didn't come for platitudes."

"So." Albert stood up and paced the room. "Then, you've come for advice?" He noted something sharp in her eyes as she nodded. "Well then. If a man has a mistress or two, I wouldn't mind. Idleness and dissipation! Rather commonplace in these hellish regions of the globe. You know," he spoke calmly, attempting to flatten the agitation in her brow and make her sit back and breathe, "I do have a theory about these tropical climes; they have a peculiar chemical effect on the mind. Too much sun aggravates the soul, fires baser urges. Why else do we see respectable Englishmen, who at home are upright and proper, turn native and take up with a 'downhomah' as they say? Why, just consider the French. You see what heat has done to their culture—a touch of the tar brush everywhere. No temperance!" He reached for his glass and found it nearly empty, and hoped she'd leave soon. His own 'downhomah' was coming for a toss.

"I'll be honest, Albert. I want to take a lover."

Albert, who had been downing the remains of his first whisky slug of the day, spluttered, then coughed.

"I know it sounds improper."

"But surely, your position, Madame?"

Her lip curled at that. "I threw a party last week and that devil didn't show up!"

"Jack? Perhaps he was at the office," he suggested, aware it was Jack who signed his pay check, not her.

"No, I called."

"Drinking with clients then?"

"No."

"Violet, a man needs his peg now and then. Reprimands will only push him away."

"He's usurped *your* position, and if it weren't for him, you'd be running that firm. *You'd* be in the corner office and perhaps—"

"I must stop you. Jack *is* my superior." He stood up and went to the window. *By God,* he thought, *how will I be rid of her?* He turned around, and winked. "You want to make your husband jealous? Is that it?"

"More than that," she snapped. "I want a *CHILD.* I've given up trying with *him.*"

Albert thrust his hands into his pockets. "I don't see how I can help."

Violet suddenly leaped across the room ending any illusion that this would be a decent conversation. Her bony hands grasped each of Albert's arms. "You wouldn't be my *first.*"

Albert detached her from his newly ironed suit and loosened his tie. With a quick glance over her petite features and endowments, he said, "If you like, Violet. I will consider your offer."

There was silence in the room. "When?" she demanded.

Albert sat down. He didn't know how to take this, and his mind drifted to the five percent. "Violet, what do you hope to accomplish if—we were to—to form this liaison? For, if Jack were to know, he'd boot me out in a flash."

"O–you! Is *that* your concern!"

"To be honest, Madame, it *is.*"

She pounced on his lap—her hands flung about his neck.

"Violet, I won't give you a child unless—" He could feel his member stirring under the weight of her female bottom that rode higher up his thigh. "Unless, you promise not to tell." He tried to remove her hands.

"Is that all?" she asked, sitting back, eyeing him in a calculating way.

"It is."

"I promise then," she said undoing his buttons.

He was sweating under the effort to retain composure, and he licked his lips nervously, not wanting to lose the opportunity for a free toss, nor his job either. "Violet," he said very carefully, weighing things, as she wriggled, causing him to flush. "I want—*need*—to know a secret. For you see, if we—that is, if *I* do what you are asking, I need, how do you say—?" He fidgeted with the armrests of the chair as her fingers went down to his trousers. "*A guarantee.*" Gasping at the touch of her quick hand, he stood up, pushing her off forcefully. Violet seemed startled, insulted. He feared he'd been too rough, but when his trousers suddenly dropped and he stood exposed, she began to laugh with hilarity, pointing at his raised member. Coloring, he furiously pulled up his pants, "Impossible! *NEVER!* Never, I will *NOT* do it!" He showed her the door. "*OUT!*"

Her laughter stopped. "You're not asking me to *leave*, are you?" When he turned the knob, she said, "I'll scream. My word against yours." He watched as she mussed her hair and pulled the front of her dress open. The sight of buttons popping off and the lacey bustier excited him, as it frightened him with the potential difficulty. She was already out in the hallway. "I'll scream now!"

"Well, go ahead, and I'll not sleep with you," he said.

Looking vexed, she came back in.

Albert closed the door and took a deep breath. "So, you've had lovers before?" She nodded. "That's good. I don't fancy inexperience." He led her back to the armchair, and allowed her to slide up onto his lap. "Now, tell me the secret you've hidden from Jack. Mind, it has to be good. It's the only assurance I've got that you're not toying with me."

"I don't know ..."

"*A secret for a child.* That's what it shall be." She leaned against him, and he stroked her hair as he looked out the window at fluffy clouds passing by, imagining her wet mouth sinking down ... "You must have a secret or two from him. A physical proof, a letter, perhaps, from one of your lovers?"

Violet leaned over, picking up her beaded clutch off the floor, and removed a stick of peppermint candy, which she offered him.

Albert was taken aback. "What?" He pushed it away. "You're wasting my time."

"*Look,*" she said forcefully, pointing it at his face.

"Well?"

"It's a piece of *glass.* A *cane* I took from a girl, a *lover* of Jack's. He gave it to her as a present." Fire blazed in her eyes, "For *fucking* him!"

Albert's eyes widened. "Shocking! But what's that to me?"

"Don't you see? I have it now. Imagine—this was the girl Jack bought my *hats* from, *and I—I innocently WORE* them, while she *gave* herself to him! Oh, it's made me wretched—ate me up, keeping it in. But, you see, I had to know for certain—so I set a trap, writing her—asking her to meet me at Barker Road Station. I signed it *Jack. And what do you think?* That *very* night she was there—in the dark, calling, '*Mr. Mooooorrrr—gan,*" Violet imitated, sneering, her lips curling back.

"No! A nasty piece of work."

"Yes. When *I* came out of the dark she was surprised. 'This is for Mr. Morgan's fiancée,' she said to me. Imagine the gall! Thought she had *me* fooled. Then I saw something in her hand. A beautiful glass walking stick! 'Well,' I said. 'This is too expensive for you, a hat shop clerk. Give it to me!' When she refused I snatched it away, and she said, 'But it was a gift!' I told her, 'You *LAY DOWN* with him for that cane, didn't you? You got it out of him by spreading your *filthy LEGS*!'"

He looked at the piece of cane in his hand. "Just glass. Pretty though."

Violet snatched it back. "She didn't deserve it!"

"And, is this your 'sordid' secret? That he bedded a hat shop girl? Every man has this kind of adventure. You'll need to do much, much better—for a child."

"There is more," she murmured, staring at him a long moment; then she said, "We were standing near the edge of the platform. It was dark and we were alone."

"You, and this girl—?"

Violet was silent, a little afraid.

"Go on, woman. My patience is wearing thin!"

"Well, it seemed she might—might get *past* me, so—so I just moved in and grabbed, grabbed hold of her hair …"

"And?"

"And there she was—balancing on the very edge of the platform—"

He sat amazed. "*The platform.*"

"Yes. And I could see the long gap of the cog rails falling away and away down to Wan-Chai. She—she was calling for *Jack.*" There, her voice broke and she went quiet again.

"Ah-hah!" Albert leered. "And *was* she pretty?" he asked, trying to pry open her anger further. "Ahhh, *must* have been, for him to give her such a lovely gift. Why, he must have bedded her *repeatedly!* Describe her face to me."

"NO! She was hideous! Crippled!" She rapidly twirled the remains of the cane, eyes sharp and wide. "I held—held onto her hair as she wavered." Albert felt her give a tiny push with her fingertip against his chest.

He started, frowning.

"Everyone thought it suicide. *Everyone.*"

"You—you *pushed* her?"

"Pushed."

Albert swallowed. "And Jack? He doesn't know?"

"I want a child."

"Then give me the cane."

"I can't. It's proof he's been untrue! He only wanted Papa's firm. He's lied all this time. I've hated him for it." She began to cry bitterly.

"But you married him!"

"Of course!" she choked. "I got Poppa to step in for me. Otherwise Connie would've *snatched* it all away for herself! She had Jack eating out of her hand one whole dance season—with a steady eye on Peak House all the while."

"Ah."

"Yes." She stood still, then calmly began to undress. "You have the details, Albert. Now. I get what I came for."

He was unable to restrain a twitch of a smile as he greedily took in the meager breasts, the narrow waist, and long legs. He let himself be drawn into the bedroom, watching her bare bum ahead of him waggle, and pinched her. Never in a thousand years had he imagined Violet Summerhays Morgan would deliver herself on a platter without his even trying. And he had Jack to thank for this, he mused, watching her lie down on his unmade bed. Violet, the fool, didn't understand she'd unwittingly given over her share of the vote with her pitiful confession. There would be no taking it back—and no keeping Jack either; she was finished. He pointed to the edge of the bed, gruffly. "There are certain things I like," he said sternly, undoing his trousers.

"That? I won't!"

"Get back here." He grabbed her by the hair and she condescended, murmuring about a child.

China Coast Navigation & Co. *25 October 1941*

"Time for tiffin," Algy said knocking, then entering Jack's office, concealing a beaded handbag behind his back. He slid down into the chair by the electric fan and leaned his face very close to the whirring blades so the fan distorted his words. "I have something to shoooow youuuuu. Someeeethingggg not sooooo pleasssssant."

"Quiet, you fool," Jack said crossly, holding up a finger while he added figures.

Algy snorted indignantly, then stood up and marched in place, singing the cockney song—"*I gave her inches one: George you're sure to come. Put your belly close to mine and waggle your bum. I gave her inches two, she said, George you're nearly through …*"

Jack stopped and pushed away from his desk, lighting a cigar. "You're a bloody nuisance. What is it you want? And keep it short, my head's splitting. I've been in the doghouse with Violet ever since little Bella was sick and …"

"I've been asking you to go out drinking, and you've given me the runaround for weeks and I'll bet that—"

"I like the last line after 'inches ten,'" Jack cut him off. "'*Yes, I gave her inches all, inches all, inches all—and she took my balls and all.*'"

"You're a cad. It's a wonder Ana tolerates you at all."

Jack's mouth turned up at one corner, smugly. "Yeah, but she can't get enough of me."

This rankled, but Algy said nothing and instead took out a cigarette, tamping it. "Violet came to see me yesterday."

Jack went to the big map on the wall and moved a green pin south, tossing a red one into a tray. "Whatever for?"

"She was nervous as a cat," he said. "Asked if I'd have a bite to eat!"

"I think she's got an inkling about Ana, but can't pin me down during office hours."

Algy lit the cigarette. "You watch out."

"I know. Connie saw us at the beach."

Algy shook his head. "You're finished."

"We'll see. Things are already out of control. That night when I came home there wasn't a mirror to be seen. The servants played dumb when I asked, 'Where the hell are the mirrors?' Amah said they were dirty, being cleaned. I looked all over and found them in the crawlspace behind the wine cellar—all broken. When I asked her, 'Is that how you clean mirrors?' she clammed up."

"Tricky business, I'll say."

"Well? What did Violet want with you?"

"I couldn't follow her reasoning exactly. Something about Albert giving her a grouse foot that belonged to her mother and Rose swearing that Albert had never *met* her mother."

Jack stood up irritated. "She's not playing with a full deck."

"No, I imagine not. She also wanted to know if you trusted Albert and if you spent much free time with me."

"She's just fishing about that night I didn't come home—or else trying to figure out the five percent solution."

"She did ask if you were conspiring with Albert against her."

"See? And what did you say?"

"I said Albert was purely window dressing as far as you were concerned."

"Good." Jack picked up his tennis racquet and began practicing his strokes in front of the large window.

"Right, but then she said, 'You know if he kills me, he'll get it all.'"

Jack froze mid stroke. "What???"

"Yes. She also asked if you might be leaving Hong Kong."

Jack sat down rubbing his forehead. "God I hope Connie keeps her mouth shut."

"Ask her."

"I dare not. Besides, I believe she and Violet are not on speaking terms."

Algy shrugged. "I think you should see this," Algy said, and held up the beaded clutch. "She forgot it at my desk."

"That's her purse, one of many."

"Have you looked inside? There's a blasted handgun in here."

Jack took it and removed the weapon. "Hmm. Loaded. But I doubt she knows how to use this."

"Unless she holds it to your head! It's a .45, my man. She needn't be accurate, only close!"

"I know, I know." Jack put the purse and gun into his desk drawer and sat back. "Now, getting to the important issues, what's going on with the new prices?"

Algy languidly pointed over at the map, "The route's been changed."

"Says who?"

"The Shanghai Rice Controller told our pilots the Chinese government is monopolizing rice distribution, and it's being backed by the Hong Kong and Shanghai Bank. You'll have to lower your price."

"Is that a fact? With Indochina and Thailand off limits, where the hell does he imagine he'll get his tonnage from?"

"That's why I told you, stick to arms. The price never fluctuates, the pilots get bigger cuts and they won't complain. A new pilot said he didn't appreciate doing mercy missions for famine relief on the in-flights just because Jack Morgan feels guilty for the food on his plate."

"Is that so? Well, they'll do as I say. That local temple is grateful for whatever I can give them. And why not help if we're making good money on runs out of the country?" He glanced at his watch. "I tell you, I haven't been happier in my life. Everything I've done has been leading me to this moment."

"What do you mean?'

"I mean the balancing act between shipping and war, determining routes—what to ship when and where, and how to get it there. I've got China in the blood. Odd for a boy from Kentucky, don't you think? And what about those planes!"

"Gah!" Algy grimaced. "They'll be your Waterloo!"

"Thank you, Algy. And you know what? I've better things to do than have tiffin today with you." They both got up and headed out of his office. Jack locked the door.

"So, if it isn't tiffin, then it's inches all?" Algy snickered, walking Jack to the lift. Jack stepped in, but gave him a nasty glare as the doors closed.

"You should know better than to agitate him," A voice behind Algy said. "It makes him even more impossible."

Algy turned around to see Summerhays's secretary, Nancy. "So you've gone doolally over him too?"

She shrugged, smiling.

"Don't you think it'll catch up to him one day?"

"A man of his stamp? *Hardly.*"

"And yet?"

"Dear boy. I'm ten years your senior and have worked for old Mr. Summerhays for twenty-odd years. And now Mr. Morgan. Long tiffin's come with the territory and make a man of power all the more attractive, even to his wife, I imagine."

"Is that so?" he said scratching his head.

"You're so—*refreshing*, Mr. Worthing."

He wasn't sure if that was a snub. "Well, must toddle off. Important business, you know."

She half smiled, "Indeed."

Old Peak Road *28 October 1941*

HALFWAY DOWN THE PEAK road that morning, Violet stopped in the shade of a flowering Bauhinia tree outside the Ladies Recreation Club. She didn't enter but could hear the pop of tennis balls, and laughter inside. The lifestyle it represented had once occupied her whole life, but since the debacle at the Helena May she had been forced to seek out her own company. She gazed down at the ground, then picked up a fallen blossom. The botany group had declared the tree a sterile hybrid. "Poor thing," she sniffed, whispering to the stamen, then dropped it. "Jack has that problem, too." Seeing ladies coming her way and fearing another exercise in humiliation, she hurried off. *But, oh, how she longed for the idle chatter—the company of women on these walks!* As she came around a sharp bend, she nearly ran into an old man. He was looking *at* and *behind* her in a most peculiar way.

"What do you want, Sir?" she demanded haughtily.

"Oh!" The gentleman said, raising his bowler. "There is only *one* of you. I–I *heard voices!*"

Violet sneered and continued on her way, but she was so infuriated by the implication that she was talking to herself that she fumed all the way down the mountain. When she looked up again, she realized she had gone too far; she'd passed Government House

Gardens and now stood all the way at the bottom of Ice House Street in Central. Violet looked back up the incline in dismay. The sun was directly above, and the return walk was too daunting with the growing heat. *What to do.* She dallied along Queen's Road, then paused across the street from Poppa's firm. That was when she spotted her husband streaming away from the office in a rickshaw. Violet glanced at her watch—*nearly tiffin. Perhaps off to a restaurant? She would meet him there!*

She immediately hired a rickshaw herself and bid her coolie follow. They were lucky with all the noontime traffic and were able to keep the other rickshaw in sight. After several blocks it turned abruptly onto Robinson Road.

"No restaurants here," Violet said, eyes narrowing with suspicion. When her coolie took the corner, she observed the other rickshaw pull away empty from a new tower of flats. Violet dismounted and wandered up to the building.

The guard, a young man without a shirt, was squatting by the door eating a bowl of rice and dried fish.

"You look-see gweilo?" she asked.

After a brief look at her, the boy continued eating.

Violet gave a coin and he pointed lazily to the roster of tenants. She squinted. "Names, names! I don't know these people! Who are they? Where is my husband?" The boy tipped the bowl up to his mouth sweeping in stray grains of rice with his chopsticks. "Which one, boy?" He didn't respond, and seeing he wasn't inclined to move, she rushed him with her handbag. The boy leaped up, darting away with a big grin on his face and two rice grains sticking to his cheek.

"Chee-sing, gweilo!"

"I'll give you 'chee-sing.' You have cumshaw!" Seeing she was getting nowhere, she added to the bribe.

The boy came over suddenly, and with a long dirty nail pointed to flat number twelve.

"Who live there?" she demanded, almost ready to grab his skinny arm. After he shied away she handed him another coin, and he motioned to her to follow him across the street, where he turned and pointed. Shielding her eyes and looking far up, she saw a flash of color on a terrace. Violet stepped further back. A woman was leaning against a railing five stories up. She suddenly heard Jack laugh, and her stomach turned with revulsion. *Algernon's sister!*

"Every day, tiffin time," the boy said.

"You may leave!" she commanded, pointing.

"Supposey you China fashion numpah one wifu?" Violet gave him a fierce look at that, and he backed off laughing, gesturing upward, adding, "Hab got numbah one girlie, topside. Plenty short time catchee, play-play-fuckee!"

Violet was speechless and, composing herself, stalked across the street to think. Stepping into a curtain of aerial roots of an enormous Banyan tree, she hid. Shadows slipped across the tips of her spectator pumps, insects stung her, and sweat trickled down her body, but she waited. At long last, the man she saw every night, the curt silent husband, came out of the building, radiant, smiling, whistling to himself, with a swagger to his stride.

Violet took a rickshaw back up to Peak House. She couldn't cry. She would have to have had feelings for him to do that, though her *pride* was hurt. Up in her room she spread out on her bed thinking what to do. She thought of Connie and the ladies at the club. *If this became public—how they would lap it up!* Only then did she cry bitter tears. Somehow she'd imagined marriage would settle things between them, proceeding like a game of Honeymoon Bridge, ups and downs, but only two players. Never in a million years had she imagined a third person dictating his moves from the shadows. *I am quite the fool*, she thought aloud. *Father's philandering should have taught me better.* She lay motionless for some time. *It was no fling—no, it wasn't.*

Later, as the sun was setting, Rose came up to dress her for dinner. Violet told her to make her excuses and remained in bed. The next night too. On the second morning, after he'd gone to work, Rose forced her to sit up, get dressed, and go down to the verandah for a bowl of clear dried mushroom soup. Sitting in the wicker chairs, where so often she'd sat with Father, she now looked out over their land.

"Chow-chow!" Rose said, bringing out a tiny bowl with an elegant lid. "Favorite!"

Violet's hands shook as she removed the porcelain cover and raised the bowl to her lips. Hot clear liquid trickled down into her cold stomach. She drank most of it, then abruptly stood and walked out onto wide smooth lawns of Peak House. *Could he take all this from me?* She revolved slowly under the broad spreading trees, stepping over the dark shadows on the green, light shifting above her. The blazing azure harbor caught her eye.

Leaving her soup dish on the lawn, she walked down the long curving driveway, catching sparkles of light from the harbor through the trees. *She'd been a fool.* In all of Hong Kong there couldn't be a single thing, much less a woman, that Jack Morgan could desire more than Peak House and its gardens. *We're bound by this. All of it*—the lush hedges, the pagoda, the fragrant ornamental trees. *Peak House is MY jewel, MY flower! This is who I am.* Violet laughed, and then spun around and around under the big trees with immense relief, feeling her strength return.

A Rash Act

30

Northern Border with China *29 October 1941*

At dusk, Yoshi reached an outcropping where a lone birch grew, looked around, then tied a red cloth to the tree. Scurrying over rocks and boulders he found the small cave, and crept inside to wait. It must have been hours later because he awoke in darkness with a face staring into his. Yoshi blinked, and a rude hand clamped over his mouth.

"Hon' Kon' kara kita?" The gruff voice asked.

Yoshi nodded.

The man continued in Japanese, "Who sends you?"

Yoshi spelled out the kanji character on his palm for the soldier, who grunted, releasing him and motioning him to follow. They inched down a path between boulders and crossed a ravine, and a half hour later they entered camp. Soldiers were joking, sitting around eating a fine dinner. He was handed a bowl of rice with prawns, and he stared, shocked. He and his men had starved in China, but these men were getting fat. A few soldiers asked questions, curious about Hong Kong, and Yoshi finally opened his mouth pointing to his stub. "Ah! The best sort of messenger!" they laughed. Hiding his face, Yoshi bolted his food, and once finished, was led over the soft crunch of pine needles to another part of camp. Passing between tents and tethered horses, he couldn't help but stroke the smooth beasts as he passed. When the man in front of him signaled, Yoshi paused under a long pine bough, listening. From the clearing ahead he could hear a man commanding in rude Japanese. From the grammar alone, Yoshi discerned that no one in the presence of this man was his equal: it must be Lieutenant-General Sakai himself—the General chosen to commandeer Hong Kong's surrender. As he waited, Yoshi watched two men grooming a gelding in the darkness, buffing it till its coat shone copper.

"Let me see it," the voice commanded drunkenly and the horse was led into the firelight. The General took big steps around the animal, medals sparkling, arms clasped behind his arched chest. The blood-bay gelding had quiet black eyes, its mane and tail plaited, its hooves blacked for parade; it was magnificent. The soldier who'd brought Yoshi murmured something to the General, while bowing and apologizing simultaneously, then still bowing and walking backward, peered toward Yoshi, gesturing hurriedly for him to go forward.

The General roared, "Well, bring me the papers already, you fool!"

Yoshi bowed deep several times and Sakai came a little closer and laughed. "He looks like a damned peasant. He even stinks! He's lucky we don't shoot him." All of the soldiers laughed uproariously.

"What are you laughing at?" Sakai whipped out his swagger stick and struck the groom on the back. "I told you, I want a *WHITE* horse when I march into Hong Kong. Not *this!*"

The man cried out a stream of apologies and honorifics, explaining, "We have only one white mare, General. We looked within a five-day march from here and it was all we found, Sir. The Chinese peasants have dyed white horses green Sir."

"Ehhhhhhhh?"

"Camouflage, Sir."

"Bakayarro! Bring it out, fool!"

The grooms came back with a magnificent white mare but the General was hissing through his teeth, walking back and forth. "Bring me the torch," he commanded. A light was brought out and the general took a closer look, then swung around. "A flea-bitten *gray*!" he cried, pointing to a fine freckling in the coat. "I want a *white* horse when I march into Hong Kong! I'm the conquering commander! We've less than a month, assholes!" The men all shrank away bowing, apologizing while Yoshi quavered, hoping he could escape too. He began bowing and walking backward, but the General saw. "You there! Peasant!" he shouted. "Give him this," he growled, handing an envelope to his attendant.

The attendant was a soft-spoken man and whispered to Yoshi in a low educated voice, "This is for the head of the language school in Hong Kong. You know Colonel Suzuki?" Yoshi nodded; he was head of Japanese intelligence in Hong Kong, and Uncle's boss.

"Good luck, young man," the attendant whispered; "things may get very bloody before we reach you. Gambatte!"

A guard met him at the perimeter and walked him out of the camp to safety, leaving him alone in the forest. Yoshi shivered, listening to the retreating crunch of footsteps on leaves. *Hong Kong about to fall in ONE month?* The images of blood and death he'd left behind in China rose up out of the darkness all around him. Faces of villagers he'd killed, faces of dead companions, all wavered in the spaces between trees. Cholera, murder, hunger. *But I don't want more bloodshed.* He looked around quickly. Leaves crackled. Swooping ahead of him were black, flickering shadows. *Yoshi!* He whirled around. Listening hard he heard it again, further off. *Yoshi-chan! Was it O-bachan? She wasn't dead, was she?* It was right behind him! He whirled around. "O-bachan? O-bachan!" Nothing. No answer. *Was it his ghost with a centipede? He didn't want to know.* He continued walking, but faster now, reciting Shokei in a quavering mumble … *Tabi no haji wa kakisute. My shame in this world will soon be forgotten, springtime journey.* He sniffed. *It was a rotten muddy odor.* Then something pulled at his hand. Yoshi shrieked and began running madly for an opening in the trees where he could see moonlight coming in. They were all around, many of them, touching, trying to hold him back—the dead peasants, bemoaning their suffering. *How many had he killed? Obaaaachaaan!* he wailed from his gut and simultaneously broke free of the forest.

Yoshi found himself standing at the head of a long valley of tall waving grasses. A full moon was sailing above and as far as he could see there were fireflies. Their fuzzy lights blurred with his tears of gratitude. Millions pulsed all around, twinkling souls, drifting on dark air. Yoshi climbed the highest slope and then threw himself down, burying his face in the sweet grass, hearing his own loud sobs for the first time since he'd left his village and his beloved O-bachan a lifetime ago.

Peak House *30 October 1941*

A STIFF BREEZE WAS stirring the branches when Jack got out of the automobile and slammed the door. The sound made a hollow boom against the Peak fog that was gathering rapidly with the dusk. He stood out by the end of the drive, taking in the gloomy view of the harbor with all the lights out. A practice blackout was scheduled as part of war preparations, and as he turned to walk up to the big house, he saw all the lights still on. Jack glanced at his watch.

"Boy," he shouted, "boy!" No one was about, and Jack put out the verandah lights himself. In the foyer the great chandelier was on as well, and he clicked it off, going room to room turning the knobs. As he came back he noticed the chandelier on again. "Good Lord! Doesn't anyone here read the papers?" He went into the foyer, and reaching around for the knob again, was startled when he felt a hand. Violet's bony fingers curled around his. When Jack pulled his hand away she switched off the light and the house sank into darkness, then on it came again, then off. The tiger trophy above appeared gruesome in the flashing light. Jack squinted. "There is a blackout in effect."

"As if I care." Again the light went off, then on, off, then on. "Why should *you?* You don't play by the rules."

He turned away, heading toward the stairs.

"You, Jack, you still didn't explain."

He sighed, then turned to face her. "I've spent the entire day questioning how *I'll* pay the *bills*. There's no rice from Indochina, no rice from Thailand. Nazis in the West, Japs in the East. China is in a famine, Europe is on the verge of one. Tell me, what answers can I give you, your highness?"

She half smiled. "I was sitting outside all day—*you* know, outside the flat on Robinson Road. I've seen you there."

Jack turned his back, unable to imagine how it had happened, and rushed up the stairs, removing his shirt and collar, aware Violet was racing up behind him. "What is it?" he spun about to face her. "What do you want?"

"Admit it, you've taken a lover!" She was holding something like a piece of chalk pointing it at him in the dark hallway.

"You're imagining things," he said looking into wide crazy eyes.

"Oh, no, I'm not!" she said thrusting the glittering thing at his face in a staccato of more no's. He stepped back touching his cheek and found he was bleeding.

"I'm sorry," she said. "But I'd do it again if I saw you kiss another woman. I'd do much worse."

Jack went to his bedroom to see the damage to his face but when he got there, he saw the mirror hadn't been replaced. "What have you cut me with?"

"Algernon's sister! Ah? *Ah-hah!* I'm right! I didn't like her when she came and fawned over Father. He had a weakness for bad women—like you, apparently!"

"So, I should confess? Is that what you want?" he asked, feeling tired.

"Who else is there? Pippa, or is it Connie again? They're all following you around like bitches in heat! Tell me! Who is it now?"

Jack wiped his cut with a handkerchief and was startled to see the amount of blood dripping down his face. It was spreading onto his shirt. "Goddamn it, what *is* that?" She darted away, laughing. "This isn't a game Violet. I mean it."

"A game?" she mocked, holding the thing in her fist.

Jack pushed her onto his bed, finally wresting it from her, stunned to see what it was. "What? Where'd you find this?"

"Was she your lover too, that *cripple?*"

"Goddamn it—where'd you get this?" He felt a paroxysm of hate rush through his body and he shook her.

When he stopped, her eyes slid in their sockets to look at him coolly. She suddenly gave a low chuckle, then spread out across his bed cover, with a sensuality that repulsed him. "I had a lover here." She licked her lips. "A Chinese man, Mr. Fun. He spilled babies all over this—" Tears came to her eyes. "I had to find another man. It's so hard, you know," she choked out.

Jack threw the cane fragment to the floor where it shattered.

"What a *MAN!*" she mocked, sitting up and gazing at her nails.

"My whole life here is a lie," he growled, and grabbing a chair in his path smashed it to bits. "This! This! All this is a lie!" He flung the pieces of wood aside, his voice rasping with futility.

"He says it's a lie," she said, looking to the side. "Shall we forgive him? Look. How pitiful he is."

"You're mad—who are you talking to, Violet?" Grabbing a list of bills from his desk he flapped it at her. "*Your* shopping! *I pay it all.* This is reality, Violet, and it's about to come to an end."

She looked back with disgust. "You, you, you. Everything is you. But I don't need you." She lay back on the bed, arms outstretched. "I never did. I didn't love you. I don't even find you attractive." She sat up suddenly. "It's odd. All the girls talked about you, just had to get you. But you see, you're not my type and I've been put in the unenviable position of having to go looking for men since you could produce no child. I've taken on a steady lover and I'll be running CCN from right here," she said pointing to the bed.

Jack pulled fresh clothes from the closet, not turning to look at her. "I don't care if you fuck the whole town."

"Come now, have you no interest who my lover could be?"

He was dressing, pulling on his evening trousers.

"You should be much more interested in what I have to say, Jack darling."

He ignored her.

"Albert and I had a very long and interesting talk today. We decided to sack you."

Jack stopped in his tracks and turned to look at her, incredulous.

"Yes. We said, here's my vote and there's yours, and hurrah! You see, they add up to more than your share. *Too baaaad.* Now you have to come and beg. Come on," she snapped. He stared at her incredulous, but she was radiant. "Without me, you're *NOTHING! You've* known that too. Otherwise, you lose *everything.* And you'll not bring your whores up here! Not while I'm alive!"

"Ah. So that's what's behind all this. *Your* precious Peak House. Poor Percy. It's why you pushed drink on him all those years, isn't it. Afraid he'd have another child. And, how many times did he quit the hard stuff, and you left it out for him! And that ring? The one you buried with Percy. You stole that from his intended, didn't you?" Violet frowned, taken aback. "And where'd you get this?" he asked pointing to the broken glass on the floor. For once she stared at him, speechless. "Not saying? Ah well. Hat's off to you Violet. You're too clever. No, you go ahead and run the firm with Albert. And have him move in here, too. Take it all. It's worthless to me. But you see, he'll want to take it from you too, my dear."

A desperate kind of fury came over her, and she erupted suddenly, face bright red, shaking. "It's my birthright! How dare you! You, you have no notion what it's like being locked up here like chattel! You've gotten all you've wanted! *I?* I've only what Poppa deigned to give! I had to steal with my eyes! Only by noticing the weakness of those around me do I have strength. Strength to keep Peak House as mine! And I've succeeded! I had to curtail Father's love impulse, for his own good. And—and even you tricked him behind his back with your decisions, going against his will. You're no better than I."

Jack turned away, jerking off his tie, fuming at the last comment for it had hit the mark.

She followed him. "You're a *man*. You've got *freedom* to do as you please. Don't look away!" She snatched at his shoulder, scratching though the fabric with her nails in attempt to hold him back. "Look at me, Jack!"

Jaws clenching, he turned to face her not knowing how he would go on living with her now.

"You placed your naked body on that deformed—*DEFORMED shop girl!* How *could* you?"

Should have, he thought. *And married her. She was lovely, so much lovelier than you—for she was kind.* "So, you took her cane—and then? Maybe—*allowed* her to fall?"

"*YOU* gave it to her! A *gift* to a vulgar shop girl!"

"An innocent child!"

"*YOU—you slept with her.* I knew it—all along!"

"You *pushed* her," he said feeling a pain in his heart, hoping she'd deny it.

"Pu–shed?" The accusation seemed to paralyze her between thoughts, her eyebrows crimping.

"Yes ,Violet. You *pushed* her, didn't you."

She suddenly broke her silence. "Oh, so what if I did? You're a *DOG*—creeping, crawling into *BED* with whatever comes your way. Sex for you is like going to the *toilet*."

Jack turned away feeling a strange buzzing in his mind and a trembling in his body. He went to his closet and jerked out his traveling case, threw it onto the bed, and began sweeping all his clothes from the shelves, thrusting them inside. *Now he knew, he could never look at her again.*

"But—what are you doing? You can't *go!* You've no *job* without me. Isn't that what you care about? And what of *Peak House?*" Violet cowed when he swung past her with the suitcase. It was so overfilled it didn't shut and he grabbed it under his arm, scraping his way against the walls as he marched down the stairs, bumping the hall table and sending the enormous Imari vase crashing to the floor. He was unaware of the servants who quavered behind curtains, unaware Violet clung to him and only when his shoes tumbled out tripping him did he realize Violet was still attached.

"Please, please!" She was trying to kiss him. "Stay, Jack. Stay! I will be pregnant soon! We'll have a family here, for *Percy*. Come back, and I'll give you your job! I'm sorry! Really, I am. Remember your promise to Father!"

He pushed her away in a sudden burst of rage, and kicked the teak newel post loose. The servants let out a wail of terror, but Violet didn't hang back. At the door she clung to the suitcase handle so he couldn't get out. They struggled until Jack let go and she fell backward into the foyer with a cry, shirts, trousers, socks, spewing everywhere. He quickly collected the clothing again, and as he tried to gather it all she lashed out with her nails. He felt the sting on his cheek but continued collecting his fallen clothing.

Violet was stunned, and when he swept past her and pushed through the front door, she let out a wounded cry. Only then, when he got out onto the great lawn, did he turn around and throw his set of keys back toward the house. They flew in a high arc landing with a dull tinkle somewhere behind him.

"Jack. Take the keys," she said in low, hoarse voice, standing in the dark like a specter. "Don't go! I can find them, wait! Just wait!" He looked back only to see her crawling, feeling for them in the grass.

Jack strode down the driveway, out the gates, and onto Old Peak Road. He didn't stop until he was all the way down by the Ladies Recreation Club. There, he paused, covered in sweat, unable to see past his emotions. *He felt his throat closing up.* Everything seemed to be caving in, his past and the future, like a house of cards, flattened—yet, *he had done this.* Jack sat down on his suitcase, confused, ashamed, and feeling far less of a man than when he was hauled shipboard all those years ago, scarred and bleeding. *How could it finish like this?*

The end of the blackout alarm sounded over the slopes and valleys of Hong Kong, loud and soft, loud and soft, close and near like the claxon of train approaching and then passing. "Evening, Sir," a soldier greeted him, then passed by in the dark, vanishing into the mist.

China Coast Navigation & Co. *31 October 1941*

ALGY LOOKED AT THE clock for the umpteenth time that morning and couldn't help but think that something was very wrong. When the lift doors made their *ting* he stood, craned his neck to look. He finally got up from his desk and went to see Nancy.

"Are you absolutely certain Jack didn't have a meeting with clients somewhere?"

"You think I'm lying? I've nothing scheduled here."

"Then ring the house."

"And if the Mrs. says he left for the office hours ago?"

The elevator doors dinged and they both looked up as Albert Chiswick stepped off the lift. He was eating a pastry with a particular cocky tilt to his head and came to stand over them, his tongue loosening dough from a molar. "I have a bit of news for you," he said, then finished chewing. "I've just been conferring with the principal stockholders, well the *majority* of them," he sniffed. "We've determined to let Jack Morgan go."

They looked at him in disbelief.

"You heard me. I'm the new chairman!"

When they failed to react, he pointed to the opaque glass door where Jack's name was printed in gold lettering. "*HE IS GONE.*" When they still did nothing he commanded, "*Unlock* that *door*, Nancy."

"Well!" she gasped looking about. "I—*I don't have the keys.*"

Albert also tried the door, rattling it.

"Listen here," Algy said. "You've no right!"

"I'll break it open if need be. Get the guard to pry it open. Now!" Nobody moved. "I see, I must do it myself, but remember this," he said pointing at them. "You have crossed me."

Company officers, hearing a ruckus, popped out of their offices for a look.

Someone announced, "Chiswick says he's bleedin' taipan now."

By the time the news had been repeated a few more times the entire firm had gathered in the lobby, talking at once as if it were a day at Happy Valley racetrack after an especially bad call.

Nancy looked at Algy, whispering, "His files are in there. Do something, quick! I'll keep him at bay as long as I can.

Algy extracted himself and hurried over to Jack's door, unlocking it with his key. No one paid any heed, even when he dragged an oil drum over from the janitors closet, its heavy metal scrape making a low, growing rumble. The clerks just stepped aside and kept arguing. "Does this mean we're all sacked as well?" someone asked.

"I don't know," Algy retorted pulling the drum along into the office.

Working quickly, he emptied the file cabinets into the drum, and then all Jack's desk drawers—until his fingers touched the cold beadwork of Violet's purse, and the elevator rang. Algy looked over the crowd. It was Albert returning with the guard and the skeleton keys. Algy stepped out of Jack's office shutting the door behind him, trembling.

"Step aside," Albert said, "and surrender that key!"

"Th—the things in this office d–don't belong to you."

"Guard! You there. Go out on the street and summon a constable. I want Worthing arrested for invasion of private property. You," he said jabbing Algy in the chest, "are going to see me in court."

Everyone stood watching in shocked disbelief.

Nancy picked up the telephone, dialing, and then announced, "Albert, it's for you. I've the police on line so you can lodge a formal complaint. You see, constables from the street, well—it would look *so bad*," she said, her hand covering the mouthpiece.

"Good thinking," he said going off to take the receiver. "Anyhow, he can't get far with that oil drum." Nancy offered Albert her chair, and when he took out a cigarette, she lighted it with Percy's big silver desk lighter.

"Yes, yes indeed. This is the chairman of China Coast Navigation." He tapped his finger on the desk and took a few puffs, nodding imperiously at her.

As the employees moved closer to overhear the official indictment over the telephone, Nancy motioned for Algy to go back in the room.

"What?" he gestured behind Albert's back.

"*Go—!*" she hissed. "*Dispose of the papers!*" Nancy was pushing something into his hand. He looked down. *The lighter?*

"Don't forget to shut the door," she murmured.

"Oy, Albert, the sod's back in there," a company clerk said. "Shall I drag him out?"

Albert flapped his hand in dismissal, "Yes, an intruder," he was saying to the chief of police.

Algy quietly shut the door, tipped all of the lighter fluid onto the papers, then soaked Jack's map thoroughly. He only had to bring the match close and all of China and Southeast Asia exploded into flame. When he stirred it up with the end of Jack's tennis racquet, the lower papers caught too. Algy stood back proudly watching the blaze growing, fanning it with his jacket to help it along. Very soon it needed no help, but spotting Jack's lighter he emptied that too. Flames shot up to the ceiling in a sudden burst, singing his hair, and he jumped back horrified. They began shouting in the office as thick black smoke suddenly began to rise—the flames evidently visible through the frosted window in Jack's door. Algy, seeing his job was done, pulled the door open—hoping for a clean beeline out of the building. Instead, he found himself facing Albert, who abruptly jerked the door back with a slam, and locked Algy into the burning room.

Algy tugged on the knob. When that didn't work, he tried to slide his key into the lock. *It fell out. The skeleton key on the other side!* The fire grew hotter at his back, and the smoke, thickening precipitously at the ceiling, began inching down, filling the room top to bottom. *"LET ME OUT! CHISWICK!" There was no answer.*

Covering his mouth with his jacket, he hurried to one of the windows, and gave a yank; it popped open. Instantly a terrible draft sucked the flames higher! Algy shut it, despairing. It was becoming more and more difficult to breathe and he staggered to the door crouching under ever-thickening smoke, head dizzy, eyes streaming—when his foot kicked something heavy: *Violet's beaded purse!* His hand plunged inside and grasped cold metal.

Over the sound of the flames and his own coughing he could hear voices imploring Albert to open the door and could now hear a fire engine's thin wail. *He was not about to die here.* Algy raised the gun at the lock—and looking away, squeezed.

The crash nearly burst his eardrums. Shouts went up inside the office as he broke through, stumbling into the lobby, pistol in hand. Albert and the entire staff of China Coast Navigation stood gob smacked like a bunch of trained seals. When Algy moved toward them a collective gasp escaped their lips. Amazed by his new power, he waved the pearl-handled revolver and the clutch purse at their faces with great panache—it worked! They backed off, parting with awe, and a path opened up for him. He moved toward the exit carefully, eyeing them, and made it half way across the lobby when he sensed them moving in.

"Get him, lads!" Albert cried out behind him. Algy began to run.

Incident at Barker Road

31

Chatham Square *30 October 1941*

His knees were pumping like pistons and sheer terror had him crisscrossing Central in a blind sprint. Algy nearly cried with vexation, for short of jumping off Queens pier, there was nowhere for him to hide. There were pedestrians everywhere willing to turn him in for a mere coin. The thought kept him going, and turning into a side street at full tilt, he hit a patch of rotten cabbage leaves and glissaded, rather beautifully he thought, until his heel caught the sidewalk. Algy tumbled, airborne—and squeezed the trigger. The gun went off, a vagrant screamed, the bullet whistled, and Algy landed in a long slide that tore open his slacks. Not being one to give in, he got up and ran again, with bloodied knee and eyes peeled in terror. But by now, he found he had run out of steam and, gasping for air a few minutes later, he collapsed into a doorway on Murray Road, thinking he would vomit.

Chest heaving, hands braced on his knees, he eventually stood up and leaned against the wall. As the noise of his breathing died down, he heard music, and peering round a corner, he noticed a marching band coming down Queen's Road toward Statue Square. Algy tucked the revolver into his handbag and hurried to join a crush of onlookers, walking along with them. Trying to appear jaunty and unconcerned, he asked a stranger, "What's the occasion?"

The man gave him a rather queer once-over, then said, "Sir Mark Young, our new governor. Here via Barbados."

"Barbados? Gosh, a beach and martini life," Algy said looking over the heads of hundreds of natives in bowlers, and conical straw hats. Only a few white topees dotted the crowd—four thousand Europeans had already evacuated. "Is that a *Royal* with him?"

"A maharajah. He's hoping to quell the anti-British sentiment in India, I presume." The man looked him over again and not without distaste. "Are you a performing minstrel?"

Algy looked down and cringed. It was not just the slacks that were torn. His shirt was covered in soot. He wiped his face; soot there too. "Uh, *no*. Not exactly."

"Ah, there he is," the man suddenly pointed toward a P&O steamer draped in flags. The official horse-drawn carriage was approaching from the praya, and the solar topee with the tall red and white egret feathers marked out the governor. They listened to the salute, and as the crowd shouted, "God save the King," a strong breeze from the water came in and lifted the governor's top feathers into a crest. "I lay you a month's wages this chap's not too pleased with his new posting."

"The Caribbean does seem a paradise from this angle," Algy mused wistfully. It was dawning on him that he was not only out of a job but faced certain arrest if he remained. He ducked out of the crowd and began his climb up toward Victoria Peak. A few minutes later he pounded on the servants' entrance to Jack's flat. Ana let him in. "Jack here?"

"He was brought in at one this morning by an Indian constable, but he won't talk. Why is your face black? Your trousers are torn!"

"Can I have a damp towel?"

Jack was leaning over the railing, smoking, when Algy came out, rubbing his face clean and carrying a fresh change of clothing.

"I wondered how long it would take you to get here. What's that? You look like a chimney sweep."

"Never mind that. How the blazes did you get sacked?"

Jack shrugged. "I've got bigger problems now. I've just called the guard at our hangar. It seems a heavyset man was poking around recently."

"Albert?"

He nodded. "I'm having them moved as soon as I can. I want to sell them."

"The planes? But why? What can *he* do?"

"Albert can create false evidence, claim they're company property."

"Correction," Algy cleared his throat. "No paperwork. I set fire to it while he was telephoning the magistrate."

Jack looked incredulous. "A fire? *In the office*?"

"Didn't you hear the siren? I torched everything you left behind."

He was genuinely stunned and after a moment's thought said, "You know, he could still put a court order out on me, and have the planes impounded until further evidence can be found to prove they belong to CCN."

Algy rubbed his ears clean of soot, pensive. "But they *belong* to you."

"It's not important. It's the *delay*, and with that anything could happen—if he sees them slipping away from him, he'll just alert the war commissioner and have the government requisition them."

"You could sell to the Japs."

"Oh, that's rich."

"Well, why not?" He set the towel down. "America's not at war with the Axis."

"Forget it. I already put in a call in to my Shanghai connection last night. He may know where I can turn them over; God knows I've done him some favors."

"Not Tu, I hope?" Algy said, pulling on the clean shirt.

"Algy, there's still plenty of gamblers trucking along on the Burma Road. They need air cover and supplies. Tu could hook me up—bloody hell, is that my shirt she's given you?"

Algy stepped out of his reach. "A lot of thanks that is! None of this trouble would have happened if you'd stuck with trains!"

"Oh for God's sake! The war's coming, you fool! Our pilots tell me the troops over the border are growing every day. Can you fathom it? Our world is about to end."

Algy shrugged. "Ana told me a constable brought you in last night. Were you drunk?"

"You're goddamned right they brought me down. I emptied the bar at the LRC."

"A nasty cut, that," Algy said looking at a scab on his face and nail marks on his neck, and winked. "You get those from the constable too, old boy?"

Jack scowled, and getting up looked over the railing. "I'm cutting my ties to this place. I'll be damned if I have to die here."

Algy leaned on the iron railing beside him, and looked down at the cluster of rooftops stretching to the harbor, then handed Jack Violet's purse.

"What's this for?"

"I can't legally stay in Hong Kong any longer." Algy grimaced. "I had to shoot my way out of the office."

"No," Jack laughed. "Really? Good show," he said thumping him on the back. "It came in handy after all."

"Yes, but I don't think a prison stay would be salubrious."

"No, it wouldn't." Jack took out his wallet, and counting out some bills said, "You'll need to find a place to stay. And don't go to your flat." He gestured to a shipping schedule on the table.

Algy picked up the paper, noting Jack had circled the last P&O vessel departure on December fifth for Australia. He threw it back down with a shrug and a huff. "I'd rather go to Barbados. You know, they have the world's largest population of endangered hawksbill turtles, and the beaches—"

"What?" he snapped, aghast. "Fuck your turtles! We've a month to sell the planes and get out. Our lives are at stake, you bloody fool."

Peak House *5 November 1941*

In the weeks after the Master's departure, the weather changed. First came a heat wave, then brisk cloudless days that blew all the cicadas away along with the last traces of summer. Ginger blossoms appeared on the slopes and even the large festive bouquet in the front hall did little to dispel the sense that something in the household had gone very wrong.

Violet now rarely left her room and never removed her red kimono. Rose too was having difficulty with the staff. A table from the servants' quarters had been carried out onto the front terrace of Peak House and right there in the open they began playing mahjong round the clock, drinking and gambling. Violet had made an appearance one evening in her kimono, startling them with her stealthy calm by standing behind a pillar with a half empty bottle. When they stood up in shock, fearing dismissal, she only smirked and took a swig.

This open sign of weakness was the last straw. After that, Rose couldn't restrain them from taking tins from the larder, stealing wine from the cellar, and dragging out Percy's magnificent Jacobean chairs and placing them under the sprawling tree out front where they feasted like kings. But there was a gloom to their celebratory binging, for unlike the foreign devils, they breathed in that air of death that blew from mother China. They knew firsthand the atrocities that were being committed to the north, and although the cries of the people and the land weren't audible, they felt it in their blood, and the voracious manner in which the servants gorged themselves revealed that the specter of their own demise hovered around them like a noose.

Frightened, Rose attempted to pull her mistress up, secretly boiling Chinese herbs into her tea, but Violet could taste them and refused everything but Old Master's whisky. Early one cold November dawn, Rose found her sitting at the edge of the verandah watching the twinkle of sampan lights on the harbor. Rose sat with her until the pale yellow sunlight began to illuminate the mountains of Kowloon and southern China. "Are you feeling better?" she finally dared ask.

Violet was stone quiet, testing the sharp tines of a pickle fork. Rose got up and hovered nearby, fretting.

At eight o'clock they heard footsteps coming up the driveway. *It was Albert.* "Violet," he commanded, "your maddening calls to the office must stop."

To Rose's surprise, Violet suddenly stood up, all aglow, childlike. "But Albert darling, I call and call and no one's there! How's it possible? Where's Nancy that she doesn't answer?"

He stopped at the verandah steps and looked up at her and Rose, squinting, mopping his brow. "I've let 'em all go. Your worthless husband's absconded with company funds. I've come to tell you. You've no money left."

"That's a lie! Jack would nev—" Violet flung the fork at him, agitated.

"Is that so?" he sneered, dodging the implement. "Then why'd he manipulate profits? Why'd he sell your father's ships and invest in his private venture? To this day, I cannot uncover his records because that louse Worthing burned out his office."

"You told me to sack him, when the last thing I wanted to do was get rid of him! Why?" Violet rushed down at Albert and clung to his lapels but he brushed her off roughly, and she fell onto the gravel.

Rose stood quietly, knowing not to interfere, but watched as her Miss sobbed on all fours.

"You're the one who took the money!"

"Stand up, for God's sake!" He kicked gravel at her. "What's become of you?"

"It's *your fault* I lost him. And you haven't even made me pregnant!" Violet wailed, looking up. "With him I had standing! Invitations!"

"My fault? What about the French girl?" he asked, turning round on the steps as Violet climbed up. "Make me some real tea, woman," he barked at Rose. "And none of that witches' piss you brew."

Rose ignored him and followed them into the library hearing Violet say, "He's forgotten her. He's got new women—women all over town."

"True, but I don't suppose you know," Albert said with a particularly odd smile, "I've heard from a mutual friend—you remember Connie, don't you?"

"*NO!*" Violet's face reddened. "He's not *sleeping* with *HER* again! Is he?"

"No."

Violet visibly relaxed.

"But her husband told me Jack's new woman has borne him *a child*. Connie saw the little girl and Jack at Shek-O beach."

It took all of Rose's strength to pull Violet from the fat man's neck, where she had dug in her nails. Rose screamed for help and the servants came in running, throwing themselves on Violet bodily, so the gweilo could escape out the front door.

When Mistress had calmed down, and cook boys laughed and lifted their legs off her, Rose pleaded in Chinese, "Can you hear me? *Missie?*" Violet lay very still, blue eyes glassy, the only sign of violence being Albert's blood outlining the half-moons of all her nails. Rose gestured for the boys to leave. "What do you want, my dear? Tell Rose."

Violet's eyes suddenly became poisonously bright. "Auntie, I want a very big glass of your wonderful tea."

Rose's face beamed. "And what about some rice? You've not eaten in days."

Violet nodded. "Rice too."

"And what about some vegetables?"

Violet nodded again.

"And soup?"

"Bitter melon, Elder Sister. Bitter melon."

Rose stood up giddily. Violet had not called her that since she'd been a child. She helped her Mistress to Percy's armchair in the library, and seeing she was comfortably settled, opened the large window to let in the daylight. Then she scurried out on her tired feet, shouting with a full heart to the kitchen staff to begin cooking. Thirty minutes later when Rose returned happily laden with a big tray, Mistress was gone.

Old Peak Road *5 November 1941*

COOLIES PASSED A WHITE woman in bare feet walking up the Peak, and who knows what they thought seeing the long red robe. Probably nothing; for the weight of a hundred catties of cabbage on one's back leaves little room for curiosity. Violet watched herself too, from a distance, as indifferent to her own fate as a stranger. *What was she saying?* She could hear the words that sounded like dry leaves whispering over pavement. *A child. A child. Jack has had a child.* The words spoken low, the steps, the rhythm—they were a drumbeat pushing her onward until she stood on the last hairpin bend before Barker Road Station. She knew what she was going to do, and she didn't care one bit.

A flicker of red could be seen moving through the bamboo—the Peak Tram. She stepped closer to the cliff where plants had wedged their roots at the edge of the precipice, and caressed the smooth green bamboo—its tall stems forming a guardrail of sorts. She leaned against them, listening—a whoosh of air was speaking through them. Behind them, there was nothing. *Nothhhhhhing*—Violet repeated the sound—like wind. *Nothhhhhhhhhing.* A sheer cascade of rocks fell far away, and it seemed a mile straight down toward May Road. Her hands parted thick quivering stems, dipping high above like fishing rods indicating a trap has almost sprung, and looked around behind her. *No one had followed …*

And then she entered. Her bare feet could not touch the ground between the stalks, for there was not an inch between the green shafts in the thick cage of bamboo, and pushing her arms and head through a gap ahead of her, she emerged enough to peer out and downward, feeling a dizzying swoon. Clutching at the quivering rods, Violet steadied herself. But far below, the very rocks themselves seemed to call to her, disguising their voices in the wind. *Barren! Barren one. Baaaaarennnn one, cooooome heeeeeeere.* Her hair blew around her face, in her eyes, her mouth, confusing her, and when looked down a neon green snake slithered away underfoot. Above the bamboo was clicking in a strange, rapid percussion, and she shook her head, dizzy, tippy—and the enormous emptiness she'd been trying to outrun with her countless words, thoughts, and parties, *that emptiness rang in her head. The emptiness that wouldn't conceive, that couldn't be filled, it was her, me, I.* The woman in the red kimono plunged ahead to get away, despairing—and suddenly falling outward, Violet shot forward in an arc. *SWOOP*!

Abruptly, she was jerked and *very, very,* hard by one foot—*jammed!* The whole world came to a dipping pause; the bamboo roots strained, small rocks tumbled. Violet was hanging upside down, red silk swirling all round, her two arms and one leg kicking—*but she couldn't free herself.* Like an inverted umbrella, one foot hooked in the bamboo, she hung. Blood rushed. Head throbbed. Face grew hot, hotter. *I want to die, I want to die!* Violet wriggled her pinched foot that held her tight and began to hear her own scream, and she was screaming—shouting for all she was worth, calling on God or the Devil to take her, she didn't care which. Kicking the free leg to loosen herself, she swung, and swung above all of Central District sparkling far below. Her outstretched hands clawed at the empty air, clawed at the buildings far below, clawed at the blue harbor flecked with ships, while her cushion-cut Golconda diamond winked back at her prettily. No one had another like it.

Evidence Comes to Light

32

Old Peak Road *5 November 1941*

Two older amahs with plump rosy cheeks came huffing around the bend, "Jio-san! Jio-san!" they greeted vigorously.

Old Ling-wu ignored them. He climbed Victoria Peak out of stubbornness and the desire to damn his doctor to hell, not to socialize. *Besides, how sick could he be if he climbed to the top every day?* He wiped his brow with the hand towel he carried around his neck, and frowned at every boisterous *Jio-san* that echoed in the forest. He was not one for spotting white-breasted kingfishers or butterflies, either. He was a working man, but having sold his coal shop last week, he'd come to a blank page in his ledger book and found himself facing a future where only death and disease awaited.

Ling-wu was bald, eighty-two, and tanned like a dried squid. Coolie-thin without his singlet on, his collarbone was a clothes hanger suspending sunken ribs and a small round protruding belly.

He cinched his old khaki shorts high and tight, but the leg holes ballooning around his bowed stick legs showed how much he'd shrunk of late. Regardless, he was deceptively strong and until now his nimble mind had been full of plots—*who was trying to trick him, perhaps the wholesale merchant in Sham Shui Po who put stones at the bottom of coal baskets? Or employees who took too many breaks and stole from him?* He had to pay the local triad for protection, provide coal for the bigger bosses; and when he wasn't worried about that, he was losing sleep over the Japanese blockade of the entire China Coast that made his shipments of coal scarce. Worse still, customers unable to pay for coal had begun cutting down trees instead! *Damn the trees!*

He'd set out that morning at half six from Old Victoria Street in Central while it was still dark. He had enough coins for dim sum, and the thought of popping hot, translucent har gau with freshwater shrimp and succulent, soupy pork siu lung bau into his mouth urged him on. By May Road the sun was out and he stopped to remove his shirt, tying it round his waist. A half hour later he stood in the forest at the bubbling spring. Incense smoldered there and little mandarin oranges, gifts to the Gods, dotted the rock face. It was his halfway point. Ling-wu clapped his palms together bowing over the sandalwood smoke, then continued onward. Sometime later he emerged into the sunlight high up on the mountain—but he could hear something echoing. *A monkey?* He peered around a cluster of banana plants, then looked down over Victoria Harbor, blinking in the glare. He hiked up the road further. *It was getting louder. Someone was screaming.* Fully expecting a robbery in progress Ling-wu raised his gnarled staff to strike off any approaching assailant coming around the next bend. He was surprised, however, to find a lone Hakka woman with a child strapped to her back, balancing a basket of stones. She was standing in the path and seeing him, gestured over the edge.

Ling-wu looked, and spied a pink thing the size of a Wan-Chai rat in the bamboo. Coming closer he saw it was wriggling, trapped in the teeth of the dense plant. It had no mouth, but it appeared that from this thing the screams were emanating.

The Hakka woman cried, "Old man, it's a crazy gweilo, save life and you'll earn much money."

Ling-wu stepped ever closer, squinting. *A gweilo foot!* But it seemed the rest of the fat-kwai was in the next world, for the screams were terrible, as if devils were already devouring the flesh. Considering the danger, he turned to the Hakka woman. "Who will pay me?"

"I work for the house there," she said pointing down the road. "She's a very rich neighbor. I would save her worthless life, but I've my grandchild to think of. I'll help if you give me half the reward."

"Yet if I fail, and the devils pull me through, I'll get nothing!" They stood watching the foot wriggle and he could see a flicker of red fabric between the bamboo. Red was an auspicious color—*good fortune.*

"Go down there," the bossy Hakka commanded, "and I'll give you a hand."

Ling-wu entered the bamboo where the roots had entwined in the stone mortar of the road, boldly defying gravity and the precipice. Straddling the jammed pink foot with his own bare feet, he peered down the gweilo's leg to the upside-down voluminous twisting mass of red and gold silk—*Hai-yah! Was that her jade gate?* He'd have laughed had it not been superimposed over the breathtaking drop above Central. Ling-wu stepped back, assessed his position, and wished he'd inspected the Chinese calendar that morning. It was always bad joss to save anyone from death and alter their fate—and the bamboo clump was all a-quiver from his added weight, and the gweilo foot was about to slip through. He waved for the Hakka, but she stood just out of range of his arm, peering over the edge.

"Hurry," she said, "take your neck towel and wrap it round the foot! Make a noose! You will be rich!"

He felt nervous edging out, his legs trembled, and the screaming made thought difficult; but he squatted and leaned ever farther out and tried to lower the towel through the gap in which the foot was lodged. *Impossible!* He saw he must lean still farther out to loop the towel about her ankle, then noose it enough to pull. He thought of the money.

"Hurry! She's slipping!"

Ling-wu cursed the old woman under his breath but edged out and plunged his hand through the gap. Stones dislodged from under the bamboo, hurtling downward. "How rich is she?" he croaked.

"Very rich!" the voice above him said.

He leaned over further. It wasn't easy to noose the ankle when the other leg was kicking wildly. "She is trying to kill herself!" he shouted.

"Pull, old man. *DO NOT YIELD!*"

"Easy for you," he muttered. His arms were kicked twice by the free leg and the pain throbbed in his forearms, but he'd noosed the ankle, then twisted, and finally began to pull on the towel. It was a job like no other. She weighed at least a hundred catties of coal, *but coal didn't fight back!* Ling-wu cursed, and squatting, feet bracing wide on roots, arms pulling hand over hand, he dragged the crazed, thrashing woman back into this world, one leg, then the other, then the two arms popped through the gap. He needed the Hakka woman's help, and turning his head to look behind him for her, he felt a mighty heave on the towel and turning back received a full blow from the butt of the foreign devil's heel to his nose. Up went his hands, down dropped the towel, and Ling-wu, attempting to stand, instead shot forward, flying through the gap from whence the screaming wretch had come.

Robinson Road *5 November 1941*

AFTER A LONG NIGHT at the godowns, Jack made his way to his new home after sunrise and, taking off his jacket, entered the front hall on tiptoe, hoping not to wake Bella. Under the cover of darkness, he'd had the planes moved to another hangar and had spent the night helping pilots sand off *Bella Pacific*. He shut the door behind him gently, but the sound echoed over the crates packed and ready for their departure. He wanted to be ready, and had authorized his pilots to make a few more gun runs into China—something he hadn't done for the past year. The Hong Kong Harbor Police had upped their wartime preparations, nearly shutting off all illegal business; but it was a risk he had to take. Leaving Hong Kong took cash, and if he couldn't find a buyer for the planes, he would be in trouble.

As soon as he entered the dining room Ana greeted him with a kiss, and set a steaming cup of tea down for him. Algy was seated opposite, reading the morning paper over the remains of breakfast.

"How about another spot of tea and a kiss for me too?" Algy pouted.

Ana laughed playfully. "If you can get Jack to let us all leave Hong Kong today and forget the planes, you can have both tea and a kiss."

"That's *my* paper!" Jack said snatching it from Algy. "And, how is it that you've trained my staff to prepare *your* breakfast every day?"

"I put my order in the week before. Let's see, tomorrow's Wednesday, so we should be having kidney with toast and mushrooms."

Ana laughed, ruffling her fingers in Algy's hair and kissing his cheek. "Now, work on Jack, Algy-dear, so we can leave."

"Ana, I sweat my blood for those planes and I'll be damned if I leave them *here* for the Japs. *Or for Violet!* How is it you don't see that? That money's for Bella's future! And I don't see why you're spoiling this lazy bugger. I didn't see him at the hangar last night."

"What good is money if we don't make it out of here alive?" she said firmly.

"And just how do you expect me to start up in Australia with no money? After all I've built up here? Am I to be a dockhand? I've already worked in coal mines and I'll not have more of that. You need to leave the thinking to me."

There was a sharp cry in the other room and Ana looked at him crossly. "Now you've woken Bella," she said and left the room.

Amah came in with his breakfast tray and set it down before him as he scanned the *South China Morning Post* headlines. "Algy, listen to this," he said, surprised. "'Exodus from Batavia. Japanese steamer *Takachiho Maru* arrived here to-day and will proceed to Batavia on November 6 to take on board about 600 Japanese residents from East Java; after that it will stop to …'"

"Jack, wait." Algy was spooning marmalade from a jar into his mouth. "Forget that for a moment."

He looked up irritated.

"I've a spot of bad news, I fear," he said, gesturing with the spoon. "Just met Nancy in town and she said they've frozen your accounts, pending investigation. If they can prove you transferred cash out of the colony you're in a heap of trouble. She also mentioned the Java plantation. People are talking up a storm."

Jack sat back rigidly, "I switched money out when I bought the planes, but I don't know how they could freeze my regular account. And stop eating out of the jar, damnit!"

The doorbell rang and Jack got up to answer before it woke Bella again.

An officer in full uniform stood in the hall, holding an envelope in his hands. "Are you Jack Morgan?"

"What is it?"

The officer didn't say a word, but his face broke into a strange, condescending leer, and he thrust an envelope at Jack so all he could do was take it. Once the paper was in his hand, the officer said, "This is an official summons to appear in court and you've been legally served. That is all." The constable made him sign, then vanished down the stairs.

Jack went back into the flat dismayed and found Algy had disappeared. Sitting down, he tore open the envelope. There were no charges; it was just a summons to appear in court on December 12. He set it down and his eyes went to the newspaper. *What if December 12 never came?* He scanned the newspaper article again and then his mind went over what he already knew: 80,000 Japanese troops were in Indochina, and another 10,000 were moving south from Hanoi where they were establishing tank, artillery, machine gun, and telecommunication units. Another 10,000 were moving south of Hong Kong on the South China Sea island of Hainan. He flipped to the editorial and read that the increasing concentration of troops in Korea, Manchuria, and Indochina was "possibly for purposes of intimidation in the current war of nerves with Russia." Jack laughed, throwing down the paper. *And what about Hainan?* None of this sat well with the facts. With Batavia being evacuated of Japanese civilians, and with the other information, he knew there could be only one reason; they were planning an attack. *What about Hong Kong?* The Japanese were still here—*they'd not been evacuated.* This calmed him, but he sat back to think out the possibilities. When Algy suddenly returned with a new jar of jam, Jack said, "Damn it all! Where've you been? I've just been served a summons." Jack pushed the paper over. "Never mind. Just read this."

"Better you than me," Algy said sitting down, and scanned the paper while buttering toast. "Not a chance. They'd never attack on all fronts. Completely ludicrous."

"How so? England's proven itself unable to stand up to them, hiding behind the term 'neutrality,' and America's not even in the war. Indochina has fallen, and Thailand has caved in bloodlessly. Who's to stop them? Holland's under Nazi rule, so Batavia is taking in its last breath of freedom. Think of it. Hong Kong has no way to fight them off. All our artillery is in Singapore, for God's sake!"

"Yes, but we're a fortress," he said crunching toast confidently. "Cannons cover every inch of our southern coastline and we have trenches in the north."

"Sure, we're covered to the south and that's well and good if they are planning a naval assault. But didn't you see the number of troops in Canton? You think Tokyo doesn't know what we have and what we're capable of? Don't be a fool. Our days are numbered."

Amah came in. "Missie say muchee bubbery here, lik-lik Bella no slip."

Jack threw his napkin down and Algy followed him out onto the terrace. It was a breezy day and they leaned onto the railings looking down. Algy suddenly pulled back.

Jack looked to see what had caught his attention and swiftly did the same. "Who do you think that is?"

Algy moaned. "It's me he's after. I'm sure of it! I'm headed to the clink."

"It's not you," Ana said standing inside the doors, holding Bella. "He's been there for two days watching the place."

Jack and Algy looked at each other. "But, why didn't you say anything?"

"I wasn't sure," she said putting out a hand to restrain him. "No, Jack, going out and thrashing him within an inch of his life won't help."

Jack paced the room, and then peered over the terrace in time to see the man walking off. "Look, Ana, is that him leaving?"

She nodded.

"Then it must be Albert's man. It's the planes, I'll wager. Albert suspects we're going to sell them." After a moment he turned to Ana and said, "You're going to have to stay with Bella here in the flat so they don't suspect anything. I'm thinking Algy and I need to move out. It's the only way to sell them without them supervising our every move."

"Just forget the planes, Jack. Please?"

"And capitulate to Albert? Where's the sense in it?" Jack asked exasperated. "I've left everything with Violet so I could come with *you*. But that's how it is. Do you want me to humiliate myself by begging on the streets in Sydney so you and Bella can eat? I just won't do that."

"Then who paid for the planes?" she said, crossly.

"I've a rat-infested room across from the old Mosque," Algy interrupted, stepping between them, grimacing at Ana to stop. "If you hurry and pack, we can shove off before that man returns."

Jack stepped around Algy to face her, angry now. "Those planes were bought on *interest* on profits I made *years ago. You* of all people should believe in me. I've given everything back to that firm, damn it! My blood and sweat money, that's what it is! That's all I have to give!"

"I don't care about the money. You're gambling with our lives."

Algy glanced out the window uncomfortably, then looked at his watch. "Ah, he might be back any minute now."

"I'm staying with Algy tonight," he said in firm tone. "I'll try my connection at the temple tomorrow. It will be a more secure place. I'll send word."

Ana quietly watched him pack, then held out a paper. "Bella drew this for you yesterday."

Jack took the stick figure drawing of the three of them with Bella's name in block letters. Beside it was an airplane. He couldn't help but think at least his daughter appreciated his planes. "Thank Bella for me and tell her to keep practicing her writing." She nodded. "Just a few more days. We'll be together *always*. Isn't that long enough?" He wished she had faith in him.

Ana was unresponsive when he kissed her.

"Remember, I love you," he whispered quickly as he and Algy slipped out the servant's door. Taking back alleys between dirty old buildings, they ran down the steps on Ladder Street, and disappeared into a crowd setting off fireworks that snapped like machinegun fire.

Peak House *5 November 1941*

Sister Rose knew something bad had happened when the Hakka woman brought Violet up the path. One look at the way her arm tightly clamped to Violet spoke volumes; whatever it was, there would be money involved. Rose ran to meet them taking Violet's other arm in hers, noting the bleary eyes and red swollen face. The Hakka was recounting the oddest and most incomprehensible tale. Violet didn't bat an eye as the woman spoke, but stared ahead in a deadpan expression, broken now and then by a look of indolent condescension.

It took some time for Rose to sort out what had occurred, what had been averted, and what was due in cumshaw. It appeared the Hakka's uncle had died when Violet had thrown herself off the peak near Barker Road. Rose listened to the woman trying to get to the truth behind the exaggeration—and then paid out, coin by coin, several months of wages. Violet coolly watched the entire transaction but then when Rose led her to her cold meal in the library, she only slumped into her previous state of anguish. Rose didn't know what to do and went to stand under Percival's portrait that hung over the fireplace, as if Old Summerhays could advise her.

"Why do you bother, old woman? You're not my mother!" Violet pushed her hair back then began picking at it.

Rose glared. "What foolo pidgin you talkee? By'mby my payee plenty cumshaw! You rong oltaim! For what?" She came over and pried the strands of hair from Violet's fist and put them in her own pocket. "You belongey too muchee bad heart."

"I didn't ask you to pay, Rose! I didn't ask that coolie to drag me back either! I should've been allowed to die!"

"Nogut! You younk, *got* plenty somethin'! Coolie no got moni, cali stone for Missie garden, cali cabis up Peak for chow-chow, cali water for dlinkee, takee night soil so you no gotum stinkum! Chinee no talkee foolo pidgin like Missie! Coolie workum till die, not killum self! You lezibaga gir'!"

"Oh, scold all you want. I don't care. I'm young and rich, so what? It still amounts to nothing. I may as well be carrying cabbages up Old Peak Road for I've no children, no father or mother."

Rose felt a pang of sorrow touch her and switched to Chinese. "I'm lonely, too. I never took a husband because of my duty to you."

Violet got up, and running her hand along the fireplace, stopped at the wedding picture of her and Jack ducking under rice and flapping doves.

Rose came up behind her and took Violet's hand in hers, removing the photograph. "When your mother died you were only five. Every night I stroked your lovely hair as you cried, saying to me, 'Elder sister, you're like a mother now. Please don't you die too.'"

Violet rested her forehead on the mantel under her father's portrait in uncharacteristic weakness.

"What is it, my child?" Rose asked, fearing the girl might try to kill herself again.

Violet slowly turned to look at Rose with hollow eyes, and whispered in Chinese, "I'm barren. Jack has had a *child* with another—*another woman!*"

Rose felt a surge of anger and cried out, *"Then—it's for Jack you kill yourself?* You fool!"

"Fool?" Violet screamed, "Can't you see the disgrace? They all said I couldn't keep him!" She grasped at her hair unconsciously. "Claire, Connie, they're laughing behind my back! But, you see if I kill myself, *no one* can laugh!"

"You *are* the fool! Come, I've a secret." Rose turned the wedding picture face down. "When I tell you, he will be finished, cast out of your thoughts forever!"

"Tell me what?" Violet asked, startled.

"Promise me you'll forget Jack," she warned.

Violet nodded cautiously.

"Good," Rose nodded. "Now I'll tell. Master Jack, he caused your father an early death."

Violet rolled her eyes. "Impossible. He was his bloody nursemaid!"

"No, no. *True!"* Excited, Rose switched to English. "Olo Mass-itah plenty cross, he soim newspapah, he pait! Kolim *liar*." She tapped her ear smugly. "I *hearum!*"

Violet's mouth nearly dropped, but she followed her to the servant's quarters where Rose fished out a newspaper from the rice barrel. Snatching it away, Violet read it in a flash.

"But Violet, where you go?" Rose asked, running downstairs after her. "You plomise—*maski!* Forgetim!"

Violet picked up the telephone in the hall with a glint in her mad eyes.

"You let Mass-itah go. Nogut! Find numbah one ha-sze-man. I helpum," she insisted, trying to cut off the call.

Violet pulled the receiver out of her reach, laughing. "You give me evidence and then tell me to find another husband, as if nothing happened? What a fool you are. You can't stop and start me like a motor car. Once I go—I go to the finish," she said bitterly. "Whatever happens, woman, it's your fault now."

Dim Sum Shop, Stanley Street *18 November 1941*

Albert pushed the remains of lunch away and sat back in his chair taking out a kretek. "What's there to know? Morgan went to the P&O booking office yesterday. But did he or didn't he buy a ticket?"

"I couldn't see. Anyway, how can it matter if he hasn't sold the planes? He can't leave before that."

Albert groaned, blowing out a smoke cloud. "Look, all I know is when the money changes hands, we'll need the police on hand."

The Dutchman shrugged, taking another plate of fried wu gok off a passing trolley. "There'll be no money for us that way. The planes will be impounded for the war effort."

Albert rubbed his chin. "He'd go to jail, though."

Leaning heavily on the restaurant table, chopsticks poised in the air, Van Leiden asked, "How about you and I holding them up? We'd get it *all* that way."

"You fool, first we need to know *where* he is! There'll be nothing without that."

"He's not been to his flat for days," the Dutchman said drizzling chili oil on deep-fried taro puffs. "If only he had another asset that was easier to grab."

"True," Albert said tapping the table as the waitress came by with tea. "Look, his company account's frozen. That alone should smoke him out."

"But why not get rid of him," the Dutchman said, gingerly chewing the hot dim sum. "We can look for the planes at our leisure."

"Because," Albert said exasperated, "he keeps them flying, earning cash, while my ships are idle from the blockades. I don't have time. I need the cash."

"What about the crazy woman? You could move into the house. I'd say it's worth a pretty penny," he said fishing for an evasive dumpling with his chopsticks.

"I've already thought that out. I need to take him to court first. With her as an abandoned wife we stand a better chance of winning. I'll marry her once I push Morgan out of the picture."

"But don't you have enough money as it is?" he asked. "I mean, you just bought a Rolls, didn't you?"

"Percy's. I expropriated it."

Van Leiden laughed. "I just don't see you married to her."

"She *was* pretty once." As an afterthought he added, "She nearly killed me, though, when I told her Jack had a child."

Van Leiden nodded, then after a moment, sat up. Both men stared at each other, dumbstruck. "The child!"

"*Yeessss* ..." Albert smiled. "The other asset!"

They sat forward, thinking in tandem.

"But then—what about the court case? Do you continue with that if we ... ?

"No." Albert called for the tab and downed the cold remainder of his Pu-er tea. "I'm going to call my solicitor right now and drop all charges against Morgan. We need to change our tack *immediately*, bring him out into the open. You go watch the flat for the kid. There isn't time. Come, we'll hammer this out on the way. We're going to need money to arrange all this."

Peak House *27 November 1941*

IT WAS ALREADY TWILIGHT when Violet applied her makeup—rushing, still doing it without a mirror. She felt the liner slip a little under her eye, and swore. She was so excited Albert had finally returned her call and made a date, even though she suspected he might be cheating her out of her money and her firm; it was just so hard being alone. Violet pulled on her nylons, now practically banned with all the war efforts, careful not to ladder them. It was wonderful to go out of the house, to have a mission, a person to meet, a friend. She took her purse and threw in her checkbook as he'd asked.

When she finally arrived in Central and sat down opposite him, he greeted her angrily. "What took so long? Look at you. Your make up's all funny."

Violet blinked, and took a breath to speak, but then said nothing.

"What?"

"Albert, I came as quickly as I could, but you've taken my motor car."

"Enough," he said, ordering drinks. "The firm takes precedence over nonsense." He threw back his head, pouring whisky down his throat like he was filling a sack. "My fourth," he gulped, "that's how long I've waited, damn it. You bring your checkbook?"

Violet twisted her hands in her lap, her eyes downcast. "Rose asks why you don't come to see me anymore."

"See you? A social call?" He was incredulous. "You tried to kill me."

"Hardly."

"No? It was as near as damnit! I still have the marks here to prove it."

Violet looked down. "Are we having dinner?" she asked eagerly.

"No," he cut her off as the waiter filled his glass. "Not in these straitened circumstances. You may thank your husband for that. You bring the check?" he asked again, pulling on his collar.

Violet bit her lip, nodding and Albert visibly relaxed. She wondered what he'd called her for. Around them waiters came and went, passing their table en route from the kitchen, the door flapping. "Albert," she said carefully, "I was hoping our relationship was to make Jack jealous. Why are we seated by the kitchen? No one will notice us together."

Albert leaned forward with a hearty chuckle. "You think having drinks with me will make him jealous? No, no, no. You need me to move in, and take you as my principal lover, but I'm not ready for that yet." He edged in closer to her, lowering his voice. "I've a better plan." He winked. "It'll force him to remain in Hong Kong."

"Good. But how?"

Albert looked smug as he leaned toward her. "*We steal the child*."

"*Steal*—?" There was a lot more clatter and noise coming from the kitchen. "But Albert, what about the *woman?* Take her. Jack and I can *keep* the child."

"You've strange ideas. Better leave planning to me," he said and looked up, scanning every passing plate like he was reading headlines.

She wrung her hands. "Take her, take the woman."

"For God's sake, Violet. This is *so* much easier. We take the kid, then do like the locals—*ransom*."

Violet stared. "Whatever for?"

"The cash—*from the sale of the planes!* He can have the *damned* child back. I'll not keep it. It's the cash we need!"

Violet studied the wineglass, the way light reflected off it, and when she tipped it back to drink she saw a tiny reflection of herself in the circle of burgundy liquid. She placed it back on the table saying in a quavering whisper, "*But then he won't come back to me.*"

"Look, I don't have time for your nonsense. Why do you think he married you? In God we trust, all others cash! There's your answer!"

She stared at him. *Maybe he was right.*

Now, forget about the woman. He won't be interested when the cash is gone. He'll come back to you."

"Why don't you just *kill* it?"

"No!" he said placing his fist down on the table. "You're not thinking straight."

"But, but otherwise he might go *back* to her. The child's the key, the child! *Everyone wants a child!*"

"Keep your voice down, you fool. I want to live here in dignity and decency after all this is done. Understand? Now write that check."

"Decency?" Violet choked, then looked down. "Fine, fine. You're right. It's the cash." Her hands went to her temple, and she took a sip of water, feeling the situation suddenly out of her control. As she'd finished writing the check he snatched it away. Violet blinked, then set her jaw. *So that's how it was to be.* "Albert dear," she said thinking quickly. "Can you tell me, who's doing this? Is it that Dutchman from Macao? Just where is he?"

"Van Leiden? Now, Violet," Albert snarled, pushing his chair back and signaling the waiter he was leaving. "Forget it!" He dropped his voice so it was barely audible. *"If I kill it, Jack won't come back. Not a chance in hell."*

"All right, all right." She wiped tears from her face with her handkerchief, upset at how she was treated. "But tell Van Leiden, I want to *SEE* Jack's child."

He unlatched her hand from his sleeve. "Bloody hell, why?"

"I just do," she said. "I *want* to see it," she begged. "Tell him Albert, will you?" They were standing by the kitchen door, waiters bumping past them. "You can have my money. All of it. I don't care. Take it, just promise I can see it—and I'll go along with anything. I just want to be part of this." She gave a tearful smile.

"Right." Albert was laughing silently as he turned to go, and when she tried to latch on for a good-bye kiss, he pulled away rudely. Even the waiters noticed the shocking rebuff. *No matter, no matter*, she thought flushing and hurried back to Peak House to think things through. *I must be quick, must be quick.* She knew she had to do something that Albert never would expect.

Back in Father's library, Violet lay down to think. For certain, no one paid heed to a woman past her prime alone in the world—no more than one would a carbuncle. But if she got that cheating husband back she'd have social standing, self-respect, parties. As far as Albert went, she couldn't stop him—she must work within his plans to get her way. Just before dawn she got up and removed an envelope full of cash from the safe and tucked it in her purse, then she climbed to the garret. Knocking lightly on the first door, she looked in, "Rose, it's me. Wake up."

"Ai-yah! What you do here?" Rose asked in a low tired voice, startled at seeing Violet in the servant's quarters. She tapped her bed for Violet to come sit beside her and, switching to Chinese, said, "You used to sleep up here with me. Remember? Those nights you were afraid?"

"Yes, Rose, I remember," she said keeping to English. "But I've a question." The two of them sat together on the edge of the bed, Rose still blinking the sleep from her eyes. "Tell me—how much to buy a child? Don't you have a cousin who does that sort of thing?"

"But we already have two mui-tsai," Rose said in Cantonese. "Do we need more?"

"I want a *baby.* A baby that will think of me—like I do you—*like* a mother. Is that so hard to understand?" Violet felt tears coming to her face and a few sobs wrenched out of her, surprising even herself. But it worked on Rose.

"We can take many, many children to live with us!" Rose's eyes suddenly sparkled as she began to cry with her in sympathy. "There *can* be a family without Mass-itah Jack."

Violet stood up, setting her teeth at the mere mention of him. It amazed her what Jack had done just for sex; destroy their perfect life together, just like that! To hell with consequences!

"You make me very happy," Rose said dabbing her tears.

"Good. Now get dressed, I'll be waiting."

She sniffed, her teary eyes going round. "*Now?*"

"Yes, now! Why did I come up here—to chat? We're *both* going. I don't care what it costs. Now, stop idling."

"Nogut, waitum!" Rose blurted out in pidgin. "Missie come, prais up. My wanpela-tasol! *Save moni!*"

"No, you're *not* going *alone*," Violet said out in the hall, tapping her watch. "Eight o'clock, be ready."

Final Days

33

Robinson Road *28 November 1941*

VAN LEIDEN WAITED FOR a sighting of the Morgan child but wasn't rewarded until Sunday, when he thought to check the servants' entrance. Around the back of the building he entered a typical Chinese courtyard with potted bamboo and low chairs. He hid himself there, and after an hour an old amah and the very child he had seen up high on the balcony appeared. The servant was scolding the little girl who was walking very slowly. "Pull hands out of pockets," she said in Cantonese. "Money can't fall out, *but money can't go in!*"

Bamboo fronds obscured his view of them but also provided cover as they turned down a staircase. Van Leiden waited, then got up from the crouched position and followed them out onto Seymour Road. He took extra care not to overtake them, and crossing the street, he walked opposite, eyeing the child as she moved in and out of the shadows cast by vertical signboards with glaring red characters. She'd be easy to hoist, he mused, certainly less than thirty catties, and no doubt the parents would pay up before Albert had to consider removing an ear.

The amah eventually paused at an incense shop and made a purchase; a few minutes later the two were entering a small neighborhood joss house with their offering. Van Leiden lit a kretek and stood on the sunbaked square while they went in. He grew very hot waiting, and spotting a young boy, waved him over. "Hey, I've a job for you." He explained his request in Cantonese, and the boy gave a thumbs up and then scurried into the temple doorway.

Van Leiden leaned against a wall across from the temple, head throbbing from the heat. It was times like this, with dust in his teeth and hot air scorching his lungs, that he longed for the sweeping tulip fields and cold blue skies of home. But Holland was under Nazi occupation. Europe was falling. Before he could dwell on this, the boy ran out of the temple.

"She comes to see her father who lives here," he said breathless. "Every day she brings his noonday meal."

Van Leiden thanked him with a coin, amused that Morgan had sequestered himself here of all places. He flicked away his kretek, and decided to walk the perimeter for a look inside; but he discovered the edifice was walled and backed in the rear by tenements. Spotting a local shopkeeper rolling incense, he asked if there was a way to see into the courtyard from above. The man pointed with stained fingers to a large, dank building.

He strolled over to the building, then ran up a back hall where night soil was left for collection, and came up to a landing where a window just cleared the temple walls. Looking down, he was startled. *They were sitting right below him on a bench in the blazing courtyard; he could even see the wrinkles on the man's face as he smiled, talking in dulcet tones to his little girl.*

A few minutes later he was on the telephone. Albert was ecstatic, but Van Leiden tried to temper him. "First of all, I'm not a child minder. Where do you expect me to keep it? I've just a one-room flat. Have you considered this?"

Albert brushed him off. "We can settle that later."

"What if it ends up with me a week or longer?"

"If you're so worried, Violet can mind her. It's a good way to string her along. She's got control of the house and all the papers are still in her name."

"Yeah, and you've only five bloody percent," Van Leiden sneered as he rang off, then wandered down Hollywood Road in search of a pub.

Wyndham Street *28 November 1941*

YOSHI LAY ON HIS futon, staring at the ceiling, listening to his wristwatch tick. If he stilled his body and mind to the serene flatness of water in a bowl, he could feel each jerk of the second hand traversing the nerves along his skin, and up his arm. *To be dead to the world was to be completely alive to it*—this he'd observed, for when his mind raced, zig-zagged like flies over a carcass, frenzied with desires, he knew he'd lost inner balance. Looking up at the ceiling, he whispered Baisei's haiku, trying to forget everything else. *Island of eternity, A turtle dries its shell out, The first sun rays of the year.* He let it sink in, pictured it, took a deep breath—*No.* It hadn't worked. Outside the tiny flat in the hallway, he heard footsteps and the crying of a child. A door banged. Birds twittered. From the street came the din from a hawker banging a pot, shouting his wares. He heard footsteps again, then a key in the lock. Instantly he rolled over to face the wall.

The door shut with a bang, and although he stilled himself so that not one muscle twitched, his uncle shouted. "Bakayaroo! That would wake the dead, worthless nephew." He heard O-ji san take his shoes off neatly by the door. "You didn't come to the meeting as usual!" He padded in with slippers on. "Eighty thousand troops wait over the border by Canton, and *each* of those men has a role and *knows* it!" He heard Uncle begin preparing lunch. "You'll be expected to walk by my horse when we march through Central. How will you know what to do if you don't attend? Yoshi, *YOSHHH!*" He growled ferociously, Yoshi opened his eyes. "So you're not dead!" O-ji san was bending over him. "Look," he pointed, "there's your new uniform. They've passed them out secretly to all of us."

Seeing he wasn't going to be rid of the old man, he glanced at the lacquer box.

"I've given you months to recover, but you still won't speak or show gratitude. How did you fight the enemy on the field? By lying still as if you are dead? Certainly you can't be depressed this long. I've given you plenty time to recover."

But O-ji san couldn't understand, for he hadn't really fought in this war, nor lost his tongue and become defaced. And the shame of it! *The blood on his hands.* Yoshi had seen the legless Chinese ghosts in the woods, shadows running, touching him, calling his name. Yoshi was terrified of karma; these vengeful spirits would be waiting for him when he died. At the thought of karma, the mantra on personal debt that every Japanese child was taught, "Not even a glass of water!" came to him. It was a reminder he owed Jyaaaku Moganu far more than water—*he owed him his life.* It was a terrible, terrible burden. Even if he could kill himself, he couldn't do so without first settling this enormous debt—*and to a gaijin!*

"Yellow dog, they call me!" O-ji san spouted on, angry. "And sitting like bacon in my chairs! Think of my sacrifice!" He poured himself a cup of cool barley tea. "A gaijin had the nerve to push me off the sidewalk today! This is what it is to allow, as the weak Chinese do, the white man to take over their country! Yellow man has become a slave in all of Asia in his own land! It is up to the Japanese to show these thieves the way out! No more gambatte! Their end is near. Three days, my nephew …"

Yoshi blended O-ji san's words into the tapestry of other noises; the drip of the sink, the caw of a bird. *All this will be gone if the war comes.*

Unfortunately he could still hear him. "Yoshi!"

Yoshi nodded, eyes riveted to the floor

"You don't look sick. You don't talk. I don't see you eat."

Can't chew in public without a tongue, Yoshi thought.

O-ji san finally exhausted himself and lay down on the tatami, lighting a Camel cigarette, puffing at the ceiling. Yoshi took up a piece of paper and began to write.

Hearing the scratch of the pencil Uncle sat up. "Eehhh?"

I have befriended a white man, Yoshi wrote and found the paper ripped out of his hand.

"What is this? Writing more notes?" O-ji san knocked him hard with the pad shouting.

Yoshi fell sideways, but sat up again, reaching for the paper.

"*SPEAK! BAKAYAROO!*" He struck him again in frustration and Yoshi waited for the blows to cease; finally pulling himself up off the floor, lip bleeding, he took up the pad, writing*: I can't speak. Commander cut out tongue, for spite—because of transfer.*

His uncle didn't wait, thinking it another ploy and grabbed Yoshi's head and jaw, prying open his mouth. Yoshi, caught unawares, let out a horrid cry, neither human nor animal, and surprised even himself with the depth of its pain and sadness. Having seen his stub, O-ji san went silent for once, not knowing what to do. Yoshi took the opportunity and wrote, *We can't win. They have industry, machines, Japan is poor. A small country.*

He read, then erupted. "Eeeehh!? We have *fighting SPIRIT! Hong Kong will fall!* You'll *march next to me,* and you'll be *PROUD!*"

But we cannot win. The war is bigger than Hong Kong. What I have seen in China—terrible, Honorable Uncle.

O-ji san threw the paper down, pacing, punctuating with his cigarette. "In Asia. Each country is ruled by the whites. We're encircled by their colonies—surely we're next! Ah? What would these English do if yellow man came and took France, Germany, Canada? Eh? Would they sit idly by if we cut their only oil supply—as the Americans have cut ours? Indochina, Burma, India, China, the Philippines, Malaya! *Our neighbors! All SLAVES!* These devils are rich from their spoils and the sale of drugs. We Japanese, in our poor country, we've only our fighting spirit in our bellies and our duty to our Emperor! We are prisoners of duty! And yet, if we lose, we lose trying! But it will be with *HONOR!*"

His uncle suddenly stopped, realizing he'd spoken the unspeakable; *of losing.* In Japan he'd have been killed for such treachery. Immediately he turned, and putting away his tea things, said to Yoshi, "We'll kill, or be killed, what choice do we have? As painful as it is, we do as we are told. We live for our group because we are Japanese; this is our pride and our great burden." And with this, he slipped on his work shoes and shut the door behind him quietly.

Yoshi sat in the stillness of the flat, the sounds of the world coming back to him. He folded a small crane and admired its perfection on his palm. Then he crushed it just to see if he could. *Death was natural*, he convinced himself, looking at the crumpled form. *Death, life, birth, sickness, what did it matter?* Getting up he removed the Japanese uniform from its rice paper, and placed it before him, feeling its smooth pressed surface. *Every person has his job.* Basho's poem came to mind as he sat up, reciting it with deep relaxing breaths between the breaks. *Loneliness—hanging from a nail, a cricket.* Nothing, the haiku did not transport him as it could before the war. He reached for the radio, clicked it on. Instantly his lips smiled at the song bursting out through the burlap amplifier. "Benny Goodman!" he tried to vocalize the name, but he could only hum it without his tongue. *Oh, but how he loved jazz.* "And the Angels Sing"; it was a good tune. He'd gone to a jazz bar here one night and the memory filled his heart; red walls, crowds of people pressing for a view of the stage, hot trickling piano notes, and a beautiful woman singing. There was a kind of magic in music that poetry couldn't match, the round burbling of the trombone, the farting trumpet, and the passionate scream of the clarinet doing loops like a Mitsubishi Zero. How he admired the independent spirit of the West—*people doing as they pleased! Dreaming! Planning!* This was absolutely incredible to him, and he sighed, amazed at their freedom. And yet it would all be over. *He heard the bombs again—the intense whine. The crump, and shake of the ground.* In China it had been so loud his ears had bled. Yoshi poured himself a glass of water; then as he drank he remembered Jyaaku Moganu. *I owe him everything, even this.*

Hollywood Road *29 November 1941*

Bella's amah came out of the dark temple doorway, a cloud of incense trailing her into the sunlight. Seeing her gesturing it was time to go, Bella cried out and clung on desperately. "No, Poppa! Want to stay!"

It was the worst part about seeing his daughter. "Tell mama I love her, okay?" Bella nodded, whimpering as Amah urged her along in Cantonese with the bribe of an ice cream, and they vanished out the temple doorway.

Algy was sitting on the bench when he returned.

Jack sat down beside him. "I think I have a buyer."

"A *cash* buyer?"

"Looks that way. My rice connection paid off," he said.

"Not Tu?"

"No. The biggest pagoda builder in Southeast Asia. A Chinese Malay. He lives in Burma and Singapore, but grew up here," Jack said pointing up to the tenement behind him. "His mother still lives in that flat. Said she doesn't want anything to do with her son and his bad guanxi. She's a Christian Buddhist, and sitting here with nothing but time on my hands I listened to her. She told me he's poisoned the luck of his family with his gambling, and the murder of his elder brother."

"What's this to do with anything?"

"He's here staying at the Peninsula Hotel, with his concubines and entourage. He's trying to convince his mother to forgive him—to come away from this bastion of British imperialism."

"By jingo, what's Singapore?"

Jack shrugged, "That aside, she told me she'd only consider the offer if her son repented. She's very devout and superstitious. Says the Catholic nuns told her he needs to build more than pagodas to appease the gods. He needs to do something very big with his money in his old age for *living* people. For *China*."

"And?"

"The son agreed to see us tonight. He called me here at the temple yesterday and I convinced him his mother would rally round if he bought three American airplanes that he could use to deliver free rice to his own people—among other more lucrative uses."

"Like weapons?"

"I wouldn't doubt it."

"That's a corker!"

"I've called the solicitor to send me the papers. He's typing in the man's name as we speak."

"But you know he's not going to use those for rice!"

"No one can regulate anything. Not his mother, not me. Frankly, it doesn't matter. We've bigger problems. Remember, Tojo was nominated premier of Japan this October, and hasn't capitulated *one bit.* He's not going to remove his forces from the Dutch East Indies oil reserves, not until the US releases Japan's frozen assets *AND* guarantees all shipments to Japan! Are you following? He says the US *must stop all financial aid to China*—and that China should *surrender!* What the Hades does that tell you?"

Algy threw up his hands despairingly. "They'll attack."

"Yes, and Churchill's got no intention of helping Hong Kong. We're headed for a terrible smash out here."

"We're prepared for a naval assault."

"Here we go again. Forget the naval assault! There's a squadron of Mitsubishi Zeroes doing figures off of Hainan Island!"

"Then, tell the Governor," Algy sighed.

"Why me? Nobody listened to Governor Northcote. He finally quit and went home. I've my two girls to think of now."

"Will you sell the flat?"

"Algy, wake up," Jack said, irate. "We'll be lucky to leave with our *lives.*"

"*Right.*" Algy smoothed his eyebrow. "It is a tad *amusing* that only *you* and *God* are privy to this. But what do *I* know?"

"Ex-*actly!*" Jack snarled, pointing at him.

Peak House *29 November 1941*

Violet left Rose to dress in her garret room and came down the stairs quickly when the telephone rang. Picking up, she was surprised to hear Albert on the line, and so early.

"It's done!" his voice bellowed. "Yes, yes. Plan's set. We'll have the child next month on the second!"

Violet looked at her wristwatch, startled. "But, that's only in three days! You said *I'd* be involved." She opened her purse; the money was still there.

"No worry. Van Leiden's expecting you. You *can* handle a child? Right then, I'll ring later today," he said, not giving her a chance to respond.

Rose was coming down the stairs as Violet set down the receiver. "Rose, he's here," she said gesturing outside. The hunter green Rolls Violet had hired had just arrived from the Peninsula Hotel and was visible through the fog. The two women hurried down the verandah and the chauffeur stepped out to let them in. It was humiliating enough to no longer have a car, much less a husband, and she frowned bitterly, feeling like a forgotten spinster. She slid in across the seat, holding her purse tightly. When she looked up again, she was taken aback. The driver was studying her in the rearview.

"Miss. I want to say, I'm very sorry to hear about your father, Mr. Summerhays. We all knew him so well. He tried out our Rolls Royces several times before he bought one himself. Which color did he buy?"

Violet cringed at this gross impertinence, and looked away. "Drive on," she said and the driver closed the glass partition.

A half hour later, creeping along in a densely populated Chinese quarter, they turned into a narrow alley entirely covered by overhanging awnings. Violet looked up at dripping patchwork canvas that extended the gloom as far as the eye could see.

Rose began rapping on the glass. "Here, stop, here!"

The fog had not abated and Violet could see human forms passing in the semi-darkness. The driver hopped out and opened the door. Instantly the smell of seaweed, coal smoke, and mold greeted her, tainting the cold freshness of dawn. Violet clutched her purse to her body, and stepped out among somnambulant workers coming off night shifts.

Rose quickly took Violet by the elbow, guiding her under a sign advertising a seal cutter's shop. There, scents of hot jasmine rice and full night soil buckets brought her handkerchief to her nose. Babies were crying, people slept in the stairwell, someone was cooking, and heavy smoke from burning green wood clung to them in the spongy, cold darkness.

Rose cast a disapproving look at the handkerchief Violet held to her nose. "Tink you catchee sick, ah? Missie catchee bik plice!"

Violet stuffed it back in her purse pointing to the door. "Just do your job. I *can* afford *his* price, believe *me*."

There was the sound of a mahjong game in progress, and when Rose knocked, a shirtless man with a flabby belly opened it. Rose explained she needed a special conference with the boss, mentioning previous business connections and a distant relative in common. He just stared past Rose toward Violet with suspicion, then shut the door.

Some minutes later he opened it and as both women entered, Violet muttered to Rose in Cantonese, loud enough for him to hear. "I'll take care of this, Rose. Wait in the car."

The man had a jaundiced face and eyed her brazenly from under a shock of coarse hair. "What's your problem?" he asked in English.

"I humbly come to you by recommendation of your cousin," she said in Cantonese as Rose left. "And by firsthand knowledge of your fine work."

He seemed taken aback by her knowledge of the vernacular, and with a gesture, offered her a seat. Tea was brought out by a young child and placed before her. "You have two mui-tsai of mine in your house already, is that so?" he asked, continuing the conversation in his language

Violet nodded. "But I'm not here for this," she said carefully.

The man sat forward. "No?"

"I understand a little of your business," she said. "You see, I know you get your trade in China, and other places."

"Burma, Malaya, too," he said, "I've connections *all over* Asia."

"But I have a job, for someone—*an expert*; I need the best."

"What job?" he asked angrily. "I don't have time for gweilo housewife talk. You want children, go look back in there. I have many. You choose."

Violet opened her purse and took out three piles of banded bills, placing them neatly on the table.

His eyes opened wide.

"This is a deposit for the *transport* of a child—to *Burma*."

"Kidnapping? You're in the wrong place."

"I know you don't do *kidnapping*, but it will be *already* abducted …"

The man's eyes glimmered and his hands closed on the money. "When's this to be done?"

"On the second of December. I'm afraid to wait longer."

"You mean *stolen* from kidnappers?"

Violet opened her purse again, laying out yet more cash. "I will send a boy here with the exact address."

He looked at her carefully and then took the money, counting it under the edge of the table. "That is very soon."

"I'll pay you the remainder when the job's done."

"How much?"

She wrote down a large sum.

He sipped his tea, thinking. "And where is this pickup location?"

"A flat. Happy Valley. But this child must go to Burma. I never want it to see Hong Kong again. Understand?" She was hoping the quantity of cash would break down all barriers he had to doing it. Certainly ditching it in Burma was less controversial than murder.

The man was silent for a while, then said, "I'll have the child, but you must bring me this much." He scribbled, upping the amount on a paper then pushed it over to her. "You'll meet my man at the typhoon basin once we have it. Then I want my full payment."

They finalized the details and sometime later she was making her way out toward the covered alley. The chauffeur in sparkling white jumped out and held the door for her as she got in.

Seated inside, Rose beamed. "Pei muchee moni?"

Violet turned her face toward the steamed-up window and wiped clean a small circle to look through. Peering out at the gloom, she wondered about her husband, and how it had all come down to this.

"No talkee, ah?" Rose burst into happy laughter.

Peninsula Hotel *29 November 1941*

IT WAS RAINING WHEN Jack headed out under cover of darkness to Kowloon side. Needing to impress the client, he'd hired a Rolls and now waited in front of the Peninsula Hotel with Algy quavering beside him in the back seat. "Algy, no one will see you. For God's sake, shut up!" Their driver was staring in the rearview.

"Mr. Morgan," the man said. "What a coincidence."

Jack looked up at the chauffeur, confused. "Sorry?"

"A coincidence. You see, I also took Mrs. Morgan, only early this morning."

"Oh. Right." He nodded, but was distracted by Algy's whinging.

"Why did you have me come along? I just can't fathom it. I'm the one with the gun charges, Jack." He felt his own forehead again. "I couldn't survive prison. Even now I feel—"

"Just look professional," Jack cut him off, then turned to the driver. "Where did you say you took my wife?"

The driver was quiet a moment. "To a mui-tsai dealer, Sir."

"Look here," Algy said. "Feel my forehead. I think I've got a fever. Ever since Shang—"

There was a sudden tapping. Jack looked at Algy, "Watch and learn," he snapped, angrily, then he and the driver sprang out to greet the client and his entourage of wives.

The women had permanent curls and wore brilliant colored cheongsams, each like different a flavored candy, tart, sweet and fruity. They greeted one another on the curb while the driver held the door open with his pristine white gloves and then then slim childlike girls giggled, getting in first, sliding into the back. Inside, Algy introduced himself in English to their embarrassed laughter. All settled inside, there was a pleasant scent of liquor and deep-fried prawns that had followed them into the closeness of the automobile, bringing an immediate sense of party atmosphere. The smiling girls seemed to glitter as if in a spotlight, radiating fun. Jack and two of them were in the jump seats facing the others and Algy must have bumped knees with one because they began giggling again while Algy stammered out some sort of apology.

The client, a heavyset man in a bowler hat with a thin mustache and beige pin-striped suit, smiled broadly. "Alas, the ladies do not understand you, Mr. Worthing."

Algernon smiled flatly. "I don't understand them either, Mr. Wong." He was almost churlish, even condescending, and offended the client to the quick. Jack saw the blink of surprise on Wong's face.

Jack rapped on the glass. "Drive on, please." Turning to Mr. Wong, he said, "My associate here is in a bad temper; please excuse him. His wife just left him for another woman."

Mr. Wong almost split his sides laughing, and the girls chuckled on cue, while Jack surreptitiously crushed Algy's foot in warning. Wong bent to the girls, translating in Chinese and they all looked at Algy, listening—then burst into unrestrained peals of laughter.

"Ah, my dear Mr. Morgan. I see you have a sense of humor like my own. The English are so reserved; I find it terribly dull engaging them in conversation. You see, I went to school in England, learned the language, but they still treat me like a coolie. I think if I were a horse or a dog I'd fare much, much better."

"No doubt," Jack laughed. "I'm originally American, but rest assured, I don't prefer dogs and horses to humans!"

"Exactly, my friend, exactly! You know, we Chinese are far from perfect. We treat family and friends beautifully, but outside this group ..." He shrugged. "We might run you over and drive off by accident, but a Brit, you see—he'll back over you a few times because you inconvenienced him."

Jack laughed, proffering a cigar, seeing how the man still smarted from Algy's slight. The upper-class Chinese had the closest contact with the Brits and thus suffered the most. Having tried valiantly to fit in by sending their children to British schools and adopting Western clothes, they found they were still spat upon or ignored. "You needn't worry on that count," Jack said with sympathy. "I may be white, but the middle- and upper-class Brits aren't a forgiving lot toward me either. It doesn't matter how much money or power one might wield; the discrimination's not personal. Remember, it's a question of birth. And that simply leaves us out."

Wong laughed. "Hear, hear!"

"Just my experience," Jack said, and removing a bottle, opened the fancy wall bar with crystal glasses. "How about a toast to our new friendship!" The drinks went far toward this goal and soon they were all laughing. But Jack cast an eye toward Algy, who was glowering in his corner, about to say something, when one of the girls beside him chose to adjust his boutonniere, frightening him with her well-meaning intrusion. Jack looked to Wong. "How are you finding things up your way?"

"Ah! The problems we have with the Japs must be remedied by more air power. FDR's given Chiang Kai-shek a big boost by sending Chennault and his Flying Tigers. He's a magnificent warrior and has been a great help!"

"He's a daredevil all right—and what he does with the P-40s is astounding. Certainly, they've changed the face of the war here in China. Bombers wouldn't have served you well."

"True. Do you know I was with the Chiang's when Chennault's men did a demonstration? We were next to a DC-2 and they flew in overhead upside down, and so damned low we all threw ourselves on the ground in terror!" He roared with laughter. "They nearly clipped us!"

"There's nothing they won't do for a little fun."

Wong grinned. "I lost all the buttons on my suit! Actually, it's why I am entertaining your proposal. It proved to me that airplanes are the workhorses of the future."

"I hope you don't plan to fly in these against the Japanese. They're not meant for that kind of maneuverability. These are for cargo. But you know, Wong, I'm having a terrible time letting them go." He caught a glimpse of the client's face as the car passed under a street lamp. *Wong was smiling.* He *knew* this was a fire sale and had big cargo plans in mind. "If you take these planes, you'd be one of very few individuals in Asia with a fleet of your own," Jack added. "And you can bet Chiang Kai-shek will be impressed."

The driver hit a bump as the Rolls turned onto the tarmac. The girls squealed; then one next to Algy tipped her drink on him.

"Yes, I expect so," Wong said, trying to temper his zeal as they got out of the vehicle, but Jack could still see sparks of excitement in his eyes.

The hangar was dark, but when they stepped inside Jack switched on the lights all in one go. His three beautiful planes stood before them, cargo doors ajar—and as if on cue, three pilots descended from the three cockpits. By the belly of each plane were heaps of boxes, demonstrating how much actually fit inside. It was a clever stunt on his part, for the man's eyes bulged as he and the girls counted the crates in amazement. Every minute that ticked by Jack found more painful. He must sell, yet as he took in the elegant form of the planes, he knew he was losing everything he'd built up over the past fifteen years. "I'm sure I don't need to tell you how much I've earned on the last shipment of arms," he added quietly.

"This is impossible to refuse." Wong dared a little smile. "But," then he paused.

Jack felt his heart stop.

Wong's gaze followed the pilots. "I must have them as part of the package."

Jack felt his mood soar, but said, "You drive a hard bargain, Mr. Wong. Why don't you climb aboard, and look around. I'll discuss this with my men. What are you planning—flying these out of Burma?"

The man shrugged. "Actually, it depends on Japanese troop movements."

Jack nodded, and let Algy take them to see the other planes, while he went and met with the pilots in a huddle.

Jack came down the steps a few minutes later. "Wong, my friend, you have yourself a team! They get $750 a month from me in US dollars. I've been also giving them $500 for every Mitsubishi Zero they shoot down, but that's up to you." He was glad to bargain for his pilots, but he felt a growing regret with every step closer to the deal.

"It appears I'm a lucky man tonight."

"You are. And if you like, you can take them up for a test flight."

"No need," Wong laughed. "I've already had my assistant inquire about you. He's also spoken in depth with the mechanics here. But I do have one very big concern. I want the planes out of here as soon as possible. I am afraid your government may requisition them. I was warned specifically of this by numerous parties, and I see you're not taking risks yourself with the lights off outside. If you want to do this, it must be now."

Jack put his hand on Wong's shoulder. "If you have the cash, you can fly out of here with your mother and the girls and your first load of rice or arms tomorrow under cover of darkness."

Wong translated for the ladies and they all clapped excitedly, hearing they'd be returning home by plane. "Let's seal this with some drinks," he said gesturing to the Rolls. "I'm particularly interested in shipping weapons!"

The entire party moved out across the runway to the car, when Jack heard a step behind him. "You know," Algy said peevishly, "you should report our driver."

Jack stopped, and lit a cigar watching Wong talking to the pilots. "Why's that?" The driver was serving drinks, and the radio was blaring out "Stompin' at the Savoy" over the tarmac. Everything seemed to be closing in on him, his career imploding.

"He knows very well he's not to pal around with clients or reveal where he's taken them."

"You mean Violet?"

"Yes. And what did she want with mui-tsai's anyway? Why rent a Rolls when she already has one? Damn suspicious, I'd say."

Jack took a deep breath of air, then sighed. "I've no idea and couldn't care less. I should have backed away from the marriage with that initial telegram, but that's water under the bridge," Jack said feeling his heart breaking as they walked toward the party, leaving the hangar and his beautiful planes behind.

"A toast!" Mr. Wong held up a bottle. "A toast for your planes, Morgan! *My planes!*"

Selling Bella

34

Happy Valley *1 December 1941*

Van Leiden stood at the only window in his flat gazing out toward Causeway Bay, smoking leisurely, when there was a knock. He hid his opium pipe, then ducked under the clothesline that ran through the room, and unlocked the door. "Oh, it's you," he said eyeing Albert in the hall, then opened wide, letting him in. "Look!" he said, pointing. "Ten square meters! No room to move, much less hide a child!"

Albert strolled in glancing at the cot then gave the clothesline a tug. "Use this to tie her up," he said, adding, "Here. I'm done with this." He tossed a dirty magazine onto the cot. "You nervous about tomorrow?"

"Of course. What if she screams in here?"

Albert shrugged, "Use a gag." He leaned against the wall where he could get a breeze from the window, but was starting to perspire. "Look, I spoke to Violet. Use her to help with the kid."

"*Her?* Let's just hire an amah."

"Too risky."

Van Leiden took a cricket mallet out from behind the door. "This is what I have for risk."

"Bother that! We'll have the money before you know it. Besides, look what I have." He held up a Leica. "You can photograph Violet with the child. Evidence. It'll keep her from being able to return to Morgan."

"But when do I get my share?"

"I've no ransom yet—fifteen percent of nothing is still nothing."

Van Leiden was silent.

Albert sucked on his cigarette and blew out a long puff. "I told Violet you'd go up there for tiffin today. It'll get your mind off this, anyhow. She'll give you a couple hundred to help you arrange the job."

"This better go without a hitch," Van Leiden warned, feeling Albert wasn't sufficiently concerned about details. Nevertheless, he saw him off in a rickshaw, then took one himself in the other direction.

At Peak Tram station, he paid his fare and took a seat at the rear where there was a lingering scent of durian and garlic chives. He scanned passengers for a good looking mui-tsai he might bed, but there was nothing but old toothless kitchen amahs with high foreheads and small dull black eyes. They were dressed in black pants, long sleeved tunics, each with a white jade bangle, as they balanced baskets of butcher-wrapped meat or produce on their laps. The seats filled up quickly, latecomers taking hold of overhead straps. One of the latter stood far too close to him, clutching a live rooster upside down, and as the car began its climb, she leaned into him with the bird. A fearless orange eyeball stared at him so intently he could see the iris focusing in and out—the black hole in the center expanding and contracting like a camera lens. The bird tilted its head for a better look at him, studying his face, if that were possible—and considered him from a consciousness that knew no more than what it was itself, slabs of meat, gristle, bone, connective tissue, and fluids. This cold indifferent vision of him unnerved Van Leiden; it was how he saw others, and he didn't like being reminded of his own puny status. Admittedly, he was a failure. But it was easier being a white man abroad than a sap at home. He knew by now that his book on the Far East sex trade would never be written, and whatever talents and advantages of birth he'd had, he'd squandered. Self-hate knew no bounds. Hearing his stop announced, Van Leiden pushed the chicken away and bolted off the tram.

"Madam," he said blustering up the walk some minutes later, "How is that you look so divine?" Huge dangling sapphire earrings caught his eye as she coolly turned to face him in a blue tailored dress with white butterfly sleeves that set off her red hair. Large intelligent blue eyes scrutinized his cheap suit and scuffed shoes from the position of wealth and taste; he found it painful, but kept smiling. She was startlingly beautiful, but haggard, far too thin. She gestured with indifference toward a fluttering tablecloth piled with tea items out on the verandah. He'd been hoping for a look inside, and peering into the vast open interior, he was able to spot a satinwood side table. "Hepplewhite?" he pointed with real surprise. Like all the Dutch, he had a passion for antiques, hoping for an invitation inside.

Violet brushed back a strand hair from her eyes with a withering glance. "I've *heard* the Dutch were born with a *brick* in their *stomachs*," she cooed, but her pinched brows overflowed with condescension.

Van Leiden pulled out a chair for her, then took one himself, irritated because she'd gotten the joke wrong. "A Belgian, a *Belgian*. I'm Dutch."

Violet's thin red lips tightened, a smile, not a smile.

He had heard some of these dead cold English types could actually be impassioned lovers in the sack and he imagined turning her over like a doll—to see if her pubic hair was red. He swallowed a chuckle while Violet Morgan listlessly dabbed butter on a scone, fashionably bored. He already hated her.

"Our mutual friend seems to think you are capable of procuring the child and has instructed me to pay you." She looked up as she touched a thick envelope by her plate. "*Are* you capable?"

Van Leiden gulped. "I—I'm going to do the job to my standards. I won't *kill* anyone, if that's your concern. After all, the plan is to make your husband return, is it not?"

That took the edge off her. "*Yes*, yes that's *true*. We're having a *domestic* dispute."

Van Leiden nodded, suddenly wondering if she was balding or had ringworm.

"Albert tells me you know where the child will be and at what time. How did you ever manage such a fait accompli when Albert couldn't?"

Annoyed by her sloppy French, he squirmed in the wicker seat, hiding his own disdain. "Not so easily. They don't believe in taking the child out; the recent spate of kidnappings, you know. Human ears fried in bean oil keep showing up in the post." He stuffed a few more tidbits into his mouth, this time a pink salty shrimp spread, and caught her eye as he chewed. There was something wild, unsettling about her—and he must have been staring for she abruptly grabbed a tiny olive fork and nervously began testing the sharpness of the two tines on her finger.

"Mr. Van Leiden," she said, not looking up and still jabbing the fork, "I want this done smoothly. Not only do I want my husband back, but Albert tells me a lot of money is at stake." He noticed two drops of blood globe up on her finger.

"Yeeesss," he said slowly, fascinated by her apparent derangement. "We believe he plans to leave but must sell his planes first." The prongs made several small sets of holes. *Surely it must hurt.* "It's—ah—yes, it's a *lot* of money. We'd like to retain it for your firm. As you know, there are rich Chinese who've escaped from China—opium tsars with ready cash to invest." *Could those tiny scabs on her arms be the same cuts? But why?* "We need to be absolutely certain he doesn't sell to one of them," he said, utterly distracted. "What's your interest in this, money or revenge?"

A lascivious and unguarded grin spread across her teeth, then her lips abruptly pursed shut. Catching his gaze moving down to her bleeding fingertip, she made a quick fist, hiding her hand. "Where will this child be housed?" she demanded, pointing the fork at him.

He didn't know if he should tell, and when he hesitated she tapped the envelope by her plate as if she knew he needed money.

"Mr. Van Leiden, you must give me your address. I'll help. I understand you're not familiar with children." She held a pad of paper and pencil across the table for him. When he didn't take it, she kept pushing it toward him in a jerky fashion. He complied at last, but unwillingly, writing out the address. Violet snatched it away, and then read it aloud in a sarcastic plummy voice.

He stared, livid, then prodded, vindictively, "And what do you know of your husband's lady friend? She's rather *attractive*."

"Attractive? I don't know what *men* find attractive. She was associated with him, but," she gave a smug smile, "I am told he moved out. So. Your information is incomplete."

"Interesting," he said, his eyes scanning her bare arms again and tiny scabs. "But you see," he said, "the once *great* Mr. Morgan has come down rather far in the world. He's currently holed up in a grotty temple compound off Hollywood Road. Incredible, no? A pity."

An eyebrow went up. "Aha!" She was not insulted in the least.

"Quite a fall for your *taipan!*" he said, with another dig.

But her eyes widened in interest. "Is that so? And you're certain he's *there?*"

"Yes," he clarified, frowning. "But he has not moved *away* from her, as much as he is afraid of *our* discovering *him*."

"*He is afraid of the law!*" Violet corrected sharply. "The court order, Mr. Van Leiden." Standing up abruptly, she added, "So good of you to come, let me see you out."

He remained seated, but his mouth fell open. "Oh! No. But I'm sure with his child gone that tart can't hold a candle to *you!* I heard of your beauty *long* before I set eyes on you."

"Indubitably." Violet pointed to the steps. "I'll see you soon," she said. "In Happy Valley."

Van Leiden frowned, getting up. "And you still mean to *assist* me?"

Violet took his hand, giving it a warm squeeze along with a sly look. "*Absolutely.* Here." She handed him the envelope. "I'm counting on you. Good-bye."

He took the money, confused by her mixed messages. "Thank you. You'll not be disappointed," he said taking his hat and casting a forlorn eye over the remaining sandwiches.

"I hope not." She gave a sweep of the hand and turned away. "Pity you couldn't stay longer," her voice trailed off.

Van Leiden marched away down the gravel path, his stomach growling. *What a bitch!* At the juncture with Old Peak Road he stopped and looked back at the magnificent colonnaded house. The grass and shrubs were overgrown as if no one had been tending them but it was just the sort of domicile he'd dreamed of. The thought of Albert getting it all seemed so wrong. *Why, only one flattering comment and he'd had her eating out of his hand!* As he stood there, he realized he'd been terribly remiss. Young and ardent, he could easily cut Albert out of the picture—especially regarding sex. He was a dynamo in bed. *Why, she'd even squeezed his hand! What was that, but a come-on?* Van Leiden gulped, undressing her in his mind, and nearly ran back up the path, chucking his hat into the shrubbery as pretext, certain he'd be in bed shortly.

He received no response at the front door and greedily entered the front hall, which was hung with framed sporting photos—hunts, elaborate picnics. Up on the main wall, there were various antlers, a carved tusk, and even the mounted head of a white tiger. It was all rather dusty, and not a servant in sight. The floor creaked underfoot as he paused looking around a tall Chinese vase. *Was that her dress on the floor?* He stepped over it.

The library door was also open and he walked stealthily into the room; it was dark as night inside, and he felt himself getting aroused at the thought of her being undressed. All the windows were shuttered and curtained, so his eyes immediately went to the mantel where a candle was flickering in front of a photo—*a kind of an altar.* To his surprise, just as he touched the strange red mottled photograph a huge thing leapt at him from the sofa. He screamed in horror and fell backward, tripping over a coal bin, hitting the floor with a clatter. Above him stood Violet, red hair loose, stark naked with trickles of blood running down her arms and thighs. "Get out!" she screamed in a hoarse voice, jabbing the olive fork at the air between them. "Get out of my house!" He gaped up at her. Well, she *did* have red pubic hair.

Western District *1 December 1941*

It was afternoon, but Number One snake head was still asleep. Po-Sing the mui-tsai dealer stood over him, and then went to sit back down at the mahjong table and took out the red-headed gweilo lady's deposit, fanning through it. It was far more than the job was worth. He jotted down potential expenditures he might not have considered, when Li-fook, snake head, stirred, groaning.

"Ohhh. I've a headache."

"No drinking tonight," Po-sing warned, tucking the list and cash away. He called for the amah and minutes later a bowl of congee garnished with pungent black century eggs was placed before Li-fook, who dug in. "So," he asked his friend. "Are you ready?"

Li-fook scratched a bug bite on his wrist and grunted. "I saw your driver last night," he said, slurping. "He'll go to Happy Valley for the pickup."

Po-sing nodded. "I told him everything." There were footsteps and the bamboo curtains clicked as Liu came in, nodding and sitting down beside them. He was as tall as he was thick, and his black eyes were fierce, but what stuck in mind was the scar that had split his lower lip into two flaps. He was known on the docks as Lotus-Lips, but only Po-sing got away with calling him that to his face. Lotus-Lips-Liu sat at the table awaiting direction.

Po-sing handed him the address and Liu scanned it several times, his three lips trembling; then he crumpled the paper, stuffed it in his mouth, and swallowed it. He ate everything that might indict him. He tapped the side of his head, indicating he had written the address in his gray cells.

Po-sing said, "You're to go at sunrise. The driver will take you, and you're to wait until the Dutchman leaves his flat—they said ten o'clock, but we want to be sure. When he returns with the child, you know what to do. The driver will bring you back to the typhoon shelter and Li-fook will have the sampan ready. The gweilo will be there with Li-fook when you bring the child on board. Understand?"

The other two exchanged glances. "A gweilo?" Li-fook murmured.

"Yes, she wants to see the face of the child before she gives final payment."

Liu grunted, looking down, uncertain.

It was a serious job, and no one said anything for a minute or two as they sipped their tea. Po-sing knew what they were thinking. Taking a child *out* of Hong Kong all the way to Burma was tricky.

"What about the turnip heads?" Li-fook finally asked. Their business had taken a downturn from all the war activity going on.

"You have the machine guns. Just stick to shore and travel by night as usual. You've done the route a hundred times. When you get to Shek-O, change her hair to black and find Chinese clothing that fits."

"Eh?" The two men looked up.

Po-sing smiled. "A *gweilo* child—light hair color. I have a big buyer in Burma," he said. "*Very rich customer.* This is Number One mui-tsai my friends. Big money."

The other two laughed, feigning relief, as they finished their tea, but they looked at each other when they left the building to urinate off the back dock into the harbor. Po-sing watched them out the window and heard Li-fook say, "If we get caught in the colony with a white child we will lose our heads."

Liu grunted, undoing his button, and then pointed his cock to the detritus below. A swollen corpse was bobbing just under them next to a big clump of seaweed and both men aimed toward the target, laughing as their streams crisscrossed in an effort to be first. Po-sing dropped the bamboo shade. He didn't like that she'd changed her story and that the child hadn't yet been secured. But he knew Happy Valley well and had already checked the supposed address the previous night. Besides, he had his deposit already. Even if nothing came of it, it was an excellent trade.

Peak House *1 December 1941*

VIOLET WATCHED THE DUTCHMAN scurrying off down the driveway from the library window, then shut the louvers. Stepping over the scattered coal on the floor, she reached for the wedding photo on the mantel. *Jack, Father, and friends—friends who didn't even speak to her.* She looked at their faces. *I've lost everything.* Violet picked up the olive fork, testing it. She was always relieved by the small globules of blood that trickled out of her body, so relieved she cried. Violet now poked it into a soft bruised spot on her inner thigh, crying a little, for it hurt. Then she pushed in deep. She gasped. Blood rose up around the tines. *He'll come back. I know. He'll consider it. My blood line is superior.* Violet smiled through her tears, biting her lip to ease the pain. *I'll show Jack the picture and he'll remember how good it was. He NEEDS another chance.*

Later, after she'd rested, Violet spent an hour dressing for the occasion, applying makeup at her vanity that still had a gaping hole where the mirror had been. She leaned forward as if the glass were still there, applying red rouge to her lips. Round and round she plied the red color, breaking the stick, and it fell down. The action drew her eyes to a photo on the floor. She stooped over picking it up. Handsome Jack—at a lawn tennis party at the Ladies Recreation Club. She noticed other faces in the background. Connie. Pippa. *Sluts!* Violet took out a pair of scissors and jabbed the paper several times, then cut out the offending faces. Just as she did, they reappeared. Violet picked up the scissors again and cut Jack's image out of the remaining paper and tucked this in her panties. Then, standing up, she was about to take up the dress she had laid out, when Rose entered. "What do you want!" Violet's voice was hoarse with the strain she was feeling. "Get out and let me dress in peace!"

Her amah left, but Violet suspected she was hovering outside the door and waited for a moment before she jerked it open. Rose shrieked in fright and ran away, while Violet laughed. Then, going back to finish dressing, she spoke aloud. "It's nonsense—that woman—always hovering about! Buzz-buzz-buzz. One can't think, she uses all the air. Hovering, hovering. *You ok, Missie*?" she mocked. "Buzz-buzz. Of course, I'm all right if you'll make yourself scarce. I can't breathe with you servants, bugs on wall; go eat my food, but not my nerves! What do you think? Why else did I fire all of you?" She glanced quickly to the side. Ever since Father died she'd seen shadows out of the corner of her eyes. She thought Jack saw them too, for when she looked, he had also always looked. They never spoke of it, though. She was convinced it was Poppa. When she finished dressing she sprayed herself with Acqua Di Parma, Jack's favorite, then marched down the stairs, only to be approached by Rose again.

"Missie, pen bilong muas kulah—*nogut!*" she said as Violet walked off down the driveway, then shouted, "Clazy style! Led nogut!"

"Red is my favorite color, Rose. It *is* good. See you later!"

The lane at the side of Man Mo Temple was not so crowded with noonday shoppers when Violet got down from the rickshaw. The heat was terrible and the loose cobbles made the going tough in heels, but she was amused by the stares she got, and stood taller, sure of herself, certain that the photograph in her panties would grant her passage.

Violet entered, and blinking in the darkness, found the temple deserted. Heavy, smoking coils of incense burned silently above, adding a wonderful hellishness to the red-red hall. *Led-nogut!* she mocked Rose aloud, smacking her red lips, then laughed quietly. She walked to the back of the temple, skirting glass-encased relics, gold idols, and found a little door that led out back. The air in the little courtyard was smoking hot off the pavement and she took a few steps then called out, "Jaaack! Jaa–aaaaack!" There was something about the name she had always loved, how it came out of her mouth, how it possessed the man, how it announced that he was hers. A monk stuck his head out a door, then moments later Jack himself emerged from a moon gate at the far side of the garden. "All these are wilted," she said pointing to the plantings.

He was staring at her. "What do you want?"

"Is that how you address your wife?"

"How'd you know I'm here?" he accused, blue eyes cold with suspicion.

"Rose comes here," she lied. "Haven't you see her burning joss for me? She waved at you only yesterday."

"No," he said, surprised, though the lie seemed to put him at ease. "What have you done to yourself?"

"Me?" She thought of the photo hidden on her, and let out a nervous peal of laughter. "You look handsome as ever, Jack," she said holding out a hand to touch his face, but he flinched.

"Violet, you need to see a doctor. Tell Albert to take you."

"A-ha! So it *is* jealousy!"

Jack was standing in the sunlight, squinting, staring at her from under heavy brows with an expression that perplexed her, and then he shrugged and picking up a hoe, began to loosen the soil.

"I came here to give you one more chance," she said to his back. "Isn't that noble of me, considering you took all that money?"

Jack stopped digging. "I didn't take one cent from you, and you know it."

"Ah! The *honest* cheater! Weeeeellll, don't worry. I *tooooo* have lovers. We're even on *that* count. But you know, Albert tells me everything and I have him 'round my finger. You'll be especially glad to hear—he's given up on taking you to court. Surprised?"

Jack turned to look at her, eyes narrowed. "Why would he change his mind?"

"I told him a scandal's the last thing *I* want."

"Do you *know* what you want?"

"A second chance! I want you to come home and live in Peak House. You can have your job back. I don't care about the money."

"Violet, I don't *have* your money. What's Albert been saying?"

"Forget him!" She grabbed hold of his arm. "You can have your lovers, only please, come back with me." He stared at her hand until she released him.

"That's finished, Violet. I don't want you laboring under any illusions. But you can tell me; does Albert know I'm here? Someone's been following me, though I haven't seen him in days."

"Following?" she scoffed, and looked around the sun-beaten yard, at the dry baked soil, the flies. "Come now, Jack. Is your life here *so* good? I hear you've left that woman."

"Violet," he snapped at her, "I've a ticket out for the fifth, and I plan to go. I'm leaving *you* everything I've built up over the past *fifteen* years. Do you realize what it takes to walk away from that? I'll never get those years back. And look at you!" He stared at her, eyes blazing, and then abruptly his voice softened. "Oh, Violet. You're not well. Albert's using you."

"That's a rather heartless accusation, but then—our arrangement was never about heart. That's why you and I can live together so well, complete understanding. It's why I'm here."

He looked dumbfounded. "No, Violet, I did care for you once, but it was all confused with the job, your father—my responsibility toward him. I wanted roots and a home—*more than I wanted things.* It took a lot for me to see that. The blinders are off now."

"Oh, I'm sure," she said knowingly. "And what about Papa's Rolls? You did like it so. Tell me, am I wrong? And the tea dances? The *servants?* The *house!*"

"What's wrong with the Rolls, Violet? I heard you hired a driver."

She stared at him blankly. "Albert requisitioned it. I have no car."

"Can I ask you a favor?" he suddenly asked. "Don't tell Albert I'm here. Can you do that for me, Violet?"

She looked at him and the dirt he'd been turning over, the neat aisles of wilting plants behind him, and nodded. Surprisingly, he'd *ignored* her appeal, *her offer of the house!* "I like to garden too, Jack," she said. "We could do it together." There was a depth to his eyes, warm, sticky like pity, and she almost got lost until she noticed her own dark shadow reflected on his corneas. *Her own image—one on each eye.* "Jack?" He turned away and was working the ground, hitting the hard dry clumps, all the muscles in his body hard. She couldn't tell if he could hear her, for all he did was chop-chop-chop. It made her cross being so ignored. "Jack!" she said angrily, remembering his bastard child. He continued working. Violet stiffened her lip, furious, then asked irrationally, "So, did you *see* the pretty little *child* outside?"

Jack looked up startled. "*What child*?"

He grabbed her arm, squeezing it painfully hard, staring into her eyes, frightening her. Violet tried to pull away from this strange ferocity. "I was only joking!" she quailed.

"What do you know? *TELL ME!*" His look scalded her, and she felt herself shriveling in his gaze, drying up in that focused stream of—of yes, *HATE*. In a flash she *knew*—knew *Jack Morgan of Peak House was gone.* Now his world was divided into *hate* for her and *love for his CHILD and the OTHER woman. Love she'd never experienced—never would.* Violet forced a laugh, but the awful realization made speech nearly impossible. "Why the one *outside*," she choked, pulling her arm away. "Begging for food." She paused. "Do you have a coin to lend me? That's all I was asking."

His face relaxed. "No." He turned away and continued digging, indifferent.

She thought she would faint. She steeled herself and watched him, waiting for him to realize he was wrong. His muscles were thick and he was sweating. She didn't even like him. "I don't see how that *woman* thinks she'll break into society with you. She doesn't even have a *NAME* for herself! Think of it. *It's preposterous.* You really need to come back." He said nothing, working, chopping dirt. "I'm going now," she said testing, but the sweetness in her voice trailing over the silence had an edge of hysteria in it. "Anything more you want to say, Jack dear?" *Even she could hear it.*

"No. Try to see a doctor," he said benignly, not looking up.

Violet imagined a map of the world and how small and dark Burma seemed, and how even smaller a child would be, lost in that immense land, like a pin in his heart—*one that you cannot remove, one that you cannot find, one that burns deep inside.* As her rickshaw glided away up the road, she felt pierced herself, *withering*, unable to stop the alarming numbness that was spreading gray and dry though all her organs. Violet closed her eyes, aghast. Up above the sun was hammering down on her and Violet felt in a fever, squinting in the brightness, faint. *He pushed me, Father,*" she said, licking her chapped lips. *"It's all his fault. He pushed. Pushed.* Percy was sitting beside her in the rickshaw, but he looked ashen, and a mite sad. "You always liked *him* better, Father. *How could you? How!*" She reached out her hand to touch him, but the red plastic seat was empty and burned her fingertips. "Poppa?"

Happy Valley — *2 December 1941*

LOTUS-LIPS HAD GOTTEN UP before dawn, feeling edgy like he did on every trip out, yet he felt the excitement in his belly, too. He stood at the edge of the racecourse, stretching, practicing tai-chi poses while jockeys trained their horses before the heat of day. He took deep relaxing breaths, lowering his chi to his dan-tien, centering himself—and then he felt ready, balanced enough to kill. A half hour later he was standing outside the Dutch gweilo's flat in sweeper's clothes. Taking a broom, he began at one end of the building, and swept rhythmically, as he approached the door, then passed it. When the tall man left the flat an hour later, Lotus-Lips nodded, but the Dutchman didn't even notice his would-be killer. Liu watched him walk off down the street, then picked the lock. Inside found a cricket mallet by the door, and sat down to wait, slapping the smooth wood against his calloused palm.

Wyndham Street — *2 December 1941*

YOSHI HELD THE ORIGAMI crane made of silver paper above his head, turning it in the sunlight, against the pale blue sky. *Too bad we can't fly away together. But Yoshi knew what was coming.* He sighed, then leaned back on the steps outside of his flat and removed the meishi from his pocket, fingering its well-worn surface. It was time to repay the man, but he'd put it off so long it was nearly too late. *Jyaaaku, Jyaaaku Mooganu,* he said practicing the name. All week he could feel mounting tension among the Japanese. Finally, this morning O-ji san had taken out his Thompson submachine gun and cleaned it carefully before going off to work as barber—perhaps for the last time. By nightfall he might well be signaling the Japanese air attack with tracer bullets from the rooftop. Yoshi wondered again, *How will I tell Jyaaku to leave?*

As he sat there two Japanese girls passed by him in floral yukata; so lovely. From birth every Japanese girl was taught to take tiny mincing steps, toes pointing inward to show modesty. No Chinese girl could imitate their walk. He smiled as two more dainty ones passed—amazed that they were prostitutes at the massage parlors, yet still so demure, so gentle. They waved, then, giggling, covered their mouths with their hands. Sunlight danced off their hair ornaments. *He would marry one if he had the chance!* Each of them had trained as a nurse to care for injured forces after the victory. *Maybe I'll be shot,* he thought, yearning, imagining their cool hands running over his feverish body, stripping off his clothes, then bouncing on him … He was jolted to the present by a loud bang and he dropped his crane into a puddle. Reflecting his red shirt, it appeared to be lying in a pool of blood. Yoshi left it there.

Standing up, he tucked Jyaaku's meishi in his pocket, and began ambling slowly toward Robinson Road and the address he'd memorized since his first day here. Everything now seemed touched with potential death, and he looked upon the scenery and people with poignant nostalgia. Passing flower stalls, old furniture shops reeking of lacquer, Indian restaurants exhaling waves of curry, he sniffed deeply, wanting to always remember every detail of this last peaceful moment. At last, he turned left onto Old Bailey Street, taking the steep incline upward.

Inside the gaijin's building, he climbed up to the fifth floor. An elegant curvaceous woman answered, her eyes the color of green tea. Yoshi held up the meishi with Jack's name on it and she asked him something, her face concerned, then she switched to Chinese, trying again. He shrugged. She was becoming impatient and he finally pantomimed airplanes dropping bombs and then pointed to Jack's name again. The woman was preoccupied; she was attempting to put on a necklace and was also looking behind her and talking to an amah who was dressing a young girl. She gestured him to come in as she wrestled with the catch, then again spoke to him in one of those horizontal languages Yoshi shook his head, then wrote in the air. *What he really needed was a dictionary.* Frustrated, she gestured him to wait, sitting him down at a table covered with scrap paper, pencils, and crayons. The little girl was sitting on a chair near him, smiling, while an amah kneeled at her feet, buckling her shoes. When the telephone rang, the lady set her necklace down on a bureau and disappeared.

Yoshi sighed, then nodded at the child, who giggled. The amah suddenly grumbled in irritation; a buckle had broken. Getting up, she left the room, leaving the child and him alone. Yoshi tilted his head, making a face, but the girl raised her hand toward the bureau. Yoshi got up and looked. It was a tiger on a chain. He picked it up and the girl jumped up and down excitedly. He laughed, and came over to her, hanging it around her neck. The tiger slipped under her blouse.

"Do chie!" the child said, thanking him in Chinese and clapping.

Yoshi bowed in response, then grabbing a scrap of paper with scribbling on it from the table, he quickly made a crane for her and placed it in her palm. The child was ecstatic and as the amah returned with another pair of shoes, Yoshi sat back down. *He really needed to go home and get his dictionary.* He watched quietly as the amah kneeled, attempting to put on the shoes, while the child waved her crane happily, kicking her feet. Annoyed, the amah snatched the crane and pushed into the baby's pocket, then took her hand. Then the two of them headed out the staff door, the baby waving back at him with her free hand. "Do chie!" she called out gaily.

Yoshi watched them go. It was a moment he could never forget all his life, but hearing the gaijin woman still talking on the telephone in the other room, he too slipped out of the flat, closing the door. *He would regret this decision, always. If only he had followed them!*

Robinson Road *2 December 1941*

Van Leiden left his flat at ten that morning, took his escape vehicle, and parked it on the corner of Upper Lascar row, leaving the chloroform bottle on the passenger seat for easy access. He then turned about and walked uphill to Morgan's flat and headed down the back alley. His plan was to abduct her on Aberdeen Street, carry her the one block to the car, knock her out with the chloroform, drive back to Happy Valley, and tie her up before she woke. *Simple. Very simple, he only had to follow the plan.* Van Leiden put a kretek in his mouth but didn't light it, and checked his watch. He had to be wary not to be spotted. He'd spent too much time already in front of the flat last month waiting for Jack, and knew the servants had seen him. Sweat poured down his face now as he squatted, hiding at the back of courtyard, brushing a palm frond out of his face.

A good hour later the amah came out the servant's door with the kid. Van Leiden gulped, watching as they took the same stairs they had the day before. Sunlight reflected off the girl's golden hair, and she took one step at a time, baby style. His heart pounded as he stood up, watching, chewing on his tobacco instead of smoking. They finally got past the stairs. He looked at his watch. *At this pace, it was torture.* He followed slowly, though every instant his mind shouted—*Run! Run! Do it now!* Creeping along at a snail's pace he tried to look like he was window shopping, pausing to look at cricket cages, jade trinkets, letting them get farther and farther along until they were nearly a half block away. He sighed. They passed a flower stall, and a bakery, and then he lost sight of them in the glare of a glass shop door opening. *Had they gone in?* A vegetable cart passed in front of him obscuring his view, then another and another. *What if he lost them somehow?* The moment the last cart passed by, he leaped ahead, rushing toward the bakery, not noticing an old merchant bent double, wobbling, balancing two heavy buckets on a yo-yo pole. Rising up, the man turned and struck Van Leiden in the gut with the bamboo pole just at the bakery entrance. Caught unaware, Van Leiden gasped, and a piece of tobacco broke free, flying into his windpipe. His hands flew to his neck; he couldn't breathe! His lungs stopped. His throat shut. He wretched. Hacked. *Everything stopped.*

Wheezing, he choked, coughed his gut out, drooling, bending over, tobacco bits and spit flying out of him, until he was vomiting up his breakfast on the sidewalk. One, two, three heaves—finally he gasped, and straightening up, took a deep, merciful, wheezing, squealing breath of fresh air. It was just that moment the amah and the little girl stepped out of the bakery and looked straight at him from only two feet away.

There was instant recognition in the old woman's eyes. She jerked the child to her side and began to run, waving her free arm.

He didn't really worry—*after all, what could the old bitch do? Certainly she couldn't outrun him.* He spit out a remainder of tobacco from his mouth and wiped his vomit off with a handkerchief, tossing it aside. The old woman was some twenty feet away now, crossing the street—*and crossing the wrong way, away from the temple!* Van Leiden stopped at the curb, dumbfounded. Then he realized with dismay the paranoid old bitch was waving at a constable—and pointing back at him! *Her eye caught his—and hers grew wide.* Van Leiden sprinted into action and she began shouting, "Ta Kip! Kau Meng!" as he ran at her, furious. It all happened so quickly—but in a flash he'd covered the distance between them, and snatched the girl. The amah, thrown off balance, fell back onto the road as he turned and ran for his life.

Van Leiden could hear the constable's shrill whistle behind him, a shrieking of car tires, but he only ran faster—heart pounding, child slung across his chest, kicking all the way. He was a great sprinter, but suddenly a few blocks down the hill it dawned on him—*he was running away from his escape auto! Good God! How do I get across town to my flat?* Van Leiden cursed, knocking people left and right—child wailing all the while he tried to think and not to fall. *He couldn't think.* So he ran. He didn't stop until he reached a dark lane all the way down in Central behind the Hong Kong Hotel. Gasping and choking from the effort, he clamped his hand tighter over her mouth, then looking up and down the alley, noticed a hotel car idling outside the service entrance. The driver's door was open, and the boot too, and piled with luggage. Van Leiden didn't wait. He dashed across the alley, threw her down on the seat beside him, and putting his foot down on the accelerator, tore out into the traffic on Queen's Road Central, boot flapping, pedestrians darting out of his way, shedding luggage out onto the road behind him. She was screaming—an ear-piercing pitch. He thought he was going to crash. *Oh, to have the chloroform now!*

Fifteen minutes later he was half-dragging, half-carrying her up the back steps, nearly fainting with what felt like an oncoming heart attack. *Thirty catties—my ass!* He hadn't thought he'd be running so far with the weight—and that she'd be kicking the daylights out of him. Van Leiden's lungs were wheezing like a bellows as he fumbled one-handed for his flat keys, the other still over her mouth; he was at great disadvantage. At last, however, he unlocked the door. Pushing his way in with relief, he didn't even have time to set her down. Out of nowhere there was a rush of air and something struck him hard on the skull—and then again, and again, clubbing mercilessly, knocking him to the floor. As he fell, he released the screaming child, and lay cowering, trying to block the ferocious onslaught to his face and head. His last vision was the boot coming down with a crack on his neck.

Causeway Bay *1 December 1941*

At the Typhoon Shelter, Violet hopped off her rickshaw and walked along the water's edge, heels clicking on the wooden dock, little dull thuds. The smell was brackish, and as she looked out over the tops of hundreds of bobbing sampans, she spotted the central one, the mother ship, where they cooked meals. She sniffed—the smell of spicy deep-fried chili crab drifted over the water. Looking around, she noticed no one paying her any heed—*I'm just an English lady out for her constitutional,* she thought, smiling. She walked up and down the praya in an inconspicuous beige shift and matching silk pumps, quite enjoying herself—a real Mata Hari in pearls and favorite cloche hat.

After a few minutes, a young Chinese boy came running to her. He whispered, *Burma*. Violet cooed with excitement and quickly followed him down a dank flight of steps to a ladder that disappeared further under the dock. He pointed for her to go under, and she stepped downward with trepidation, holding tightly to the rails, lowering herself rung by rung until cold water washed up over her sling back pumps. "Oooooh!" Violet looked up to see where the ruffian had gone. "Damn him!" She wriggled her wet toes in dismay and was about to climb back up, when a sampan appeared out of nowhere. A man sitting in the dark under the tarpaulin gestured for her to remove her heels, then get on. She did as she was told, heart pounding in her throat.

Inside it was dark and stank of fish bait. Violet crawled in further, a shoe in each hand, her beige purse looped over her wrist, the uneven floor bruising her knees and immediately laddering her nylons. Violet tried to get comfortable, sitting on bent knees as a man at the back put his weight into maneuvering the single oar. Pump, pump, pump—only the lightest gurgle of water—and like a fish, they glided out onto the bay. There, they hid in plain sight among countless sampans, waiting, bobbing, anonymous in a floating village. Sounds from town came to them, but as if from far away, a kind of dreaming. The man indicated for her to wait, and Violet nodded, feeling her calves go numb, then her knees; finally both her legs and feet throbbed with pins until she felt absolutely nothing. It seemed a near eternity and she'd almost fallen asleep from the gentle rocking when a sudden wild tipping of the vessel roused her. The sampan had come to shore again and a heavy man had leaped aboard with a large rolled bamboo mat. *A market pig!* The trussed roll was squealing as he thumped it down between them. The paddler instantly began to waggle the oar in little mad staccatos. The shore pulled away rapidly.

Violet stared in excited disbelief. She attempted to ask a question, but the men ignored her, so she sat back wringing her purse handle, staring at the package. Sometime later, when they were out over deep water, the heavy man ducked back in with the alacrity of a gorilla. His countenance was hardly human with his three horrid lips and knife-point eyes. He came in very close, smiling, so close she could smell garlic, camphor, and she saw strange freckles on his face—*Oh! Specks of BLOOD!* Violet felt her heart squeezing in her chest and moaned, pulling her purse tightly to her chest, covering her priceless pearls.

He gazed coldly at her, almost laughed, but instead pointed a sharp blade at the bundle. Relieved, Violet nodded. With a deft flick he slit the bindings and the mat burst open revealing a blanketed cocoon. Lying before her was a very red-faced, hot little child. It was having trouble breathing and its hair was mussed all over its face. Violet pointed to the gag, and as they were far out by now, the man removed it. Instantly a wail came out and he clamped down his dirty hand. Violet leaned closer, intrigued, brushing hair from its face. "Nothing will happen to you, my dear, not if you are quiet. Do you understand? *No screaming.*"

The child appeared to nod and the man released it. Violet watched, transfixed. It was a *beautiful* child. Violet felt a terrible pang of regret. *Oh, if only he'd waited—it could have been ours! We could have had one like this. Why hadn't we?* A chain around the child's neck sparkled. Violet looked closer—*the Cartier tiger!* She hadn't seen it in years. As she attempted to snatch it, the giant grunted, gesturing for money. Frightened, Violet withdrew and, opening her purse, handed him the envelope. Then she turned back to the child. "That's an impressive necklace you have there."

The child touched it. "It's Mummy's."

Violet felt her lips tighten. "Yes? And what's your name, little girl?"

"My name is Bella," she said, wiping her hair from her face with an awkward baby-like motion that was very sassy and reminded her instantly of that whore of a mother. "I'm *Bella Morgan*."

"*Morgan?*" Violet felt her blood boil and she growled, growled through clenched jaws, the sound like hot tar and gravel churning, "*Baaaasstarrrrrrd! You are not a Morgan!*"

"Poppa, Poppa! *Jaaaacccck!*" the thing screamed, shattering her eardrums.

Violets hands pressed hard on her ears till there was no sound but her own heartbeat, thudding in her head. She'd witnessed it in his face at the temple, and now again—*this love so large—large as the scream shattering her head. It was his revenge. "I never had love! Nobody will love me, ever! His heart is full. No room for me!"* she cried aloud, wailing along with the child, her ears still covered, feeling she was losing her mind. The gorilla hit her across the face, his hand like a brick. Violet fell sideways, recoiling from the savagery while he gagged the child. She kept as far from him as possible after that, and didn't dare look into his eyes.

Now and then she heard occasional whimpers above the swirl of water as the sampan glided back toward Central. It seemed a long time before they finally pulled up to the steps and she was able to climb out on Pedder Street wharf. She pulled on her pumps and when she did turn to look, the sampan was just turning round. Violet caught a glimpse of a tiny pink foot from under the tarpaulin, a mere lotus bud. Then the sampan slipped away.

Raising her hand, almost as if to wave, she paused, staring. "*Your father pushed me,*" she said, explaining to the wind. "Pushed."

EPILOGUE

Hong Kong *1997*

"GRANDPA?" I SAID, QUIETLY. I touched his shoulder gently as a breeze blew in through the window. "What happened then? It was December 8, right?" He had finished speaking a few minutes ago and was now staring intently at nothing I could see. The ticking clock had resumed its prominence in the silence, and like clicking abacus beads, seemed to measure the darkness in the room with quick fingers.

He blinked, then reached for his cigar case, saying, "They were insane with blood lust, you know, from all that fighting in China. Very few had any decency left. They were primed to kill." He lit the cigar, puffing, while rain began falling outside. "Early Saturday morning they swarmed over our borders, attacking like clouds of locusts. People awoke in surprise and disbelief."

"But what happened to Bella?"

"Oh, our little Bella," he sighed, quiet a moment. "Well, Jardine, I don't exactly know. Think of it this way. In that week I'd lost a child, my job, my home, Ana, and my country. I fought along with the others, and eighteen days later the white flag went up. I was marched off to Stanley Prison with Bella's picture in my breast pocket. It wasn't until recently, so many years later, that I could piece together what occurred." He paused, his face reddening. "You see, Violet left behind a confession. Her solicitor slipped it to me at her funeral as they were lowering her casket into the ground. I'll show it to you later."

"Oh? What did it say?"

"Let's say it filled in the gaps." He shook his head in disgust. "I read it right there while she was being buried. I felt like a thunderbolt had hit me—and at that moment a Canossan nun tapped me on the shoulder. A Sister Bernadette. She asked me in a whisper—*why had I turned away Bella, when she'd returned from Burma*. Imagine the gall! After the misunderstandings were cleared up over tea later, she explained how she'd known Bella—met her years before at a mission in the hills above Mandalay, a leper colony. She explained that two Hong Kong Chinamen arrived under cover of night carrying a white child disguised as an Asian. They were seeking refuge from the Japanese troops. Supposedly, they were headed into Mandalay itself, but the Japs had beat them there and they didn't know what to do. The missionaries invited them to remain, and they did since the Japanese didn't dare to approach a leper colony. But the war wasn't ending. One night after a month, they simply departed, leaving the child behind."

I was speechless, then managed to ask, "Bella—with lepers?"

"It's not as contagious as you'd imagine. Mother Theresa bathed lepers all the time and didn't contract it. Sister Bernadette said Bella was very good with them."

"You mean Bella *stayed?*"

"Bella grew up there, and later married a Buddhist priest from Mandalay—*your father.* He died soon after, though, of cholera, before you were born—sorry."

"My head is spinning."

"Yes, I imagine so. The surprising thing is that this Sister Bernadette turned out to be a friend of that very same priest I'd met on the train in Suchow, Father John." He looked out the window and sighed. "It's odd, how our paths crisscrossed, left and right, but somehow Bella remained lost to me."

I sat dumbstruck, listening—but not sure I was taking it all in any more.

"Poor Bella's original amah died from the fall in the street that morning when Bella was ripped from her arms," he said, continuing. "And, as for the Dutchman, the police responded to a call about a foul odor in Happy Valley—and found him rotted, his head battered into a pulp. Unfortunately, there was no obvious connection to Albert or Violet. If there had been we might have tracked Bella down. Mind you, the Japs bombed us less than a week later so the official search ended there."

Auntie Tam brought out some tea and closed the windows while Jack began to describe that following week and the chaos of war, but I couldn't help but feel a growing sense of loss. As he spoke, I imagined little Bella in the bottom of a sampan, drifting farther and farther away. It seemed impossible that he hadn't known more or couldn't have stopped Violet somehow.

"We all had to report to duty," he said reluctantly. "I was with the Rajputs and Punjabis protecting the boundary with China on Kowloon side. We had dug tunnels along the hills, invisible to the oncoming Japs, except that their spies had been highly efficient. They had a mock-up of our battlements dug in China, so when they came they just dropped grenades down our air vents. No fighting needed. So many of our boys died in those tunnels. The biggest joke was that Percy's barber showed up on horseback after our surrender—the first commander at Stanley Prison camp."

"But what happened to Ana that week—when you were fighting the Japanese in Kowloon?"

"She was conscripted into the Volunteer Nursing auxiliary."

"And … ?"

"And then on Christmas morning she was at work with Dr. Black … at St. Stephen's College Emergency Hospital …" He looked away then put his cigar out, and took a deep breath. "At 5:30 Christmas morning the doctor decided to surprise the patients with a ration of tea, a present. I'm told Ana was handing out tea trays when two Canadian troopers covered in dust stumbled up the road. They said the hospital had to be evacuated immediately but

Dr. Black gave them several shots of whisky and sent them on their way, refusing to move critically ill patients. Fifteen minutes later two hundred drunken Japs came up the road laughing, arguing. Dr. Black barred them from entry and was shot in the head for his effort, bayoneted a dozen times on the threshold."

"But …"

"They entered. Began to bayonet all the critical care patients. When they had trouble pulling the bayonets out of the patients, because they'd gotten stuck in the mattresses, they changed tactics and began striking their rifle butts against amputation sites or just shooting them in the head. The screaming of the dying was unbearable. Nurses were ordered to carry out the dead while slipping in blood. The mattresses, doors, desk tops—everything was carried out onto the road and a bonfire was lit with gasoline."

"At some point Yoshi came looking for me at our flat and found Ana injured and alone. He was burdened with a great feeling of debt to me … Anyway, somehow Ana escaped from the hospital with a terrible wound to the head." Jack's eyes were brimming with tears. "*If only I could have been there.* Yoshi carried her to a safe house for medical attention where Chinese guerillas were conspiring against the Japanese. I don't think they even suspected Yoshi wasn't one of them."

I swallowed hard. "And what of Algy?"

"Oh Algy … *My dear friend.* He wasn't the best soldier, you know." Jack nodded with a wry smile. "Before the war we had a lot of marches and parades on the King's Birthday each year. Every time Algy was the one who dropped his rifle. At practice, I remember if orders were given to withhold fire, he would let loose a volley of shots—all wide of the target. The cockneys in the Middlesex beat the dickens out of him regularly for his errors until his sergeant finally took pity on him and he was packed up to join the Hughsiliers—a bunch of seventy-year-olds who'd fought in World War I. The Middlesex boys had a howling laugh when they heard about his 'promotion' and cut his fly buttons off for good measure."

"Seventy-year-olds?"

"Yes. A respectable lot of old fellows—all Percy's age. They were posted up at the Power Station. There was the head of Jardine Matheson's, the chairman of Hutchison's, a famous Shanghai wine merchant, the secretary of the Jockey Club, and a few other taipans of import-export companies. The head chef of the Hong Kong Hotel was there too. He was later our chef at Stanley Prison and made amazing food out of nothing. I can still remember his tasty fricassee of fish with coolie rice. Anyhow, after the station was ablaze, those old men, as you call them, went and fought hand-to-hand combat in the streets. They were valiant and personally held back the Japs one entire night and the next whole day, all the while knowing they would die for their efforts."

"But *Algy* …"

"After I was interred in Stanley Prison the chef came and told me Algy had gone out to light a cigarette back at the Power Station, standing on the skyline like a bird on a wire. Took a bullet in the stomach. The old guys insisted in taking him with them when the station began to burn—but he disappeared into the night, and put a bullet in his own head. I remember, the last time I saw him he'd cut the buttons off *my* drill shorts and there *I* stood with my fly *wide open*, having to report to duty without a button in sight! When I tried to grab him, he laughed and dodging me had the gall to say, 'No need to get shirty, old boy.' Oh, Algy— He was a *brother* to me."

I put my hand on his arm. He'd spotted the framed picture of the two of them in front of an airplane.

"Anyhow," he looked away, taking a deep breath, buttoning in his grief. "He was a big help searching for Bella those last few days before the attack. We kept thinking she was somewhere in Hong Kong, behind some tenement wall, crying. Ana was on the streets calling Bella's name day and night, screaming herself hoarse as if by chance a window somewhere would be open and our little girl would hear her mother's voice."

"But what happened when the war began? I mean Bella was still missing. How could you stop searching?"

"We had no choice. All around, buildings were being looted, there were bursts of machine gun fire from every side, and no food was coming in. People were dying all around. It's hard to imagine it today when you walk down the streets, past fancy shops and bakeries—what happened here. The war brought people together, but these old relationships are gone, and the painful lessons we learned have been lost too. When Hong Kong rose back up after the war it was never the same. The blood has been washed clean."

I stood up and walked to the window. The rain had stopped and a sunny haze illuminated Kowloon and the airplanes, coming and going from Kai Tak airport, winked high in the sky above monumental skyscrapers. "And what about your planes?" I asked, turning around.

"Wong bought them. He cleverly disguised the payment, hiding it in a baby's coffin and sent it over. Ana screamed when she saw it. I told her, 'It's the ransom money. We'll pay it for Bella.' But the note never came. We searched up one street and down the next, two crazed white people shoving her picture into Chinese people's faces. *But how could we make them care?* In every alley there were corpses, bodies of loved ones, and every Chinese I showed my picture to had already lived through some far worse tragedy just getting to Hong Kong."

I sighed, overwhelmed with a sinking feeling. "And Yoshi is still here—the doorman?"

Jack nodded. "He was certainly someone I thought I'd never see again." He pulled out a drawer and removed a few small pieces of paper. "Yoshi made this at my kitchen table from a scrap of paper and gave it to Bella that day she walked out the door." He slid something across the table to me

It was an origami crane thumbed to a buttery softness with a dirty repetitive design on it. Looking closely I saw it was faded block letters running the length of it: *B E L L A M O R.*

"Open it," he said gesturing impatiently, and getting up, walked to the window to look out.

I did so, carefully. Inside, the paper revealed a personal embossed letterhead with *Jack Morgan, Peak House, Hong Kong,* across the top.

In the middle were stick figure drawings, two adults and a child beside a plane. The rest of the page was covered by 'Bella Morgan' practiced neatly, over and over in a child's hand.

"Bella had it with her all those years later when she was found dead on that crossroad," he said from the window. "It was all she had to remember me and her mother by." I stood up and putting my hand on his shoulder, looked out the window with him. The streets below were almost completely dry now and the burr of activity had resumed as usual. I wondered what he was really seeing out there. But then I knew.

I knew he still saw and heard the planes at sunrise, rumbling in the sky, dropping everything they had on this island—saw the soldiers wounded left and right on the streets, saw expatriate wives marching to the internment camp singing, "There Will Always Be an England." And even I could see it too—the blood dripping from Japanese bayonets, the bruised, raped nurses, the hills by Stanley Fort littered with Japanese bodies. And the water of the strait—burping up Chinese cadavers on its wavelets while those still alive gazed up at the sky with nowhere to run.

Grandfather sadly glanced over at me, and suddenly I could see my eyes reflected in his. *We were alike—this lost old man and I—we shared this past, together.*

"Our little Bella was swept away with the war," he said. "She took everything I had with her. For years I imagined I heard her crying. I kept all that money ready for her, sealed it up in a wall, hoping … I didn't put it in the bank, and it was a good thing too because the Japanese took over all assets, you know. It took me three days to seal it in with bricks and mortar—and not too soon. The looting started right away. People were taking up movable things first, then, after the trees were all gone, every scrap of wood in town was ripped up, parquet floors, doorways. After the war, only the shells of buildings were left, but Bella's money was untouched."

"But Ana—you didn't tell me …"

A weakness came over him and he seemed to shrink onto his skeletal form with a long expiration of breath, lowering himself into his arm chair—*this man who'd lost everything …*

Auntie Tam came over quietly. "*I'll tell you*," she said, and sat down on the arm rest beside him. She spoke in a low voice, in Cantonese. "I met him, remember, in the orphanage? He came back a few days later with a badly wounded Indian soldier with a turban on his head. This guy had a crooked metal rod stuck in his arm and was bleeding everywhere. 'I can't pull it out,' Jack said. 'Please help my friend.' Our nurses took care of the Indian, and I said, in exchange, Jack had to take me to Hong Kong side for supplies."

"But Ana?"

She held up her hand for silence. "He said to me, 'You'll die returning to Kowloon side, you're a kid.' But he knew he couldn't stop a stubborn Chinese like me. So he and his soldiers took me. But in the end—*I took them.* I found a sampan and I hid them so we could cross the strait. I rowed past many turnip heads. I'm so brave, your grandpa said. Then he promised—'*If I live through this I'll take care of you.*'"

"You believed him?"

She nodded. "He's a crazy English. Keeps his promise. After the war ended, he got out of Stanley Prison and came to find me. You see, I knew the famous David Loie—you ever hear of him? I got involved with his guerrilla movement. I took care of injured people and insurgents David was hiding from the Japanese—one of them happened to be our Ana. She was injured badly from that head wound. After the Japanese surrender in the Peninsula Hotel lobby, Jack found me with her at David's. Imagine that! He took us to Hong Kong side, me too, like he promised. He bought me the flat next to his." Tam pointed proudly down the hall where I could see the big, dark, teak doors at the end. "He was very good to me. Bought all my furniture, TV. My mother came too, and he paid all her doctor bills before she died. But there was more to it."

We looked at Jack, who was staring down at the floor.

Hearing something, Auntie got up suddenly, and leaving the room, slipped down the hall, disappearing between the dark teak doors.

My grandfather sighed. "I don't know how much she understands."

I sat up in disbelief. *"Who?"*

"Sometimes, she seems to *know* who I am, and *sometimes* she's forgotten." He looked at me. "Anyway, Auntie is dressing her so you can see her today. You know, all this time I've been talking, I've been wondering what I should tell her. Maybe you will shock her back to her senses. Maybe. But somewhere, behind that damaged mind is an Ana who knows."

I sat stunned. *Could it be? She was really here—yet hadn't recognized Jack in all these years?* Incredulous, I tried not to stare.

"Here, take a look at this. It was the other thing Bella had with her, besides you."

I took the paper in my hands, struck by the strange handwriting. Jack came over and rested his hand on my shoulder, leaning gently on me as I read aloud.

> *This letter say you not who you believe. Many year ago you baby in house of white man, Hong Kong side Name Bella Morgan. Mui-tsai dealer sell you, make big money. This make much trouble for me find you, undo bad luck before my Miss she die. I put money here for ticket. Jack Morgan your father. Good man. They Hong Kong people. Come home, not too late.*

"But who wrote this?" I asked, incredulous, examining a red seal and the childish, ornamented script.

"Rose hired someone to write this and included money in the letter for the passage back. Bella received it in Burma, and returned straight back to Hong Kong with you. I keep imagining her reaching Admiralty Pier, carrying her newborn—*you*—in her arms, hoping to see us somehow. Oh God, if only I'd known." He put his hand to his brow, shaking his head, sighing. "Instead, she went to Peak House to see Mrs. Morgan."

Mrs. Morgan? I was still, so still I could hear my heart beating. "You mean, *Violet*—Violet never divorced you? After all that time?"

"It was a way to keep me tied to her, I imagine—revenge of sorts." He put his hand in his cardigan pocket and removed a silver charm, dangling it. *It was the tiger, its diamonds winking, dancing in the light.* "Bella showed this as proof to Violet, thinking they'd have a joyous reunion. *My poor Bella.* Violet threw her out in a fit of rage and, with nowhere to go, Bella wandered across town carrying you, completely at a loss. She must have been exhausted, hungry, and disoriented when she stepped off that curb in Jardine's Bazaar."

I blinked, flinched. I could see, hear the oncoming bus. The tires shrieking. I took a deep breath. "But why—why did Rose send for her in Burma?"

"Why? Well, Rose was afraid Violet would accrue bad karma, and Violet was like her own child. She even donated money to the orphanage for you, if only to help Violet. You know, it had to have been difficult for Rose—those were her life savings she spent on you. I found out all this from the Canossa nuns who'd been sworn to secrecy, but they relented after Rose had been dead for some years. All those presents the nuns gave you as you grew up—those really came from her. Your school books, clothes, birthdays, anything you asked for, poor Rose paid. I heard she gave you some caged birds because you wanted them. The nuns worried you'd become too proud, but Rose insisted."

I leaned back in my chair "It was Rose? And she's dead?"

"Tam can show you her grave."

I blinked back tears and pointed to the tall coffin-like doors in disbelief. "And—*and Ana* has been in that room all this time?"

"Sometimes I think she's hanging on just because of me. She had a stroke, but I think I'm the handicapped one."

I looked at him, wondering. Ana had told him she'd love him until he learned to love Violet just one little bit. Could it be that year after year, Ana waited, but he hadn't learned anything? "You won't move on," I said flatly.

His mouth became a tight line and he removed another envelope from the drawer in front of him as if he'd not heard me. "This is the letter I mentioned. The one Violet wrote just before she died. Read it if you like, while we wait for Tam. Maybe then you won't judge me so harshly."

The expression on his face was unreadable and I took it from his hand, smoothing open the paper. It was written only last month in elegant script on her own Peak House stationery; *Violet Summerhays Morgan …*

Jack's child,

I am writing to you, even though you are dead, as an experiment in conscience. You see, my doctor says it isn't too late and won't let up pestering until I do. I'm trying not to laugh. Well, he's an optimist or a fool. But he knows the truth. I sent you away to Burma in 1941 and I told no one.

I remember the last time I saw you, Jack's child, in 1970, when you came up the steps at Peak House with your child, heavy in your arms. You must realize how I felt. There on my verandah stood a young pretty woman who looked just like my husband—my immoral husband—and you were asking if I was your mother! It was too much to bear. What was I to say—Yes, I was Violet Morgan, but no, I was barren and my husband had gone off like a dog to another bitch to spawn? Of course I shouted at you—you with HIS smile on your face—and the polite self-effacement of the Burmese. How it irritated me. And your English was poor, your clothes—cheap! I saw the desperation in your eyes as you waited for me to break into sobs of joy—as if we could be a family! It's hardly my fault you were struck down by a bus. Put yourself in my shoes. If you knew what love I've been deprived of all these years! Your suffering was nothing compared to my misery.

At least he loved you. That day in the Temple grounds when I mentioned seeing a little girl outside—I saw all I needed. You were his child and you held him—heart and mind. That image of Jack's face cost me my happiness. I could never have that part of him. Even Father wanted to remarry and let Peak House come under the care of another woman. Imagine that. I believe he wanted me to marry just to get me out of the house. So when I heard you crying in the sampan, crying for the Jack I'd lost and never possessed, I was seared with a pain unlike anything I'd thought possible—it's a scar I carry even today.

You're buried now, over in St. Michael's Cemetery. Rose has taken care of your child, buying my way out of Hell with her meager coins. And I? I should have been stronger, bolder during my time, but I was only a woman. And know this—had I kept him, I'd have become bitter with age, compulsively checking his pockets and collars for a clue who he might be sleeping with next. In the end, women make these cheaters fat or alcoholic just to keep a leash on them. I did that with Father. I suppose short of cutting off their legs, it's all a woman can do.

There! Now are you pleased I am not your mother? As for her—I didn't know her, nor do I care to. My world is complete without that pleasure. SHE RUINED MY LIFE! Oh gosh. I've ripped the paper here! Well. That silly doctor will interpret the rip in some perverse way. Bother him.

Jack has had many women since the war was over. He's not a loyal man—he'll be loyal when he's dead, the bastard. Your mother, I hear, is some sort of invalid or vegetable, cared for by a Chinese woman who dotes on Jack, of course. Though, I must say I am surprised at how badly his life turned out, after beginning with so much promise. Not a taipan anymore! Can you hear me laughing? I suppose I returned the favor of misery to him as well, though he doesn't even know it. It was my biggest and only gift to Jack Morgan; a tapestry of misery has woven our lives together. That's how it is. But imagine, I am alive and so is he. We wait for death at different addresses. I am on The Peak, and he is somewhere in the nasty Mid-Levels. How's that for fate?

I can hear the traffic outside and the nurse is coming to me with my pills and meal. How things have changed. The last British Governor, Chris Patten, will shove off soon, the red pillar boxes will be gone, and the Queen's face will disappear from the coins and stamps. So it's 1997 and the Chinese will take over. Who cares?

The light outside is very bright and down below, with Papa's field glasses, I often spot the flock of white cockatoos flying over the skyscrapers. When I zoom in I see they have landed on rooftop air conditioners. I can see those black eyes, and how their yellow crests open up like pretty fans. Such a strange sight! Did you know on that December day in 1941, our British soldiers realized it was all over; they were going to die. And what did they do? They let their cockatoos free just as the Japanese marched into town.

Our Tommys are now gone, dead in some squalid wet cemeteries here, far from Britain and home, but their birds are still here. I watch them fluttering in the sky, and I look at my wedding photos. So many have died. Betty's child Thomas died when he was eight and John left her. Susan remarried, and Connie's husband cheated prodigiously! Albert, that fat gin-soaked scoundrel, died in Stanley Prison—starved to death. Imagine that—Kismet! I think I did rather well considering it's a new world outside. Below me, I see skyscrapers I've never entered, streets I've never walked—all on land reclaimed from the harbor, but in a way I've won. I've outlived them all and I still own Peak House. Yes, the air is polluted and on most days I can't see past the trees—and yes, I still miss Father and even Jack in his white dashing suits. But sometimes when my Philippina amah comes to brush my hair at night, I can hear voices, talking and laughing in the library, and very soon I too will be in the cemetery with Popa—and yes, even you. Won't that be a gas?

I can't imagine any good will come of this letter, but the tiresome doctor will be pleased. Silly man. He's not even good-looking, but he is young. Ah, to be young again! I would not hold back the second time around. Not at all! I would be ruthless, for that's what counts in the end. Ask Jack.

Violet Summerhays Morgan,
Peak House, Hong Kong 1997

I set the letter down in disbelief, as if I'd been in the presence of that woman. I looked at him, incredulous. *How on earth had he married her?*

"Let's just forget that, my dear," he said. "Let me take you to Ana." Grasping my hand tightly as if I were that lost child, he walked with me down the long hallway back in time.

Just as we arrived at the tall black doors, Auntie Tam pulled them open revealing a room filled with light. Lying on a hospital bed was a little crumb of a woman, all white hair, with strangely smooth skin. We came up to the bed and her eyes looked up when Jack addressed her. "Ana, dear," he said leaning down to kiss her hand, and then watching her eyes, he placed my hand in hers. "You remember Bella?" He asked this loudly and cautiously. The warm brown eyes moved from his face to mine and her hand, after a moment of inertness, suddenly squeezed mine. *Did she recognize something in me?*

"This is our dear *Bella's child*," he was enunciating. "She's come home to us, Ana. *LITTLE—BELLA'S—CHILD*."

Her clear green eyes became very round as she looked into mine, and it seemed from the tiny movement of the eyebrow and the iris that she was almost straining to speak or understand through them. *Straining.*

"Grandma," I said in desperation, "Grandma, I can't read your mind."

Her thumb pressed my hand hard, and moved back and forth, as if to comfort me.

"I love you, too," I said back to her, though I didn't know what she was thinking; still, I stroked her arm. "Come, Grandpa," I said seeing him helpless, and so he sat down wearily beside me. "I think she wants us all together."

"I think so, too," he said with a heavy sigh, giving a little affectionate squeeze to Ana's knee. Her eyes flicked to his instantly, and *I saw a flash of knowing pass between them*, and that instant, Jack Morgan had smiled from the heart. Young, handsome, bashful, and still in love; a young taipan.

A little bird darted past the window and I recalled the budgies I once owned. Ana didn't want him to *love* Violet—she wanted him to stop *hating*, to make room in his heart so he could fly away with her. Yet he was stuck on his perch with the cage door wide open—stuck on hate, stuck on Bella, stuck on the war, and the future they had lost. *It was eating him alive.*

Suddenly, all the colors and images of the past came to me: Algy, the drowning coolie, Jack's mother, the parties on the peak, Rose's quiet suffering, Ana and Bella on the beach at Repulse Bay, and Connie's dagger eyes. Connie's gossip brought it all down. Yet it didn't even matter, for it all expired in the pale blue sickroom with the clean white sheets, with the sounds of the jackhammer on Hollywood Road, and the blazing light of the present moment. A fantasy, a dream, it was all gone—all that planning, striving, living—*gone*, so that just two old bodies remained. I sat between them, holding both their hands, a link between them, and I thought, China, England, war and strife—all the past and present converged in my veins, and my blood. *I was here to remember. But I was here to live.*

"Tell me more," I said, "so Ana can listen."

Tam put her arm around my shoulder, and taking Ana's hand said, "If only she could talk!"

"If Ana could talk, she would sing—sing the way I hear her in my mind. Put on that record," Grandfather said, "so you can hear Ana too."

I stood up and went to the window instead, opening it to the strong sunny breeze from outside, hoping that he would learn to fly. I sat back down. Jack Morgan, my grandfather, was blinking in the light, his blue eyes sparkling, a mysterious smile on his face. I could see how every woman could love him.

"Why is Yoshi still here?" I asked Tam, who brought over a round tray of sweets and fruits.

She switched to English, shrugging. "He say he can't return to Japan after helping Chinese, but I think we his family. You know? Every time he see you, he see long ago Bella, day she leave. Many ghost in his life. Hai-yah! He say he wait for red centipede!"

"Oh."

Grandpa stood up and coming behind me hung the tiger around my neck. "It's yours, Jardine. You're a Morgan woman now."

"Yu guo tian quing. Rain pass, sky clear. Have a lychee," Tam said offering me the tray. "Yoshi say she have Bella face. What you think, Jack?"

Jack laughed, "Tiger like me!" He grabbed my hands in both of his, and looking into my eyes said, "So, my dear, do you forgive me?"

I looked deep into his eyes, and saw myself, saw everything as if it were written in a clear blue sky.

The End.

GLOSSARY OF *PIDGIN, JAPANESE, AND COMMON TERMS:

Pidgin was widely in use in the 1930's along the South China Coast

amah: domestic servant
arite: okay
bad heart: evil minded
bed business: sex
b'long, b'longey: is
blut: blood
Bund: riverside promenade in Shanghai
buyum: pay
by'mby: after a while, again
cabis: cabbage
catchee: have, get
catty: unit of measure, 1lb. 4oz.
cheesing: crazy

cheongsam: tight silk dress with high collar and slit up the side
chit: bill, letter
chop-chop: quick
congee: rice porridge
cookim: burn
coolie: common laborer
cumshaw: tip
dai pai dong: street market food stalls
dewil bilong man ee dai: ghost
dia: expensive
"the dragon": Feng Shui dictates that the Dragon on the north slope of Victoria Peak comes tumbling down the steep mountain threatening all the buildings in its path, affecting the luck of those inside. All modern buildings in Central District, especially those on this slope, are designed to avoid blocking this powerful dragon.
fa-kwai: foreign devil
fa-wong: gardener boy
folo pidgin: foolish nonsense
gaijin: foreign devil
gambatte: endure
godown: warehouse
got plenty something: rich
guanxi: connections
gweilo: foreign devil
hab got wa-tah topside: foolish
Hakka: "guest people" who migrated from North China to Hong Kong, a familiar sight in all black with wide brimmed hats with fringes
hap: piece
hab-time: leisure time
ha-sze-man: husband
hea: here
Hitotsu yaki o irete yearu beki da!: I should teach you a lesson!

ina-fu: girls with no elastic left in their drawers, comfort women
inakamono: country thing, country bumpkin
inari: fox; Japanese legend has it foxes are shape shifters taking human form to do harm
i-no-streit: mistake
Jack Tar: sailors in the British Navy; in this case refers to homosexual practices at sea
joss: luck
joss sticks: incense
junk: Chinese fishing boats with sails
kabocha-me: pumpkin head
kau meng: save life
kilman: murderer
kolim: call
kostu: almost (close to, nearly)
kretek: clove cigarette
kulah: color
Kum-bo: Campbell
kutim: cut
laughee in side him mouth: laugh to himself
lezibaga: lazy (lazy bugger)
li: Chinese mile, about a 1/3 of a mile, differing in measure under each dynasty
lik-lik: little
lobberman: robber
lukim: see
mas: must
maski: forget
massi-tah: master
meishi: business card
Mex: Chinese silver Yuan coins, originally Mexican silver dollars, the exchange rate during the 1930's being 2 Mex per US$. Copper hexagonal coins with holes in center were also used but were of little value even as tips.
minka: country house with thatched roof

mismis: woman
mui-tsai: child purchased as potential wife or servant
nedim: need
Nantao: Chinese part of Shanghai
notgut: useless
O-bachan: honorable grandmother
oita, kono yogore: You heard me, you scumbag
O-ji san: honorable uncle
ol: they
olsem: like, as
oltaim: always
O-mizu: water
O-nichan: elder brother
O-sembei: rice cracker
olo: old
once piece: one, a
ou-sy: outside
pait: fight, argue
pen bilong maus kulah: lipstick
pilim: touch
play-play: foreplay
plopa: goods
pukkah: proper
pulim: seduce
praya: pier
rong: blame
ryokan: country style inn, minimalist and traditional
sahib: master
savvy: understand
shamisen: three stringed Japanese instrument
sindown: stay
smellum: perfume
snake head: human smuggler
soim: show
stap: stay
stink water: perfume

ta kip: robbery
taidza: idiot
taipan: boss
taitai: rich housewife
talke: tell
tasol: just
tatami: floor mat and unit of measure
taxi dancer: girl paid for partner dancing
toktok: conversation
troimweium: throw away
tuan: Malay form of respectful address, Sir
tu de: today
United Front: Alliance between the Communists and the Kwomintang to fight the Japanese
waitum: wait
walkee-walkee: alive, fresh, as in fish
wanpela-ta-sol: alone
wantchee: want
weigoren: foreign devil
wo-men ch'ih k'oo: we eat bitterness—a peasant's greeting during this time
yukata: cotton summer kimono
yumcha: dim sum

Questions for Group Discussion:

Who is your favorite character and why?

Is there anything sympathetic about Violet? What do you think about her relationship with Jack and what each hopes to get from the other? Would you marry a man you didn't love if you had similar goals? What does she think of the role of women?

Jack reinvents Percy's business without telling him how he's doing it. Is he unethical? Does the end justify the means?

Why does Ana find Jack appealing? What doesn't she like about him? Is she a typical weak female? Why does Jack fall for her?

When does Jack become aware of his internal conflicting goals? How does this relate to the women in his life and Jardine? What does he want to be forgiven for?

Both Violet and Ana are raped. How are their views on sex and their bodies similar or different? How does this affect their lives? Whose view can you relate to?

Would you have gone off with Fritz instead of Jack? Why or why not?

What do you think of Algy's infatuation with Jack? What does Jack think? How might being gay have been in the 1930's? How does Ana relate to Algy? What is Algy's role in Jack's life?

What do you think about the life of Rose, and her sacrifice? How does Rose view her employers? How do Tam and Jardine view the British in Hong Kong today? What do you think of culture and Jack's view of it? What do you think of how language seems to shape the perspectives of Yoshi and Rose?

Is Yoshi sympathetic to you? How does he feel about the war? Does he have a choice? Jack says it's different being a free citizen versus being a subject of the Emperor. How would you have acted if you were a subject of the Emperor of Japan at a time when the people believed the Emperor was actually God?

Jack draws a distinction between being a citizen of an occupied country (China 1930's) and being a citizen of a free country never occupied (Japan). He seems to think that the Chinese sense of trust in others has been broken down by civil war and occupying armies. Do you agree that that can change a person's point of view or character? What does Jardine have to say about this?

Do you find it interesting that the Japanese felt totally justified with their role in the war—as much as the British? How does the world situation today seem different or similar to that of 1939? Is Jack right that the "great game" is still being played?

Jack says the youth of today are unaware that they are trading away their freedom for designer bags and electronics. Is he just an old man out of touch? After all the wars and crimes, how does a country pick up the pieces? Jack says Jardine is the key to the future, her mixed blood. What do you think?

A Conversation With the Author, Milena Banks

What was the inspiration for *Riding the Tiger*?

I moved to Hong Kong from Tokyo in 1994 and discovered a towering modern Chinese city with little apparent connection to the past. Everyone there, Chinese or English, was already obsessed with the approaching 1997 handover. What was going to happen to Hong Kong when the British left the colony and it became Chinese again? Would there be freedom? Would there be a financial collapse? Would there be violence? I began to wonder where old Hong Kong had disappeared—the men in solar topees, the rickshaws, the opium … I thought if I could uncover the past, I would be able to see the future. I imagined meeting some very old English residents who had secrets to hide, and I tried to connect them to the young Chinese I saw around me, vibrant, noisy, eating fast food, and dressing in Chanel or punk clothing. The characters I created are fictional, but I draw on emotions I experienced growing up. The character Jack popped into my head visually when I found a family photo of a handsome dashing relative in a World War 1 airplane, leather jacket, attitude, and all! It was easy to imagine him in a lot of trouble.

What or who influenced your writing the most?

I love Joseph Conrad's *Heart of Darkness*, Rudyard Kipling's *Plain Tales from the Hills* and E.M. Forester's *Passage to India*. Having been born in the former Yugoslavia, and then having moved around a lot in the United States and Puerto Rico as a child, I became obsessed with colonies, and by moving so many times and breaking attachments developed a nostalgia for lost worlds and people. All three of these authors embody my sense of wanting to belong to a new culture and simultaneously being offended by it— missing the culture I had just been forced to abandon. My style is cinematic because every time I moved, I knew I would be leaving again, so in my mind I was constantly trying to find perfect moments. Then when they occurred, I would search for words that would capture the sight, smell, and feel of the place for me forever. Words were my photographs and memories.

Who were your favorite central and minor characters? Did you have to research the 1930's a lot to get the details and setting right?

Jack was my favorite, though I had a great time channeling Violet! She was so crazy it was amazingly liberating to have no boundaries. Besides Algy, I really liked Tam. Her broken English excited me because she was like so many uninhibited Chinese I met who would get out their ideas in English with creative verve. I also really admire the confidence and energy many Chinese people have in general and feel they have a lot in common with my Yugoslav background. Interestingly, several people told me not to include Yoshi at all but I really wanted to create a novel where the British, the Chinese, and the Japanese could tell their side. I hope I did justice, especially with the Japanese with whom I feel a deep kinship. As far as research—it took five years of reading and thinking to develop the plot. The entire novel was written over a period of fifteen years, seven of which it sat forgotten in a drawer. The most valuable sources were *The Soong Dynasty* by Segrave, *The Private Life of Old Hong Kong* by Hoe, *Shark's Fins and Millet* by Sues, and *Japan at War* by the Cooks. *Sin City* by Shaw was an eye opener too. The other great source was the *South China Morning Post*, and all their microfilm records from the era. It was easy to get lost in reams of absolutely fascinating trivia and advertisements. The novel was originally twice as long because of this and I had to lop off tons of irrelevant details and even whole chapters with John, the priest, who was almost entirely removed. This was a labor of love, for Hong Kong, and for all the Asian friends I've made over the years. Many of the detailed descriptions of places were my favorite spots to visit. I was a member of the Helena May Club and lived on Old Peak Road—both feature prominently. I also often took tea at the Peninsula Hotel on Kowloon side and imagined how William Holden or Clark Gable hung out there while filming in the colony. I'm hopelessly romantic.

There are a lot of politics in the novel, historical and Jack's opinions. How does that fit in with what you feel the future of China will be?

1997 is long past and China has moved on. The Chinese are the strongest, most resilient people I have met so I have no fears for their culture and political future—I am more afraid for the West, which has in recent decades become slack in its motivation and self-reliance. Coming from Tito's Communist Yugoslavia and having experienced China in 1986 as a teacher, when it first opened its doors to the West,

I have my own well developed opinions on government! I have come to realize that it's not China we have to worry about, it's ourselves! As far as Jardine goes, she *is* the new world, integrated yet fractured by history and racial conflict. Will the past eat her up or will it buttress her ambitions? Who can tell? I hope people will enjoy the book and find it thought provoking. I have no answers.